PHANTOM PASS

ANDRE M. LOUW

CATALYST PRESS
Texas, USA

In North America, this book is distributed by
Consortium Book Sales & Distribution, a division of Ingram.
Phone: 612-746-2600
cbsdinfo@ingramcontent.com
www.cbsd.com

In South Africa, Namibia, and Botswana,
this book is distributed by Protea Distribution.
For information, email orders@proteadistribution.co.za.

FIRST EDITION
10 9 8 7 6 5 4 3 2 1

Print ISBN: 9781960803375
Epub ISBN: 9781960803382

Library of Congress Control Number: 2025936340

FOR MY MOM

Joretha Louw (née Theart)
(1938-2023)

For teaching me to read,

and for instilling in me

from a very early age a love of books.

I know you can't read this now,

and that breaks my heart,

but this is still for you.

With all of my love.

"There is no den in the wide world to hide a rogue.

Commit a crime and the earth is made of glass.

Commit a crime, and it seems as if a coat of snow

fell on the ground, such as reveals

in the woods the track of every partridge,

and fox, and squirrel."

Ralph Waldo Emerson (1803-1882)

NOTES TO THE READER

Non-South African readers, please see the **GLOSSARY** of terms at the end of the book.

This is a work of fiction. Names, characters, businesses, places, events, and incidents are either the products of the author's imagination or used in a fictitious manner. Any resemblance to actual persons, living or dead, or actual events or locales is purely coincidental. For more information, including images of locations from the book, visit www.andremlouw. co.za.

Political, social, racial, cultural, religious, or other views or opinions expressed in this book are intended to be those of the fictional characters, and do not necessarily reflect the views or opinions of the author. Any and all views or opinions expressed are provided for purposes of advancing the storyline, promoting a sense of realism, and lending credence to the plot as a work of fiction, and are not intended or presented in any way as proof of their veracity.

Where necessary, scientific information, forensic processes, and law enforcement procedures have been adapted for dramatic purposes.

The racial descriptor "Coloured" is not considered a derogatory term in South Africa. Coloured people in South Africa are a group comprising individuals of mixed ancestry from various ethnic backgrounds, including indigenous Khoisan, African, Malay, and European descent. The term "Coloured" is an official racial classification for this group, whose members make up a significant percentage of the racial demography of South Africa's Western Cape and Northern Cape provinces.

The name "AppleMac" is used in this work as the fictional nickname of a fictional character. It has no connection with the trademarks Apple™ or Macintosh™ and it is not used or in any way intended to be used as a trademark or to denote any connection with the business, products, services, or otherwise of Apple, Inc.

None of what follows happened.

But it could have.

PROLOGUE

The wind had picked up, and there seemed to be rain coming. She sat at the kitchen table with a cup of tea grown cold in her hand, listening to the elements. Thinking of this and that. When the moon occasionally broke through the heavy clouds, its light painted silver outlines on the foliage outside. Through the large glass window, she watched the dark shapes of the trees bowing to the wind, and the leaves that would float by, then dance around as a gust picked them up to scatter them far and wide.

There was a violent knocking on the door, loud and insistent, startling her out of her reverie. When she cautiously opened it, having recognized his voice, he stormed in, banging the door against the wall. Shoving her aside, almost hurting her.

He seemed to be half out of his mind. He was mouthing things she could hardly understand. About men chasing him, that they had taken him and that he had escaped.

She was frightened, of what he was saying and of him.

She managed to get him into a chair, although he was shaking fiercely, and giving off heat that seemed to her like that of a fever patient.

He struggled at first to get the cup to his mouth, spilling it all over her table, as he drank the coffee she had poured in a hurry. It seemed to help.

At first, she thought he was drunk. He enjoyed his drink, but she had never seen him drunk. Yet, as he sat there at the table, trying to light the cigarette she had offered him—mostly for something to focus him—she realized that this was not what alcohol did. She had seen plenty of that before in her life when she had been married. As always, her mind closed up suddenly and tightly on that thought, like a bear trap.

She suggested that they phone the police.

He kicked the chair away from the table and lunged at her, the cup flying and shattering, spraying the last bit of coffee over the oven door and her shiny new kitchen cabinets.

She had one hand on the telephone on the wall, but he pushed her away from it and shouted at her. He called her foul names. She shrank away, trying to make herself smaller. Invisible.

His big body towered over her, his hands flailing at the air around her, but there was no coordination. He stood there swaying drunkenly. His eyes would focus on her and then drift away; but he was sobbing pitifully. She wanted to join him. She wanted to let out the fear that was settling inside her chest.

"Get out!" she wanted to shout, at him, and at the fear. But she couldn't find her voice.

She did not really love this man. She had wondered about that for some time, but tonight, seeing him here like this, she finally knew. The thought came like a clap of thunder, unexpected and frightening, but bringing with it a feeling of elation, of having survived something elemental, something dark and bad.

She should be thinking about making it through this night alive, not about her relationship with this stranger. But the thought still came, un-invited and yet so clear. As if it had been there for some time, just forming itself, and mocking her now, taunting her, screaming that she should have known better, some time ago already. That made her feel stupid, and she hated it.

It was the fear that made her feel—suddenly—the absence of love.

He felt his way back to the table, like a man half blind, and lowered himself slowly onto the chair again. She relaxed slightly and tried to talk to him; she tried to muster up a broad smile—a "mommy-will-help" smile—even though it pulled at the muscles of her cheeks. In the very fiber of her soul, she knew she didn't mean it. She just wanted him gone.

Mere minutes had elapsed, but to her it was forever, an eternity, a never-ending day.

His head was bent over the table, and he drooled on the rough surface. His hair was tied back, but some strands had come loose, and he flicked them out of his eyes, annoyed. They were closed now. He was still for a minute.

She decided to draw out that minute, to be sure. She approached him, feeling safer. She really did want to speak to him, to talk about what was happening; and maybe this was passing. Maybe he was sobering up and would recognize her and not hurt her.

When she laid a hand on his arm, his eyes opened.

One look at those eyes, at the naked hate and aggression, and the terror beneath it all, and she felt the fear returning, even stronger than before. As he shuffled his feet, trying to get up, she felt her bowels turn to water.

She backed away, and her feet started to slip on the expensive slate floor that he had persuaded her to have installed. As she fell backward, her arms outstretched toward him, she heard the door slam behind her and she felt the rapid movement of air as a big body passed her, and the bellow of a voice she knew better than any other.

In that millisecond, as she hovered between what felt like life and death, she remembered her teenage years in some movie theater, when they had shouted and clapped for Superman as he flew into frame—she could even hear the music now—and all was right with the world again.

But it wasn't.

As her head hit the hard kitchen floor, she heard the thud: dull, wet, with the ghost of a metallic clang, like a mallet hitting a carcass of fresh meat. The pain came quickly, and she blacked out.

But in that moment before all was gone, she was so very, very grateful. For being delivered from this evil, saved by the only man she really did love.

And always would.

THE BODY

CHAPTER 1

As he picks his way over the wet sand and shale, the light from the flashlight bobbing here and there to help keep his boots dry, he approaches the open water. Some stars are out, but the clouds that rolled in earlier in the day makes this harder than it should have been at this time of night, and this time of the year. He is grateful for the occasional car that drives past on the coast road toward the Heads, or in and out of the Woodbourne Resort. The headlights give him just enough time to get his bearings on the still-distant shape in the water.

The little boat.

"Hold up! Can you even see where you're going?" he hears from a few meters behind him. Then a muffled *"fuck!"* as Solly slips on something and nearly goes down. Clint stifles a laugh. Poor guy, he really isn't cut out for this kind of work. Solly, who can't pass a KFC or a McDonald's without having to stop. Solly, who was booked off for two months last year when the brass decided that when your ass gets too big to fit into the patrol car, your ass is the problem, not the car. Solly, who managed to lose some kilos, and then, within a few weeks after coming back, picked them up again. Solly, who filed the official complaint about the impracticality of the patrol car seats in the first place.

Solly mostly sits in the back now as they do their rounds.

The call had come in about forty minutes ago, just after sunset. Some tourist called it in, after leaving the golf club restaurant. A Brit or a Canadian—Sipho in the charge office is not great with accents—had spotted a small rowboat floating a few meters offshore in the lagoon. Not worthy of panic, one would say, but the *rooinek* was convinced he saw an arm dangling over the side, and thought someone might be in trouble.

By the time Sipho put out the call, Clint and Solly were the closest unit. They were making their way back into town from Plett, where they had chased down a report of some Rastas who were partying in the caravan park, and some white kids spotted going in and out of an old, rust-streaked caravan where serious smoking was apparently taking place. The Rastas were gone when they got there, and the young whiteys—surfers by the look of it—gave them some attitude but didn't have any drugs on them.

Solly trips, nearly missing falling face down in the mud.

"Nee fok man!" Clint shouts at him. *"Kyk waar jy loop!"*

Solly mutters an apology. Clint swings his flashlight toward the boat, which is only about ten meters away, drifting aimlessly on the calm, pitch-black water.

Clint keys his radio. "Station, unit 6, we're at the site and have a visual on the boat. All looks OK this side, maybe just a rowboat that came loose up at Thesen or Leisure Isle. Will check it out. Over."

He comes to a stop at the water's edge. Solly joins him a second later, out of breath. A burst of static from the radio, some geese crying over-head, and Solly's labored breathing are the only sounds.

"How we gonna get to it?"

Clint isn't going to debate the matter. He wants to get this done quickly, so that they can get back to the station and to the paperwork. He has a date with that new girl at the library—taking her to Spur, not very fancy, but fuck it—but with this call they might have to settle for late night drinks somewhere.

"I'll have to wade out there. It's not deep. Just give me a minute to get my boots and pants off."

As he sits down, trying to keep his uniform dry on a grassy patch, Solly blurts out. "Hey! There *is* someone in there! Look. *My fok!*" Clint follows Solly's light. There is an arm, clad in green material, dangling over the side of the boat. The hand looks white, but it's hard to tell in this light.

He raises himself up, partially undressed. "Hello! Hey!" Clint shouts at the boat, hoping to see some movement of the arm. Maybe some drunk fisherman will raise his head over the gunwale, blinking in the glare of the flashlight. But the only response is the lapping of the water against the boat. It continues to rock gently.

Solly holds Clint's uniform pants and keeps the flashlight trained on the boat as Clint wades into the water. It's colder than he expected. "*Jissis*. This better be worth it," he mutters at nobody in particular.

He approaches the boat, cringing at the weird feeling of the weeds brushing against his legs and the mud squelching between his toes. Like it's trying to pull him down into the cold dark.

Solly's light can't reach him, and he can't see a thing. He nearly stumbles, but then his hand closes over the rough wood, and he instinctively pulls the boat toward him. Giving up on trying to see inside, he turns and pulls the boat toward the shore. After a few steps, the bottom of the boat scrapes against the sand. He gives one last hard pull to get it up far enough onto the shore. Solly is on hand immediately, and he shines his light into the interior.

They both stare and start to swear.

It's a white man, probably in his late sixties, long, gray hair tied back with a piece of leather and wearing only a blue denim shirt. The body is propped up on the bench that runs the length of the boat. A rope around the neck is tied to the bench. One arm is draped over the side. The naked lower body is drenched in blood from the horrendous wound where the genitals used to be. The mouth yawns open in what looks and feels like a scream.

But the eyes are the worst. They're just not there.

The flashlight disappears as Solly reaches for his asthma pump.

Clint spits some bile into the water, then mouths, "*Ma se moer*," under his breath as he wipes his lips. He keys the button on his radio to tell Sipho it's going to be a really, really long night, thinking he'd better call Flossie and tell her the date's off.

Finally, the rain starts to fall.

CHAPTER 2

Josh was woken by the phone next to the bed. Amy was still asleep after he finished with the call, one leg over him, and that cute little snore, sawing away gently at some tiny, invisible piece of timber. She would never admit to it, even though he adored it.

He lay there and thought about what he had just been told. He heard the branches from the pine trees outside as they scraped against the roof, and the rain beating on the windowpanes. The sound soothed him, threatening to put him back to sleep.

He struggled against the comfort of being in a warm bed lying next to a warm body, and opened his eyes. He extricated himself, slowly so as not to wake Amy, and padded into the bathroom for a piss. Afterwards, he walked over to the kitchen in the small flat that they had rented—*better to go cheap and find a bigger place later once we know whether we're staying*—and put the kettle on for some coffee. He was cold, excited, but mostly terrified.

The call had been from a sergeant at the George regional HQ, working in Serious Crimes, his own division. There was a murder in Knysna, the body found a few hours ago. And his name had come up—*fuck me*—in a request from Gavin Whitall, one of the head homicide detectives in the Southern Cape, if not the whole of the Western Cape province.

As he poured the boiling water and stirred the instant coffee, he wondered at Whitall's request. Josh had only been on the beat for four months. There had been the sudden transfer from Cape Town to George a mere six months after completing his training and qualifying as a rookie detective. Amy was upset, but was later—much later—convinced that, as they had both known from day one, the nature of the job required him to be transferred to wherever he was needed. George was hardly the worst place they could have ended up. He had dreaded a move to Johannesburg, a city he disliked, or even worse, some rural shithole in the Eastern Cape or Limpopo. They had ended up in arguably the most beautiful part of the country. Where he could try to impress the bosses, and Amy could peddle her tattoo artistry to the many tourists who flocked to the area throughout the year. Things could have been worse. And now, it looked like he might actually get his teeth into a real investigation with the big shots.

He had heard of Whitall, of course. The guy was a legend. After a solid career as a detective in various murder and robbery units across the country, he had moved to the Scorpions, where he was credited with some really high-profile investigations, of which a few actually led to convictions. After the political demise of the Scorpions, he had returned to Cape Town and was later transferred to head up the investigations branch in George.

Whitall was one of the most experienced and well-respected investigators in the service, nationally, and probably one of the only top cops who had never been implicated, even remotely, in any sordid political intrigue. Some said it was because he was a *rooinek*—born in England and moved to South Africa in his early teens—so he carried none of the baggage of the Afrikaner cops who had been around in the Apartheid years, and were now, since 1994, viewed with suspicion by the political powers that be.

Josh finished his coffee, thinking of the day ahead. He had been asked—ordered—to report to Knysna station by 10h00. He'd better shower and get going, especially if the roads were going to be wet.

He'd message Amy from the road, hoping they could still do the live blues and pizza night at Mariners that evening. He suspected they wouldn't.

The drive had taken a bit longer than he'd expected for a Saturday morning. It seemed a lot of rain had fallen in the early hours, and traffic through Kaaimans Pass flowed like mud. He had opened his driver's window going down the pass, the smell of the rain never failing to calm him.

As Josh jogged into the station, the rain had subsided to a drizzle. He walked to the desk and was greeted by the duty officer with a smile, asking him to go down to Whitall's office. The station was quiet. Apart from the few bedraggled people sitting on the hard benches in the charge office—some with bandages as a sign of just how good a Friday night they'd had—the corridors deeper into the building were a ghost town.

The door was open. He knocked as he tentatively walked in. The man at the desk was reading a file but he looked up smiling, and pushed his glasses onto his head. He stood and stretched out his hand, giving Josh a firm handshake.

"Holland? How are you? Thanks for coming on short notice." He waved toward the only other chair as he sat back down.

"Colonel Whitall, it's an honor to meet you, sir."

The man was of medium height, slightly stocky, and handsome in a rugged, *I-don't-give-a-shit* kind of way. Short, curly blonde hair that was graying at the temples. He certainly didn't dress like top brass, either.

"The name's Gavin, OK? And you OK with Josh?"

Whitall seemed very chilled, and Josh immediately took a liking to the man. He nodded and shifted in his seat.

"We can get acquainted later," Gavin continued. "Sorry for the rush, but we have a bit of a shitstorm developing here. I need some help, and I heard we have a young trainee detective with some legal background." His rather bushy eyebrows were raised inquisitively, and Josh nodded.

"Good. That might come in handy. Let me tell you what we've got before we go out there."

Josh settled down into the chair as Gavin explained the events of the past twelve hours.

"A body was found after 21h00 last night in a small rowboat floating in the estuary just off the Woodbourne Resort, on the road out to the Heads. There was a telephonic tip-off from a Norwegian tourist, who saw the boat from the golf course turn-off. The victim is a white male of advanced age.

"The body was horribly disfigured. Castrated, with the eyes removed. The cause of death is unknown, but we expect the post-mortem results any time now from Forensics in Mossel Bay. The Knysna forensics building is undergoing renovations—you may have heard about that." Gavin pulled a face at this before continuing.

"A rope was used to tie the victim to the vessel. It's currently being transported to the SAPS forensic science lab in Plattekloof, with the hope that it might provide some evidence. It's unclear where the boat came from; there was no evidence of it having been launched from the lagoon shore for hundreds of meters either direction. We're currently going with the opinion of one of the officers first on scene: that the boat had drifted from either Thesen Island to the north or Leisure Isle to the west. We are investigating tide activity, but wind conditions were light yesterday and it's improbable the boat had been blown around the lagoon."

Gavin drew a hand through his hair, and Josh sensed his frustration.

"Of course, this is not, as first suspected, a boat that had simply got loose of its moorings. The body and its placement suggests that it had been set out into the water by a person or persons unknown."

"Has the victim been identified, sir?"

"Gavin, please," Whitall replied. He dropped his eyes to the file on his desk for a minute, and rubbed the sides of his nose where his glasses had left red indentations. He stood suddenly, grabbing a set of car keys and a pack of cigarettes from the desk.

"And yes, he has. It's why I asked for you."

En route on George Rex Drive,
in the direction of the Heads
Knysna
11H23

"Where exactly are we going, sir—Gavin?"

They drove an unmarked, silver Toyota Corolla, maybe Gavin's personal car. They passed the golf course on their left, some Saturday morning warriors in their ridiculous checkered pants and colorful golf shirts tramping around the greens despite the drizzle. He stared over Gavin's shoulder as they passed where he gathered the body had been found. There were three SAPS vehicles parked as close as possible to the water's edge, and ten or more police officers scouring the shore, trying to look busy. He realized that the station was a ghost town this morning because most of the personnel were out here on the lagoon.

A dark red dinghy was pulled up onto the sand and attached with a neon green line to the bull-bar of one of the SAPS *bakkies*, as the tide had started to come into the estuary and the water level was rising.

"We're going up Sparrebosch way. You know Pezula?"

Josh was not a golfer, but he knew that Knysna was blessed with some of the nicest golf courses in the country. Apart from the municipal course they had just passed, there was the internationally acclaimed, Jack Nicklaus-designed Simola course on the other side of the lagoon. Close to the Heads, on an imposing piece of headland with spectacular views of the Knysna lagoon and town, was Pezula, an estate course with a five-star hotel, where the rich could live the high life of birdies, caviar, and gin and tonics.

Gavin took his eyes off the road, and looked at Josh for a few seconds. "You may have heard of our vic. Mark Whitcombe."

Josh did a double-take.

"The advocate? Bigwig legal guy from Cape Town?"

Gavin nodded. "Yep, that's the one. Senior Council, one of the top advocates at the Cape Bar for more than thirty years. Sixty-seven years old, retired four years ago after making a fortune in litigating cases here and elsewhere. The UK, Hong Kong, and God knows where else."

Josh whistled. "The guy's legendary. He used to work with Chaskalson, Sachs, that crowd. I remember teaching my students some of the cases he argued. I think he even served a few stints as acting judge in the Supreme Court of Appeal."

They turned onto Duthie Drive through Fernwood Estate, up to the golf course on the cliff.

Gavin told Josh identification was not official yet, but they would know soon enough. They were going to interview the widow now.

At the gate, Gavin flashed his badge. Security directed them to the Whitcombe house, which was next to the 14th green. They pulled into the driveway of a house that looked pretty much like every other on the street: large, with lots of glass, and an electric blue Porsche SUV in the driveway.

As they got out of the car, Gavin said, "Let me do the talking, OK? I want you to have a look around, be my eyes if you can."

The door opened as they walked up the gravel path to the imposing front door, with its ornate Oriental carvings and lots of steel. An attractive lady—Josh guessed she was in her mid to late fifties—came out and offered her hand. The security guys at the gate had called her and she greeted them with a slight smile. Her eyes were puffy, and Josh could see that she had not slept the night before. She showed them into the huge entrance hall, which was tastefully decorated and very modern. A tall picture window to one side offered spectacular views of the golf course and the woodlands beyond.

Veronica Whitcombe offered them coffee. They declined, and she motioned them to a massive leather couch in the large sitting room off the entrance hall. She took a seat facing them in an expensive-looking chair of Scandinavian design.

After proper introductions had been made, Gavin commiserated with Mrs. Whitcombe over the tragic death of her husband. He made a point of stating that, of course, no official identification of the body found had been made. He was about to continue when she interrupted him.

"Colonel, I know your rules and regulations require you to err on the side of caution. I understand that. But the man you found is my husband." Josh saw the skin around her eyes crinkle, her lips drawn thin.

"*Was* my husband. That's why I phoned the police station and reported him missing." Her story was succinct.

Mark Whitcombe had, following his retirement and their move to Knysna, bought a small cottage on Marlin Road, near the Loerie Park Sports Grounds, closer to town and not far from the lagoon. Here he had set up a small office, where he disappeared to most days of the week and, recently, most weekends. She had no idea of what he did there. She was confident he actually did spend his time there, though; Josh and Gavin both looked uncomfortable when she snidely said she was pretty sure he wasn't seeing another woman. She thought he might be writing a book about his career, an autobiography. She gave a rather unflattering smirk at this. It was clear that this was probably not the happiest of marriages.

The couple had never had children. They both kept to themselves for the most part. He had his high-profile career. She had birdwatching, charity work, and her award-winning gardens in the various houses where they had stayed in the past thirty-odd years.

When Veronica Whitcombe again offered them coffee, Gavin decided to get to the point.

"Why did you report your husband missing? You say he was in the habit of disappearing to his office. When did you last see him?"

She looked flustered at the question but rallied quickly.

"I know how things work. I've seen the TV shows. Nobody believes someone has really gone missing unless they've been gone a few days, right? He left here Thursday morning just after breakfast, probably around eleven."

Gavin gave Josh a brief look before he turned back to her.

"But how could you be sure that he hadn't just decided to sleep over at his office?"

Josh spoke up for the first time. "Did he drink? Maybe he didn't want to drive?"

She shook her head, drew up her shoulders, and looked from one to the other of the two police officers seated on her expensive leather couch.

"You don't understand. I didn't think he was missing. I knew he was dead."

CHAPTER 3

They were both a bit punch drunk after the interview. This was Josh's first next-of-kin call, and he had heard horror stories from more senior detectives. Uncontrollable anguish and sorrow, shock, sometimes even temper tantrums and physical attacks on the unfortunate messenger. All things considered, it could have been worse. They had driven up the hill expecting to simply comfort a widow, and hoping to establish the identity of the victim before the post-mortem results confirmed it. But they came back with so much more.

Veronica Whitcombe had done more than paint a picture of an unhappy marriage to a workaholic egomaniac, who saw himself as some great intellectual and made the lives of those around him a living hell. She said more than once that she often thought how lucky it was that they never had children. A progeny that her loving husband could "fuck up."

This early in the investigation, and with no suspect on the horizon, Gavin was obliged to ask some rather delicate questions. Yes, Veronica was Mark's sole heir. To the house, the Porsche, and a Jaguar, as well as a beach house in Ballito. There was a flat in the UK and some local and overseas investments. And yes, there were substantial insurance policies. But she was amused at these questions. It turned out that Veronica was independently wealthy, having been born Veronica Campbell, rather late in life to a former KwaZulu-Natal sugar baron. She seemed to take pleasure seeing them squirm at the realization that the investigation would not be so cut and dry.

What she did, however, offer the detectives was the news of a few emails and a letter received the previous week. Apparently, Mark had received some threatening correspondence, from an anonymous source, which was linked to something earlier in his career. That much he had let drop after a few whiskeys the weekend before, refusing to say anything more to his wife.

Veronica produced Mark's laptop from his study, and she told them that they were welcome to take it if they would provide a receipt. He might have had another computer down at the cottage; there used to be a PC in the study at home, but she thought that Mark might have moved it down to the cottage. At Josh's question, she said that Mark's cell phone was not at home, that he must have taken it with him. No phone had been found on the body or in the boat. Josh took down the number, which Veronica had read off her phone's display.

The letter was also handed over, unfortunately without the envelope that it came in. Gavin handed it to Josh, who bagged it after having a quick glance over its contents. It was on nondescript notepaper, and consisted of three typewritten lines:

"You have three days.
This is the last communication.
Send an email stating where you will hand over the files.
Tick tock."

As far as Josh could see, there was nothing of evidentiary value. Barring extreme luck with fingerprint analysis, he doubted that they would get anything from it.

Of course, the letter was also incongruous. If it came from the same source as the emails—and the letter itself commanded Whitcombe to respond by email—why send a letter? Why not put the threat in an email?

When they got back to the station, Gavin had immediately handed the laptop over to their in-house tech fundi, a young Coloured warrant officer named Ricardo "AppleMac" Jantjies. He was widely acknowledged as one of the best computer guys in the Southern Cape SAPS. There had been some requests from Cape Town to get him into a squad out there, but AppleMac stayed with his elderly grandmother in Joodse Kamp, and he wouldn't leave her for the fame and fortune of the big city. So he kept his status of lowly W/O, but his office was bigger than Gavin's.

When he was not working on digital evidence and cracking suspects' phones, he was left alone to run his IT business on the side. Nobody wanted to see AppleMac get stabbed in some shebeen raid or hurt in a car chase.

They were all confident that he would find any dirt that there might be on Whitcombe's laptop, and hopefully trace the threatening emails. He would also take care of the victim's cell phone records; AppleMac had a friend or an ex-girlfriend working at every one of the major service providers, and he usually got results fast. The letter had gone off to the Question Document unit. Gavin had also procured a key to Whitcombe's cottage from Veronica. A team of officers and AppleMac would pay the cottage a visit that afternoon.

The single best line of inquiry to come out of the interview with Veronica—and which it was hoped would be borne out by the investigation into the letter and emails—was the name of a former client of Whitcombe's. It was a story that went back some years.

In 1995, shortly after the dawn of democracy, Mark Whitcombe had been at the Cape Bar. Over fourteen years, he built a reputation for commercial litigation, specializing in large insurance and admiralty claims. But he had also been active in the anti-Apartheid movement since the late 1970s, and he made a number of contacts amongst members of the then-exiled liberation movement. Of course, being a gun for hire, he also cultivated relationships on the other side of the fence.

In early 1995, he was approached by Reghardt Brink, a former security police squad commander, who had been referred by a prominent Apartheid-era conservative politician, a distant relative. Brink had been arrested in 1993 for the 1986 bombing and assassination of a prominent African National Congress leader in Beira, Mozambique. With the Truth and Reconciliation Commission hard at work and the ANC newly in power, Brink was suddenly thrust to the fore as a poster boy for redress—even vengeance—against the sick fucks who had killed so many in the darkest hours of Apartheid.

Brink was convicted of the killing of ANC firebrand Senzo Shabane, an operative who was rumored to have been in charge of training freedom fighters in Mozambique and Tanzania in the 1980s, as part of the plan to take the armed struggle to Pretoria.

Brink was prosecuted and eventually convicted in the Cape Town High Court in August of '94. In '95, he appealed to a full bench of the court against his sentence of twenty-seven years. He approached Whitcombe to argue his appeal.

It was unclear why, but the appeal failed, and Brink was sent off to Victor Verster Prison near Paarl, the prison from which Nelson Mandela had been released only five years prior. There Brink stayed until August 2017, when he was released after a well-publicized appeal to the Supreme Court of Appeal in Bloemfontein. Josh remembered media reports at the time citing the 1995 appeal's "inefficient counsel" as one of the prime reasons for overturning the conviction. Apparently, there had been possible tampering with or falsification of evidence in the original trial, by prosecutors and other parties unknown. Josh also remembered reading that Brink had embarked on a civil claim against the Minister of Justice and Constitutional Development for wrongful imprisonment.

What made all this of interest to Gavin and Josh was the fact that, according to Veronica, Brink had suddenly appeared two months ago at the Pezula security gate, demanding to speak to Mark. Mark had refused to see him, and had avoided further contact, even though Brink phoned a few times, screaming at Mark and frightening Veronica considerably.

Things culminated in a bout of fisticuffs in Zachary's Bistro at the Pezula Hotel one Saturday evening in September. Brink appeared at their table, started to shout and swear at Mark, and then assaulted him. Mark got in a few punches before Brink was thrown out by security. The couple had not phoned the police or laid charges against Brink.

But by all accounts, it seemed Brink was not Mark Whitcombe's biggest fan.

Phones were ringing at Knysna station that Saturday afternoon. Since they'd returned from Pezula, Gavin and Josh had been busy setting a theory in motion.

While they waited for the pathologist's report, Gavin initiated a BOLO for Reghardt Brink. He had been seen in town relatively recently, and even though they were not sure whether he was still there, they were confident that an all-points bulletin would produce some results.

It was now after 17h00 on Saturday, twenty-four hours since the discovery of the body. Homicide lore was pretty unanimous on the point that the first forty-eight hours after a murder were crucial. They only had so much time to make a dent in the case; if there was a possible suspect (which was a description everyone on the team agreed fit Brink to a tee), they needed to act fast.

Their evidence was slim. They had a body. They had Veronica's story. They had little else.

Josh knew they were walking a tightrope. Focusing on only one suspect had the potential to burn an investigation even if you eventually managed to prosecute them. The judicial standard of proof "beyond reasonable doubt" meant that even if you brought a suspect to court and managed to bring sufficient evidence for a conviction, any halfway-decent defense attorney might be able to provide reasonable doubt by showing that the police focused on one—and only one—suspect from day one. If there was no evidence of a broader investigation, and specifically the discounting of alternative possibilities, the exclusive focus could turn into a nightmare for prosecutors.

But there was simply no other target on the horizon. They were caught between the danger of inertia and the need for momentum, and decided to go for the latter. Calls were put out, and computers started chatting to each other over the internet. It would not be long before Brink was spotted and gathered up. Or so they hoped.

A couple of journalists had stopped by an hour prior, from the Western Cape's premier Afrikaans language paper, *Die Burger*, and from the *Herald LIVE* out in Port Elizabeth. News of the murder had made the *Knysna-Plett Herald* that morning, three short paragraphs on page two of the paper. The identity of the victim had not yet been disclosed, but it would probably be on the front pages the following day.

Gavin had personally spoken to the journalists, and they—and any future newshounds who came snooping around the investigation—were under strict instructions not to publish certain information about the discovery of the body. They were allowed to report the basics, including the fact that "the body had been mutilated," but under no circumstances could information about the body itself, clothing, or the rope found in the boat be published without the prior written consent of the lead investigator, Gavin.

He wasn't planning on giving such consent.

After 17h15, the team arrived back from Whitcombe's cottage. They walked in with mixed body language. Christiaanse, Jones, and Van Wyk, the W/Os who were asked to perform the search, seemed quite happy, and they marched cockily to the coffee machine in the squad room. AppleMac, trailing slightly behind them, seemed in a bit of a funk. Gavin motioned to Josh to join him and they walked out of Gavin's office to hear the news.

Josh was preoccupied. Amy had phoned ten minutes ago to ask what was happening, and she was pissed at his radio silence since his message that morning. He was in the doghouse. He suggested that she ask Rieta out for the pizza thing. Rieta Smit, their overweight and ultra-Christian neighbor, was occasionally a fun companion on those evenings when they needed some distraction. She'd hate the blues music and its expletives, but Josh couldn't care too much right now. He would just have to smooth things over when he got back to the flat.

"You guys OK? Had a good time?" Gavin smiled.

Josh saw the quick glance Christiaanse threw in AppleMac's direction—something like a veiled, *Shut the fuck up if you know what's good for you.*

"Hi, Colonel. We just got back." Christiaanse was a weasel-faced little punk, closer to forty than thirty. He wore all Cape Flats gang-type garb: the funky sneakers (big brands, but probably rip-offs), tracksuit, chains, and an Adidas cap, earning him the nickname "8-mile" around the station. Josh had seen the type before, in training, and at his brief posting in Grassy Park in the southern suburbs of Cape Town. He was surprised that the station commander allowed Christiaanse to go out dressed like that while wearing a badge.

"And?"

Christiaanse looked his men over. "We checked out the cottage. It's nothing more than a three-by-five little shitbox."

Gavin seemed less enthusiastic now. "Maybe just tell us what you found inside?"

Christiaanse looked a bit pissed, but launched into the basics.

The team had entered by means of the key provided to Gavin by Veronica Whitcombe. There was no alarm or security system of any sort. The small cottage consisted of two rooms, an office, and a small bathroom with a toilet and basin. The office was a bit of a mess. One large desk with two chairs. Papers scattered all over the place.

There was a metal filing cabinet in one corner, but it was open and contained few files. On one wall there was a poster of trees, some kind of jungle scene, proclaiming that man was killing the planet at a rate irreconcilable with humans' status as the most intelligent species on the planet (or something along those lines, Christiaanse said with a smirk).

There had been no vehicle parked by the cottage. Veronica had said that Mark drove his Jaguar sports car on Thursday, but mentioned that he used to park the car in the parking lot of the Bosun's Pub & Grill, an eatery just off George Rex Drive and within a few minutes' walk to the cottage. The area around the cottage was a bit seedy, close to the Knysna industrial area, and there had been a spate of car break-ins.

While the team was at the cottage, an officer had found the car in the Bosun's parking lot. He had driven out to Pezula to get the spare key from the widow and had then driven the car to the SAPS impound lot in George. Mark's key was missing, along with his phone.

Gavin nodded, brows furrowed. "That's it? Everything? We were told that Whitcombe was possibly writing his autobiography down there. Was there any evidence of that?"

Christiaanse shrugged. "Not that I saw."

"Anything in that filing cabinet? Or a computer or a laptop?'

Christiaanse nodded at Van Wyk, who looked, to Josh, defensive. "I went through the files. All a lot of *kak*. Environmental bullshit. A bunch of cut-outs from newspapers, magazines. The Amazon rainforest being burned and raped, our seas being overfished and shit, that kind of crap."

Gavin caught Josh's eye. This early in the investigation, and with so little to go on, the cottage seemed disappointing.

"Was there a landline?" Gavin asked. Christiaanse nodded.

Gavin turned to Josh. "Remind me to get the number for the cottage phone from the widow. We should call up those records. If Whitcombe spent as much time in the cottage as she says, he probably made and received quite a few calls there, and with the cell phone missing, there might be something to work with to tie up his movements on Thursday and yesterday."

Gavin walked to the desk where AppleMac was packing his stuff into a black backpack with Far Cry, Tomb Raider, and peace sign stickers. "Apple, what about you? Anything catch your interest?"

AppleMac glanced at Christiaanse, and then back at Gavin, smiling.

"Not a thing. No computer or laptop. But the dude was wired. Those babies were there, but not when we got there."

"Why do you say that?"

"There was a router for a Wi-Fi signal installed, but it was unplugged and I found two external hard drives on a chair. Obviously disconnected from a PC or a laptop that was being used, but someone took the hardware, I'm afraid."

Josh looked at Gavin. This was to be expected, of course, but it also meant that whatever Whitcombe had been doing in there on the computers was probably gone for good, and that while the state of the body seemed to quite unequivocally point toward murder, the absence of the computers seemed to point toward a true motive over and above a freak see-you-and-kill-you scenario. Whitcombe's body was found on the lagoon, but his back-trail had just revealed some sort of criminal attention. Those computers had been taken. Unless Whitcombe—or for that matter, Veronica—had removed them.

According to the team, there had been no break-in. Only someone with access to the cottage's keys could have gained access. Josh thought that Gavin might be seriously considering applying for a warrant and taking another trip up the hill to Pezula.

With nothing more to add from the cottage debriefing, Gavin sent everyone home. He spent a few minutes with AppleMac and asked him to start checking out social media and online for both Mark and Veronica Whitcombe, after which Josh threw in a suggestion: Brink, too. Gavin asked AppleMac to please remain available on short notice, even though he was not on shift the rest of the weekend, just in case they did recover the hardware.

Christiaanse and Van Wyk left amongst some loud banter about a pool challenge at some bar in town. Gavin and Josh let them go, and retired to Gavin's office.

KNYSNA SAPS STATION

18H14

After they were both seated, Gavin glanced at Josh and lit a cigarette. The Knysna station was a smoke-free zone, but exceptions were made for the more senior officers.

"OK, Josh, let's do this. You know that a major part of your involvement with this case is training. This is your first real 'action' in an official investigative role, and I want to start getting a sense of your feelings and your thinking on this thing." He tipped some ash into a "World's greatest boss" mug on his desk. He looked at Josh with a hint of a smile.

Josh had known this was coming. He looked down for a second and gathered his thoughts.

"OK, initial impressions. We have a very brutal murder. I've worked a few cases in the Cape Flats, drug cases. No knife to the throat or six bullets in the body here. This seems to be a very personal motive. Hate? Jealousy? I don't know. We have Brink as a decent suspect with a decent motive, but can we discount a more personal, crime-of-passion type motive? I'm thinking of the injuries. He got his dick sliced off."

Gavin nodded as he mashed the stub of the cigarette into the coffee mug. "Keep going."

Josh gained momentum. "We have nothing else right now to suggest such a motive or another suspect closer to Whitcombe, so let's look at Brink. The offense against him by Whitcombe, if there was such a thing, is pretty old. 1995? That's ages ago. Yes, he spent all the time since then in prison, but does it seem rational to expect him to hold a grudge that long?"

Josh picked up on Gavin's raising of the eyebrows at the word "rational" and he immediately continued. "Yes, I know, the state of the body hardly screams 'rational'; it seems like something born of emotion, but I still wonder. After more than twelve years in prison, and at—what is Brink now—about sixty? Is it probable that Brink would disfigure his victim like that?"

Gavin shrugged, and dragged the mug full of ash to the edge of his desk. He had a smiley face mug full of coffee, too, which sat by his car keys. He probably didn't want to get the two mixed up.

"OK, I hear you. But did you see the files that the NPA sent through this afternoon? On Brink?"

Gavin had requested, and was supplied with, the original files from the Brink investigation that led to his prosecution in 1993. The National Prosecuting Authority's offices in Wynberg had them couriered over earlier in the afternoon. Brink's sordid history as unit commander for the security police in the 1980s jumped out of the pages. He had participated—allegedly, as not all of the allegations had been converted into charges—in a number of vicious killings of suspected Apartheid enemies, and even a suspected murder in East Berlin in 1987 of a KGB Colonel who was long suspected of having been the top Soviet operative in the ANC's elite MK training units in Tanzania. Josh had glanced through the files. Indeed, some of those long-ago killings had been just as gruesome as the crime they were currently investigating.

Gavin wrapped up the meeting with an expansive yawn.

"You've been here since ten this morning, I'm guessing that you could use a break. I'm off home, the wife's got a little braai thing organized." He smiled, and Josh felt strangely affectionate toward his new boss. "Do me a favor? If AppleMac's still out there—he usually hangs around, I think our Wi-Fi's faster than what he's got at home—will you ask him to please focus on the laptop that the widow gave us? He can work on it tomorrow, and I'd like a report on Monday morning. In the meantime, I'll see whether we get any results in finding the computers he suspects were taken from the cottage. I'll phone Veronica Whitcombe tomorrow morning to ask whether she knows anything about them. If I get any shit from her, I'll get a warrant to search the Pezula house. OK?"

Josh was happy to have the Sunday off. He knew that if the BOLO on Brink produced any results, he would be phoned to come into the office. He kind of hoped he would. It was early days in the investigation, but he already felt they were not proceeding at the speed they should. A tip-off on Brink's whereabouts would be great, and he wouldn't mind leaving Amy to entertain herself if there was a chance to grab the guy.

"Sorry," Gavin spoke up as Josh headed out the door. "Also ask Apple to check those two external drives he found in the cottage."

Josh had forgotten about the drives. People used external drives to back up valuable information. If someone had taken the computers and left the drives, they may have fucked up.

As he climbed behind the steering wheel of his old green BMW, Josh thought over the cottage search. The lack of computers at the scene didn't disprove Veronica Whitcombe's suggestion that her husband had been working on his autobiography. Could a Mark Whitcombe memoir of his illustrious legal career pose a threat to anyone? Whitcombe could have a whole collection of pissed-off clients from back in the day.

And the "environmentalist" material that Christiaanse and Van Wyk reported finding—how might that fit into the greater scheme of things? It was still early days, but Josh thought that it might bear keeping an eye on whether Whitcombe was actively involved in any environmental causes.

Josh shook his head, pushing the case out of it and thinking instead of Amy. *Let's get her some flowers or, even better, a good bottle of wine.*

He drove off in the direction of George.

CHAPTER 4

When he arrived home, Josh was pleasantly surprised to find that Amy was upbeat. She had a bottle of wine open already, so he put the one he had bought from a liquor store in Sedgefield, just before they closed, on a shelf.

She had not asked Rieta to the blues joint, and had ordered pizza in. There were a few slices left for Josh. He decided to apologize right off the bat.

"Honey, babes, I'm sorry, I've neglected you all day."

She gave a sweet, if somewhat tired, smile. He was working, yes, and she had to get used to it, but he felt bad. With the past few months being nearly exclusively focused on training, he was rarely gone over a week-end, and he knew that she stressed constantly about her start-up business. Saturday was a day of little in the way of opportunities to work on what needed to be done, and more time to worry and pick at all the reasons why a mobile, pop-up tattoo studio might not be the best idea, especially out of season in Knysna.

Josh felt a sudden burst of affection for her, and he leaned over and kissed her, stroking her hair.

She smiled at him and kissed him back.

"Sorry, monkey, I've been a bit of a bitch. I know." As he sat down across from her, she pulled a face. "Your work has to come first, right? I love that you support me in what I'm trying to do, but you're paying the bills. I get that." She looked down, then raised her green eyes to his. "I know there are times I'm going to have to be alone." Her smile crinkled, and a dimple appeared on her cheek.

That smile, and those eyes, always got to him. He put down his wine glass and moved toward her. This was the first time in nearly two weeks that they had chatted like this. There had been a bit of a rough patch after he forgot about a meeting she had with a lady about a potential short-term rental opportunity for a small stand at the waterfront in Mossel Bay. The owner wanted to check her out, to offer her a shot at setting up her tattoo parlor for the December holidays. Her Jeep had been giving problems again, and she had asked Josh to drive her through. He had forgotten and had not put in leave for the day.

She lost the contract and he had been given the cold shoulder ever since. Now she seemed relaxed about it. Josh glanced sideways at the bottle of wine sitting on the kitchen counter, trying to spot the label. If it was the wine that did it, he wanted to know which one to get in the future.

The day's rain had subsided. The clouds had drifted away, leaving one of those beautiful Southern Cape evenings that so many people cited as their main reason for giving up the big smoke in all corners of the country and moving down to this idyllic piece of paradise. He suggested, and she agreed, that they should drive out to the beach.

The sun was setting as they drove into the parking lot in Victoria Bay. They took the bottle of wine that Josh had brought home and the few slices of pizza that were left, along with a fuzzy blanket, down to the beach. Besides the moon, the only bright thing in sight was the slight fluorescence of the white water as the waves came in.

Three surfers—two guys and a platinum-blonde girl—enjoyed the surf that seemed to be dying down as darkness settled. They would pack up pretty soon.

Josh and Amy cuddled under the blanket, sipping wine, and discussed the week that had passed. She asked him about the murder case, but he was reluctant to let it intrude on their private time.

The surfers greeted them with broad smiles as they walked past. When they were alone, Josh kissed Amy and nuzzled her ear, and she giggled.

"Hey, you pervert, the surfers may be gone, but some sweet old folks like to walk their dogs here, you know?"

He chuckled. "Yep, *doggy* is kind of top of mind."

She burst out laughing, kissed him long and passionately, and then suggested they pack up and go home. The invitation was in her voice, and in record time he had disposed of the empty pizza box and the wine bottle in a nearby rubbish bin. They trudged through the sand back to the car, hands all over each other.

SUNDAY

10H23

After a leisurely breakfast in bed, Amy had left for the gym around 09h00. Josh stayed home and messed about with her Jeep. The thing still had trouble starting, and neither of them was ready to send it to a local mechanic who would charge an arm and a leg for something that Josh might be able to fix himself. He knew next to nothing about engines, but he worked from the premise that if he tightened everything that should be tightened and checked that all cables were in one piece, he would eventually find, and fix, the problem. As he walked back into the kitchen to fetch a cold beer, the phone rang. It was AppleMac.

"Hey, Captain, how you doing? Sorry to bother you on the holy day, but I thought you'd want to know soonest."

AppleMac's contact at Vodacom had come back with the dirt on Whitcombe's phone. A record of numbers dialed and calls received would be emailed to the station on Monday morning. But the interesting part was that the phone still showed up on cell phone towers. Josh was stunned; he had already made up his mind that the phone was somewhere at the bottom of the lagoon.

"Where's the signal coming from?"

"Over in my neck of the woods, Cap, Joodse Kamp and Concordia."

Josh knew that Joodse Kamp was a poor settlement situated between Xolweni and Concordia, on the hill overlooking the lagoon. Less than three kilometers from where Whitcombe's body was found.

CHAPTER 5

Josh walked into a buzzing squad room. Most of the seven desks were manned, with officers on their computers or on the phone. He saw Christiaanse and Van Wyk shooting the shit at the water cooler. He guessed they were discussing the weekend's drinking and that they were being as helpful to the investigation as they had been in the briefing on Saturday.

Gavin came out of AppleMac's office and spotted Josh, a smile on his face. "Hey, you made it!" Josh had the feeling that there had been some news. He greeted his commanding officer and commented on the state of the place. Gavin's smile broadened. "Yes! Looks like things are starting to happen." He motioned Josh into his office.

Gavin clapped his hands together. "We got a hit on the BOLO on Brink. A patrol unit out past Stormsrivier Bridge turned into the Tsitsikamma Total Petroport. They showed Brink's photo around and got a hit from a cashier at the Wimpy. Apparently he grabbed a burger and chips.

"The officers managed to get CCTV footage from the garage forecourt. Brink got into a red Toyota Avanza, and left, driving east. We got a partial registration number and we have a report out on the radio. I've been assured that the Eastern Cape units are following this as priority. There was a hijacking in Port Elizabeth last night, and a tourist was robbed in his tent out at a game farm near Humansdorp, so there's a bit of action out there, but the Avanza's number one on their list. I'm hoping we'll have some news before noon."

"Have we had any news on the post-mortem and the rope sample sent to Forensics?"

"No. Fuck, I get so pissed off at the forensics bastards—those slackers out in Mossel Bay. The ETA for anything, on both counts, is tomorrow by 17h00. How the hell do they think we're supposed to get things solved when we have to sit on our asses waiting for evidence?"

Josh understood the frustration. Yes, there were budget cuts all the time, and a severe shortage of skilled personnel, especially in forensics and the other satellite services that required qualifications. But he also wondered how hard it could be to do your job when the evidence gets literally delivered to your door. Just start up your computer or polish the lens on that microscope and get on with it. It wasn't as if those lab technicians had to scour the streets for evidence like the poor sod cops.

Josh tried to steer the conversation away from forensics. They were on a high here. They had action, and some prospects in play. "Did AppleMac tell you about Whitcombe's phone?" he asked.

Gavin looked up from lighting a cigarette. "He mentioned something about the signal being picked up out at the squatter camp, up on the hill. Any movement on that?"

"I think we go after it," Josh responded eagerly. "Even if we get the phone records from Vodacom, there might be other stuff on the phone. Pics, videos."

Of course, the phone showing up in Joodse Kamp didn't mean that Whitcombe had been there. They knew next to nothing about the retired advocate's final hours. He could well have been mugged or had his phone stolen somewhere. In fact, Josh now recalled Christiaanse and his team reporting the state of the cottage: papers everywhere and the computers missing. There had been no forced entry, but that didn't mean that Whitcombe hadn't been attacked there.

Gavin nodded. "You guys get me the phone and then we'll see where we are. We'll have to connect Brink to Whitcombe anyway. That little brawl back in September doesn't do it for me in terms of motive, and definitely not in terms of opportunity. That's nearly two months ago. We would need to place Brink still in town or in the area and, hopefully, in contact with Whitcombe over the phone or on the internet. You get me that, and we can nail the fucker."

Josh was in a patrol car with AppleMac and two officers.

When he saw Christiaanse and Van Wyk still at the water cooler when he and Gavin returned to the squad room, he decided to ask for the two officers who had found the body on Friday night: Fortuin and Fourie.

They were actually quite pleasant guys. Clint Fourie was clearly Batman to Solly Fortuin's Robin. Solly was nice enough, but not the sharpest tool in the shed.

Clint drove, Josh riding shotgun and AppleMac in the back with the big guy. Just before they left, AppleMac had pulled the email from his Vodacom contact off his computer with Whitcombe's cell phone records for the past two weeks. Thus far, they only had Veronica's number and the home phone of the Pezula house to eliminate. An officer worked the computer back at the station, trying to get a handle on the other numbers dialed and calls received. They hoped to have a complete picture by that evening, so that they could start following up on Whitcombe's contacts and try to patch together a picture of his movements.

The bad news that AppleMac reported as they climbed into the car was that his Vodacom contact, Trixie, had just phoned to say that the cell phone's signal had finally died. While signal triangulation off cell phone towers couldn't pinpoint an exact address, this was still bad luck. The last position before the signal went was somewhere in the region of the Masifunde Library on Concordia Road. Josh knew they would have to go door to door in the surrounding neighborhood.

He chatted to AppleMac on the way out of town. The IT tech lived with his grandmother of ninety-six, in one of the oldest houses in the settlement. She and his grandfather, deceased some fifteen years before, had moved there from Uniondale in the late 1980s. Since then, the area had become more of an informal settlement, with the huge influx of poor and jobless Africans from the rural Eastern Cape, looking for work in Knysna and Plettenberg Bay. Shacks and lean-to's were now the order of the day. *There goes the neighborhood,* seemed to be AppleMac's general attitude toward developments. He was constantly worried about his "ma"; crime around Joodse Kamp and Xolweni had increased sharply in recent years, but he couldn't budge her to move elsewhere, even into the town of Knysna itself.

As they drove east on the N2, Josh asked AppleMac about the hard drives.

"Sorry, boss, I didn't get to that yet. I had a bit of a domestic emergency yesterday. I'll have a look when we get back to the station."

Josh didn't ask about the emergency, but he suspected that AppleMac had spent Sunday catching up on his IT business. He couldn't blame him; he himself had spent the day fucking around with Amy's Jeep and watching Netflix.

As they turned left off the N2 onto Assegaai Road to make their way up the hill, Gavin phoned Josh's cell. More bad news.

"Hey Josh, bit of a clusterfuck this side. An EC patrol out of Port Elizabeth found the Avanza, parked in front of a guest house in Jeffrey's Bay. Turns out the driver's a retired teacher from Despatch, who was out this way visiting his daughter and her family out in Happy Valley. They sent through a pic. The guy looks a little like Brink if you squint real hard. Fuck me, that cashier at Wimpy must have been on meth! So that's a fucking bust."

Josh let off a few choice words of his own. The net had just stretched much wider.

Chances were that Brink had gone west toward Cape Town, so the Western Cape units would scour the main routes, primarily the N2 highway and towns en route such as Swellendam, where one could leave the N2 and take quieter roads toward Robertson, Worcester, and the N1. From there beckoned the road north, and Johannesburg, which would have to be a prime focus, but Josh knew that even the west coast would be in reach for Brink. The guy was AWOL with a whole country to traverse. Worst of all, with the Toyota lead not panning out, they didn't even have a vehicle to search for. They would just have to wait.

Brink's files from the NPA didn't raise any particular Cape Town angle. Brink had been based in Johannesburg and in the north for years, having only retired to a small house near the naval base in Simonstown in '92, which is why he was arrested, tried, and convicted in the Western Cape High Court in Cape Town, and why Whitcombe at the Cape Bar crossed his radar for the eventual appeal.

According to the files, there was a sister who married a farmer out in Clanwilliam toward the west coast, back in the 1980s, but she had died while Brink was in prison, and apparently Brink and his brother-in-law never got along. Chances of him fleeing in that direction were slim, but Gavin had mentioned that a Cape Town team was in the process of paying the farmer a visit.

Gavin said that he was not going to sit around the station waiting for news. He would take the drive up to Pezula to talk to Veronica Whitcombe again, to get the phone number for the cottage and to find out whether the cottage computer had made its way back to the house at some point. Josh still had the autobiography angle in the back of his mind, and he asked Gavin to ask her about that, and if there might be notes or early drafts floating around the house. Gavin agreed that it was a good angle to pursue, and he promised to ask. He wished Josh and the team luck with the search in Joodse Kamp and rang off with a warning to be careful.

The informal settlement was home to several drug gangs, especially the Funky Guys, a gang of Rastas who were suspected of being the main manufacturers and dealers of methamphetamines, or *"tik,"* in the Southern Cape. These guys were dangerous; some of their exploits made the gangs on the Cape Flats seem tame. Josh hadn't known that the Knysna area had huge drug problems, but he considered himself duly warned.

Masifunde Community Library
Concordia Road, Joodse Kamp
09H24

They had parked at the library, where they could hide the patrol car among a few other vehicles, of all shapes, sizes, ages, and states of roadworthiness. There was some type of women's empowerment workshop going on in the building, and there were even a couple of late model, jet-black SUVs with blue lights, with dark-suited drivers having a smoke and waving at the

SAPS team as they drove in. *Probably some ANC politicians,* Josh thought. *They were the ones who so loved the shiny cars and blue lights.*

Josh quickly organized the search. He and AppleMac would check out the library. The earlier proximity of the phone signal to the building could have been coincidence, but there was always a chance that Whitcombe had visited the library. Clint and Solly would start a door-to-door search along the street, interviewing the inhabitants and asking whether anyone had seen an older white guy in the past few days.

As Josh and AppleMac walked into the library, a few guys in dark suits came out. The politicians were leaving. It seemed that the meeting, which had been held in a large room just off the entrance way, was over. A few people milled around. Josh saw the title slide of a PowerPoint presentation projected on a white wall toward the rear of the meeting room, reading "Stakeholder's meeting of the Phantom Pass Environmental Project (PPEP), **EMPOWERING OUR LOCAL WOMEN TO CONSERVE OUR BIODIVERSITY HERITAGE**." The speaker was listed as Charmaine Dalgleish, from the Western Cape Provincial Government's Department of Environmental Affairs and Development Planning. Josh spotted a white lady who looked to be in her fifties chatting to three black women. As he walked over, he saw a tall Coloured guy moving toward the library exit.

AppleMac nudged Josh and whispered in his ear. "You know him? That's Jerome Erasmus, 'Masekind,' leader of the Funky Guys."

Josh looked over. The guy looked to be in his forties, well-built with a lot of muscle, dressed in traditional Khoisan garb, with a tall red and green *"tam,"* or rastacap, hiding his dreadlocks. Despite being inside the library, he wore a pair of Aviator sunglasses.

As he passed, he flipped the glasses down and squinted at Josh over the lenses. *"Hey djy, wat de fok kyk djulle boere?"* Royalty walking here, man. *"Moenie met my fok nie."*

AppleMac whistled softly. "There walks a very dangerous man. Wonder what the fuck he was doing in a library."

Josh shrugged, then asked AppleMac to look for the library manager and find out more about the meeting. How many people had attended, and who. He then walked over to the white lady as she finished her conversation and turned to fetch her bag from the podium.

"Ms. Dalgleish, I presume?" She turned with a ready smile and offered her hand.

He put out his own hand. "Captain Josh Holland, I'm with the Serious Crimes division of SAPS George. Nice to meet you."

"Please call me Charmaine. And *please* buy me a coffee?" Josh laughed. "I drove through from Pinelands at three a.m. to make it to this meeting. I am dead on my feet." She pointed him down a hall to the staff kitchen. "You won't believe it, but you can get one of the best cups of coffee in town right here. Want to join me?"

Josh followed her as she explained that a wealthy German resident of Hunter's Estate had donated a very expensive commercial espresso machine to the library. And then sent one of the local kids, Tebogo, to do a barista course in Cape Town, putting him up in a fancy hotel in the V&A Waterfront for a couple of weeks. Tebogo now sometimes came in to make delicious coffee for the staff and visitors to the library, when he was not working at an upmarket boutique hotel on the outskirts of town. Josh was impressed.

He was even more impressed with the coffee. Tebogo had a glint in his eye and a big smile, all glittering, white teeth. He greeted Josh and proceeded to make the perfect cup of espresso. Charmaine sipped the brew with a dreamy smile as Josh explained that they were looking for any news of someone who had been found murdered down by the lagoon on Friday night. When he showed her the photo of Whitcombe they had pulled from the internet, her eyes widened.

"That's the lawyer. I've never met him, but I've seen him at a couple of these meetings. I don't think he ever spoke up, or to me at least, but I remember him sitting in the back, taking notes. Someone mentioned that he was some kind of lawyer."

Josh was alert now. They had assumed Whitcombe's cell phone had been stolen at the time of the murder, and had found its way up the hill to Joodse Kamp, as this was where stolen property often ended up. But it seemed Whitcombe had some connection here.

"Do you mind telling me what this PPEP is all about? I've never heard of it. But you seemed to have a pretty good turnout, including some bigwigs."

Charmaine pulled a face and sipped her coffee before she started what sounded to Josh like the usual spiel she probably gave when asked about the project.

The Western Cape government's DEADP—and yes, she was aware of the irony of the acronym—was tasked with environmental planning and sustainable development. The department had, for the past few years, been preoccupied with the drought in the province, which frequently made headlines and had a significant fallout for the Western Cape's governing party, the Democratic Alliance, for their alleged poor management of the crisis. There was also talk of large rifts between the provincial and the national governments (the latter run by the ANC)—there was no love lost between the two opposing political parties—and of a refusal by national government to bail out the Western Cape in the driest, and direst, days of the drought. Rainfall had picked up the last couple of years, and it seemed that a major crisis was averted for now.

The DEADP was also tasked with biodiversity conservation projects. One of the major areas in the province where this was pursued was along the Garden Route, and especially the stretch spanning Wilderness, Sedgefield, Knysna, and Plettenberg Bay, with its vast wetlands and substantial variety of unique, endemic fauna and flora. As an added benefit—or so the department's policy makers liked to declare—a key strategy goal was to empower local communities, particularly women.

Programs were aimed at selecting natural, environmental key points, and then identifying poor communities with the purpose of training and job creation. They worked closely with the provincial and national departments of tourism, with a view to not only develop indigenous expertise and conserve the beautiful landscapes of the Garden Route, but also to secure new revenue streams (mainly from ecotourism) and greater employment security for the many small communities of "refugees" streaming into the province in search of employment and social services. Josh smiled to himself when Charmaine said that they were trying to push the ecotourism angle so that the area would someday be more famous for the tourist draw card of its biodiversity than for its decidedly non-water-wise golf courses.

The Phantom Pass Environmental Project (or PPEP) was one such initiative. It targets the Phantom Pass, the last pass on Seven Passes Road between George and Knysna, which traverses about seventy-five kilometers of stunning landscape crossing the deep gorges cut by seven rivers in the area. The last of these, the Knysna River, which feeds into the lagoon by the estuary, is overlooked by Phantom Pass. The somewhat spooky name is rumored to derive from the white ghost moth, Letho Venus, which is endemic to the forests in the area. Josh had read about the Phantom Forest eco-reserve nearby, which had won world tourism awards as Africa's leading "green" hotel for a number of consecutive years.

The idea for the PPEP had come from members of the local community. In fact, from a group of Rastafarians who had a commune in the Phantom Pass area. Josh's attention perked up. He still wondered what the gangster, "Masekind," was doing at the meeting. He would ask her later.

When the department officials started giving little road shows about the plan to select a few key points for conservation and development in the Knysna area, a community leader had approached her. Vernon October—a local name with ties to a major trade union, who was active in championing the interests of the Xolweni, Joodse Kamp, and Concordia communities—suggested that the Phantom Pass forest would be an ideal site to focus their efforts. According to October, the forest had a significant spiritual history for the local Khoisan peoples, something that the Rastafarians had been tapping into since the early 1970s when they established a commune there.

The idea was that the construction of a small tourist center, with some traditional Khoisan artisans teaching tourists how to make Bronze Age weapons and tools, complete with a mythical forest trail and maze, could be a big draw card for foreign tourists, especially Europeans. It could assist in conserving the unique biodiversity of what was very close to a rainforest biome. It was also hoped that such development would go hand in hand with a renovation of Seven Passes Road, in order to make it a more popular, off-the-beaten-track tourist route. There was even the added attraction of the Millwood gold fields nearby, the site of one of South Africa's first gold rushes, which in the 1880s drew adventurers from as far afield as the UK, Australia, and California. The Western Cape Department of Tourism had, for some time, felt that this little gem was underdeveloped as a local tourist attraction.

Josh finished his coffee and listened attentively. Charmaine was passionate about the project, even if she was clearly tired after her long car journey.

"You saw the tall Rasta guy at the meeting?"

She nodded. "Yes, Jerome Erasmus, a leader of the local Rastafarian community. He's been involved with the project from day one."

Josh was careful of his phrasing. "You do know that he's also the leader of a local gang, one allegedly heavily involved in the manufacture and distribution of *tik*?"

She nodded, looking a bit pained at the change of topic. "Of course we hear these kinds of stories, but Jerome's been very helpful in smoothing things over between the politicians and the landowners up in the Rheenendal area. This development would impact them, you know." She glanced at him, with that pained expression still on her face. "We often deal with some 'off-color' characters when we go into these poor communities. I frankly don't want to know, as long as they bring something positive to the projects."

Josh didn't respond. He couldn't judge her for that, although he thought the government might be a bit more particular about who they chose to work with, being the same guys who paid his salary for putting these "off-color" characters behind bars.

She put her own coffee cup aside, stifling a yawn, her cheeks reddening.

"I am so sorry, Captain. I really need some rest. I'm staying in a guest house out in Belvidere. Do you think we could continue this conversation later today?" She smiled.

Josh couldn't say no. "That sounds good. I'd like to talk to you about the lawyer, Mark Whitcombe. We didn't get to that."

"Of course. As I said, I never spoke to him, but we can talk later. And I'd love to tell you more about the project if you have any further questions."

Josh got up and handed her a card with his cell phone number and email address. She gave him her own card, and the address of the guest house where she stayed.

He joined AppleMac at the entrance to the library, promising to fill him in on the conversation with Dalgleish, but first he wanted to see what Fourie and Fortuin found out on the street.

Turns out they had been busy.

CHAPTER 6

The rain had blown in again overnight. By 11h00 it was pissing down, uncommon this time of year, so near to summer. December was when this part of the world opened its doors to the equivalent of what Americans know as their "spring break." December was sun, sand, sex, and drugs you would never do again (or promised yourself not to). But lately, Knysna felt like a chilly English seaside escape. It was just wrong.

All officers involved in the investigation were supposed to meet at 08h00 in the squad room at the Knysna station. Everyone wanted to keep the "solve it in forty-eight hours" mantra alive, but they were no closer now to an arrest than they had been on Friday night when the body was found. There was a sense of urgency that was trickling down from Gavin to the lowest members of the team. The popular sentiment was they'd get a solve by this evening. It was bravado. It was stupid and premature. Josh was still new to the game, but even he could see that.

At 07h30, they were notified of a location and time change for the briefing. Now they were to rock up to some conference room at the Protea Hotel down in the Knysna Quays, the town's version of a hip and happening harbor-style development.

Gavin had sent out the request to meet at the Protea Room 1-14 (*Conference Facility—No Smoking Please*) for the meeting to start at 11h00. They were asked to park out in the shopping center's parking lot. Apparently, SAPS couldn't afford to book parking at a half-empty hotel—whose property and patrons were protected 24/7 in the tourist season by SAPS—without incurring a huge bill.

As Josh walked in, he could see AppleMac setting up the projector. He was one of the last to arrive and immediately thought what an impressive turnout it was. Of course they were all obliged to be there, but even in his short few days at the Knysna station, it was clear that some of the officers would find somewhere else to be for the inevitably boring meetings. Or maybe it was just the fact that the meeting was to start at 11h00 rather than 08h00. They all settled down when Gavin walked in, in the company of a bigwig in full dress uniform.

There were a few names on the program this morning. Gavin, AppleMac, and Josh were scheduled to report back on the investigation thus far, progress (none), and the way forward. Gavin would kick things off.

"Ladies and gentlemen. Thanks for coming," Gavin announced as he walked over to the podium and placed his coffee cup on the desk next to it. He gathered his glasses from his shirt pocket and put them on while shuffling through some notes in his hands.

He looked up. "We're not in the squad room."

There was a titter across the room.

"Sorry, that was for everyone except the detective squad. The observant ones, or at least the ones who get paid to be. For the rest of you poor suckers, we're in the Protea Hotel downtown. Those desks you're at are not your own, just in case it looks unfamiliar to those who actually spend time at their desks." He was smiling.

He explained that they had received a memo from the maintenance department at provincial HQ, two weeks ago. The Knysna station was being fumigated, bit by bit over a three-week period, and it turned out this morning's bit was the squad room.

Christiaanse raised his hand and asked a question before being acknowledged. "But really, sir, how much docs this cost? Must be *mucho dineros*. Some of us are still hoping for bonuses this year."

Some joker in the back pointed out that he had seen Christiaanse sniffing around the facilities, and pre-ordering his lunch, which was included in the conference fee. There was loud laughter from across the room. That seemed to shut Christiaanse up for the time being.

"Before we get too comfortable—" Gavin threw a pointed glance at Christiaanse, "—this is going to be an important briefing. We have with us—and we're very honored to have him, of course—the Cluster Commander for Eden district, Major-General Isaac Hlungwane." He pointed toward their uniformed guest.

There was muted applause across the room. Josh saw some eyebrows raised, and a few whispered comments. He had not been in the Southern Cape for long, but Josh guessed that members of the top brass were universally received with some skepticism, if not resentment, among the rank and file.

Hlungwane nodded, looking stern. Josh sensed that Hlungwane was pissed to be here, and would not make this a happy occasion for any involved. He nodded at Gavin to get on with things.

"OK, everyone, let's get settled here. I have a few things to say, and then Warrant Officer Jantjies will give us some feedback on the digital evidence. Then Captain Holland will tell us what he and the team—where's Fourie and Fortuin?" Hands went up from the third row. "Well, what that team has done in the past couple of days." Gavin paused, watching the faces of the officers. "Until now we've been focusing on one potential suspect." Maybe Josh imagined it, but Gavin seemed to cast a furtive glance at Hlungwane. "But what Captain Holland and his team have unearthed seems to have opened up a new avenue of inquiry. He'll tell you all about it." Gavin took a sip of his coffee.

"We all know Reghardt Brink looks like the alpha male here. He's been on our radar from day one, because of the initial interview with the widow, Mrs. Whitcombe. And I'll tell you that I have spoken to her since then, and I am personally still hot for Brink." A glance at Hlungwane, and once again, no response from the senior officer, beyond a scowl and a penetrating stare directed at the back of the room. Gavin wasn't fazed.

"But I think Captain Holland and his team have raised another possible avenue of investigation and we will pursue it as credible. You never know, these lines may intersect at some point."

There were some looks exchanged. Josh guessed that everyone would prefer an easy answer, but he just didn't think that there was one up for grabs in this case.

"OK, first up," Gavin continued. "No big surprise, but there's been some escalating media interest in the murder. Terence Maleka from the *Knysna-Plett Herald*—the guy's a bullterrier, most of you probably know him—and some young lady from *Die Burger*, De Jongh or De Lange?—have been phoning since yesterday morning. We've also been fielding calls from the SAPS Media Centre's Southern Cape Office, so let's have them deal with it. I want to ask Josh to contact Desiree Carolus. I'll give you her number later."

Gavin looked at Josh, who nodded. "Please liaise with her during the course of the day and for as long this takes, OK? Just remember that we have a bar on the details. We're withholding the finer details of the state of Whitcombe's body. We can discuss the wording of the statement after this meeting." Josh nodded again, and Gavin moved on.

"Now, for what I managed to find out when I went back up to Pezula yesterday morning. I had another chat with Veronica Whitcombe and to be frank, I'm starting to think that she might be hiding something. Whether it has anything to do with the murder, I don't know, but I just get that gut feeling."

He glanced at his notes. "Captain Holland and I both noted on Saturday that there didn't appear to be much love lost between husband and wife. However, now she seems to be prevaricating on her answers from that meeting. She doesn't know anything about whether there was a computer or computers down at the cottage. She doesn't know what her husband was doing down there most days. She now says she was just being flippant about him maybe having been busy writing his autobiography."

He glanced at Josh again. "In answer to the questions you wanted me to ask, Josh, she says that there are no notes or drafts of a book any-where she knows of. She was apparently just making the point that Mark Whitcombe was very self-absorbed and full of himself."

Josh nodded. *There goes the possibility of a motive coming from some wronged client or an old enemy wanting to avoid an exposé.*

"Apart from that, I got the feeling that something wasn't right between them; I mean, beyond maybe just not loving each other anymore."

He grimaced a bit. "I have this impression that maybe there was some pretty recent catastrophe. The usual suspect for that, of course, would be a mistress, some kind of affair. But I didn't get that feeling, really. On either side of the relationship. And she denied it.

"So, seeing that they didn't have any kids, I'm wondering whether it might have been something to do with money. All the trappings of wealth are there, of course, but you never know, right? I think we need to take a closer look at their financials, maybe going back six months or so. OK, AppleMac?"

Josh saw that Hlungwane looked uncomfortable, if not more pissed off than earlier. He guessed it was Gavin's reference to gut feelings. The brass were not known to like cop instincts getting in the way of stuff you could learn from a book or track on a spreadsheet.

"OK, just before we step off the subject of the widow. One last curious thing. She's been informed of the body's state, of course, and the fact that Whitcombe was found wearing only a denim shirt. She says when he left Thursday morning he was wearing chinos, a golf shirt, and a sports coat. He mentioned something about having lunch over at the golf club later."

Josh frowned and raised his hand. "So, we're looking at him having changed his clothing somewhere between Thursday morning and Friday evening? Did he keep clothes at the cottage?"

Gavin shook his head. "No, she says not as far as she's aware. I asked her about the denim shirt, and she said Whitcombe used to own one, but it was amongst a bunch of old clothes she'd asked him to drop at a home-less shelter a few months ago. She remembered because she was dead embarrassed when Whitcombe walked around Pezula wearing the old shirt."

Josh made a note.

"OK, *now* we're off the subject of the widow." Gavin cleared his throat. "We have a major development. Earlier this morning, we found out where Brink has been staying in the area."

The mood in the room picked up, a few people sitting up in their chairs.

"It seems he was lodging with an old ex-colleague of his from the security police death squad days. Guy by the name of Kobie van Zyl. He owns a run-down small-holding out in the forest near Rheenendal, really off the beaten track."

Josh's ears pricked up. He had heard the name yesterday. It was an area close to the Phantom Pass and the old gold fields. So, Brink and Erasmus had been active in the same area.

Gavin explained that a retired British teacher in her early seventies ran a volunteer animal rescue service out in the Rheenendal area, and often visited the farms and small holdings there, mostly to check on the welfare of the dogs and horses. She had a run-in with a man answering to Brink's description the previous week, when he chased her off van Zyl's property. When questioned by a SAPS patrol in the area, she immediately remembered the 'silly twat,' and told them about Brink. The man was long gone, however.

Gavin continued. "Van Zyl is a colorful character. The officers from George station who went out there to check the place out got a bit of a surprise when he pulled out an old, rusty AK on them."

There was some incredulous laughter amongst the group. Some eyebrows were raised.

"Yep, started threatening them and tried to chase them off his property. And, of course, true to form considering his pedigree, the guy called a couple of the officers 'kaffirs.'" A whistle came from the back. "No surprises; seems his bark is worse than his bite. They arrested him for obstruction of justice, for having an unregistered and highly illegal firearm, and for pointing said firearm at officers of the law—and they threw in some crimen injuria. The *doos* is currently cooling his heels in a holding cell at George station."

There was some sarcastic applause. Hlungwane still didn't budge.

"He'll be questioned about Brink, of course, and we'll check out his background thoroughly. For now, though, the most helpful info we have is that Brink was driving one of van Zyl's vehicles. It's a cream-colored Merc 230D, a 1989 model. We've put it out on Brink's BOLO. Hopefully, now we have a vehicle to look for, if he hasn't ditched it. That was about an hour ago, though. No hits yet."

Josh interrupted. "Sir, any indication of when he saw Brink last? When

Brink might have fled with the car?"

Gavin shook his head, pulling a face. "Nope. Van Zyl has lawyered up and refuses to answer any questions. We'll have to wait for that." Gavin put the papers back in his pocket. He finished off by telling them that a search of van Zyl's property hadn't yielded anything. Brink had been staying in a small room in an outbuilding, and had cleared out, leaving no belongings behind. Josh guessed the man's security police background had made him a light traveler, ready to "pick up sticks" at short notice and disappear in the wind.

"Well, that's not a lot, I'm afraid, but that's all from my side for now. AppleMac, can you give us some feedback from your side?"

As AppleMac rose from his seat, Clint had his hand up. "Sir, the boat?"

Gavin nodded and immediately motioned to AppleMac to sit back down. "Thanks, Clint, yes, sorry, I forgot. I got this from Fourie. The rowing boat has been traced to the owner." Again, Josh could sense some interest around the room.

"The owner reported it as missing or stolen on Sunday night. An old retired guy, an accountant by the name of Wilson, with a small place by the water out on Leisure Isle. Apparently, he didn't miss it 'till Sunday afternoon. It's usually tied up by an old jetty at his neighbor's house. He only uses the boat to take his grandkids out fishing on the lagoon, and they're only coming down in mid-December."

Clint jumped in. "We thought from the start that the boat might have drifted over from Leisure Isle, sir."

Gavin nodded. "Yes, I want us to check out the island sometime, maybe this afternoon. Let's see how accessible the neighbor's jetty is. Fourie, you and Fortuin can drive over." Clint and Solly both nodded. "Also, when you get out there, have a good look around to see whether we might have a murder scene out there. I don't have to remind everyone that there was no blood found in the boat. Whitcombe was probably not killed in it, but rather was moved into it after getting hit someplace else. It makes sense that the scene might be close to where the killer found the boat."

There were some murmurs of agreement.

Gavin stepped back from the podium, and AppleMac got up again. As he walked forward, Gavin looked over at Hlungwane and turned back to the group.

"The last thing from my side is just to, again, officially express my severe frustration at the service we're getting from Forensics in Plattekloof and the medical examiner's office in Mossel Bay." It was clear that he wanted to get this point across to the brass. "We're still awaiting results on the post-mortem and the rope. I guess I should be glad that we haven't had a further revised ETA on the results from them. As things stand, we're still expecting reports by 17h00 this afternoon. I really don't think the delay helps this investigation any."

Hlungwane nodded and looked away.

AppleMac looked a little nervous. "Hi, everyone. I really only have one thing to report on at this time." He glanced at Gavin. "Sorry, Colonel, I haven't had a chance to look at the emails from the Whitcombe laptop yet. Things have been a bit hectic, but I plan to spend this evening going through them and seeing what I can find." Gavin nodded. "The bad news is we got the results back from the Question Document unit on the letter the widow provided. Nothing, zippo, zilch."

Gavin cringed, with a sidelong glance at Hlungwane. Josh didn't know whether that was for the lack of a result or for AppleMac's choice of words.

Josh raised his hand.

"Sorry, just thinking aloud. You say no physical evidence from the letter, but from the text we at least know that there was a reference to 'files,' to be delivered or exchanged for something." He looked over at Christiaanse, who had led the search of the cottage. "I know you reported, and we asked, but I just want to double check. Was there nothing that could qualify as the files in question at the cottage? Or a sign of such files having been there?"

Christiaanse shook his head. "No, Captain, as we reported, just a lot of crazy environmental bullsh—" his eyes went quickly to Hlungwane, "—stuff that didn't seem to have anything to do with anything."

Josh nodded. "OK, thanks."

AppleMac continued. "What I can report on is that we got the vic's cell phone records from Vodacom yesterday morning, and we've managed to isolate the numbers dialed and the calls received for the past fourteen days, leading up to last Friday." He corrected himself. "Actually, last Thursday. There doesn't seem to have been any activity on the phone on the day of the murder."

Josh made a note of this.

AppleMac stepped over to the laptop and opened a Word document that was projected onto the big screen on the wall behind him.

It was a list of numbers. Beside each number was a name.

- *Veronica Whitcombe's cell phone, a total of 7 outgoing calls from Mark Whitcombe's phone and 4 incoming calls.*
- *The landline at the Whitcombe's Pezula house, 5 outgoing calls, incoming calls none.*
- *Papa's Pizzeria, Main Road, Knysna central, 8 outgoing calls.*
- *Daniel le Roux, 96 Thornely Road, Leisure Isle, Knysna, landline, 2 outgoing calls.*
- *Couple of unknown cell numbers, 7 outgoing calls and 2 incoming calls from one of the numbers.*
- *Imperial Jaguar, George, Knysna Road, George, 2 outgoing calls.*
- *Shaun Boutique Hotel, 109 Lynnwood Road, Brooklyn, Pretoria, 1 outgoing call.*
- *Lydia Crossley, 76 McNulty Drive, Silver Lakes Golf Estate, Pretoria, cellphone, 2 outgoing calls.*
- *Esther Rodrigues, 26 Ivydene Avenue, Rondebosch, Cape Town, cellphone, 1 outgoing call.*
- *Grant Filander, 38 Salie Avenue, Knysna, landline, 3 outgoing calls.*
- *Frank Mkwanazi Attorneys, Golden Isle, 281 Durban Road, Bo Oakdale, Bellville, landline, 2 outgoing calls.*
- *The Lookout Deck pub, Hill Street, Lookout Beach, Plettenberg Bay, 1 outgoing call.*

AppleMac stood aside, giving everyone a chance to read through the names. When he thought they'd had a good look, he stepped back to the podium, and Josh could see he was wearing an apologetic expression.

"As I mentioned, we only got this information yesterday. So we haven't yet had a chance to check it out, but this is priority and we will pursue each lead."

Josh saw that Hlungwane getting impatient, shifting in his seat with a scowl. AppleMac turned toward Gavin.

"Sir, I suspect those unknown numbers might give us some trouble. But we will check out what those calls were about."

Gavin nodded, then got up. "Does anyone have any thoughts on this?"

There was silence, a few people shaking their heads.

Gavin turned back to the IT tech officer. "OK, get a couple of guys to help you. We need to move on this. I want some results by later this week, OK?

AppleMac said they would, and asked if he could be excused. Gavin nodded and then motioned for Josh to take the stage, as AppleMac pressed a key on the laptop to return it to a blank screen.

Stepping up to the podium, Josh tried to order his thoughts. He liked to speak off the cuff whenever he had to speak in front of people. That was how he used to teach his classes. So, he took his cue from Gavin's earlier presentation.

"Good morning—sorry, seems to be afternoon already. Good afternoon, everyone."

He looked over the expectant faces. These were men and women who he knew wanted to get back to their computers and phones and chase down the case.

"Colonel Whitall presented his report of events and results in no particular order of importance. I want to do the same. So, I'll start with what we found out up in Joodse Kamp yesterday, on two fronts. Both point to a possible new suspect.

"Yesterday morning, I drove up to Joodse Kamp with Warrant Officers Jantjies, Fourie, and Fortuin. We went looking for the victim's cell phone. You all know that Vodacom picked up the signal up there until it faded out, in the vicinity of the library. I'll tell you what W/O Jantjies and I found out there, but first what W/O Fourie and Fortuin found.

"They did a house-by-house in Concordia Road and the surrounding streets. There was no sign of the phone. Of course, we didn't really expect to find it. If it's there, it's hidden under someone's mattress or sold or bartered for drugs already; but we did get something. I think you're all familiar with the Funky Guys?"

There was a general murmur, some unintelligible swearing.

"And then you also know of Jerome 'Masekind' Erasmus." Nods, and a few scowling faces. "Well, Erasmus lives in a big house on OR Tambo Street, a couple of blocks behind the library. It's no secret, everyone in the area knows of him and where he stays, although I don't think he gets many local visitors from the 'hood.' The people we spoke to at the surrounding homes don't really want to talk about Erasmus. My impression was that he is feared, and people would rather turn a blind eye to him being there."

Josh looked at Clint. "W/O Fourie, if you don't mind, I'll paraphrase from your report. Erasmus's place blends in well with the rest of the neighborhood. An old house, double story, zinc roof, needs paint everywhere, looks neglected. But where the poor paint job stops, the security features start.

"There's a wrought iron fence surrounding the property, about three meters in height, cameras in a few spots, clear signs declaring that the place is protected by armed response, and, apparently, a couple of teenage guys walking around the yard, looking organized. Like sentries."

A few team members seemed to make the connection.

"These guys were the armed response." Josh looked at Clint again, who nodded.

"Clearly the place is protected. The officers asked around and nobody in the street can recall there ever having been a break-in or anything at the house. We all know that Erasmus is doing stuff in there. Probably has a supply of drugs there. But I think everyone in the area knows that the place is protected and that if you mess with Erasmus, you'll have some major problems in terms of life expectancy.

"Anyway, W/O Fourie dodged the sentries and knocked on the electric gate, calling out that SAPS officers were in the area looking for information on a mugging and a stolen phone. There was no response from inside and no entry was provided.

"But W/O Fourie managed to sneak around by the gate and catch a glimpse of part of the yard." Here Josh turned to Clint again.

"Would you mind just telling us, from your seat is fine, what you saw?"

Clint Fourie looked a little flustered—he hadn't been asked to speak today—but he stood up and turned halfway toward the audience.

"Hi, guys. *Ja*, it was a bit of a mess. The place looks like most properties in the area. The yard is a rubbish dump, all kinds of sh—things lying around. A rusty old car and a broken-down washing machine, some other stuff, but I got the feeling..." He paused, looking a little embarrassed, "... that it's an organized mess. Doesn't look like the normal crap just strewn around. I don't know. Like the place was camouflaged to look like a mess."

He glanced at Josh as if for reassurance before turning back to the team. "What I did see seemed to prove that. There was a car parked in the yard. I could only see the front half, at a bit of an angle. Looked like a *laanie's* car, low black Audi. Fancy car, brand new."

Josh stepped back to the podium and interrupted Clint. "Thanks, Clint." Clint nodded and took his seat.

Josh turned to AppleMac. "W/O Jantjies, I believe you have some information for us on that?"

AppleMac got up, grabbing some sheets of paper from the empty seat next to him.

"Hi again, everyone. I have here some printouts from the file on Jerome Erasmus which we requested and received last night from the Organised Crime Investigations and Narcotics unit out in George. We found the car."

AppleMac was reading from a page in his hand. "It's not black. It's 'Daytona gray'—apparently that's a very dark gray that may appear black—a 2019 Audi RS5 Sportback purchased from Audi Centre in George in September this year. That's a more than 1.5 million rand car, with all the bells and whistles, according to the dealer specs. And, according to the dealership, the car was paid for in cash. There's also a 2016 Ford Ranger and a 2009 VW Golf registered in his name. Oh, and a boat."

"What kind of boat? A red rowing boat?" Clint asked.

Everyone burst out laughing.

"Sorry, it's not that easy, I don't think," Gavin said, bringing things under control again.

Van Wyk, of all people, spoke up from the back.

"Colonel, we know this guy is a *skollie*. And Narcotics knows all about him. But can we link him with Whitcombe?"

Josh was surprised. The guy actually seemed to be able to think like a cop, in between all his bullshit with Christiaanse. He spoke up.

"Thank you, W/O Van Wyk, good question. We're getting there," Josh said. "Officers Fourie and Fortuin couldn't find any trace of Whitcombe's phone from the house-to-house, as I mentioned. But W/O Fortuin did get to speak to a few quite vocal young lads who were playing 'World Cup final' out in the road."

There were a few smiles; especially from the Coloured members of the team who had grown up playing that exact same "World Cup final" in their own streets, using bricks as goalposts.

"After the website pic of Whitcombe was shown around, a couple of *laaities* were adamant that they had seen the old whitey with the long hair and the 'red Ferrari.' The 'Ferrari' had apparently been parked in front of Erasmus's house a few times over the last month or so."

Here Josh smiled at Solly and said, "Good work." He continued, "Whitcombe's Jaguar, which is in the impound lot now, is an F-Type Coupe, in 'Caldera Red.' I went onto Jaguar's website and checked it out." Josh took an A4 page from the file folder on the table next to the podium.

"I printed this out this morning." He held the photograph of the sleek Jaguar sports model up for everyone to see. "I know we have a lot of car guys in here who might laugh at me, but for the rest of us, I would suggest that this car, in that color, would look like a Ferrari to any kid, and probably to a lot of adults, too."

There were nods and even a few enthusiastic affirmations from the group.

"That puts Whitcombe at Erasmus's place on multiple occasions."

Gavin nodded, and he thanked Clint and Solly for some sterling work. He then asked them to make sure that they took pictures of Whitcombe's car and to follow up by showing it to the children who claimed to have seen the "Ferrari." He knew that a defense attorney somewhere down the line could jump on a failure to verify that this was the actual car witnessed at Erasmus's residence. Clint made a note of this and gave Gavin a thumbs up from his seat.

There were some looks exchanged, the silent (and salient) question being: what the hell did a retired advocate and a drug lord have to talk about?

Josh put the photo of the car back into the file and moved on to the library side of the previous day's investigation.

"OK, everyone. Let me tell you what W/O Jantjies and I found out at the library. And W/O Van Wyk, to answer your question just now: we found more to link Whitcombe and Erasmus there."

Van Wyk looked sullen but nodded. Josh guessed he had had his one original thought for the day and was now probably looking forward to lunch. Or drinks after work with Christiaanse.

Josh explained the events at the library: seeing Erasmus, the remark that was thrown his way, and then the chat with Charmaine Dalgleish. He tried to condense the information about the PPEP project, emphasizing the fact that Whitcombe had attended a few meetings, and that Erasmus was involved, possibly through the machinations of the local activist, Vernon October. They were going to check him out. He decided to summarize his own thinking.

"We seem to have a situation where Whitcombe and Erasmus came into contact through this government project. Of course, they may have met or known each other before that, but this is what we have to go on for now. We have no idea what Whitcombe was doing. We have the evidence from the cottage, seeming to show that he was into environmental causes, but we don't know yet what drew him to the PPEP. So maybe they met at Erasmus's place to discuss the project. We don't know.

"What does seem interesting—and this is not our main focus, I just thought about it earlier—is that Brink was staying out in Rheenendal, with van Zyl. That's part of the area allocated for the project. I remember Ms. Dalgleish telling me that the project would affect the landowners there, and that Erasmus was helping to smooth things over with them. We might even have a triangular link here around the project. Whitcombe, Erasmus, and Brink. But I think we have enough to work with in putting the vic and Erasmus together, if not for some other reason, then at least in terms of their involvement in this project."

He saw nods across the room.

Josh wrapped things up and thanked everyone. He stepped down from the podium. A second later, he turned back, looking at Gavin.

"Sorry, Colonel. By the way, we didn't quite forget why we went out there."

After tracking down Fourie and Fortuin outside the library, Josh had dashed back inside. Whitcombe's phone was not in their lost and found.

It remained a priority in the investigation.

The briefing broke up just after 15h00. The team members went in different directions to check out various angles. Josh left Gavin at the hotel, where he was to have a discussion with Major-General Hlungwane.

Rather you than me, Josh thought.

Just before Josh left, Gavin invited him and Amy to a braai at his place that evening.

CHAPTER 7

Amy and Josh got out of the BMW in front of Gavin's house, a neat little cottage toward the quiet end of a cul de sac, set between old trees and established gardens. They walked up a paved drive to the front door, which stood open. Soft music could be heard coming from inside, Norah Jones.

Josh knocked, and a minute later Gavin came to the door, all smiles, barefoot, with a beer in his hand. Introductions were made, and Gavin asked them to step inside and walk through to the back, where his wife was busy in the kitchen with "a salad or something."

The house was tastefully furnished by someone with an eye for antiques. Amy gushed about a couple of pieces of art until Josh slapped her on her behind and told her to move it, people were thirsty. Gavin laughed.

Jenny Whitall was a pretty woman, petite and brunette. She smiled broadly as Amy and Josh were introduced. Josh handed a bottle of red to Gavin. Amy commented on the décor and she and Jenny started talking a mile a minute. Gavin put his hands up and said he was going to steal Josh away for a few minutes while they went to light the braai out on the patio. Jenny reminded him that he had agreed there would be no work talk that evening.

"I know, woman, so let me get it out of the way before you two join us outside. OK?" She gave him a mock withering stare, then laughed. "At least offer Josh a drink before you go."

Gavin and Josh stepped outside onto the patio, each with a cold beer in hand. The weather had cleared again during late afternoon, and it was another stunning evening.

"Wow!" Josh said and meant it. A large, well-kept lawn sloped down away from the house toward distant flower beds planted with shrubs. Tall, old trees grew by the fence at the back of the property, giving the illusion that the garden bordered on a woodland. It was spectacular.

A large pool on the right was connected by dark wooden decking to the patio, where the braai was set up.

"I never knew you colonels made this kind of money," Josh said with a cheeky smile. "Anything IPID should know about?"

IPID is the Independent Police Investigative Directorate, the watch-dog tasked with investigating allegations of criminal conduct by SAPS members.

Gavin laughed. "If only! And no, I haven't been taking any bribes, thank you." He explained that the house had been Jenny's parents' home, in the family for two generations. And that was the reason why he, Gavin, had decided to settle in Knysna after all his various postings in the past. He was originally from here, had grown up in Sedgefield after his parents moved from the UK, and had gone to boarding school in Cape Town from the age of fifteen. He had met Jenny here in his early twenties when on holiday with his parents, and her whole life was here. "I managed to marry well," he said with a wink, as he took a sip from his beer. They toasted to marrying well.

Gavin put his beer down to light the braai. "Josh, I really don't want to talk shop tonight. Jenny will actually kill me, but I would just like us to chat about a couple of things before the ladies come out."

Josh nodded. "Of course."

"I've put on my party face, so that you can't see the seething anger bubbling under the surface." Josh raised an eyebrow. "The bloody post-mortem results are not in yet. The fuckers promised us we'd have it today, but I got an email from the pathologist's assistant an hour ago. They are sorry, some unforeseen shit came up. Apparently, the autopsy was done, but they're waiting for a toxicology report overnight. The new ETA is to-morrow morning by nine. If not, I really will make *kak* for them. I'll go all the way up to the provincial commissioner if I have to. We know each other, he'll sort it out. This is not the first time this has happened."

Josh had heard that Gavin was close to the powers that be in the Western Cape provincial structures, but he got the sense that Gavin was not one to casually drop names.

Gavin grabbed his beer and took another sip, then moved a couple of logs around on the fire. The flames from the firelighters started to lap hungrily at the *rooikrans* wood. Josh grew up with an English-speaking father and an Afrikaner mother. She would never use, or need, so many firelighters. Maybe it was a *rooinek* thing, he thought, smiling to himself.

"We did get a brief report from Forensics in Plattekloof, on the rope found in the boat. Not much use, I'm afraid. As we guessed, it is marine rope." Gavin seemed to have to think for a second. "Three strand, hawser lay polyester, for what it's worth."

Josh looked annoyed. "Damn, are we never going to get a break, *any* break, to help us out here?"

Gavin shook his head and tried to look more positive.

"Wait, there is something. Although I don't know that it'll help us much at this point in the investigation. The lab guys could trace it to where it was bought. Nautical Sports in Port Elizabeth."

Josh was surprised. "How can they trace marine rope to one supplier?"

"Because of the color. It comes in a variety, but it seems the only supplier in South Africa that sells this rope in olive drab is Nautical Sports. Apparently the most likely use for this kind of rope is as mooring warps for vessels. It's a chafe-protected rope used to fasten the boat to mooring buoys, or whatever, which might be something, because the sailing expert who the lab guy contacted somewhere in Cape Town said that the size of the rope means it was probably used for a larger vessel. Larger than your normal fishing vessel."

Josh looked doubtful. "OK, that's something, but how do we link this to anyone here in Knysna? That rope could have come from literally anywhere after its sale in the shop. And I know nothing about sailing, but surely one can use a bigger rope to moor a small vessel. Might be overkill, but it probably happens?"

"You're right." Gavin pulled a face again, and grunted. "Best case scenario is that the rope was bought from the shop by our perp, and he or she used it for its intended purpose, on a boat that requires a thicker warp."

"That would then exclude fishing boats, probably. So, what are we thinking? A charter boat? Or a houseboat?" Josh asked.

There were a number of boat charter services running in Knysna. There was also one company that offered stays on houseboats, a way to enjoy a week or two on the water within easy reach of Knysna nightlife.

Gavin shrugged. "That's about it. I'm not going to divert the investigative capacity at this point to look for *rope* when we probably won't be able to tie it to a credible suspect. Excuse the pun. Let's file that away in case it connects with something later—"

Josh interrupted. "I guess we should just ask the owner of the boat whether the boat itself was the source of the rope. You know? Whether he used that rope to moor the boat."

Gavin nodded. "Yes, of course. I texted Fourie and asked him to take a picture of the rope along to show the accountant."

Josh nodded.

There was no sign of the women yet. Josh guessed that Amy and Jenny were bonding, taking a tour of the house. He was glad. She could really do with making a friend in town. The fire was going now and Gavin and Josh each took a seat on comfortable outdoor lounge chairs. Josh stretched contentedly. It was a beautiful evening, and with the cold beer, the smell of the fire, and the pleasant company, he relaxed for the first time since Sunday.

Amy came walking out with two fresh beers, one in each hand.

"Hey, you two. Jenny sent me out with reinforcements." They each took a bottle gratefully. "And Gavin, Jenny asked me to come out to check whether you guys are talking shop. I gathered that sending *me* was for the sake of your health."

Gavin gave a hearty laugh, and Josh joined in. "OK, OK, please tell the ball and chain just a few more minutes. Then please come join us out here."

"Will do. And wow, it really is lovely out here." She walked back inside.

"She's very nice. And very pretty." Gavin smiled at Josh. Josh returned it and they toasted again.

"We probably should wrap this up. I just want to ask. I heard your briefing earlier today, of course, the facts. But what are your *feelings* about the case?" Gavin seemed sincere in his interest. "Never underestimate the power of the gut, son. A lot of what we do is about how you feel your way around a case. Even if the bigwigs don't like us to admit that."

Josh thought of Hlungwane. He hesitated for a second while taking another swallow of cold beer. He was flattered to be asked. He sensed that Gavin trusted him.

"I don't know, Gavin, I really have nothing to base this on, but I'm feeling less sure about Brink as our perp." Gavin raised an eyebrow, encouraging him to go on. "I know he's a good fit. He has been from day one. We have motive, and he seems to have fled town after the murder.

"I just think that this Erasmus angle is worth having a look at. That's where my money is. The guy is a recognized baddie, a *tik* dealer, and gang leader with a violent history. If he and Whitcombe had been in contact, and regular contact at that, I don't see that as a social arrangement. They had nothing in common.

"While I guess Whitcombe dealt with many such characters in his career—I remember reading that he did legal work for Rashaad Staggie in the early '90s, shortly before that shitbag's death—I would still find it strange that a retired senior counsel, married to a society lady, with a nice pad up at Pezula, would hang out with this guy. Surely he at least had some social standing to maintain?" Gavin nodded.

"And add to that this environmental project. I can't question these Rasta guys' commitment to their faith—well, I do find it kind of hard to reconcile the tenets of the Rastafarian faith with Erasmus's drug empire—but don't you find it strange that a guy like Erasmus would not only be involved in the PPEP, but actually seems to have initiated it?"

Gavin cleared his throat. "I agree, one hundred percent. Something is off there."

Josh glanced over his shoulder to make sure that the ladies were still inside, but dropped his voice anyway.

"Also, do you remember me saying the other day that the nature of the mutilation of the body—especially the killer slicing off Whitcombe's dick—doesn't sit well for me with Brink being the perp? I've been thinking that it might be evidence of some much more personal motive. Sexual jealousy? Jilted lover? Some twisted form of revenge?" He shook his head, frustrated. "I don't know. But I will tell you that if that was not the motive, I am a lot more comfortable in believing that this is the kind of damage 'Masekind' and his gangsters might do. Isn't this how they operate? Making their victims memorable, as a message to their enemies?"

Gavin nodded thoughtfully. "That does make sense. Well, as I said yesterday, I plan to stay on the Brink angle. Whenever we find the guy, he'll have to answer some tough questions on why he was stalking the Whitcombes. But I want you to run with the Erasmus angle. Maybe go out to Phantom Pass and have a good look at what's going on out there."

Josh was heartened by Gavin's agreement. "Definitely. I hoped to drive out there tomorrow morning. According to Dalgleish, they've started construction on the tourist center building, so there'll be workers out there I can talk to. And I'd like to talk to the Rastas too. Apparently they have a few members of the commune who live out there permanently, but I want to hang on with that until we're in a position to question Erasmus. Which I hope will be soon."

Gavin nodded. "Good idea. We don't want to spook him. He already has questions to answer over his involvement with Whitcombe. And those questions we'll place at his door through the eyewitnesses who saw the Jag at his house. I suggest we don't say anything about the project for now. As far as Erasmus knows, we don't have anything on Whitcombe's possible link with the PPEP. That might put him at ease. We can hit him with that later."

Josh agreed. Amy and Jenny came outside then, laughing, glasses of wine in hand.

They ate a delicious meal of braaied fillet steaks, boerewors, and a salad. The talk was relaxed, and the couples got along really well. The wine had helped. Josh and Gavin were now sipping an expensive whiskey, which Josh got the impression only came out on special occasions. Most of the evening's talk had been about Josh's rather unusual route into his current job.

He had grown up in the small town of Villiersdorp in the Overberg, just a few kilometers from Theewaterskloof dam, the largest dam in the Western Cape, which provides most of metropolitan Cape Town's drinking water. His mother still lived there, following the death of his lawyer father a few years ago. After school, Josh had completed his LL.B. degree at Stellenbosch University. After that, he had gone to the University of Cape Town, where he completed an LL.M. in private law. Then came two years doing his articles of clerkship at a small firm in the southern suburbs.

By the time he was admitted as an attorney and could practice law, he had decided it wasn't for him. He didn't want to spend his days in courtrooms and chasing after clients for the payment of his fees. He had returned to the Law Faculty at UCT, where he took up a position as a lecturer in contract law. After five years and a promotion to senior lecturer, he realized that the only way to make professor was if he did a PhD. So, at the ripe old age of 32, he gave up law and academia. He had always had a hankering for law enforcement and felt that he could contribute as a detective.

After spending the compulsory two years in SAPS—a dreary stepping stone for Josh, most of which he spent posted to the seediest areas of the Cape Flats and Kraaifontein—he was selected for detective training. And now here he sat, as one of the oldest trainee detectives in the country.

Amy and Jenny really hit it off. Jenny was an artist, specializing in landscape paintings, with subjects mostly covering the Southern Cape area and the Karoo. She had a small gallery in Thesen Harbour Town, in the upmarket Thesen Island marina development on the estuary. She was planning an exhibition for December to showcase a different style of work. She had completed a series of paintings of the indigenous peoples of southern Africa, with an emphasis on tribal iconography.

Upon hearing that Amy was a tattoo artist, Jenny suggested linking their work around the exhibition. Amy might do some tribal art tattoo designs which would be offered as an add-on to the gallery. Jenny might do prints of some of her work, which would be signed and sold to tattoo clients as part of a package, each print paired with the applicable tribal tattoo.

In the end, Gavin had to chastise Jenny and Amy for talking shop all evening.

The party ended just after midnight, and Josh and Amy made their way back to George. Amy drove. Both couples assured each other that they would definitely do this again, and soon.

CHAPTER 8

Josh had left home just after nine, feeling slightly hungover from the previous evening. He blamed the whiskey. He was driving up to Phantom Pass this morning, so he decided to skip the drive into Knysna to the station and go directly there. He took the Seven Passes backroad rather than the N2—it would be slower going, but there would be less traffic. He was also curious, after Charmaine Dalgleish's description of the area, to see the forests and the rivers in all their glory.

It really was a spectacular drive. In places he thought that it was a good thing he hadn't taken Amy's Jeep. He had considered it, in case he had to traverse rough ground and he needed the added ground clearance or the four-wheel drive. But it turned out that the road was perfectly passable for the BMW. And he would have hated to get stuck out here if the Jeep packed up again.

He followed the directions he had received from Charmaine and turned off the main road into a heavily sheltered by-road, under the thick foliage of some obviously very old trees. The narrow road was marked "B7" with a crude cardboard signpost. It didn't look like very official government business, until he saw the bulldozer and two other roadwork machines parked to the side, and then the opening in the forest where construction on a rather sprawling, bungalow-style building was well underway. They were not to roof height yet, but even from the car, the design of the building was clear. There were two other cars parked at the building. One was a white *bakkie* with a Knysna building supplies company's logo on the side, and the other was a bright yellow Mercedes convertible.

Josh got out and walked closer to the building works, as a white male in his late fifties—wearing a bright green tartan dinner vest above distressed jeans, a shining diamond ear stud, and a hardhat the color of the Merc—approached with a smile and a hand outstretched. Josh greeted Simon Fowler, the architect for the project.

He introduced himself and saw Fowler frown. He didn't seem pleased by the presence of a cop on his building site.

Josh explained that they were investigating a crime down in Knysna, which had turned up a connection with the PPEP project, and that he was just here for a first look. Fowler seemed very averse to this kind of attention, and immediately tried to deflect the police interest in "his" project. He pointed out the "virgin forest" surrounding them, and their "extremely low carbon footprint with the limited amount of construction equipment being used," with a vague wave of a hand toward the heavy machinery Josh had seen as he drove in.

Josh placated him by asking whether he could be shown around. Fowler was only too happy to oblige. Josh was not an idiot and he sensed that the guy was trying to get rid of him as soon as possible. He wasn't suspicious of Fowler, though, and he kept thinking that if a guy had come into his station asking for a tour, he would also want to send him on his way soonest.

Fowler explained that they were about five weeks away from completing the building. There had been some hiccups early on, with the supply of materials out here "in the sticks," so far off the beaten tracks of Knysna, and so far from the pool of local labor. With a backhanded swipe at politicians and how they operate, he explained that the DEADP had insisted they use only workers affiliated with the Tourism and Allied Workers' Union, or TAWU, until some bureaucrat finally realized that the bulk of the members of that union were not trained in construction work.

Tour operators, booking agents, and hotel reception staff were not well-known for their ability to build a tourist center from the ground up. Fowler laughed at his own wit here, and then explained how he had personally had to step in and say some harsh words. They were eventually provided with experienced construction crews, and things were now back on track for completion by the end date stipulated in the contract. By his own account, Fowler had saved the day.

Josh didn't like the guy. He was self-important, and to be honest a bit of a snobbish and "cultivated" shit, but the mention of TAWU rang a bell. He looked around and asked a silly question about the capacity of the building while trying to think. He then remembered that Vernon October, the gentleman who allegedly introduced Jerome Erasmus to the PPEP project, was a senior official in that trade union.

Josh mentioned the groups involved in the project, asking how they all fit in. He tried to bring up the involvement of the Rastas, to hear whether they were contributing or to what extent, if any, they had a say in what was happening. Fowler looked uncertain. He knew of the group, so Josh mentioned Erasmus's name, implying that he knew the man and was simply asking whether Erasmus had any hands-on involvement. Fowler just shrugged.

"I've met him, of course." The architect's eyes darted away. The impression Josh formed was that Fowler knew Erasmus was the main player in the project, but that he didn't actually know him well, if at all. He was trying to appear more important than he really was. Josh thought of the older model, yellow Merc convertible. The man was a poser. OK, he got it.

"That group has not really been involved with the execution of the project. Obviously, I'm handling the gist of that here, ensuring that building goes to specification and that the government's grand ideas get turned into reality: a brilliant new tourist destination, world-class and *very green*."

He smiled at this, and Josh got the impression that the guy was giving an acceptance speech at some environmental Oscar awards.

Josh had heard enough. He shook Fowler's hand and said that it was clear there was nothing untoward at the site, and that they had clearly been misinformed by their witness. Fowler at last seemed to grasp the plot, and he asked what crime was being investigated. Josh felt a perverse streak coming on, and he said that there had been some noises from within a provincial government department about the use of white professionals such as engineers, technicians, and architects on what were supposed to be black upliftment projects, and that some bribes had allegedly changed hands.

The architect looked dumbstruck. And—Josh thought—guilty. He wanted to laugh.

"Thanks for showing me around. And best of luck out here." After Fowler gave him an absentminded farewell, Josh made his way back to his car and then carefully backed out to avoid the big JCB moving in. So very green, indeed!

He drove off, seeing in the rearview that Fowler was still standing there, looking at the car until it rounded a bend in the road.

His cell phone beeped. It was Gavin calling, and he picked up immediately.

"Josh, where are you? Still out in the forest?"

Josh heard the excitement, and something else, in Gavin's voice.

"We have some action. Van Zyl's Merc, the one Brink's driving, has been found. No sign of Brink, though."

"Where?"

"Wait for it: at a bar, the Calabash Bush Pub, out in Bain's Kloof."

Josh whistled; that was a bit out of the way. More than four hundred kilometers from Knysna, in fact. He remembered thinking that one possible route Brink might take was from Swellendam on the N2 by the quieter roads to Robertson and Worcester, where he could get on the N1 to drive north. But he had bypassed the N1. Bain's Kloof was past Worcester and back in the direction of Cape Town. In fact, it could be a route, via Wellington and Malmesbury, to the west coast.

"What do you plan to do?"

Gavin sounded hyped up. "I want to go out there. The two of us. Now. Things are quiet here; we're waiting on a lot of stuff still, but I want to get momentum going. I want to see the car, get a feel for where Brink is headed. Maybe we'll find some evidence of that in the car and then we can organize a manhunt."

Josh replied, "That sounds good."

"Are you done out there?"

Josh replied, "Yes. I'll tell you about it on the way. How should we do this?"

"I think stay where you are. I'll come fetch you and bring an officer along to drive your car back to the station. Would that be OK?"

Josh considered this. He would phone Amy and let her know. The Jeep seemed to be running again, but if she had problems while he was away, he'd phone AppleMac and ask him to take the BMW through to the flat in George.

"Sounds perfect, I'll wait here."

ENGEN MOSSEL BAY 1-STOP (ON THE N2)
13H15

Gavin had picked Josh up just after 12h30 in the Corolla. He had driven like a madman on the N2 past George, Glentana, the Groot Brak and Klein Brak rivers, and now Mossel Bay. They stopped at the 1-Stop to refuel, and Gavin asked Josh to run into the shop and get them some energy drinks, chocolate bars, and cigarettes for him.

As Josh arrived back at the car, the attendant was finishing the fill-up and was washing the back window. Josh got in and handed the goodies to Gavin.

"Sorry, it just struck me, going through Mossel Bay. Did the post-mortem results come through this morning? Like they promised?"

Gavin laughed. "Shit, yes, at last!" He opened the pack of cigarettes. "I gave the report a very quick read. It came through about ten minutes after the report on Brink's car. So, I was a little distracted. It's in my briefcase in the back seat if you want to have a look later."

"OK, great, just glad we got it. Anything stand out?"

Gavin glanced over, looking unsure. "Hard to say. We'll have to check it in detail. But let me give you the main points. I want you to be as up to speed as I am." He gathered his thoughts for a minute, and then relayed what he knew.

"Whitcombe's time of death was estimated as between 22h00 on Thursday and 01h00 on Friday. He died from a hard blow to the head from a blunt instrument, which caused an epidural hematoma. A blood clot formed underneath the skull, probably from a tear in an artery that runs just under the skull, called the middle meningeal artery. That's associated with a skull fracture, and there was a pretty bloody substantial fracture, apparently.

"The weapon could be literally anything pretty heavy or swung hard enough, but it seems like a flat surface, no edgings or sharp ridges. The impact was frontal, to the side, hitting his temple, lower forehead, and upper left eye socket. I'm thinking the blood around the eyes obscured the bruising at first glance, which is why Fourie and Fortuin didn't note any of that in their preliminary report."

Josh nodded, listening attentively.

"The mutilation—castration and removal of the eyes—were done post-mortem. At least the poor guy didn't suffer through that. The blade for the former part appeared to have been somewhat blunt. Hence there was more blood than normal for that type of 'operation.'

"No hair or fibers on the body, I mean none. Apart from the fibers from that old denim shirt. It's a bit weird to find no hair, though." Josh nodded again, frowning. "What they did find was evidence of diesel on the body and in the hair. We'll check that out. Probably from some location where the body lay for some time, an hour or more, before being put in the boat.

"Finally, a thorough autopsy indicated that Whitcombe had cancer of the stomach. It didn't kill him, but he was dying."

Gavin paid the attendant and put the car into gear.

"What about that toxicology report?" Josh asked. "They said that it had held up the release of the results."

Gavin nodded, as he drew away from the pumps and lit a cigarette, lowering his driver's side window to let the smoke out.

"That's a separate report. I didn't get a chance to look at it yet, but it's also in the briefcase. Have a look if you want."

Josh started to reach over, then decided against it.

"No, it's OK, we can check it later. But I'd like to consider what the PM report does for us, in terms of the murder and the crime scene. Here we are, chasing Brink's ghost. Maybe there's something we can use when we catch up to him. You want to spitball a few ideas?" Josh asked, aware that Gavin was hyped up now with the thrill of the chase, and the idea of netting Brink.

But Gavin nodded. "Yes, let's talk. I want your thoughts."

Josh's first comment was that, for him, the biggest news was that the mutilation of the body had taken place post-mortem. "So does that rule out torture?'

Gavin nodded. "I also thought that. We're still putting the threatening emails and letter through the wringer, of course, and we still don't know who sent them. But the mention of 'files' shows that someone was after information. I also thought torture can't be ruled out."

Josh continued. "Then you mention the complete lack of hair and fiber evidence on the body. Which would suggest that it was cleaned. But there was a lot of dried blood."

"Yes, that is strange."

"We know Whitcombe didn't die in the boat, or rather, the mutilation didn't take place in the boat, right?"

Gavin grunted.

"If he died elsewhere, the body wasn't placed in the boat while there was still bleeding. So, we are looking at the murder taking place elsewhere, and the body then probably lying somewhere for a period of time, where some cleaning up could have taken place. That suggests somewhere in-doors, and out of sight. The killer must have access to premises where they could take their time, out of sight and without fear of discovery."

Here, Gavin jumped in.

"Sorry, I've been in a bit of a rush, so I forgot. On that point, Fourie and Fortuin went out to Leisure Isle this morning. They spoke to that Wilson guy. The owner of the boat."

Josh looked interested. Gavin glanced across at him and caught the look.

"No, unfortunately, it's a bit of a wash. Wilson knows nothing and saw nothing, and he says anyone could have taken the boat. The jetty where the boat was tied up is across the road from his neighbor's house. The houses are on the landward side of Links Drive, and the jetty isn't fenced. They checked Wilson's place out, including the double garage, and they didn't find any signs that someone was killed there, or that a body was stored there. No blood, signs of violence, nothing. They think Wilson's in the clear, and that the body was never at his place."

Josh looked disappointed, although he knew it didn't invalidate his theory.

"Oh, and by the way, they showed him photos, and Wilson couldn't identify the rope. He said that he had the boat tied up with a piece of clothesline the last time he'd left it there. He's never seen that rope before and he doesn't know how the hell it ended up in his boat. Then again, he had the same to say about Whitcombe's body."

Josh nodded. That at least could likely eliminate the man, who, if he had had anything to do with the murder, would probably have been smart enough not to leave the body out on the water in his own boat.

Just after they had passed the turn-off for Vleesbaai on the left, Gavin's phone rang over the speakers. He had it on Bluetooth, and the voice came over the Toyota's sound system.

It was a W/O Engelbrecht, phoning from the SAPS impound facility on Meul Street in George Industria, where Whitcombe's Jaguar had been taken. The commander of the facility had informed Gavin a couple of days ago that they were stretched to the limit. A large number of minibus taxis operating illegally around the nearby Thembalethu settlement had been impounded the previous week, and most of the staff were tied up in processing the return of these vehicles to their owners. There was a lot of paperwork. On top of that, there were five vehicles in the queue waiting to be searched and to undergo forensics testing. Gavin was told that the examination of the Jag would probably have to wait at least seven to ten days.

Gavin had asked them to at least do a cursory search before they put the car on ice, and for the W/O who performed the check to call him with results. That man was now on the line.

"Colonel Whitall, you asked us to check the vehicle's satellite navigation system. I've just done so."

Gavin sat up straighter, hoping that there would be some useful information.

"I'm sorry to say, sir, but there was nothing I could find that seems helpful. There are no saved destinations, apart from two restaurants in

Plett and the municipal offices in Mossel Bay. I've just sent you an email with those addresses. And there's no record of searches on the satnav."

Gavin wasn't happy, but it had been a long shot. He thanked the W/O and, before he dropped the call, asked whether the expected wait for the full examination of the vehicle was still as long as he had been told.

There was a tone of regret in W/O Engelbrecht's voice as he said good-bye, as he had to disappoint Gavin a second time in less than a minute.

Around 250 kilometers later, mostly on an empty N2 highway and then the quieter roads after Swellendam where Gavin got a few chances to show off his overtaking skills, they were through Robertson on the R60, about halfway to Worcester. Josh sagged in his seat, the morning's hangover gone, but he still felt pretty lethargic. He thought about Amy. Last night was great for her. She couldn't stop talking on the way home, about Jenny, and the idea for the art exhibition. He glanced sideways at Gavin. The couple were being extremely nice to them. He hoped to repay the favor someday.

His thoughts came back to the present and to the road they were driving, between Robertson and Worcester. He *hated* it. He knew it from back in his student days, when he and some friends had sometimes ventured to Ceres, Bonnievale, and other surrounding towns to camp out—*well, to be honest, to drink*. The road is long and for the most part quite straight, with nothing in the way of scenery beyond the low, uniformly brown Karoo bushes that cover the expanse of sloping hills on either side of the roadway. But the road itself had deceptive low rises and dips, and you would invariably come around a slight bend and find some guy oncoming in your lane, while overtaking someone else, having failed to see the approaching traffic. You always thought that you could see further ahead than you actually could. He could never help but get nervous on this stretch.

Gavin went too fast into the turn by the little bridge just past Nuy Winery, as most drivers did. He mouthed some sort of apology but didn't slow down. A few kilometers down the road, Gavin's phone rang again.

"Hello, Colonel Whitall?" a voice asked over the car's speakers, breaking up a bit.

Gavin answered. "Hi, yes, speaking. Who is this?"

"Sergeant Vilakazi, sir. From SAPS Wellington."

Gavin sounded a bit impatient. "Yes, sergeant, we are on our way to you guys, approaching Worcester now. Any developments around the suspect's vehicle?"

"Er, sir. We've found a body; in the vicinity, on the pass. We believe it's your suspect."

CHAPTER 9

They had planned to drive to the SAPS station in Wellington to meet the team, and then proceed from there to the bush pub to view the vehicle. But now Gavin decided to drive straight out to Bain's Kloof. He asked Josh to phone the Knysna station and tell Fourie to speak to the SAPS pathology services in Paarl. Gavin wasn't sure, but he thought Wellington (and the pass) fell under the Paarl forensics lab and mortuary. He wanted the post-mortem report on Whitcombe to be emailed through to the relevant persons there.

Gavin then phoned Sergeant Vilakazi back and told him that they were about thirty minutes out from the pass. He asked the team on the scene to meet them at the bush pub.

Josh thought that he had actually been to the pub once, years ago. He remembered that the vibe was great, and the pizza some of the best he'd ever had, a surprise find out there in the middle of nowhere. But they would not be having pizza today.

CALABASH BUSH PUB (ON THE R301)
BAIN'S KLOOF
16H37

Gavin pulled the Corolla into the bush pub's parking lot. There were four SAPS vehicles parked there, and a few officers who stood talking in a huddle that reminded Josh of rugby players having a chat before crouching down for a scrum. There were a few civilian vehicles, including, in a back corner of the lot, the cream Mercedes of 1980s vintage. All four doors, the trunk, and the hood were open as a couple of officers searched the inside of the car. Gavin and Josh got out and stretched their legs. The fan of Gavin's Corolla ran like mad, and Josh could smell the brakes. *Cooked, medium to well-done*, Josh thought.

The detectives walked over to the group of SAPS personnel. A Coloured officer in his late forties spotted them and stepped away from the group.

"Colonel Whitall? You made very good time. Nice to meet you."

"Thank you, sir, likewise." Gavin and Josh shook hands with Brigadier Tom Wilsenach, the station commander for SAPS Wellington. He had a pleasant face and manner, and he looked more like a manager than a cop.

They walked over to the group of officers, and Wilsenach introduced them, including Sergeant Vilakazi, a young officer who looked nervous but seemed raring to go on the investigation. He looked somewhat in awe of Gavin.

A patrol unit had pulled into the pub's parking lot just after 11h00 that morning, so that one of the officers could use the bathroom. The other officer checked the vehicles parked there and he recognized the Merc from the BOLO description as one of three vehicles that were currently on their radar through local and province-wide bulletins. The registration number matched. He fetched his partner, after which they informed the bar manager that they were looking for a suspect whose vehicle was parked outside. After a quick round-up of the handful of patrons in the bar and the restaurant next door, with ID checks, it was found that the driver of the Merc was not there. The officers went outside to secure the vehicle, and the call was made to the station. A few minutes later SAPS Knysna was informed.

The vehicle had been found unlocked, with the keys under the driver's sun visor.

"OK, we'll look at the car just now. What about the body, sir?" Gavin addressed Wilsenach.

"That was reported about an hour ago. I don't know how well you know Bain's Kloof?"

Josh replied that he had driven it a few times, and had once spent a weekend camping at the Tweede Tol campsite on the pass years ago, but

Gavin was unfamiliar with the area.

Wilsenach nodded and he turned to Gavin. "OK. It's a very narrow, winding road, with spectacular views of the valley and the river below. There are a few stopping points where you can pull over. One of them is at the Kramat."

Josh knew that a Kramat is a holy shrine of Islam, which marks the grave of a Muslim Holy Man, or Auliyah, a "Friend of Allah." There is a circle of Kramats surrounding Cape Town, with more than twenty recognized Kramats in the Peninsula area.

The body was reported by an elderly couple from Mitchell's Plain, on the Cape Flats. They were out touring Ceres to visit a maiden aunt and had decided to stop to see the Kramat and offer up a prayer. SAPS Wellington units were dispatched, and Sergeant Vilakazi and his partner, who had joined the patrol unit at the bush pub earlier, also drove out to the site. Being so much closer, Vilakazi was there first, and after having a look, he called the body in as an apparent homicide. He was aware that the BOLO suspect was not at the scene of the vehicle, so he immediately started to think that this might be their man. There was a delay as the officers tried to look after the elderly couple, who were severely traumatized. When they were safely in a police vehicle on their way to Wellington station, Vilakazi made the call to Gavin.

Gavin turned toward the young sergeant, smiled, and thanked him. "You did well, Sergeant. But now we need to match the body to the car." Gavin looked at Wilsenach. "Brigadier, will you give us ten minutes with the car, and then we'll go and see the Kramat? I assume the body's still there. I don't want to intrude on your time."

Wilsenach replied, "Yes. Our crime scene team is still working on it. We haven't relinquished the body yet. We've also got traffic control involved; we've set up a stop-and-go system just after the bridge. The road is too narrow to traverse with our vehicles parked there, so we're regulating traffic around the spot. Fortunately, it's in the middle of the week, nothing near the traffic volumes over a weekend. Check out the car and talk to my people working it. Then please go out to the site. I'm sorry, but I have to drive back to Wellington for a Community Policing

Forum meeting at 18h00."

He looked somewhat contrite and obviously felt the need to explain. "You'll forgive me for saying this, but your suspect is an outsider. We have some serious crime out here in Wellington, mostly on the farms, and our local civvies help us a hell of a lot. I need to show solidarity. Will you buzz me when you're done? After 20h00? If you'd like, and if it's not too late, I'll take you out to dinner, or have you over at my place."

They thanked him before he strode off to his car. They turned toward the old Mercedes.

The crime scene techs had started to sign off on the car, filling out their paperwork. A quick glance from Josh told him that the car wasn't very clean inside. They had collected all the papers and other stuff (even things like empty cigarette packets and cool-drink bottles), and all of the likely surfaces had been powdered for prints. A young black woman in crime scene overalls approached them.

"Good day, sir," she greeted Gavin. "I am Sergeant Xolani Molefe. We've bagged everything we found in the car, and we have a number of prints we will be sending to the lab, ASAP. I'm waiting to sign off on the report now. Will you wait for it?"

Gavin expressed his thanks, but he told her no, with a shake of his head.

"Thanks very much, but would you mind sending me your report by email?" He gave her his card with his email address. "We have another scene to visit. But could you maybe just give me the highlights now? Did you find anything you think might determine where the suspect was heading and where he'd been? Or why he might be lying dead a few kilometers down the road?"

Sergeant Molefe showed them the results of the material collected from the vehicle for further processing. It was not very bountiful. There were some chips packets and a few cool-drink cans, which should yield useable prints. There were, unfortunately, no road maps or other documentation which might point toward the route Brink had planned to go, and no navigation device, nor cell phone. Generally, it was a disappointing search.

"I don't see any luggage here," Gavin said. "Did you find any? A bag, or a suitcase?"

Molefe shook her head. "No, nothing."

Gavin frowned, and looked around, and then he turned to Josh. "Explain this to me, if you can. The man flees Knysna, on the run, gets a car from his old brother-in-arms, and makes a break for this area, going west—a hell of a long way. It doesn't look like he's planning to go back the same day, if at all, but he doesn't pack anything? Anything? Clothing? Personal items? Fucking socks?"

Josh also looked puzzled. "You're right, that just doesn't make sense. Where's his stuff?"

"The search of van Zyl's smallholding in Rheenendal yielded nothing. Brink had taken whatever clothing and belongings he may have had with him. Which means that he might have been staying somewhere in the area here."

Josh frowned. "You mean he was maybe in a guesthouse or something in the area? And that he might have just been visiting the bush pub to eat or for a drink?"

Gavin nodded. "We'd have to look into that. Maybe this wasn't a stop here on the way to wherever he was headed. Or, of course, maybe he was mugged, and his luggage was taken."

The only potentially useful find was an ID document and a wallet, found in the cubby hole inside a shopping bag from a Plettenberg Bay clothing store. The ID was for a Michael Jeremy Gordon, issued in 2018. The Department of Home Affairs was moving toward an ID card system, but the green book ID documents were still issued if your original was lost or stolen. Gavin looked closely at the photograph. It was undoubtedly Brink.

The wallet contained eight 100 rand and 74 rand in smaller bills and coins, and a laminated employee parking permit for the Iziko Slave Lodge in Cape Town, a museum in Cape Town a short distance from the Company Gardens and next door to the Parliament complex. The permit was in Gordon's name, and the vehicle was listed as a Mercedes-Benz, cream in color.

Gavin looked long and hard at Josh. "This is a destination."

Josh bit his lip. "It's thin." He looked at Gavin and shook his head. "I really thought we'd get more, you know?'

Gavin nodded. "Yes, but remember, this guy is—or was—a professional. He came up through the ranks in the dark old days. He would know how to arrange a fake ID. Although, and I'm no expert, this looks real and is maybe just a replacement document acquired through genuine channels. Of course, it's bullshit, with a bullshit name.

"What I'm interested in is this parking permit. Why? What is he planning on doing at this place? I know parking in Cape Town is mad, but I don't see him faking an ID and a permit to get parking for this rust bucket."

Josh had to agree. "Should we have a look at this museum?"

Gavin replied, "No. I'm thinking that he planned to position himself somewhere close to something else. A target? Maybe planning to park the car there and have a base to operate from for some reason?"

"OK, but it seems a bit weird. Who has a fake parking permit made, and why?"

Gavin thought for a minute, frowning. "Imagine if we were chasing a terrorist. With this info, we would be thinking, here's a guy wanting to have a place he can keep his vehicle close by, for ease of movement or a quick escape, without catching the attention of law enforcement. You know? With this he has a genuine safe harbor for the car."

"OK?" Josh still looked doubtful, not quite following the picture in Gavin's head.

"If this were a suspected terrorist, we would ask: what's the point? What is he trying to get close to? And, maybe more pertinently, why have to worry about secured parking? Maybe because the target you are looking at has security checks and stuff? A vehicle parked on the street for a prolonged period would raise eyebrows, and will maybe get you investigated and arrested."

Josh blurted it out. "Parliament?"

Gavin nodded. But then he also quickly shook his head. "Just thinking aloud. Let's go see what's waiting for us on the pass."

They arrived at the Kramat site ten minutes later. Three SAPS vehicles were parked closest to the mountain side of the narrow road that traversed the pass. One of them was an ambulance stenciled with the Paarl Forensic and Pathology Services logo, waiting to receive the body. There had been some skillful maneuvering of the vehicles to get off the roadway as much as possible. Even so, as Brigadier Wilsenach had mentioned, they had closed the road with a stop-and-go system, and officers were allowing cars through four or five at a time from either side of the pass. Because of the congestion, Sergeant Vilakazi, who was accompanying Gavin and Josh in a police *bakkie*, had asked them to leave the Corolla at the bush pub. Vilakazi's partner dropped them at the Kramat site, and then he left. He was to pick them up later.

They walked up the hill from the roadway, past the cement sign inscribed with "Die Kramat" by the roadside, over the loose sand and low bushes on the way to the Kramat itself, bordered on one side with an ancient-looking low stone wall. The burial mound, in the shape of a rectangular concrete sarcophagus, was covered in the colorful and intricately embroidered fabric called *chaddars*, left by acolytes.

It was a reverent scene, and Josh looked around him in awe at the surroundings, the tall cliffs towering over them and the deep valley across the road below them. He felt a slight breeze blow against his face, bringing the rather pungent but pleasant and clean scent of the fynbos on the mountain. It was all so at odds with the reason he was here. He had a sudden, strange feeling of complete peace.

The mood was broken by the figure hidden under a white sheet, with SAPS markings on the edges. The body lay next to the burial mound, stretched out parallel to it, like a lover lying beside a partner in bed. The head pointed down to the road.

"I have to prepare you, Colonel. There is quite a lot of blood and some brain matter." Vilakazi moved toward the body to pull the sheet back so that they could see, but Gavin stopped him, a hand on the younger man's arm.

"Sorry, Sergeant, just a minute. Has the scene been properly checked and photographed?" Josh could see that there was a disorganized mess of footprints and marks in the dry sand around the body. "Have the techs signed off on the scene?"

There were four overalled technicians busy around the edges of the site, the mound, and the stone wall. Vilakazi nodded and looked over at one of the uniformed crime scene techs, a light-skinned Coloured woman. Glenda Jacobs moved closer and greeted them. Gavin introduced himself and Josh, and she gave a grim smile, appropriate to the nature of the scene.

"Colonel, we've covered the immediate area. There is very little evidence, I'm afraid. We found the sand trampled to death—we understand that a couple found the body, and that officers subsequently came to check out the scene." She looked somewhat embarrassed when she glanced at Vilakazi, hastily adding: "All protocols were followed, of course." Josh could see that Vilakazi appreciated it. "But unfortunately, all the feet may have obscured evidence of movement."

Gavin didn't look impressed in the least, but nodded.

"So, we can approach the body and remove the sheet? Are all photos and measurements taken?" She nodded.

Vilakazi stepped closer again and then he carefully pulled the sheet back over the head and torso of the victim.

A white man, in his late fifties or early sixties, lay on his back with his arms outstretched. He was dressed in a khaki-colored shirt and jeans, with a very pronounced exit wound in the face, the left eye and the whole left side of the face a gaping and bloodied hole. There was a lot of sand on the face and nose, some in the wound. Blood covered the chest area, and the shirt stuck to the skin. Sand was also stuck in the bloody mess left on the fabric. Josh felt a tingle of revulsion as a beetle crawled over the front of the shirt and disappeared under the collar.

Both detectives had seen enough pictures of Brink from the NPA files and the internet to realize that this was their man, even with half his face gone.

The first thought Josh had was that Brink had shaved his head. Their file photos, including media reports at the time of his release from prison, testified to a 62-year-old white male with a full head of dark brown hair. That was also the face on the photo on the "Gordon" ID found in the Merc. The body that lay in front of them was bald, with a clean-shaven head and a small goatee showing some gray. Josh guessed that Brink shaved his head when he fled Knysna.

Officer Jacobs stepped closer and ran through the list of findings at the scene, specifically in respect of the condition of the body.

"As you can see, sir, a white male, around sixty years of age, fully dressed, wearing a pair of leather boots—Caterpillars, in fact—and a very nice leather belt, good quality, expensive." She looked embarrassed. "No identification on the body, nothing in the shirt pockets or in the pockets of the jeans.

"Wounds to the body: a shot to the back of the head, entry just above the occipital artery on the left-hand side and a massive exit wound, which took out most of the left side of the face. And we have two bullet wounds, entry to the front of the chest, that we believe were inflicted subsequent to the head shot. That would mean that he was shot in the head from behind and would have fallen face-down. So, he was turned over for the chest shots from the front." She looked away, as if disgusted by the work she had to do, and the things she had to see.

Gavin looked thoughtful. He turned to Josh. "You know this, right?"

Josh did, and he grimaced, flooded with memories he would rather forget. He had done enough work on the Cape Flats in the past couple of years, and he remembered a nearly identical grouping of wounds on the body of a police informant two years ago in Lavender Hill.

"An execution," he stated flatly.

Gavin nodded. "Yes, this was not a random act. Not a car hijacking or a mugging gone wrong. This was someone taken out, by a person who's done this, probably many times, before."

Josh asked, "Any evidence of the shooter? Was this an automatic? Do we have anything on the weapon?"

Jacobs nodded. "We obviously have not done ballistics yet, Captain, but we found two shell casings." She pointed. "There, and there. The one was found right next to the burial mound, the other in a bush about two meters away from the body. We are still looking for a third casing, but it will turn up."

Gavin said, "OK, so obviously an automatic, and…?"

"They are 9mm shells, we suspect—although, again, of course subject to ballistics analysis—from a Glock."

He nodded his thanks to Jacobs.

Josh then decided to jump in, before they relinquished the scene. "Officer Jacobs, I know you're doing fingerprints, but I'm particularly interested in what you said about the body being turned over following the initial kill shot to the head."

Gavin nodded.

Josh continued. "If the body was turned over, will you look specifically for prints or for other evidence on the clothing? They may have laid their hands on him. We can maybe get some prints. I'm thinking specifically of that nice belt you've been eyeing."

Jacobs nodded and said that they would pay attention to it.

Gavin turned to Vilakazi. "Nothing else of interest found?"

The sergeant looked toward Jacobs for confirmation, and she interjected.

"Er, sir, I don't know whether this is relevant to this investigation—" Gavin motioned for her to continue, "—but we found a pair of briefs, men's underwear, dark blue."

She whistled to an assistant who was scanning the area behind the low rock wall. The young man looked up and came over, and she asked him to show the Colonel the "onnie." He put his hand in the white evidence bag he carried and extracted a clear plastic bag, which held the underwear, and was covered with a crime scene label. The briefs looked a bit tattered. Gavin looked at Jacobs, an eyebrow raised. He asked her whether it was possible that this slightly out-of-the-way scene, the Kramat, might be the location for some amorous nighttime encounters.

She blushed and said that she didn't know, and that she had checked and the body was dressed in underwear under the jeans. But the briefs had been found on the other side of the burial mound from where the body lay, very close to the corpse.

Josh also thought that it was probably irrelevant, but he was glad that they had bagged it and would take it along to Forensics with the other evidence.

Gavin looked like he had seen enough, and again asked Jacobs, with a sideways glance at Vilakazi, whether there was anything else. They both shook their heads.

"Nothing, sir, sorry."

They drove to Wellington from the pass, and Gavin and Josh checked into the guest house Lucinda had booked for them. It was a quiet spot. They had nice rooms, both with outside doors opening onto a stunning garden and pool. They wouldn't use it, but it did allow Gavin to smoke outside.

After both retiring for a quick shower to get the road dust off, the pair joined Brigadier Wilsenach for a surprisingly lavish dinner at an Italian restaurant in town, and the bill was on the station commander.

They had an interesting conversation. Gavin was a bit reluctant to discuss their investigation in much detail with a superior officer, which Wilsenach seemed to understand. There were too many questions still, and they were all aware of the fact that, at that very minute, they were sitting in a restaurant far from where the case had started, having arrived here because of yet another crime which at present showed even fewer potential avenues for solution. They didn't have a fucking clue where this was going.

Wilsenach did have one piece of news for them, though, and they discussed it in the car on the way back from the restaurant. The questioning of the patrons of the bush pub's restaurant had brought some new information. A young couple, students from Stellenbosch University, had been cycling on the pass that morning. Upon their arrival at the Calabash around 10h45, they were nearly hit by a car that raced out of the parking lot, tires squealing, in the direction of Wellington. A dark blue Mazda sedan, a few years old they guessed, with two black men in the front. They didn't get the full registration number but saw that it had Cape Town plates ending in the digits 832, and there was a bumper sticker with the logo of the Kaizer Chiefs soccer club on the back.

Gavin and Josh both thought that these two men could be their guys. None of the other patrons or the bush pub staff recalled seeing two black men in the pub or in the restaurant during the morning or seeing a blue Mazda in the parking lot. All indications were that Brink was abducted from the parking lot. He may have been followed and then grabbed just after he parked the Merc at the bush pub and bundled into the car—with or without luggage—before they made a quick getaway.

Josh was thinking aloud. "And the Kramat is only a few kilometers down the road. One of very few parking spots on the pass where one can pull a vehicle over to the side."

Gavin joined in. "So maybe the intention all along was to hit Brink, but the bush pub's parking lot was too busy and there was a potential for witnesses at the scene. So, they throw him in a car, take the first opportunity to stop and drag him up the hill behind the rocks and bushes, where there's no one around."

Wilsenach's men had put out a BOLO for the Mazda, although information on the vehicle and its occupants was rather scant.

They arrived back at the guest house just before eleven. Both men were tired from the day's drive and developments, but they were still a bit hyped up. They decided to have a beer from Gavin's mini bar out on the patio before retiring to their rooms.

For both of their respective theories, it was a surprising turn of events. There seemed to be nothing random about Brink's killing; it was no hijacking or robbery. It appeared more likely that while the SAPS BOLO was out for the man, someone else had also been following, someone with a motive to take out their prime suspect. To get to him before they could catch him and question him. Or perhaps Brink was not dispatched because of what he might reveal about Whitcombe's murder but rather because he was himself a target of the same perp? Maybe he and Whitcombe were targets of the same killer, each in their own right?

They chatted for twenty minutes and then seemed to succumb to the fatigue of the past few days. Josh joked about his hangover that morning, and Gavin smiled. Yes, he admitted to having had the same, and he blamed the fifteen-year-old single malt. They were tired, and tomorrow would probably be a long day. Gavin had mentioned earlier that they were expecting results from a number of angles, not least of which AppleMac's report on the Whitcombe emails, and now from whatever might turn up on Brink's body. They decided to regroup the next morning at breakfast.

CHAPTER 10

They drove through to the sprawling suburb of Durbanville, about thirty kilometers east of Cape Town. Josh had visited there a few years before, when he still worked at UCT. A previous girlfriend lived in Welgemoed, the posh area of Bellville. In those days, Bellville, the large northern suburbs city, and Durbanville, its upmarket neighbor, were still clearly separated, not only geographically but also in terms of status. Friends of the ex-girlfriend, who lived on the fringes of Bellville, would always give their address as "Durbanville."

Back then, the influx of foreigners from Somalia and Nigeria that had "plagued" downtown Bellville for the last couple of decades—this seemed to be the old-timers' shared view, mostly as a result of increases in crime—had not yet penetrated north of the N1 highway, which served to split Bellville and Durbanville. Now, it seemed to Josh that there were new housing developments all over the place, and the lines were definitely blurred, if they indeed still existed.

Gavin had asked Josh whether he would mind if they dropped by the Durbanville SAPS station. He had thought through much of the night, having had trouble sleeping, and had come up with the name of someone he believed could bring something to the investigation.

There was little else they could do at present. The BOLO for the Mazda was out, and the autopsy and the ballistics reports on Brink would take a day at least. Gavin hoped for a better turnaround time than they'd had from Mossel Bay.

Erna Pretorius was nearing retirement. She was wheelchair-bound, having suffered a serious motorcycle accident twelve years ago. Gavin had worked with her when she was a partner in a private investigation firm based in Milnerton, near Cape Town. They had collaborated, officially and unofficially, on three different cases in Gavin's past. Ironically, while many cops retired or left the force and then pursued opportunities in the private sector, Erna had done things the other way around. Following her accident, she had decided to go for the better and cheaper government medical aid, and had given up her PI work for a posting in the SAPS crime intelligence directorate. She could also do a more effective job spreading her web across cyberspace from a desk, with no need to go out on the road and chase perps.

She was currently based at the Durbanville station, mainly tasked with the northern suburbs and west coast. Her partner, a French woman who had immigrated to South Africa and now worked as the winemaker at a nearby wine farm, had persuaded her to make the move out of the bustle of Cape Town to a quieter existence in the "burbs." Erna was—or so Gavin said—as sharp as she had ever been, and he wanted to pick her brain on the Whitcombe investigation. She owed him, he said. Josh didn't ask.

He had shared an update with Amy in a late-night WhatsApp chat. She sounded concerned, but he tried to downplay his concerns. They would find the killer. It would just take time. She empathized, and said that she really missed him. She had a meeting with Jenny Whitall that morning to start conceptualizing the art exhibition. That made Josh happy. The guilt he had been carrying around for months—for uprooting her, for asking her to build a new business and a new life from the ground up in a strange place—felt just that little bit lighter. He said a silent word of thanks for Gavin and Jenny.

Erna Pretorius's office looked like the scene of an explosion. There were files all over the place and no apparent sense of order. If there was a system, its name was chaos. There was a ficus plant in a corner, but Josh could swear the poor thing was leaning toward the door like it was planning its slow escape. He wanted to cheer it on.

Erna was a mountain of a woman. She was seated in a wheelchair decorated with bumper stickers, the most politically correct one stating, "If you can see my brake lights, fuck off." The general impression was of a big lady with a big hairdo and, as he would find out, an even bigger personality. The sides of her head were shaven, and the Mohawk was a cacophony of colors: purple, pink, and blue. She wore thick-rimmed glasses, in a very bright red, and a conspicuous silver nose ring. She also wore one of the broadest smiles Josh had ever seen.

After the expected catching-up-with-Gavin conversation, and some laughs (hers, an overly loud and anything but discreet guffaw of delight), she fawned over Josh, with some very direct, and quite uncomfortable, sexual innuendos. Gavin had given Josh some background, and he knew that she had been an openly lesbian woman for many, many years. When she told Josh that he looked like an "eminently lickable young Mel Gibson," he snorted, burst out laughing, and then finally asked her to "fuck off!"

That was all it required. Her smile got even broader—Josh hadn't thought it possible—and then she trusted him and he, her. So, Gavin got down to brass tacks, and started describing to Erna the shape of the shit-storm wave they were currently surfing.

Erna sighed, and had another huge gulp of the "Ridiculously Thick" lime milkshake she'd had a clearly overburdened administrative assistant fetch from the Steers a few blocks away. She listened attentively to Gavin's recounting of the Whitcombe investigation, with Josh jumping in now and then to add details Gavin had glossed over. She sat mostly with her head back and her eyes closed, and she threw in a question or two occasionally. Josh was impressed; the questions were always on point.

She put the half-empty milkshake aside and looked at Gavin.

"I think your case is more complex than you think, Gav. It's not just a revenge killing of a lawyer by his former client, fifteen years later; although I do think the backstory is to be found squarely in the history between Brink and Whitcombe." She glanced over at Josh, and then back to Gavin. "But I also feel that Josh has a point in wanting to look at the Rasta gangster. I don't like him, but I like him for Whitcombe's murder." She smiled a beaming smile at Josh. "See, Mr. Gibson, this lady is trying to protect your honor." She said this in a very cheesy American South accent, straight out of *Gone with the Wind*. Josh chuckled.

Gavin frowned. "OK, Erna, but what do you mean about the Whitcombe/Brink backstory? How do you feel it features, if it's not, as we've discussed, just Brink getting back at the guy for messing up his appeal and having him spend twelve years in jail?"

Josh had seen Gavin frown at her seemingly outright rejection of the revenge killing theory, the one for which Gavin had been advocating since Saturday's interview with Veronica Whitcombe. He could hear the hint in Gavin's voice, implying that surely this theory made a hell of a lot of sense.

"Brink was released from prison nearly two years ago. It doesn't fit for me. If he was that pissed off at his former legal counsel, and those feelings had been percolating for twelve years in a cell, why wait that long to start stalking the guy? If he was as emotional about the whole thing as your theory suggests, I just don't understand that time frame. Maybe there was something else, still linking the two, but it happened much more recently." Gavin blinked at this. It looked like it had gotten him thinking.

She closed her eyes again and then gave him a squinting look. Gavin had told Josh he had never met a cop with a more accurate radar, gut, or whatever you wanted to call it. Josh recalled Major-General Hlungwane's disgust at the thought of a police officer relying on such primitive methods. But Gavin said he had seen her on a few occasions pull a "massive fucking rabbit" out of a hat with her instincts. She could connect dots where some people couldn't even see dots.

"There is another player on the field here, Gav. He or she might be connected to all three of your central actors—Whitcombe, Brink, and Erasmus—but there is someone else in the wings, somewhere. I have this feeling that it had something to do with the Whitcombe/Brink appeal. There is—and this is just my gut feeling—a much longer *and more involved* history behind all this."

Gavin frowned again. "OK, so what do you suggest, that we look at the paperwork on Brink's 1995 appeal? The work Whitcombe did or didn't do? Or what?"

She nodded, and then she shook her head. "Yes, and no, by all means, look at the case, look at the files, read the transcripts."

At this Gavin glanced over at Josh. Yep, with his legal background, he would be the one to go through those in detail. He could already see the nights spent reading dry, old court transcripts and legal briefs, but he was up for it.

"But my gut tells me you need to go back even further. The crime Brink was originally convicted for in '95. The killing of the freedom fighter."

They had not paid much attention to that case, and Josh suddenly realized it was because they hadn't really done much homework on it. Brink's first meeting with Whitcombe—hiring him to do the appeal case—was as far back as they had thought it necessary to go. He now found himself wanting to know more about the Senzo Shabane killing in Mozambique nearly thirty-five years ago.

"OK…" Gavin looked a bit uncertain and doubtful. "That's a very old, Apartheid-era crime, committed in another country."

She nodded. "Yes, I know, but you asked for what my gut is telling me. You also told me that your main suspect was killed yesterday by what looked like professional killers, two black guys. My gut then shouts, 'Who might command black professional killers?'" She looked a bit embarrassed now, not an emotion with which Josh would have thought her familiar.

"I know this is a stretch, but your victim in the Mozambique killing was an ANC freedom fighter. In this day and age, who does that description of the guys in the Mazda fit best? Gone are the days when the only pros operating under the radar in this country were old, white Apartheid security people or right-wing nuts with professional training under the old regime. Or the odd recce from the border war days. Right?"

Gavin's attention perked up. She continued. "Who are the black stealth operators nowadays? We have an apparently completely dysfunctional intelligence community, secret service, and other agents working for or with or completely separate from the 'National Intelligence Agency.'" The scorn in her voice was obvious. "And who wields the power to control and to mobilize those guys? Now?"

Gavin nodded slowly. "Politicians."

She nodded. "Who is the go-to group of politicians who have been in the news so often, at least since the start of the Zuma years, for their political infighting and dirty tricks, and all the alleged machinations behind the scenes, involving the use of this new breed of spooks?"

Gavin nodded again. "The ANC."

She mimed toasting a glass with him. "Shabane was an ANC armed struggle leader, right? Jeez, Zuma himself was ANC 'intelligence' in the struggle years!"

At this she laughed, but it was true. The former president, who was currently facing corruption charges for allegedly stealing billions and corrupting most parts of the government, was a former ANC intelligence leader in the fight against Apartheid.

"So, could there be ANC people still in the game, who may have been involved with Shabane?"

This time Josh also nodded. Of course there could. But he was skeptical. "OK, but why now? It's a 35-year-old crime."

For the first time, she shook her head, seeming less confident now. She pulled the milkshake cup closer and took a mighty sip. "I don't know. And I don't even know if I'm right." She glanced under her brows at Gavin.

"Don't shoot the messenger, Gav. She also has feelings." She made a mock sad face, wiped away an imaginary tear, and then saw that Gavin still frowned. "It's just a feeling, OK?" She finished the milkshake and threw the empty plastic container at an overflowing dustbin by the door, missing spectacularly.

And then she politely told them to *fok off*, as she needed her beauty sleep. Josh grinned. It was still an hour until lunch.

THE BODIES

\ bä-dē \

NOUN, PLURAL

CHAPTER 11

BP SERVICE STATION
BUFFELJAGSRIVIER (ON THE N2 TOWARD GEORGE)
FRIDAY, 25 NOVEMBER
10H45

When he woke at six, Josh had a message from Gavin. He'd decided that they might as well hit the road to Knysna, even though there was no great hurry to get back. Josh agreed, and asked Gavin if they could take a quick detour to see Josh's mother in Villiersdorp.

Josh's father, a retired attorney, had died in 2015. For the past few years, his mother had knocked around in the big, rambling house on Caledon Street, in the quietest corner of an already quiet village. He often worried about her, and tried to phone at least twice a week, although he knew she had a tight-knit circle of friends and good neighbors. He hated that he couldn't visit often, but it was just too far from George for regular trips.

So they took a detour through Grabouw, taking the scenic R321 which meandered for more than thirty kilometers through farms with fruit orchards. Josh was disappointed when they went over Viljoen's Pass, which had been plagued by forest fires in recent months and now looked like a lunar landscape, gray and uninviting. The road eventually took them over Theewaterskloof dam to the quaint village of Villiersdorp.

Marie Holland treated them to coffee and some delicious homemade lemon meringue pie, sourced from a neighbor, Tannie Susan, her specialty. Gavin chatted enthusiastically to Marie, and she asked him about Josh's progress as a detective. She was still not one hundred percent behind his career move. A local Afrikaans girl, she had married the handsome young English lawyer in town many years ago, and had always hoped that her only child would follow in his father's footsteps and have a long and distinguished legal career. It was so much more respectable than being a policeman. Gavin suppressed a chuckle at that. But she supported Josh and she was glad to hear that Gavin was so impressed with him, even though she asked Gavin at least five times, within Josh's earshot, to keep an eye on him, as "it was such a dangerous job" they had.

As they drove away, Josh expressed his fear to Gavin that his mother's mind was starting to go. It was something he had suspected for some time. He resolved to encourage her to start building puzzles again, something she had always enjoyed but seemed to have given up. Gavin agreed; there was dementia in Jenny's family, and he had done some research on it, and things like puzzles and Sudoku could retard the downward slide.

After that, they both seemed a bit melancholy, growing quiet as Gavin steered them back toward the N2.

They filled up the car and waited for an order of steak and cheese *roosterkoek* in Oude Post, something the restaurant out in the middle of nowhere, and in a service station of all places, was widely famous for. Gavin returned from stepping outside for a cigarette and a quick call to the SAPS Knysna station.

"Well, at least we're in for some new information," he told Josh. "I just spoke to AppleMac. He's gone through everything and says he can report on the Whitcombe emails and the hard drives that were found in the cottage."

They ate heartily and got back in the car. Josh drove. Traffic was still light on the N2 outbound from Cape Town at this time on a Friday, mostly SUVs with mountain bikes mounted on the back—the lucky ones who could take a weekend off. They managed to make quite good time back to Knysna, and back to work.

KNYSNA SAPS STATION
FRIDAY
16H00

It was nearly going-home time for the admin staff. You could feel the energy. Christiaanse and a couple of his cronies were not on the later shift, so as usual they hung around the water cooler and pretended to discuss cases, while they were really planning the evening's entertainment.

There were only two chairs in AppleMac's office, so Josh had to grab one from the squad room so both he and Gavin could take a seat at the IT tech's desk. There was a little projector set up, beaming its images onto one of the walls. It looked a bit primitive, but AppleMac assured them that he and a couple of colleagues had watched quite a few Premier League matches that way; and then he seemed to realize he had imparted this information to a senior officer, and decided to shut up about his little projector.

The young man kicked off his report, looking very serious.

"Colonel, Captain, I have managed to work through all the material I was entrusted with—and I wish to express my sincere appreciation for the trust you have bestowed upon me, in light of its potential importance to the investigation—"

Gavin jumped in. *"Ag nee man Apple. Fok man!"* He looked angry, but Josh knew that he was trying to keep from bursting out laughing. "Please don't talk like you're pitching some bloody general. Just give us what you've got, OK?" At this, Gavin smiled and then so did AppleMac. He reddened and looked down with a grin.

"Sorry, sir. I was a bit flustered, OK? This is *kwaai* stuff for the case, and I didn't want to fu—mess up. May I start over?" His pleading look was priceless.

Josh nodded, trying hard not to laugh. Gavin looked like an indulgent parent whose patience has been stretched too far already.

AppleMac wiped the slate of his face clean, and turned serious again.

He had a few things to report. The first was a bit of a bombshell. Whitcombe's phone—the one they had searched for fruitlessly up in Joodse Kamp on Monday—had been found.

An undercover narcotics officer, who knew Erasmus quite well, had managed to lay his hands on it. The phone was a new Samsung Galaxy S10, which had been released locally only a few months before. Whitcombe was apparently up for a contract renewal and had gone for some fancy kit. The undercover officer had placed ads on the usual used goods sites—Gumtree, OLX, a Facebook group for secondhand stuff, and a couple of other platforms. He had spread the word that he was buying an S10, in any condition, for good money.

A sixteen-year-old junkie from Concordia sent a WhatsApp message to the cop, and had told him that he was in possession of such a phone, in great condition, but without the security password. The story was that it had been sold to him by an elderly neighbor, who had been given the phone by his granddaughter, who had a nice job in PE, but grandpa needed the quick cash for some groceries and other necessities—and, of course, he was a bit senile and had forgotten his own password for the phone.

Josh and Gavin both smiled, as did AppleMac. If only these junkies would be a bit more original. The phone was clearly stolen, or, at best, found on the street.

AppleMac continued. "The cop ended up paying two thousand rand for the phone, a phone worth around seven or eight times that new. Of course, there was no SIM card in it, but we can retrieve data saved to the phone. It has quite an intricate security setup—they come standard with the phone." AppleMac looked happy, about to share an IT-nerd inside scoop. "In fact, this model used to have an advanced ultrasonic fingerprint scanner hidden under its screen, which was affected by a security issue. A glitch which the manufacturer managed to address recently. The devices were upgraded. This particular model now has a fingerprint sensor built into its power button."

Gavin and Josh both tried to look suitably impressed, and interested in the eventual outcome of all this techie hullabaloo, which, in light of AppleMac's tone of voice and suspenseful delivery, Josh took as high drama in IT land. There was probably a blog or two about this.

AppleMac seemed to realize he was alienating his audience. "The point is that the junkie was, of course, talking *kak*. There was no password security on the phone." He quickly continued. "Anyway, to cut a long story short"—there were two grateful smiles to be seen—"Whitcombe used the fingerprint security option, so we could nail it."

Gavin had a knowing grin. but Josh was confused.

"W/O Fourie drove the phone down to Mossel Bay this morning. He took prints off Whitcombe's body at the morgue. He managed to activate the phone, and he kept pressing buttons every few minutes 'till he got back, so the thing wouldn't lock again." Here AppleMac looked especially pleased with himself. Josh felt it was fully justified. "We, of course, had prints copied that we could use in case we needed to unlock the phone again."

Wow, Josh thought. *These young guys do know their shit.*

Gavin also looked suitably impressed, but he wanted answers. "That's great, really, it is. But, what did you find on the phone? Anything we can use here?"

AppleMac looked chastised, but rallied. "As you know, with no SIM card, most of the call information, address book, and that kind of stuff is gone. So we are limited to whatever was saved on the phone itself, as opposed to the card. Most smartphone users will save a lot of stuff—media, pics, vids—to the Cloud or sometimes to their phones, rather than the SIM card. We got lucky. There were some pics and vids saved to the phone, and we managed to access them."

"Please tell me it's not porn," Gavin sighed.

The young officer threw him a rather sour glance. "To be honest, sirs, we don't know what we have. Of course, there are some inane pics, and a vid or two. All kinds of *kak* that Whitcombe and his wife photographed and filmed. Plants—someone mentioned that she was into gardening—and just random sights, birdwatching even. Wow, these people are white!" Josh tried hard not to laugh. He could see Gavin's grimace.

"Apple, is there a point to this?" Gavin asked. "You know, ultimately? Do you really want me to smoke in your office?"

This time Josh did laugh. AppleMac was great at what he did, but he was the ultimate millennial snowball. He would probably fumigate his office if even one cigarette was lit in there.

So he cut to the chase. "Colonel, there is really just one thing that stands out. Well, a couple of vids and a few pics of the same subject matter."

Gavin put the cigarette packet back in his shirt pocket. "OK, what's that all about? Tonight still, please!"

There was no rancor in the comment, and AppleMac seemed to relax. He fiddled with his PC, and then he motioned with one hand toward his projector and the image of his computer's desktop projected on the wall. A window opened and a video started to play.

It was mostly dark, but you could make out the basics. The first video's opening scene was of someone, the videographer, walking from light into a dark passage. Everything went black for a few seconds.

Somewhere off camera, seemingly behind the camera, a light was switched on, maybe a handheld torch. The video moved on through what seemed like a rough-hewn passage underground. A few people moved further into the tunnel. The sound was very low in volume, some talking, but it was hard to make out individual voices. The picture moved around a corner, and then another one. And then it arrived at a wall of dirt. It panned around a couple of times, and then the video ended.

Gavin frowned. "Is that it? What was that?"

He looked at AppleMac. The tech officer looked a bit disappointed. Maybe he had expected a more positive reaction.

"Sorry, sir. That's what we have, and about six more variations of it. All just a video of someone filming what looks like some cave—or, in fact, two different caves. As you've seen, it's a bit hard to tell what's going on there, what they're filming, but I've watched this a number of times and it does seem as if there are two separate underground locations."

Gavin glanced at Josh, puzzled. He decided to light a cigarette anyway. Now AppleMac frowned—in *his* office!—but he was outranked.

"I really don't know what to make of this." Gavin puffed some smoke out from the corner of his mouth as he frowned at the screen. "Is this the only video we have on the phone? Nothing else? Just these dark passages?" AppleMac nodded. "You mentioned photographs?"

"Yes, sir, sorry. A few still shots, out in what looks like a forest-type environment, of the openings to caves or underground passages, about twenty pics. I went through them as well, and I think –this is really just my opinion from viewing these pics and the videos—that it might, again, be of two different scenes, in two different locations. I would venture a guess that the pics and the vids are of the same two locations: tunnels underground reached from above ground at the spots where the pics were taken." He brought the pictures up on the screen and flipped through them.

Gavin had an idea. "Josh, does any of this look familiar? It's a forest setting, and you were out at Phantom Pass on Wednesday. Could this be in that area?"

Josh frowned, and thought for a few moments. "I couldn't say, really. I didn't see any of this kind of thing out there. And the Millwood mine shafts are closed to the public." He scratched a finger over his cheek. "But I wonder now, do you think this could be in Rheenendal?" Gavin looked interested. "We have Brink out there, staying with van Zyl. We have Brink and Whitcombe connected through the apparent stalking and assault at the restaurant up in Pezula. So Whitcombe's phone records this stuff out in a forest. Is that too much of a stretch?"

Gavin thought, then he nodded his head, slowly. "No, there might be something there…but I must say, I think we're just going to speculate here with no real way to go. I think we should check out van Zyl's smallholding to see whether these caves are out there." He glanced at AppleMac. "Thanks, Apple, this is good. It's something that means something, but I think we're not close to interpreting this in any meaningful way at this time. Is this really all of the video and photographic evidence off the phone?"

"Well, sir, as I mentioned, there were some other pics, but really just domestic stuff. Nothing that seems to link with these images—so no, I think this is it."

Gavin nodded and stubbed the cigarette out in an empty KFC box.

AppleMac looked a bit disgusted. Gavin saw it, and told him to throw his trash away in the future.

CHAPTER 12

They were still at it, the three tired men gathered in AppleMac's office.

After having looked at Whitcombe's cell phone footage, AppleMac launched into the rest of the evidence he had been sitting on for most of the week. They looked at the contents of Whitcombe's laptop as well as the hard drives found at the cottage, and at the cell phone records. Gavin had also asked AppleMac to look into Whitcombe's social media presence and financial records. They dreaded, but also hoped, that it would be a long night with plenty of useful information to sort through.

"The bad news, first off, is that there was very little information on the laptop itself," AppleMac started. "I got the impression that Whitcombe probably did a very regular—I mean, maybe once every couple of days—wipe of everything. The internet search history contained only one item, a Google search for 'best prawns Plett.'

"Of course, there are ways to recover info from a laptop's hard drive, which we haven't tried yet; ways that could reveal information deleted by the user. But I thought we should hang off on that, because it can also damage the hard drive and ultimately obscure or destroy data. Was I wrong?"

Gavin shook his head. "No, not if we can still consider it for later. I'm interested in what the first search revealed."

AppleMac looked pleased. "The guy had very run-of the-mill apps and programs installed that were used relatively frequently—things like Facebook, internet banking, YouTube, food delivery, and an Aston Martin car configurator.

"The YouTube search history was also mostly for cars. I think he was shopping for an upgrade to the Jag. There were also some music searches, mostly 1970s rock bands like The Who and Led Zeppelin, and some cricket stuff. Weirdest batsman dismissals, closest endings to a Test match, that kind of thing. Oh, and quite a bit of environmental stuff—talks given by scientists about climate change, how to preserve threatened species. Most of those are about South Africa and, more specifically, the Southern Cape; all quite innocent stuff, nothing criminal or shady that I could see. The most controversial, if I can call it that, was a couple of searches on methamphetamines and their production."

Gavin perked up at this, but AppleMac put up a hand. "No weird 'how to build a bomb' or 'how do I make my own drug stash' kind of stuff, but he did seem interested in the production of meth. *Tik.*"

Josh was fascinated. He knew that this was no exact science, but AppleMac seemed to be certain that Whitcombe was not some shady operator on the dark web, into kiddie porn or something as sinister. The drug stuff seemed out of place, but nothing earth-shattering. The man had a long legal career and had represented at least a few alleged drug dealers. It didn't ring any immediate alarm bells. Although it was interesting in light of the evidence of Whitcombe's association with Jerome Erasmus.

AppleMac looked shifty again, and both Gavin and Josh realized that some bad news was coming. "As for the two external hard drives we found at the cottage…the picture is a bit more bleak."

Gavin looked annoyed. "Tell us."

Both the drives had been professionally wiped. AppleMac started explaining how one could use software to do this, to ensure that all information is erased from the drive, much more effectively, and completely, than would be the case if one simply deleted files. Data destruction programs are, apparently, widely and easily available for this purpose. AppleMac suspected that a program called DBAN had been used.

"This is a bootable program, meaning that it could have been accessed and used off a CD, a DVD, or a flash drive."

"So, what does that mean? Is the content of those drives completely, and permanently, gone?" Josh asked.

AppleMac nodded, and then shrugged. "Yes, for all intents and purposes, although we can send the drives to the SAPS Computer Forensics lab, but I don't know whether they will be able to recover anything."

"What about the Cloud? A lot of people now also back up stuff to the Cloud, right?"

AppleMac nodded but then said that there was no evidence of any Cloud access having been set up on the hardware. Gavin grunted, and then motioned with his hand for AppleMac to move things along.

Josh interjected. "Well, at least we know there was something on those drives worth hiding or destroying, right?" The other two nodded. "And we know that the drives could have been wiped at the cottage, by someone using that program…DBAN? On a flash drive or something? We still don't know for sure whether the cottage was searched or ransacked before or after Whitcombe's death, but we do know that someone could have wiped the drives there, right?"

Gavin nodded, but asked, "Why not just take the drives? Why go to the trouble of wiping them? If you take them the cops will never know they existed."

Josh gave another grimace. "Good question." AppleMac didn't have an answer.

"OK, I haven't exactly been wowed up to this point." Gavin threw a dark look at the young tech officer, but then smiled when he saw how glum AppleMac looked. Gavin got up from his chair and stretched. "I'm kidding, Apple, it's OK, man. I know you're just the messenger here, but I was hoping for something with a bit more substance. So far it seems we have some irrelevant shit, and we've lost some probably very relevant shit; or, at least,we didn't lose it—that's one bright point. It was destroyed before we got there."

AppleMac nodded, looking disappointed. "There is some more positive stuff, sir."

Gavin brightened at that, but said he was going to fetch some coffee before they continued, and that he planned to phone his wife. He suggested that Josh might also want to let Amy know that he would be home late. Neither inquired about AppleMac's domestic situation.

Josh nodded and thanked Gavin. He was dead tired, but they needed to get through this stuff as soon as possible. Gavin asked, but only Josh wanted coffee. AppleMac was on a strict diet of fruit smoothies, and he would mix something together from his stash in a bar fridge next to his desk. Josh decided not to ask about the KFC box Gavin had used as an ashtray.

Ten minutes later, they started on the threatening emails Veronica Whitcombe had showed Gavin and Josh at their first meeting.

There had been four emails, anonymously sent, from an email address listed as bobo9412@gmail.com. They were all short messages, addressed to "Mlungu":

"You know who this is. I want what we discussed. Now. Contact me with details and price."
　　[Received Friday, November 4th at 18h23, read by
　　Whitcombe on Saturday, November 5th at 06h12.]

"Still waiting. You have 24 hours to let me know. Do not fuck with me."
　　[Received Monday, November 7th at 10h58, read by
　　Whitcombe at 11h24.]

"Your proposal unacceptable. Am considering sending a friend to talk to you face to face. You want that?"
　　[Received Monday, November 7th at 16h37, read by
　　Whitcombe at 16h42.]

"Will do your new plan. Keep phone on. Expect contact tomorrow. And visitors. Keep to the agreement and everything will be fine."
　　[Received Tuesday, November 15th at 12h32, read by
　　Whitcombe at 12h33.]

Gavin and Josh both squinted at the text, concentrating.

"Before we get into where these messages came from—" Gavin looked hard at AppleMac, "—and you can help us with that?"

AppleMac nodded. "Not definitively, sir, sorry, but we do have some info."

Gavin looked less than happy. "OK, let's consider a few things first. One. Do we have any replies to these emails from Whitcombe? In a sent items folder?"

AppleMac shook his head. "No, Colonel, I couldn't find anything. I assume—if one reads those messages, especially the third and fourth ones—that there was communication between the two parties over the phone. But not by email, at least from Whitcombe's side."

Gavin nodded. "That begs the question why our emailer would use email in the first place if there was phone communication already in place between them. Note that there's no phone number provided in those messages, so that wouldn't explain why the emailer would initiate communication by email if there was already telephonic contact."

Josh jumped in with an idea. "The first email suggests that they were already talking. The sender wants 'what we discussed.' AppleMac, I know you'll tell us later about Whitcombe's social media presence, but did you find any other potential means of communication online? WhatsApp, or Facebook Messenger maybe?"

AppleMac shook his head. "No, sir, Whitcombe does not appear to have been on WhatsApp, and he never sent anyone a single Facebook Messenger message."

Gavin said, "OK, they were talking by phone then."

"Another thing…" Josh looked a bit embarrassed, but he went ahead anyway. "I don't know whether this means anything. But look at those dates and times of the emails received and read." The other two glanced over at the projected image. "I'm just speculating here, but can you see that it took Whitcombe nearly twelve hours after receipt of the first message until he read it? It came in after 18h00 on a Friday and Whitcombe only read it after 06h00 the next day." They nodded. "Look at the subsequent three messages. They were all read much sooner after they were received. The last one was read just one minute after receipt."

They nodded again and looked at him. "I'm going out on a limb here, and this probably doesn't mean much, but I would suggest that Whitcombe wasn't expecting that first email. He only noticed it the morning when checking his emails. What if the use of email itself was a threat, an implied one? They had been talking on the phone, but now our sender wants to show Whitcombe that he also has access to his email address. He can contact him in new ways, with new possibilities of harm or exposure?"

Gavin seemed to get it. "Don't be embarrassed, I like it, it's possible—and you use that word 'exposure.' I guess it's time to start considering what the text of these emails means. This reads like blackmail, doesn't it? Extortion of some kind. Remember the letter that Veronica Whitcombe gave us about the 'files'? Looking at these emails, I'm confident—and I know that this will sound melodramatic, but I would stake my career on it—that Whitcombe had blackmailed our sender. He asked for something—money most likely, of course—in exchange for some files, information. About what, we don't know, but I like that theory very much."

The others both nodded.

Josh picked up Gavin's trail. "I would suggest we consider that those 'files' contained one of two things. It could be new information that the sender wanted, for whatever purpose, or it could be information contained in those files which belonged to the sender or somehow incriminated him or her. A kind of 'pay me or I disclose the contents of the files' thing?" Gavin nodded and the lawyer in Josh finished. "Of course, only that second scenario would point toward blackmail. In the first scenario, it might just be a perfectly legal commercial transaction, the selling of some useful information at a price. Even if our sender's tone seems quite threatening, there's nothing in the law against driving a hard bargain."

Gavin took this all in. "OK, so that, of course, brings us to who the sender is." Gavin looked impatient to take this conversation, and this paper trail, to a level where he would have someone to chase.

Josh put up his hand. "Sorry, Gavin, just a thought. We're talking about blackmail." Gavin raised an eyebrow. "It just struck me. We know nothing about the 'files.' We don't know whether the sender had tried to buy information or was trying to hide it." Gavin nodded. "I just thought of something Erna said. Remember, about us having to look at the Shabane killing?"

Gavin seemed put out now. He was tired and wanted to wrap things up. Josh could read his expression, but he raised his hand again, as if in self-defense. "Wait, I don't want to go into that. I was just as skeptical of her theory at the time. I remember asking her why a 35-year-old crime would bother someone enough to get professional killers involved. To eliminate a witness or a murderer?"

Gavin nodded, listening now.

"I'm really just connecting those two things. We have a possible old motive for very recent crimes. We have evidence pointing toward a recent attempt to blackmail someone, possibly to hide information. You see what I'm getting at?"

Gavin did. Pretorius's theory, as unsubstantiated as it was, might actually fit here.

He squeezed the younger man's arm and said, genuinely, "Nice one. OK, I agree, we must look into that."

The talk became more general. Fatigue was setting in across the room. Josh got up to stretch his legs and wondered how Amy was doing. She had sounded good on the phone, still excited about the collaboration with Jenny Whitall. In fact, she said that she planned to meet Jenny for coffee the next morning at the Dros in George to "talk shop" again.

AppleMac started to deliver his notes on the search for the sender.

"Can I just say one thing?" Josh interrupted. "Not to cloud whatever AppleMac has to say about the technical part of tracing the emails." As Gavin was about to respond, he also threw in, "And not wanting to paint us into a corner before we have that info."

Gavin looked intrigued. "Of course. What do you have in mind?"

Josh was out on that limb again, the territory becoming too familiar.

"I was thinking of the email text again. Addressed to 'Mlungu.' If I'm not mistaken, I am a 'Mlungu.' Right?"

Gavin and AppleMac both nodded. "Yes, a 'white man.'"

"Exactly. It's a term used by Africans to describe whites. Does it make sense that the use of the word might indicate that our sender is African?

One who knew that he was speaking to a white person?" Gavin slowly nodded, but Josh could see that he wasn't really convinced.

AppleMac took this as his signal to begin. He explained that they had scanned the email headers of the emails Whitcombe received in his Outlook account. There was nothing to expose the sender's identity in the messages themselves, nor in the email address. They had found the IP address of the sender; this, in itself, also did not disclose the sender's identity. Using the SAPS's official software, they could track the location of the sender as being somewhere in Cape Town. The software couldn't give them a more specific location.

The more positive news was that the emails had not been sent over a public network. If it had, the search could have left them with only an indication that the emails had been sent from somewhere in South Africa. It appeared as if the emails were sent over a private network. AppleMac then started to renege on his promise to limit jargon; after they encountered MUAs and MDAs and "network clouds," along with a few even more obscure terms and acronyms, Gavin had heard enough.

"What are you telling us, Apple?" He wore a scowl that looked ready to turn nasty.

AppleMac got the message, and wrapped up his narrative quickly. "Colonel, we were able to trace the origin of the emails to a user on a private network in Cape Town, one that actually had quite decent security features, and nearly eluded us."

"You mean like a private company? Is this guy sitting in a bank or in an insurance company?"

"No, sir, a private network, not a private company. We traced the user's IP address to the greater grid of Parliament's server. More specifically, we could zero in on the server for the parliamentary security services."

Gavin and Josh were dumbstruck, and stared at each other. "Parliament?" they blurted out at the same time. AppleMac just nodded.

Josh knew that the parliamentary security services operate under special legislation, the Powers, Privileges and Immunities of Parliaments and Provincial Legislatures Act of 2004. The Act provides that members of the parliamentary security services may enter the parliamentary precincts and perform policing functions in certain circumstances with the permission of the Speaker or Chairperson of Parliament, or otherwise where there is immediate danger to life or safety, or a threat of damage to property.

Josh knew this, having taken an interest in the matter in 2014 and 2015, when the Speaker of Parliament had allowed security forces to remove members of an opposition party from proceedings in Parliament, during some very heated debates concerning then-president Zuma and the allegations of corruption against him. In those events, the sticking point had been that some mysterious "white shirts" had been involved, alleged members of SAPS services who had been co-opted to fulfill parliamentary security duties. It was, understandably, constitutionally suspect, especially as those parliamentarians who had been removed were the most vocal critics of the president.

Gavin cleared his throat. "OK, that's a bit of a shock, actually." He frowned and shook his head as if to clear it of cobwebs. "And you can't get closer to the identity of the emailer than that?"

AppleMac shook his head. "No, sir. All we can say definitively is that the parliamentary security services' private email network was used. We cannot link the IP address to a specific user. By the way, I assumed that you would want to sign off in advance on any attempt to contact the network administrator and determine whether such a link can be made to an individual registered user? So we didn't even try that."

Gavin nodded. "Yes, thanks, we don't want to show our hand yet." He shook his head again, looking pissed off. "But I'll be damned if I know what our hand is here."

They took another ten-minute break for Josh and Gavin to grab more coffee. As they stirred their mugs, Gavin yawned conspicuously, and Josh said what both of them were thinking.

"Parliament." Gavin looked up, nodding. "The Slave Museum permit found in Brink's car, remember? You think there's a connection there?" Gavin considered it, as he stirred his coffee, then threw the plastic spoon into a bin.

"That could really just be a coincidence, you know. We don't know why Brink was organizing parking in Cape Town in advance, and specifically there."

Josh shook his head. "But if, like you said in that analogy, we were looking at Brink's movements like we would a terrorist's, the Parliament complex would make sense."

Gavin grinned. "We all make mistakes."

As they walked back down the passage, he stopped, and turned to Josh with a smirk. "Some of us, of course, also sometimes have that rare stroke of genius."

Josh smiled. He could see that Gavin was on the same page. They had an angle involving a security unit based at and operating solely within the parliamentary complex. They had Brink who had apparently planned to park his car next door; more than that, going out of his way to obtain or fake the necessary paperwork to do so. They couldn't let it go.

When the two detectives settled back into their increasingly uncomfortable office chairs, which Josh guessed had been with the station since the dark days before democracy, AppleMac continued. Gavin had indicated that they should step on to the remaining agenda items, in respect of the digital investigation.

None of them really had the energy to discuss the results of the more detailed search of Whitcombe's cell records, which AppleMac had touched on at the hotel briefing on Tuesday. He did confirm that Fourie, Fortuin, and Christiaanse had worked the computers for the last couple of days, to get the information on those numbers. They had also started to put together what he referred to as a "hypothetical caller-based activity log," where they would attempt to piece together Whitcombe's physical movements during those call times. Eventually, of course, they would interview the people on the list.

It was just after 23h00 on a Friday, after a long week for everyone concerned, so Gavin suggested AppleMac email them the pertinent information and that they could get together to discuss it either over the weekend or on Monday. This was crucial information and both Gavin and Josh agreed that they should be fresh when they considered it. Gavin did, however, ask AppleMac to give them a condensed report on the Whitcombes' financials.

AppleMac explained that their investigation on this angle was con-ducted through the Whitcombes' bank, and the South African Revenue Service, or SARS. While the legislation governing SARS contained provi-sions safeguarding the privacy of a taxpayer's personal information, there were also provisions for cooperation with SAPS in respect of criminal in-vestigations. AppleMac reported that they had, thus far, received good co-operation and apparently full disclosure from the relevant SARS officials.

The couple both banked with ABSA, a remnant of the old, white "Apartheid banks" like Volkskas and Saambou. The Whitcombes were married out of community of property and did not share a joint marital estate. They also did not share a joint bank account, but kept separate accounts.

Apart from the bank accounts, there were a number of investments. Some were held with other South African banks, and there were some stock portfolios of companies listed on the Johannesburg Stock Exchange. There were also foreign investments held offshore, mostly in the UK. Josh remembered that Mark Whitcombe had been active in litigation in the UK and in other parts, specifically Hong Kong, in the later decades of his career at the Cape Bar, and he suspected that opportunities were there to have squirreled funds offshore, or rather to never bring them into South Africa in the first place.

AppleMac reported that the overall value of the couple's respec-tive bank accounts and investments totaled just over 47 million rand (excluding the two properties, one the house at Pezula—valued around 6.2 million rand—and the other a beach house in Ballito on the coast in KwaZulu-Natal—valued at around 4.1 million rand). They didn't have a valuation for the flat in Coombe Hill in London, which the couple had bought nearly twenty years ago, but prices had gone up in that area and it was expected to be worth upwards of 10-15 million rand.

Gavin and Josh were both surprised. This was more than they expect-ed, even for a top advocate of many years standing. AppleMac mentioned that SARS had reported that the bulk of the estate came from money in-herited by Veronica Whitcombe in 2008, after the death of her mother. Her sugar baron father had left his total estate to the mother upon his passing in 1991. More than two-thirds of the total value of the estate was Veronica Whitcombe's share, derived mostly in the form of the capital from her inheritance, along with three siblings, who each inherited one fourth of her mother's estate.

Gavin stopped him. "Is there anything that jumps out? Anything more relevant for our purposes?"

AppleMac shook his head. "No, sir. At least, if I get your meaning, not anything that looks shady. All sources of income, investment interest, et cetera seems to be accounted for. We had one of the SAPS accountants in the George office look at the total picture."

Gavin grunted. "OK, thanks."

AppleMac interrupted him. "Sorry, just one thing. The accountant did say that there was a transaction on an investment account held in Guernsey, in the UK Channel Islands, in the name of Veronica Whitcombe. Apparently, an amount of—" AppleMac bent down to his laptop and pressed a couple of keys, "—an amount of 3.2 million rand was released from that investment. The request was emailed through to the Whitcombes' broker by Veronica, and the money was released in early September, September 12th to be exact. But she phoned the broker five days later to inquire about the transaction, and she was surprised and angry to hear of it."

Gavin and Josh both sat up a bit straighter. AppleMac glanced at them and then pressed more keys on the computer.

"The accountant contacted the broker, based in London, on Wednesday evening. We got a response yesterday. He had been concerned, thinking that there might have been some unauthorized activity on the investment account—fraud or hacking, you know—but the broker says that he had personally phoned Veronica Whitcombe on the 18th of September to check and inquire whether anything was amiss and whether the Whitcombes required assistance. Veronica said that she had forgotten they had decided to release some funds—apparently, the accountant says, there was a substantial penalty for early release as the investment is time-locked—and that all was fine. But the broker is not convinced and thinks there may have been something fishy going on, and that Veronica

Whitcombe had not even been aware of the withdrawal until it turned up in the broker's monthly email report to the Whitcombes."

Gavin and Josh looked at each other. Gavin said, "So it looks like Mark Whitcombe in some way authorized the withdrawal of a substantial amount of money from his wife's investment account without her knowledge?" AppleMac nodded. "And he has no control or power of attorney over such account?" AppleMac nodded again.

Josh thought ahead a bit. "Do we know where the money went?"

AppleMac responded, "Yes. It was received into Mark Whitcombe's ABSA savings account on the same day, September 12th, and then it disappeared."

"How could it just disappear from the account?"

AppleMac scrolled down the page of his notes. "Shortly after entering the ABSA account, in a matter of twenty minutes or so, the money was transferred through an inter-bank payment to an FNB account held by a company in Cape Town…12Tri Pharma (Pty) Ltd."

"And?" Josh was impatient now.

"The accountant did a check, and he contacted FNB. The company's account had been established three days before the payment from Whitcombe's account. It was closed, and all funds withdrawn, an hour after the payment. At this point, we have no further information. The George office has promised to put someone on it. They will check out the FICA documentation and speak to FNB to see whether we can trace 12Tri Pharma."

The Financial Intelligence Centre Act of 2001 required financial institutions, as "accountable institutions," to keep quite rigorous information about account holders. The purpose was to counter money laundering and the financing of terrorist and related activities.

Gavin and Josh both looked at AppleMac. This seemed significant.

There were, of course, a few stock motives for murder. Money was one of them, and quite a popular one. This was a substantial amount, and they needed to find out the backstory.

CHAPTER 13

Amy had left him to sleep late, and he woke to the sound of her cleaning the flat. That was sometimes a bit of sexy time. Josh loved to make what he knew were cheesy French maid jokes, and she liked to dance around and do the cleaning in less than an appropriate maid's uniform.

But this morning it grated on him. He was still tired from last night's late return from the station. She had earphones, but she preferred to have the music on loud. Even when she couldn't hear it over the sound of the vacuum cleaner, and he could hear very little else, despite burying his head under a pillow. He took it for a few more minutes and then got out of bed and stormed into the bathroom.

He sat at his study nook a few minutes later, a fancy name for the used office desk, with the wonky leg and multiple coffee cup stains, for which they had paid a neighbor 50 rand. He opened his laptop, and saw that Gavin had sent an email through just after 07h00. It contained the post-mortem report, the toxicology report, and reports by AppleMac on the emails and financials he had covered with them last night.

Josh opened those last two files first and scanned them to make sure that he hadn't forgotten something or that AppleMac hadn't missed anything in the briefing, but it all seemed to tally with what they had discussed. He saved the files for future reference.

He took a sip of his coffee, and then a deep breath, before he opened the PM report. He hated these. Maybe because he had always been blessed with a good imagination—the main reason why he had believed he could make a good detective. But when it came to the reports of autopsies his mind always went to the gory details, and he wasn't looking forward to it. But he needed to think through all this and see whether he could give Gavin some worthwhile input.

The main points were as Gavin had told him in the car on the way to Bain's Kloof, but Josh appreciated reading the more detailed explanation of the findings recorded in the report:

1) TOD/PMI was estimated as being between 22h00 on Thursday November 17th and 01h00 on Friday November 18th, calculated from the level of rigor mortis and post-mortem lividity.

2) Whitcombe died from an epidural hematoma. A blood clot had formed underneath the skull, probably from a tear in the middle meningeal artery, which runs under the skull. The hematoma was associated with a skull fracture, which had been caused by a hard blow to the head with a blunt instrument.

3) The weapon was likely a heavy object, or a lighter object swung with great force, with a flat surface and no sharp ridges. Whitcombe was hit on the front of the head, slightly side-on, impacting the temple, lower forehead, and upper left eye socket. It had created significant bruising around that area.

4) The mutilation of the body was performed post-mortem. The genitalia had been excised with what appeared to be a bladed instrument, but blunt, creating excessive tissue scarring and bleeding. Rust, soil, and dirt had been found in the wound.

5) There were no hair or fibers found on the body, except for some fibers from the denim shirt that Whitcombe had worn. The pathologist noted this as anomalous and suggested that some cleaning of the body could have taken place, or that the killer had taken special precautions to cover themselves prior to the attack.

6) There was trace evidence of diesel on the body and in the

hair. It was marine diesel oil, which has a higher density than diesel fuels used on land, such as in commercial or passenger vehicles. This looked like RMA 10, a marine diesel oil with a lower proportion of heavy fuel oil mixed in.

7) The autopsy indicated cancer of the stomach, quite advanced, yet untreated at the time of death. The pathologist's estimate was that Whitcombe probably had a year or two left to live if no treatment was administered, and that in either case eventual death would have been painful and protracted.

After reading through the report, twice, Josh sat back and closed his eyes, letting his mind sift through the information. They had both immediately focused on the post-mortem mutilation of the body, observing that this seemed to exclude the probability of pre-mortem torture. Now Josh considered the rest of the information more closely.

To him, the use of a blunt bladed instrument—which it appeared may have been rusty and also may have been the source of the soil and dirt found in the wounds—pointed to an opportunistic mutilation of the body. The killer had apparently not brought along surgical instruments. This confirmed his initial feeling regarding the injuries: this looked like either a crime of passion, driven by high emotion, or otherwise the mutilation had been done as an afterthought. If the latter, and said afterthought was not itself borne of emotion, Josh thought this might point toward a calculated effort to mutilate the body in order to distract investigators and point the finger of suspicion elsewhere.

He remembered telling Gavin at the braai that the mutilation, to him, looked like the kind of thing one could expect from Erasmus and his gang of vicious killers and drug-peddlers. He now added a mental note that someone else might have mutilated the body for that very same reason: to point the finger at another party.

The killer had taken precautions not to leave hair, fiber, or other trace evidence behind at the scene. Josh thought for a minute, remembering that Brink had recently shaved his head. If they looked at Brink as their prime suspect in Whitcombe's murder, this may have been in order to avoid the transferral of hair. Or, if the radical haircut hadn't been planned in advance for purposes of the murder, it could still explain the lack of hair evidence on Whitcombe's body.

And then there was the stomach cancer. At present there was no evidence of treatment having been sought and administered. They had no way of knowing whether Whitcombe or anyone else, including his widow, and his killer, were aware of the condition. If Whitcombe was aware of his condition, and of the fact that he had a limited life expectancy as a result, that could have affected his motives in whatever he was doing. They already had evidence of anomalous conduct by the man.

There was the apparent sudden, and possibly obsessive, interest and involvement in environmental causes. Was this a display of conscience from a man expecting imminent death? There was the evidence of consorting with Erasmus, which from the first was something that struck Josh as very out of character for Whitcombe. And then there was AppleMac's report on the financials last night, which seemed to raise the possibility that Whitcombe had stolen money from one of his wife's investments. If this were true, could it be the actions of a man facing early death, and one that would by all expectations be an ugly one?

Josh closed his eyes tight and rubbed them, feeling the start of a headache coming on. He closed the laptop and yawned. He would have a beer and see if he could coax Amy into an afternoon spent on the couch, watching some mindless TV series. He would read the toxicology report that evening or on Sunday, so that he would be ready to discuss any implications for the investigation with Gavin on Monday.

WILDERNESS
SUNDAY, 27 NOVEMBER
10H28

When Josh and Amy woke just after eight, they were both a bit restless. It was a Sunday morning, but it felt like a month since they had gone somewhere together. The last time, in fact, had been dinner at the Whitall house the previous Tuesday. But now they both felt that it would be a shame to waste what looked like a perfect Garden Route day. Josh left his cell phone on the kitchen counter, after recording a brief voicemail message to say that he would return any calls later that afternoon—just in case Gavin phoned about the case.

They loaded their kayaks into the back of Amy's Jeep, which thankfully started on the first try, and then made their way out toward Wilderness via Kaaimans Pass, Josh at the wheel. Amy had her feet up on the dashboard and sang along with the radio most of the way. Josh laughed when she went off key, which was often, and each time he got a playful slap on the arm and a fake pout.

In Wilderness, they turned left onto Hoekwil Road, and proceeded through the beautiful scenery over the Serpentine River until Josh pulled in by the gate of the Island Lake Holiday Resort and the small lake with the same name. As they got out of the car, Amy snuggled close to Josh. They both stared out over the water toward the sea on the other side of the hill. It was a truly spectacular day to be here. There was not a breath of wind, and it was slightly overcast, which meant that it wouldn't be too hot out on the water in the blazing sun. Josh gave her a cheeky kiss, and then stepped around the back of the Jeep and lifted out the two kayaks and a set of paddles.

Amy jogged up the hill to a large outbuilding next to the main reception of the resort. As she knocked on the door, it opened, and a bearded giant of a man stepped out, smiling broadly. Tim O'Connell, a "bloody Irishman" as Josh liked to remind him, worked as a handyman and outdoor activities coordinator at the resort. The couple had met him at a pub shortly after moving to George, and they had become fast friends. They often kayaked together when they had the time. Tim fist-bumped Josh as he joined Amy up on the hill, and then apologized to them. He had to drive out to Sedgefield to look at a boat he was considering buying. But they were welcome to take the kayaks out onto the lake. They thanked him and said goodbye as he locked the door and strode over toward the main building. He waved at them and shouted that he'd see them next weekend if they didn't drown themselves today.

The water was deliciously cool, and they glided along, making long wakes on the surface, their paddles giving off that slight splashing sound

Josh always associated with holidays. They were surprised to have the lake mostly to themselves, and they guessed that on a windless day like today, most locals and the few early December tourists were probably on Wilderness's spectacular long beach, just on the other side of the N2 highway.

They did a few sprints, with Josh giving her a small head start each time. After the second one, he decided she didn't need it. She was thrashing him. He needed to do this more often. He wasn't in the best of shape, he realized—too much time sitting on his ass reading police reports. Amy needled him about it, and he couldn't argue. So they agreed to just chill and take a gentle paddle around the edge of the lake, steering clear of the heavier reed patches. There were a couple of anglers in a rowboat by the small island in the middle of the lake. They waved, and Josh and Amy returned the greeting but steered well clear, not wanting to scare the fish away.

When they got to the broader expanse of the Touws River, of which the Serpentine was a narrower tributary, they decided to turn back, paddling slow to enjoy the peace and quiet, the sound of the birds, and the occasional splash as a fish jumped somewhere between the reeds.

As they rowed leisurely back to the entrance to the resort, Josh spotted a big, dark-colored *bakkie* parked about forty meters from Amy's Jeep. The vehicle was pointed toward theirs, and its lights were on. There was no one around, although it looked like there were two dark shapes in the cab. Probably some weekend anglers come to check out the lake.

But as Josh lifted the second kayak into the back of the Jeep, he noticed that the *bakkie* was still parked by the shore a little distance away. Its lights were still on, and he could hear the engine idling.

Josh opened the passenger door for Amy and then walked around to start the Jeep. It took on the fourth try, and they looked at each other, frowning. He promised that he would ask around the station in the coming week and see whether he could find some backyard mechanic who could look at the starter motor, which he suspected was the problem. As he reversed into the road, she recited some meme she had seen on Facebook: "When a man says he'll do something, he'll do it. You don't have to remind him every six months."

As they drove past the *bakkie*, which Josh now saw was a dark green Ford Ranger, he saw the dark shapes of the occupants inside the cab. His mind registered bright colors—red, green, and yellow—and a head of long dreadlocks ducking toward the dashboard of the vehicle. As the Jeep rode past, Josh's mind jumped to the Rastas he had seen at the library up in Joodse Kamp with Jerome Erasmus. His smile was gone, and he felt the skin around his mouth tighten as he glanced in the rearview mirror. After reversing, the Ranger turned 180 degrees, and started to follow.

Josh was acutely aware that his service pistol was in its holster in the drawer of his bedside table back at the flat, and that he had left his cell phone on the kitchen counter. Amy's phone was in her backpack in the back of the Jeep. He didn't want to worry her, and he couldn't stop anyway. The Ranger had gained on them. It was now no more than thirty meters behind them, speeding up.

When they got to the junction where Hoekwil connects with Bo-Langvlei, instead of continuing on as they had originally intended, Josh swung the wheel to the right and continued along the long bend of Hoekwil as it turned ninety degrees back toward the ocean and the N2. He sped up a little. In the mirror he saw the Ranger come around the bend, staying with them, and it matched his pace when the Jeep started to pull away a bit. Josh now had to consciously keep himself from flooring the accelerator, but he eased the throttle open to 90 km/h. Amy didn't seem to notice their speed. She was looking out of the window at the guest houses they passed, set back in lush trees and wetland brush.

It wasn't long before they completed the gentle curve of the road around the eastern shore of Island Lake, near the George Lakes Yacht Club entrance. The Ranger was even closer than before. As the Jeep approached the stop sign at the end of Hoekwil onto the N2, he slowed with a jerk. Amy gave him a strange look, and he mumbled an apology. The Ranger also slowed. Josh glanced to his left and saw a small truck approaching in the direction of Wilderness. Behind it was a stream of cars in both westerly lanes. There was nothing coming in the easterly direction.

Josh didn't go. He sat there for a few seconds, until Amy frowned and was about to speak up. Then, after one last glance to the right to show him that the easterly lane was still empty, Josh threw the wheel over hard right and floored the accelerator.

The Jeep shuddered out onto the N2 and lurched in front of the on-coming truck, which had to brake, its horn blaring. Josh put his arm out the window and waved to the driver to apologize.

Before Amy could get a word in, he said with a forced laugh, "Sorry, I misjudged that one." She looked at him strangely, but let it go.

As they gathered speed, he saw that the Ranger still waited at the turn-off, faced with the long stream of cars in the truck's wake. It would take the Ranger a while to get onto the N2 in pursuit. Josh floored the pedal and pulled further away. When they approached Salinas Beach just before the start of Kaaimans Pass, Amy had to put a hand on his shoulder and remind him of the speed cameras on the climb into the pass. He eased back the throttle, thanking her, eyes on the mirror. He couldn't see the Ranger anymore.

17 ROSMEAD STREET, GEORGE
SUNDAY, 27 NOVEMBER
16H15

After they returned to the flat from lunch, they vegged in front of the TV. Amy phoned Jenny Whitall to arrange a meeting on Tuesday at the Thesen gallery to discuss the upcoming show in December, which was still being planned in earnest.

Just after four in the afternoon, Josh once again found himself en-twined with Amy on the couch. He had woken with a start, Amy still asleep beside him. He kissed her lightly on the forehead, and then he carefully wriggled out from under her, having to do some imaginative engineering to ensure that she wouldn't fall off the couch as she turned in her sleep. The TV still played, some reality show he hated but didn't want to switch off in case she woke up.

He made his way to his desk. The morning's rowing had tired him out more than he thought. He had fallen asleep about forty minutes earlier, but the "power nap" was a fucking myth to him. He felt like shit and decided it would be a very early night.

He powered up his laptop and opened the tox report. He had gone to bed last night feeling a bit like a naughty schoolboy who hadn't done his homework. He had promised himself that he would read this report last night after dinner, but he and Amy had gotten a bit amorous, so he never got to it.

Whitcombe seemed to have been high as a kite when he died, according to the substances in his system when he was found the previous Friday night. The blood alcohol level in his body was three times the legal limit for driving a motor vehicle. Because Whitcombe's eyes were missing, the lab could not perform the usual test to determine the level of alcohol (or ethanol) by testing the vitreous humor, the clear jelly from inside the eye. So they had to resort to testing samples from a number of sources: the liver, kidney, cerebrospinal fluid, bile, and gastric contents. They had performed direct injection gas chromatography on the samples to detect alcohol.

There was something else as well. The lab had found 0.3 grams of flunitrazepam in Whitcome's system, a potent benzodiazepine better known in popular culture as Rohypnol. The date-rape drug. The drug could cause loss of muscle control, loss of inhibitions, loss of consciousness, and amnesia. Effects are usually worsened when combined with alcohol. Tests had shown that a dosage as small as 0.001 grams can impair an individual for eight to twelve hours.

Josh sipped coffee and tried to filter this information. Veronica Whitcombe had told them that her husband enjoyed alcohol. The odd glass of red wine at dinner, a couple glasses of whiskey. The alcohol level in his blood appeared anomalous—extraordinarily high for his drinking profile. The guy had been pretty fucked up at the time of his death.

The flunitrazepam was just, simply, not supposed to be there. It was generally not a self-administered drug. There were few benefits for the individual involved. This would mean that someone had administered it to Whitcombe.

After Veronica Whitcombe's statement that he had worn more formal clothing at the time of his last sighting, they had checked with both the

Knysna golf club and the Pezula estate. Whitcombe had said that he was going to have lunch "at the golf club." He was not seen at either establishment. Josh had to strike these as possible venues where someone could have slipped him Rohypnol in a social setting.

He suddenly remembered that Knysna had another premier golf course, Simola, on the other side of the estuary, and there were quite a few golf courses in Plett and George, actually. They had no evidence linking Whitcombe to any of those courses, but they would have to check them out, too.

They had also checked the Bosun's Pub & Grill, the establishment near the cottage where Whitcombe's car was found. He had not been there, and Veronica Whitcombe said quite definitively that he hated both the food and the vibe there; his interest was solely the safety of his car in their well-lit and frequently busy parking lot.

That left Josh thinking. They simply didn't know where Whitcombe had been in the nearly thirty-six hours between leaving his home and the discovery of his body. As Josh thought about this, he recalled that AppleMac's report earlier in the week on Whitcombe's cell phone showed an outgoing call to a beachfront restaurant in Plett. AppleMac had also reported that the only remaining Google search record on Whitcombe's laptop had been for "prawns in Plett." There was the possibility that the man had visited a restaurant there on Thursday or Friday. He made a note to contact the restaurant, The Lookout, or something like that. It could have been where Whitcombe was administered the flunitrazepam. But he seriously doubted it. Considering the effects of the drug, he couldn't see Whitcombe driving back from Plettenberg Bay having been slipped a "rufie."

What fired his ever-developing detective's synapses the most was something he and Gavin had discussed on the drive to Bain's Kloof, and which now also might fit with Erna Pretorius's theory. Gavin and Josh had both initially thought that Whitcombe may have been tortured, considering the mutilation of the body. The post-mortem nature of such mutilation now seemed to disprove that theory.

Yet, Pretorius's theory, along with AppleMac's evidence regarding the threatening emails on Whitcombe's laptop and the letter that the couple had received, seemed to point to blackmail of a suspect or suspects unknown.

Josh wondered whether Whitcombe could have been ambushed—maybe at the cottage, maybe elsewhere—and drugged by the blackmail victim, or someone acting on their behalf. Flunitrazepam was hardly known as a truth drug, something to be used in interrogations if you needed some answers from your subject. In fact, Josh, from a layman's perspective, thought that it was probably the furthest thing one could find from some sort of truth serum, seeing that it knocked the victim out, and rendered them pretty much unresponsive.

But it made sense. The blackmail angle regarding Whitcombe and some third party had bumped around in his mind for the past couple of days. If one were to act on the supposition that Whitcombe had blackmailed someone, and that the items he had proposed to sell for a price were "files" containing whatever information was of interest to the other party, Josh thought that administering a drug like flunitrazepam to Whitcombe may have been a way for the blackmail victim to put the fear of God into him, with the intention to interrogate him.

Josh tried to imagine himself in this person's position. You want to interrogate Whitcombe and find the files, but truth drugs can be notoriously unpredictable. If you harm Whitcombe, or even kill him, those files might be lost for good or, depending on their nature and what precautions Whitcombe may have taken for their disposal after his death, might be on their way to someone whom the victim would not want to see them.

Suddenly, flunitrazepam made sense. Scare the guy. Scare him a hell of a lot. Put him in a near coma, and maybe have your guys terrorize him while in that state without actually torturing him, maybe without even touching him. When it's through his system, he is still able to hand over the information. But now, with the knowledge that he'd be toast if he didn't ultimately produce it. Josh liked it, and thought he would pitch it to Gavin.

Amy brought him out of his thoughts with a kiss to his cheek. She was up now and ready to start dinner. She had insisted, a few months ago, on doing the Meatless Monday thing. He wasn't a fan, and on most

Mondays he got a cheeseburger somewhere during the day—something he was sure she would catch him out on soon. But Sunday evenings were fair game. She was doing a spaghetti bolognaise, and he was very much up for it. He had not slept well all weekend, and he felt that the protein boost might help.

As they started cooking, he switched on the TV. Carte Blanche was on. He fried the mince and she was on sauce and pasta duty as they watched another exposé on a politician in government caught stealing more than 300 million rand, from a drought relief scheme in the Eastern Cape Province. Allegedly, of course.

It was depressing stuff, but at least there were a couple of funny scenes where the politician was caught on hidden cameras, hiding from reporters in his luxury home.

CHAPTER 14

The first thing on Josh's agenda after arriving at the station was to phone Desiree Carolus at the SAPS Media Centre's Southern Cape office, to discuss the media reports circulating about the Whitcombe murder. She had left about ten messages for him at the station since Friday evening. He really appreciated that she hadn't bothered him on his cell over the weekend—he was pretty sure she would have the number. Her news was obviously quite urgent, but she respected the investigators' free time. He liked that.

Thus far, they had succeeded in keeping the Brink angle—at least as far as his killing near Wellington was concerned—out of the media. But, seeing that they were following much more obscure leads in the form of Erasmus and the possible blackmailing angle, there was very little of substance they could provide to the Fourth Estate, to placate the baying hounds without endangering their investigation. Thus far, they had been lucky; while the media could frequently act like entitled teenagers expecting results unreasonably quickly, they were a little over a week into the investigation and no real criticism had yet been leveled at SAPS or the investigation team.

The mainstream media coverage had initially focused on the mutilation of Whitcombe's body—even though the journalists were under orders to not print details, it was still sensationalized, which no doubt sold papers and clicks—but since then the coverage Josh had seen had focused on the retired advocate's career and some of the high profile cases he had been involved in, as well as the widow's family history. He knew that the hard questions were still to come, but for now, he was content to leave things to the officers who dealt with the journalists on a daily basis. Desiree was a seasoned professional, with more than ten years' experience dealing with the media, who perpetually tied up their switchboard as they demanded information, "Now!"

As he spoke to her over the phone, Josh realized that his high hopes had been premature. The latest twist—and the reason she had tried so fervently to reach him—was that an investigative journalist from the popular eNCA satellite TV network had been assigned to do a week-long exposé of their investigative efforts thus far. Desiree mentioned that Hlungwane—their taciturn Cluster Commander—was livid, and he wanted heads to roll. He apparently viewed this interest as an indictment of him, personally, and he had been heard to say that there were racist, "white monopoly capital" interests at play within the media. Hlungwane was known to have been squarely in the Zuma political camp before the recall of the former president, and Zuma and his people had always held a dislike for that network in particular.

Josh ignored this, but he did understand that there was significant pressure on them. He remembered, in 2005, years before he ever came to Knysna, a violent murder in the town. Jessica Wheeler's body was found on the grounds of St. George's Anglican Church on Main Street, ironically just across the road from the police station. She had been killed by suffocation, and her mouth had been pushed into the ground. There was sand found in her stomach. A local DJ at a night club was convicted and sentenced, but the crime and the outcome of the prosecution still left a bad taste, and it was—for many people across the country—a nasty memory of violent crime in the beautiful tourist town of Knysna.

Josh also remembered, from his days at university, being taught about the seminal 2001 Constitutional Court case of Carmichele v. Minister of Safety and Security. It involved the assault in 1995 of the claimant, who had stayed with a friend in the secluded village of Noetzie on the coast, just over ten kilometers from Knysna on the road to Plett. Ms. Carmichele had been assaulted by a man who had been accused of rape, after he had been released on his own recognizance. The court made a significant finding that the members of the SAPS and the public prosecutors in Knysna had negligently failed to comply with their constitutional duty to take steps to prevent this individual from causing the claimant harm. This was a watershed case on the tort law responsibility of the state toward victims of violent crime. It was taught in every law school.

So Josh understood Desiree's anxiety. Whitcombe was yet another high-profile case, and SAPS—and the town of Knysna—could expect to suffer some serious reputational damage if things were not handled properly.

Desiree asked Josh to consider an interview with the eNCA journalist. He said that he would discuss it with Gavin in their briefing later that morning. Josh felt that he was definitely not the person to take on the role of spokesperson in a national media interview. Gavin would be the guy for this, and he hoped that Gavin would agree.

Knysna SAPS station
10H45

Josh and Gavin had an hour to discuss the PM and toxicology reports, which they had both spent time reading over the weekend. They gathered in Gavin's office and both brought notes and papers which they spread over the small desk.

Walking in, Josh had seen a small stack of newspapers on a chair to the side of Gavin's desk. Gavin had told him that he had picked up the habit years ago during a few higher profile cases. He called it his "tower of power."

Every day, he saved a copy of any newspaper that carried a report about the crime he was investigating. He had a couple of contacts at stations in other provinces who sent him copies from their local papers, if the crime made it into the press there. It was not vanity, nothing of the sort. He was not looking for his name in print. In fact, Gavin very much preferred it when his name didn't feature at all. Gavin said that keeping record of the press coverage had helped him out a couple of times in the past, especially when he was challenged by journalists who claimed that certain information was in the public domain already, and could thus be rehashed in their stories. It was a quick source of reference that usually left him with the high ground, from whence he would come down on such journalists and read them the Riot Act.

They sat in Gavin's office with cups of coffee, looking at the documentation spread between them. Gavin was the first to speak.

"Before we get into the Whitcombe forensics reports, I just got word a few minutes ago. Two developments on the Wellington side." Josh was immediately interested.

"The Brink autopsy report is ready. The pathologist promised to email it to me and copy you sometime this afternoon, but she read the high points to me over the phone."

He lit a cigarette. "Unfortunately, nothing major in respect of the body itself, pretty much what we knew from the scene. The sergeant there was right about the sequence of the shots; one to the back of the head, then the body was turned over after landing face down, and then two shots to the chest. The weapon was about twenty centimeters from the back of the head for the first shot, so there was a lot of gunshot residue on the skin of the head and neck. There was no GSR for the chest shots on the clothing or skin, so she assumes that the shooter stood over Brink's body and fired from a height of around 1.2 meters, the gun hand facing down." Gavin took a drag of the cigarette and then dropped some ash in his "World's best boss" mug.

"Did they do ballistics yet?" Josh asked, shifting in his seat.

"Yes, fortunately, they seem more on the ball out there in Paarl than our friends in Mossel Bay." He was still sour about the long wait for the Whitcombe reports, and he would probably not let it go anytime soon. "All three shots were fired from the same weapon. Even though the bullet from the head shot wasn't retrieved—you saw the exit wound—" he pulled a nasty face, "—the entry wounds are consistent between the three shots fired. From the two slugs recovered from Brink's chest, it's clear we were right, or that the sergeant at the scene was. They're from a Glock G19 Gen 5, in 9mm Luger, a semi-automatic that holds fifteen rounds in the magazine. A pretty common weapon, unfortunately."

"But we have the casings from the scene."

Gavin nodded. "Yes. And they managed to find the third one after the body was removed from the site; it was in a fold of one of those wrappings covering the tomb. With the rifling and the firing-pin marks, they say that they should be able to match the weapon if we ever find it."

"Good. Anything from the body itself?"

Gavin shook his head. "No, no other wounds or bruising, no indication of rough stuff prior to the shooting. But—" Here he smiled at Josh. "You remember that sergeant admiring Brink's leather belt?" Josh nodded, smiling himself. "And you suggested they should check it. They found prints on the belt, decent ones. Two sets. They've eliminated Brink's, of course. They're still running the other set through the database, and the patho says they hope to have the results by tomorrow morning at the latest."

Josh was ecstatic. "That's bloody great! So the guy who turned the body over—"

"Yes, or the shooter, although I agree it would make sense for someone else, if there were two people, to have turned the body."

They still worked on the assumption that the two black guys in the blue Mazda that raced out of the Calabash parking lot were their prime suspects in Brink's killing. Now they were finally starting to get some results, tangible things they could follow up on. "You said there were two developments on the Wellington side. The Glock and the prints?"

Gavin shook his head. "No. I also had a call from SAPS Cape Town Central station. One of their units found the Mazda."

Josh grinned like a schoolboy.

Gavin raised a hand. "Hold your horses, son, there's unfortunately not a lot on the car, but they've impounded it and they are busy going through it with a fine-toothed comb."

The car had been found on Zone 13 Street in Langa. It was a 2008 model Mazda 6, a 3.0 liter, V6 four-door sedan in blue. The car had a number of dents, and one quarter window was out and had clear plastic taped over it. The registration number on the back plate (the front plate was missing) was CA 415-832. There was a yellow and black Kaizer Chiefs football club sticker on the back.

The car was registered in the name of Enoch James Mulaudzi, a 54-year-old resident of Langa who lived in a small house on Zone 13 Street with his wife. Mulaudzi was an employee of PRASA, the passenger rail agency, and he worked as a janitorial staff member at the Metrorail Infrastructure and Rolling Stock Depot in Salt River. He had no criminal record, and no firearms registered to his name. He had bought the car in 2013, and was up to date with licensing it for use on the road. There were no traffic violations or fines recorded on the vehicle.

"Mulaudzi is from the Eastern Cape. It appears he's been working in Cape Town for the past twenty years, the last thirteen of which were at the Metrorail depot."

"Has he been questioned?"

Gavin had a wry look. "One of the CT Central men spoke to him. He has no idea how the car could have been out near Wellington. He hadn't been driving, and he doesn't know who else might have been. He is convinced it's a mistake, that our eyewitnesses got the registration wrong. He says he barely ever uses the car during the week. He takes the train to work—leaving at 05h30 in the morning and usually only back after seven in the evening—and now and then he'll run to a shop in the car. Otherwise, he and the missus sometimes take a drive on weekends, over on Baden Powell to Muizenberg or to Stellenbosch or Somerset West."

Josh was doubtful. "Any sign of a break-in? Could someone have stolen the car?"

Gavin shook his head. "And brought it back? Not likely."

Josh frowned. "Borrowed it? Does he have other family, or friends who might have taken the car for some purpose?"

Gavin shrugged, and said they just didn't know.

"I assume they'll let us know about any prints found in the car. For when we get the results of the prints on Brink's belt?"

"I've asked Forensics out in Paarl to email the results of the prints on the body to me and to Major Van Rooyen, the point man at Cape Town Central on the BOLO and the search results for the Mazda. If we get a match, we should at least be able to tie the car and the two guys to Brink's murder definitively. Well, at least one of them."

Josh wanted to mention something, though. "Sorry, Gavin, I was just thinking of something else earlier. You know we were wondering about the lack of luggage in the Merc?" Gavin nodded, lighting a cigarette and pulling deeply from it. "Well, I was thinking. We were speculating that maybe the two guys had tried to mug Brink at the bush pub. But there was too much traffic, so they piled him into their car to take him elsewhere, and then settled on the Kramat as a quieter scene. It just struck me earlier that maybe we can explain both those things. What if they were after something that Brink had with him?"

Gavin tipped some ash into the mug and nodded again, looking more interested now, so Josh continued. "They knew he had something, and they were there to get it from him. They needed a quiet place to search for it. And when they got it, they executed him. Because having gotten hold of what they were after, they needed to silence him.

"And do you remember the pair of men's briefs that the forensics team found at the scene?" Gavin nodded. "Well, I remember you saying something in the pub's parking lot before we went to check the body, asking about the fact that Brink didn't even pack socks? Well, that got me thinking. What if they had Brink's bag at the scene, and as they searched it, those briefs dropped out? That's why they were there."

They had speculated out at the bush pub scene that Brink might have stayed somewhere in the area, where his luggage might be found. But the SAPS units from Wellington, Worcester, and Ceres had all canvassed the region, and there was no evidence of Brink having stayed anywhere in the area. In fact, nobody had reported even seeing him in the area, which brought them back to their original theory that it had been a random stop at the Calabash on the way to his destination, seemingly Cape Town.

Gavin agreed; it was something to consider. And it could align with the missing files issue in the Whitcombe case.

After grabbing some coffee, and after Josh had caught up with some emails about the case, they decided to chat for a few minutes about the upcoming interview with Erasmus. The Rasta gangster was expected at 14h00. Neither looked forward to it. Both felt that they didn't have enough on the man's involvement with Whitcombe; not yet, at least. They would have to play it by ear and hope that the gangster wouldn't bring a lawyer.

The one thing they both agreed on for the interview, emphatically, was that they would not bring up the PPEP angle. They wanted to see first how he reacted as an apparent person of interest in the advocate's killing, and they hoped that they had enough information from the eye-witness reports of Whitcombe's car spotted up in Joodse Kamp on multiple occasions. If there was something to the PPEP angle—and this was quite probably how the two men met initially—then they would prefer to keep Erasmus guessing on whether they knew anything about it. It couldn't hurt.

Just before their informal meeting broke up, Josh swallowed hard and decided to go for it. He told Gavin his suspicions about the Ford Ranger having followed him and Amy from Wilderness the previous morning, and that he thought that it might have been Rastas, maybe Erasmus's men.

Gavin frowned. "Are you sure?"

Josh was quick to shake his head, emphatically. "No, not at all, that's why I debated telling you. I can't be sure, not at all, but I got this feeling…"

Gavin nodded slowly. He didn't look convinced. "I don't see why Erasmus would want to do that. We're not on his radar, right? He didn't know about this afternoon's interview until this morning, and he still doesn't know that we're the ones who want to talk to him, right? I think it's likely that he's expecting this to be a Narc unit interview."

Josh shrugged. "I was thinking…you asked that Narcotics guy on Friday afternoon to drop by Erasmus's place this morning and ask him to join us for the interview this afternoon. What if he told Erasmus then already?"

Gavin squinted his eyes slightly. "That's a serious allegation. You mean the guy is in cahoots with Erasmus, and that he was warning him?"

Josh shook his head slowly. "I don't know, I'm just thinking aloud here. Maybe it's nothing, maybe those guys weren't Erasmus's men, and they weren't even following us."

Gavin didn't say anything, but he still looked worried.

CHAPTER 15

On Friday afternoon, Gavin had asked a Narcotics officer from George, Captain Gershwin Carels—who knew Erasmus after having had some official interactions with him over the past couple of years—to "extend the invitation" for Erasmus to visit Knysna SAPS on Monday afternoon.

The officer had delivered the ultimatum: Erasmus was being looked at in an investigation handled by Knysna station and he was cordially asked to avail himself of an opportunity to clear up some issues—to "assist the police in their inquiries," as the old chestnut went. If he were willing to report at Knysna station at 14h00 that afternoon, they would not have to issue a warrant to question him and potentially search his house for evidence regarding the Knysna investigation. He was not told what the investigation was about, but he had probably guessed that it was drug-related, another attempt by the Narcotics team to paint him into a corner again. They had tried to do so many times in the past six years since he had taken over from Brendon "Grootman" Goliath, the former 28s gangster from Pollsmoor who had moved out to the Southern Cape, following his release on a ten-year-old armed robbery conviction in Wynberg magistrates court.

Reportedly, Erasmus was originally hired by Grootman as muscle, before Erasmus organized a "change in leadership" for the 28s. Grootman's body was found in his car at the bottom of a ravine, though a post-mortem surmised he was dead before he hit the ground. Erasmus graciously accepted his new promotion.

Erasmus arrived to the Knysna station in the low, sporty gray Audi that W/O Fourie had spotted out at the man's house the previous Monday. Josh watched through the window of the charge office, where he and Gavin chatted with the desk sergeant. He was impressed; it really was a beautiful car.

Two Rastas—obviously muscle—exited from the back. Josh recognized the two men who had been with Erasmus at the library the previous week. A black man in an expensive suit got out of the passenger seat, carrying an equally expensive-looking leather briefcase.

When they entered the station, Gavin and Josh were waiting with a couple of officers. They greeted the Rasta and his attorney. The muscle stayed out of sight, taking seats in the charge office, from where they stared down any members of the public who looked like they wanted to have a seat on those hard—but more comfortable than standing—wooden benches while they waited hours for their complaints to be dealt with. There were a couple of grandmothers, and a pregnant woman, but they all stayed standing and averted their faces.

Desmond Chauke was a senior partner at one of the largest law firms in the country, Lubisi Thurston Cachalia, or LBC, based in their Sandton office. Johannesburg was Africa's legal hub, and housed the top law firms on the continent. His firm was a really big player. Chauke's specialization was criminal law and he was on record as also having been involved in a substantial number of high-profile celebrity cases in the past few years, not only in criminal matters but any kind of legal dispute that would bring media attention and large fees. He was a pitbull. Josh remembered reading a *Sunday Times* column dedicated to his professional career the year before, praising him as one of the first really experienced and talented black African lawyers to emerge in post-1994 South Africa who had not pursued a career in the judiciary.

Josh was justifiably wary, and he exchanged a look with Gavin, who seemed to be just as aware of the pedigree of the guy they were up against. And neither of them missed the fact that, unless Chauke just happened to be in Knysna today, a phone call from Erasmus following the Narcotics officer's phone call to him after 9:00 a.m. that morning had gotten this big fish on a plane to George to attend an informal questioning session.

Unless, of course, as Josh believed, Erasmus may have already had news of the pending interview by Friday evening. Either way, they could both sense something big, dark, and slimy rolling underwater in the deep. Erasmus's use of this high-caliber heavy hitter was a clear message. He would not go down easily. They would have to be on their toes at all times.

There were rules and procedures, and both Gavin and Josh could picture Chauke standing in front of a judge in a crowded courtroom, roasting the SAPS investigators for how they had mistreated his client, and making flowery constitutional arguments in the process. Josh grimaced. The courts love those nowadays. He was worried, especially as he reflected on the fact that they had very little real evidence to link Whitcombe with Erasmus. He hoped that Gavin would bring some experience—and genius—to the "question room," as some of the old-timers still called it. Today, he sincerely hoped that it would be the answer room.

The four men were seated, two teams squaring off across the table from each other. Erasmus wasn't wearing the *tam* on his head today, as he had when Josh had bumped into him up at the library in Joodse Kamp. His dreadlocks hung halfway down his back. And he also wasn't wearing sunglasses today, and both detectives noted the small tattoos under his eyes: teardrops. They knew that this was a universal symbol of mourning in the context of prison tattoos, also popular amongst some Cape gangsters. It could symbolize the loss of friends, or—especially when the outline of the drop was filled in—an avenged death. Erasmus's four drops were all filled in. The man had piercing green eyes, testifying to a mixed parentage, with the reddish look of someone who smoked a lot of weed. They were disconcerting when their glare fixed on you.

The Rasta, dressed in jeans and an expensive-looking blue t-shirt that showed off big muscles, had insisted, through his lawyer, on being given a cold drink as soon as they had stepped into the room. Gavin had sent a sergeant to fetch a Coke from the vending machine outside the charge office.

Chauke had made quite a dramatic show of getting seated. He needed a space for his briefcase, and Josh watched, cynically amused, as the man seemed to work up a head of steam about the poor arrangements for their *(his)* visit. He was eventually persuaded to just put the case at his feet, next to his chair. After everyone was seated, and he had whispered in his client's ear, he made another show of getting up, slowly taking off his jacket, and hanging it over the back of his chair. Josh wanted to yawn, both literally and sarcastically, but refrained.

Erasmus was the most chilled person in the room. Outside, he had not greeted the officers and had not said a word to them. He looked like he was about to burst out laughing about something. Josh had wished he could bury his fist in the guy's smirk. But now at last he spoke.

"Wat soek djulle met my? Huh? Het djulle fokol anners om te doen nie?" He had a glint in his eye. He knew that he could talk to them however he wished; he had a prime cut of high-priced lawyer beef next to him, and he was going to enjoy this.

Gavin looked down at a page of notes on the desk in front of him, and Josh looked elsewhere, at a corner of the room. Chauke cleared his throat, and he observed that his client had expressed a perfectly legitimate question. *Why were they here?*

Josh nearly laughed aloud when Chauke continued to say that only the innocent ever asked why they were being interrogated. The guilty knew full well. Apart from the drippy, bullshit sentiment—and, for all his grand pedigree, Josh thought that Chauke's delivery was a bit ham-fisted—that was clearly just not accurate. He cleared his throat and decided to look away again, before he showed unwelcome emotion.

Gavin finally looked at Erasmus. "We are not recording this interview, as it is not an official interrogation. You, Mr. Erasmus, have not been arrested for any crime or on any charge. You admit that you are here voluntarily? In fact, you are, at this current point in time, not even a suspect in any official police investigation that I am aware of."

Josh caught the irony in his voice in the end, and he wanted to laugh again—if it had been funny. Erasmus was a suspect in many, many suspected crimes, but this was not their business here today.

Erasmus threw a quick glance at Chauke, and then he nodded at the question. *"Aweh,"* he mouthed, while looking sideways at Gavin. Yes, he was here voluntarily.

Gavin made a tick on the pad in front of him. Josh saw Chauke lean forward slightly to steal a peek, under the guise of polishing his glasses.

Chauke seemed to catch Josh's look from the corner of his eye, and he slid his glasses back on and then sat back in the chair, looking imperious again. "I would just like to put on the record that my client has agreed that we conduct this informal conversation—"

"Interview." Gavin interjected.

Chauke hardly missed a beat. "Interview"—with a nod at Gavin—"in English. I hope you will understand that in my appearances before the Constitutional Court and the Supreme Court of Appeals, I hardly ever—"

Gavin interrupted. "Agreed, we have no problem with that. In fact, your client is the only person who has spoken Afrikaans in this room since we had a seat."

Josh decided to jump in. "Or his version of what passes for Afrikaans." Erasmus glanced at him, eyes squinting. Josh wanted to get into the game, and, if possible, piss Erasmus off. You never knew what a pissed-off drug dealer might say or do that would help their cause.

Chauke gave a magnanimous smile. "OK, so here we are. You want my client to answer some questions. My client has no knowledge of what you are after, what you think he might know, or why, for whatever god-forsaken reason, you might think that he might be able to assist you. We will conduct this conver—interview in English, and we will all be civil." He glanced at Gavin, and then briefly at Josh. "We are all gentlemen here, and we all know what the courts think of strong-arm tactics aimed at innocent members of the public, right?"

Gavin didn't deign to answer, and he immediately launched into his questions. He looked across at Erasmus.

"Mr. Erasmus, did you know Brendon Goliath, also known as Grootman?"

Chauke nearly jumped out of his chair. "Objection! What is the relevance of that question?'

Gavin lowered his head and tried to look only slightly exasperated. Josh thought he didn't do a great job of it.

"This is not a courtroom, Mr. Chauke. I don't think I need to remind you of that." Chauke gave a thin smile, as he stared at Gavin over the top rims of his Hugo Boss spectacle frames. "And I do not believe I have any legal obligation to prove the relevance of any question I ask of your client or, for that matter, for any such question to be relevant to anything at all. This is an interview, and we are simply asking your client for information. This is not a court, and we are not interrogating your client on some charge, attempting to solicit evidence for use in a court of law."

Chauke looked down at the desk. He rearranged his legal pad and his expensive pen to be even more symmetrically lined up, if that were possible. As yet, he had not written a thing. When he looked back up at Gavin, his eyes seemed to suggest that Gavin could continue.

Gavin looked at him for a few more seconds, until things started getting uncomfortable, and then he turned back to Erasmus.

"As I asked, did you know Brendon Goliath?"

Josh was a little shocked when Chauke, again, seemed to throw his toys out of the cot. "What is the purpose of this question, Colonel Whitall? I will refrain from questioning its relevance, but surely my client is entitled to ask why you would ask him whether he knew any particular individual?'

Gavin looked as pissed off as Josh was, but he rearranged his face into a slight smile, and Josh realized that Chauke was baiting them. This was an informal interview. Erasmus was under no legal obligation to be here. He was participating—"cooperating" would be much too strong a word, thus far—by his own volition.

Josh looked at Gavin, who seemed to catch his drift, and he gave a small nod. They were both aware that if they pushed too hard, the lawyer would find a reason to end proceedings, real or trumped-up. They would have to watch it.

When he turned back to Erasmus, Gavin tried to look more chilled. He actually smiled. "We are trying to establish your client's rise in the organization that he currently heads." He glanced at Chauke.

Chauke was livid. "Organization? What organization is that? What evidence do you have that my client heads any kind of organization at all?" He could see Gavin's face, and he probably just wanted to get in a gratuitous dig. "Do you mean like a bridge club, or a pub quiz team? I would have to consult with my client before he answers anything along those lines."

Gavin had to raise a hand to placate the professional attack-dog. "We are simply acting on information we and other officers have received about your client's position as head of the Funky Guys, a gang—well, let's call it an 'organization'—operating throughout the Southern Cape and based at his home in Joodse Kamp, right here in Knysna."

Chauke smiled, a crooked smile, looking as if he had expected this question. "Let me state, categorically, that my client has no knowledge of the alleged 'organization' you speak of. Your SAPS Narcotics division has, for a few years now, made similar allegations against my client, none of which have ever been remotely proven." At this moment, the man started ticking off points on the five fingers of his left hand as he continued. "He has been harassed, embarrassed, and persecuted, for a number of years, by—"

Gavin shut him up with a wave of his hand in the air. "OK, fine, we don't need him to answer that question, let's move on."

Chauke looked surprised but rallied quickly, and he looked more smug than usual as he glanced at his client. Maybe to convey that this was how you saw your big legal fees in action. He had just shut down the SAPS inquiry about Erasmus's gang affiliation.

Gavin turned back to Erasmus. "How do you currently earn your living, sir?" Chauke was about to jump up when Gavin continued, trying to preempt another tantrum. "We saw you arrive in an expensive car earlier, and I was just wondering how you can afford to pay for it."

This time Chauke did jump up, and he started doing circles behind Team Erasmus's side of the table. "Enough! You do realize that you are trampling on my client's constitutional rights?"

As Gavin looked poised to respond, to point out again that this was not an interrogation and that Erasmus was not being denied any of the guarantees under law to remain silent, Chauke launched into his diatribe.

"I know that you attempted to teach me about the law just now." The man looked like he was about to have an explosive fit of laughter. "But I must again question the relevance of this line of questioning. How is my client's trade or occupation of any importance to you, the State?"

Both Gavin and Josh picked up on the use of the word. The man was trying to lay a basis for allegations of trampling on his client's rights by the powerful mechanisms of the State's investigative machinery.

Gavin looked ready to back off the question, once again. They didn't really need to know where Erasmus's money came from, even though they all had their suspicions. And Josh knew very well they would never get a straight answer.

Chauke continued. "My client has a constitutionally guaranteed, fundamental human right of trade, occupation, and profession. He can do whatever he wants to earn whatever living he earns. And that is no business of the State, or its Gestapo officers in this room."

Gavin pushed his chair back, looking like he'd had enough of this asshole, but Josh jumped in with a comment.

"Mr. Chauke, I think you know as well as I that there is a difference between a 'right' and a 'freedom.' Section 22 of the Constitution guarantees to all the country's citizens the 'freedom' to pursue a trade. In fact, it says that they have the right to choose a trade, occupation, and profession freely." Chauke looked slightly shocked, so Josh continued. "You also know that Section 22 itself qualifies that freedom by saying that it can be regulated by the *State*: 'The practice of a trade, occupation, or profession may be regulated by law.'"

The lawyer looked a little put off, and ready to start an argument. But he simply asked, in a mockingly sweet tone, "What is your point, Captain?"

Josh wasn't intimidated. "My point, sir, is that as you so rightly point out, we are the State." He motioned to Gavin and himself. "We are constitutionally entitled to regulate your client's freedom to practice his trade of choice." Chauke just stared. "We were simply asking him what trade he is engaged in, as we happened to notice that he seems to be quite successful at it. If I work another twenty years at my job, I might be able to drive that German car that you and your client arrived in. We are simply curious as to how he manages to afford it, without any visible means of income— sorry, legal income—that we can see."

Erasmus smirked, but Chauke looked like he was about to have a stroke. As he was about to erupt, Gavin put a hand on Josh's shoulder.

"Gentlemen, I think this is the perfect time to take a short break."

Chauke and Erasmus stared, and then they turned to each other, bowing their heads closer together as they started to have a whispered conversation. Gavin winked at Josh and motioned for him to leave the room. The two cops walked out, promising to be back in ten minutes.

The other team patently ignored them, as they continued to whisper sweet nothings to one another.

KNYSNA SAPS STATION

INTERVIEW ROOM 2

15H10

They were back at the table. Erasmus still smirked. Chauke was seated next to him, finishing a text on his cell phone. He was obviously well aware that Gavin was ready to recommence the interview, but he was intent on showing his own importance. He had other cases and clients and they should just wait for him to finish this urgent correspondence.

Gavin ignored him and moved on to his next question. Chauke scoffed and dropped the phone on the table.

"Mr. Erasmus, I need to ask where you were on Thursday November 17th and Friday November 18th. That's a week ago. Between 08h00 on the Thursday and 22h00 on the Friday."

Erasmus looked at Chauke, and they huddled again. Josh glanced at Gavin, and made a face. Chauke broke the huddle and asked why they needed this information.

Gavin managed to keep a straight face—he had had enough of this guy's obstruction of the interview. He was being difficult for the sake of being difficult.

"Mr. Chauke, I believe that we've covered this ground already. We are asking your client for information, about his whereabouts on certain dates and at certain times. He really does not need to know why we're asking. He needs to tell us—and be truthful in doing so—where he was and what he was doing at those times. If he decides to refrain from telling us, we will then consider whether he is trying to hide anything, and whether we need to consider arresting him for obstruction of justice and his unwillingness to assist us in our investigation."

Chauke looked daggers at Gavin, then at Josh, while Gavin continued.

"If your client chooses to hide this information, and not to cooperate in this interview, we will be within our rights to draw an adverse inference, and believe that he is trying to hide something from the police. And that usually gets us all excited." He produced a broad grin, for effect. "It gives us a mission to pursue, to find out the truth. Would your client prefer that?" The grin now turned into a sweet smile, looking as if honey might drip from his lips.

Chauke wasn't done, though. "I am sure you will understand that my client has not been told what this investigation of yours is about, and why he, specifically, is being questioned. He would be perfectly within his rights to worry about where you are going with this. For all we know—" and here he glanced conspiratorially at his less-than-interested looking client, "—you might be fitting him up for some imagined crime that he did not commit. Surely you can understand his reticence in being forthright under these circumstances?" The man folded his arms and looked like he had just spoken the last word on the subject.

Josh jumped in, afraid that Gavin would start shouting. "Sir, we are not trying to finger your client for a crime. We are asking him to disclose some information. Facts." He let that float in the air for a few seconds. "We are asking him about facts. The same as if we asked him what he had for breakfast this morning. He can decide to tell us, or not to tell us. Either way we cannot fit the circumstances to make him look guilty of anything. But, of course, if his facts correspond with our facts, he might require more investigation. Your client agreed to cooperate, but thus far we have had zero cooperation from either of you two gentlemen." He used the term very lightly.

Chauke gave a thin smile, and then he conversed with Erasmus again. While his client whispered in his ear, and without even looking at Gavin, the lawyer said, "We still do not know what you're investigating. It appears as if my client is being strong-armed into—"

Gavin had reached his breaking point. He blew up.

"Listen here, sir, I don't give a fuck what your client may think about what we're doing here. For the last time, we are just asking questions, and requesting information within his knowledge. If he doesn't want to assist us, we will take a quick break and I will phone the fucking state prosecutor's office and take legal advice on whether we should arrest your fucking client and keep him overnight while we assess how best to proceed, in the face of a recalcitrant witness in an official police investigation."

Chauke gave a sarcastic little laugh. He clearly took some pleasure from having pissed Gavin off. Then he whispered into Erasmus's ear again.

The tall Rasta listened for a few seconds, then shrugged and moved away from his lawyer. He looked Gavin in the eye.

"I spent a couple of days in Plett. Those two days you asked about. With a friend."

Gavin and Josh shared a quick look. At last.

"A friend? Can they confirm your whereabouts at the time? Will they?"

Erasmus nodded.

"Your friend's name?"

He squinted at Gavin. "Gentlemen don't kiss and tell." He looked like he was about to laugh, but he continued. "Her name's Shaileen Davids. A *kwaai stukkie*, big tits, knows how to make a man happy. Twenty-two, nice and tight in all the right places."

He looked at Gavin, and then at Josh. He clearly enjoyed playing this game with the cops.

Josh grimaced. The girl was probably nothing to this man, but he just couldn't imagine himself being such a prick about someone he was intimate with, ever. This reinforced everything he had thought about the Rasta from the start. When he first heard of him, and then met him at the library up in Joodse Kamp, he had thought that he might be biased and just disliked the man based on his criminal reputation, but he was a complete dick. That was clear now.

Gavin nodded. This was better than nothing. The man at least attempted to provide an alibi.

Erasmus now seemed eager to say more. His eyes crinkled, and he looked as if he were telling a very funny joke. "She likes to play when I want to play. You can call her, I spent three days with her, and we went out to Happy Valley on the Thursday, I think, for a drive, and some fun."

Josh asked, "What does Ms. Davids do for a living?"

Erasmus grinned. "Fuck knows, she's a druggie, does a lot of meth." He laughed at his own joke. Chauke looked at him with a frown, and he placed a hand on his client's arm. Erasmus brushed it off. "Or so I've been told by the lady herself. I really try hard to discourage her. That shit will fry your brain, you know. *Daai goed is kak*." He smiled broadly at Gavin.

Gavin smiled back. He had regained his composure now. "We'll need a number and an address for Ms. Davids, please." Chauke nodded, signifying that he would get it for them.

Gavin decided to move on. "Do you know a man by the name of Mark Whitcombe?"

Erasmus blinked, and he looked at his lawyer. Gavin and Josh had the same thought: that was a hit.

Chauke again started to whisper to his client, and Erasmus looked down at his hands. His eyes went shifty for a second, and there was something in his face; but the smile formed again on his lips, looking a bit forced. Chauke raised his head and started to fire on all cylinders again.

"I have decided, finally, that my client needs to be told what this is about, now! You have been trying my—*our*—patience for some time, hiding behind the fact that this is what you like to call an 'interview,' but that won't fly anymore. Section 35 of the Bill of Rights guarantees my client a right of access to information; to know what you are after him for, and what he is being suspected of. We will no longer participate in this sham if you refuse to provide more information."

Halfway through the little speech, Josh was already shaking his head. "Mr. Chauke, we have the utmost respect for you and your client, and for your undoubtedly great legal expertise, but you continue to misunderstand the nature of these proceedings."

Chauke gave a sarcastic smirk at this, but Josh continued. "The rights guaranteed in Section 35, which you refer to, are provided to 'arrested, detained, and accused persons.' Your client—currently—is none of those. We are interviewing him for information, just as we would a bystander at the scene of a car crash or a robbery. He is not being accused of anything. We will decide, on the strength of the information he provides, whether there are any grounds to accuse him. If so, he would become an accused person, and then you'll be welcome to raise his constitutional rights again. In the meantime, we are waiting for your client to answer the question."

Gavin was all smiles now. Chauke looked irritated and he whispered to Erasmus again, who shrugged him off and looked at Josh.

"I know the name. He's the whitey lawyer, old dude, who was killed? It's been in the papers."

The two cops exchanged a glance. They had expected this. The case had been in the media for most of the last week, and this response was an easy out.

So Gavin continued. "The question was whether you knew Mr. Whitcombe."

Before Chauke could jump in, and he looked keen to do so again, Erasmus stifled a yawn and said that he had heard of the guy.

"Heard of him?" Gavin looked quizzical. "Before or after the media reports?"

Chauke moved closer to his client again, but maybe Erasmus was becoming tired of the man's bullshit as well, as he ignored his lawyer and continued speaking.

"I've heard of him, before. Not sure where, you know?"

This time Gavin and Josh leaned close together, and they had a little muffled chat. Chauke was looking, and when he apparently realized that he was now sitting waiting for these lowly-paid public servants to proceed, he dropped his eyes to his phone, swiped the screen, and looked as if he were checking his emails. Erasmus hummed some tune. It sounded like hip-hop.

Gavin looked up again. "Mr. Erasmus, is your answer that you only knew of Mr. Whitcombe? That you never actually met him?

The man stopped humming, and he shrugged. Gavin could see that he was not going to give a straight answer, so he decided to jump to their evidence.

"We have eyewitnesses who saw Mr. Whitcombe's car parked in front of your house out in Joodse Kamp, on a number of occasions; about five or six times over the last month or so. Does that ring a bell?"

Josh smiled to himself as Captain Predictable threw another fit. He started to worry about Chauke's blood pressure.

The lawyer was up on his feet again, spittle flying from his mouth. "What the hell do you mean coming here with 'eyewitnesses'? You tell us that my client is not under investigation, and yet you have witnesses lined up against him? To testify to God knows what kind of bullshit about him?"

Gavin raised a hand. "Woah, counselor, just relax please. We are not investigating your client. In the course of our investigation—of Mr. Whitcombe's murder, *not* of your client—some witnesses provided information to us. At the time, your client was not a suspect. We were looking for evidence of Mr. Whitcombe's movements and witnesses provided us with evidence of that, by stating that they had seen the victim's car parked at Mr. Erasmus's house on a number of occasions. We are now asking your client to respond to that, to explain it to us."

Chauke was still on the warpath. Josh was starting to wonder at the fact that the mention of Whitcombe, and of the fact that this was clearly a murder investigation, had not appeared to faze Chauke one bit. The man was still on his high horse.

"Who are these witnesses? What are their names? My client has a constitutional right to confront his accusers, out in the open, for the truth to come out. This is looking more and more like an ambush!" He looked at his client, then back at Gavin. "A bloody *witch-hunt!*" Inspiration must have struck, because Chauke looked from Gavin and Josh to Erasmus, and then back at the two white cops again. "Maybe a bloody *racist* witch-hunt?"

Josh had to refrain from shouting at the man. "Mr. Chauke, do we really need to remind you again that your client is not being accused of a crime? He is not arrested, detained, or even accused. We are asking him questions. We have witnesses who testified to seeing the car there, on multiple occasions, and we would love to know what your client's response to that is. Did he meet with Mr. Whitcombe at his house? If so, what were they meeting about? What did they discuss? That is what we want to know."

Gavin jumped in. "And, Mr. Chauke, if either you or your client was to become aware of the identity of our witnesses, let me remind you that you should stay away from them. If your client attempts to contact any witness in this case, we will arrest him. OK?"

Chauke clearly didn't take kindly to the threat, but he simply nodded and then took his glasses off for another clean, glancing at Erasmus.

Josh reminded Erasmus of the question. The Rasta pulled a face, looking bored, and then responded. "OK, we met a couple of times, liked to talk about shit." He licked his lips. "But I didn't know the 'whitey' man, we weren't friends. We was just chatting, talking all kinds of *kak*."

Before the cops could respond, Chauke had his glasses back on and he had a question. Josh could see that he was now preparing for court, somewhere down the line.

"Before we get into any meeting or meetings my client may, or may not, have had with this person, would you please tell us about the car these 'eyewitnesses' claim to have seen? At my client's house, allegedly?"

Josh looked a bit uncomfortable, so Gavin decided to handle this. They couldn't get around it. They might have to fall on their swords here. "Mr. Whitcombe was driving a British sports car, a red one, and it was spotted by our witnesses on multiple occasions parked at your client's house. The car is currently in our impound lot here in town. It is a very conspicuous vehicle, a pretty rare model on our roads."

Chauke frowned. "Did you show these witnesses photographs of the car?"

Josh reddened a bit. This was something that they were still planning to do. Fourie and Fortuin had been asked to take photographs and show them to the three boys whose details they had taken, the ones whom they had identified as the most trustworthy of the little gang of rascals who had been lounging around Erasmus's road.

Gavin sensed his discomfort, and he explained. "We are in the process of doing that, but the witnesses identified the vehicle to our satisfaction."

Chauke sensed weakness and pounced. "Ah, I see. You question my client about this, and confront him with a so-called 'eyewitness identification' before you have acquired confirmation? That is sloppy police work, if you don't mind me saying so."

Gavin and Josh both minded him saying so.

"How exactly did your 'witnesses' identify the vehicle, if they hadn't been shown pictures of it?" Chauke was now starting to show his talent for trial work.

He again took his glasses off, to fix a penetrating stare on Josh, then Gavin. "If you say that this British sports car is a rare model on our roads, what is the likelihood of your eyewitnesses—situated in Joodse Kamp settlement in my client's street—recognizing it and being able to describe it to the police?" His mouth twisted into a vindictive smile.

Josh looked at Gavin, and he received a slight nod. He might as well tell the whole story. He explained how the witnesses had identified the car as a "Ferrari," and had accurately described the driver. He then explained that Whitcombe had been driving the red Jaguar F-type, which was a very close match to the look of the Italian sports cars.

Chauke was immediately out of his seat again, throwing his glasses so that they slid across the table and Josh had to stop them from going over the edge onto the floor. In all honesty, he was tempted to let them go. But he was afraid the man might sue SAPS for damage to property.

Chauke started going off about assumptions, and conclusions, and jumping to them. He then explained that clearly the so-called eyewitnesses had never actually identified Whitcombe's car, and that, as they sat here—he was standing at this time, of course—there was not a shred of evidence linking Whitcombe or his car to Erasmus's house. This was all circumstantial evidence, and the police were sloppily drawing some very wild conclusions from it. They had had enough, he and his poor, embattled client. They were about ready to leave.

Josh stood himself, if only because he hated having the other man standing over them and talking down to them. He raised both hands and asked Chauke to "chill."

"Excuse me, sir, we can discuss your concerns about the identification of the vehicle. Something we will sort out very soon once we've shown those photographs of the vehicle to our witnesses. And I should add that we *did* show a photograph of Mr. Whitcombe to these witnesses, and they all identified him as the driver of the car." Chauke seemed to take this on board, and he looked a bit disappointed. Josh continued. "But may I remind you that a couple of minutes ago your client admitted to having met Mr. Whitcombe on a few occasions? And that they had spoken?"

The wind left Chauke's sails.

Gavin decided to jump in as soon as possible. He looked at Erasmus. "How did you meet?"

Erasmus looked like he was gatvol of his lawyer's theatrics now, and he just wanted to get this over with. Both Gavin and Josh picked this up, and they were excited about it. Erasmus looked away from Chauke.

"I don't remember, I have a lot of followers, on social media. I think he contacted me there."

Gavin was quick to reply. "We checked. The man had little if any social media presence, nothing really on Facebook, Twitter, or Instagram."

Erasmus looked pissed, like Gavin had flat-out told him to his face that he was lying. "I don't give a shit, that's what I remember, but hey, I might be wrong."

He smiled. They knew that he had lied, but could they prove it?

Back in his seat, Chauke was rallying again.

"My client's recollection is not subject to cross-examination, so please stop harassing him. If you want to, get a warrant, or arrest him. Go for it, as you have nothing at this point to link my client with this Whitcombe person, nothing!" He looked like he had suddenly thought of something. "Even if your witnesses pan out, and still stick to their 'story...'" He pronounced the word so that they were sure he thought it was bullshit. "How will you prove that my client was at home if that car was parked at the house? My client does not control that street, and cars can park wherever they wish. If he was not at home when this man—*if* this man—parked there, good luck in bringing this evidence to hurt my client."

He looked at Gavin and Josh, in turn, and then he laughed. "You're shit out of luck. Sloppy police work, as always. We'd love to see you in court." He looked at Erasmus for confirmation.

The man smiled broadly, and then he said, *"Fok dit. Genoeg gehad van djulle kak."*

He rose, and Chauke joined him. After he had fetched his jacket and his briefcase, they turned and strolled out of the room without a word of goodbye.

Gavin and Josh were not sad to see them leave, by any measure, but they both knew that this had been somewhat of a fuck-up.

When they were gone, Gavin was refreshingly honest, and self-effacing. He apologized to Josh for coming so close to losing his temper. He was the experienced one—and Josh knew that he had interviewed and ultimately prosecuted some of the highest profile criminals in the country. Gavin seemed to be truly embarrassed. He was supervising a trainee detective and he had probably come close to teaching Josh a few of the most important interrogation "don't do's" rather than anything positive.

Josh nodded along and made the right noises, but he actually thought Gavin had done a hell of a job to not only not lose it completely in the face of the irritating lawyer, but also to bring some clear and direct intent into the process. Josh thought that Erasmus had chilled toward his highly-paid mouthpiece toward the end of the interview. This could be because Chauke was such an irritating asshole. But it could also be because Gavin exuded a sense of purpose, and a "don't fuck with me" attitude.

They had agreed earlier to discuss the Whitcombe forensics reports that evening, but Gavin said that he was bushed, and he suggested that they get to that the following morning. It had been an eventful day, and, in light of the interview, a pretty disappointing one. Even if this was not unexpected given the circumstances. The one positive was that Erasmus had definitely had some kind of reaction to Whitcombe's name. He had known the man, and admitted it.

Gavin told Josh that he was going to ask Narcotics to fill them in on every little thing they had on Erasmus, and what he did, from now on. He was definitely still on their radar.

Josh smiled. This was his suspect, and he was a long way from letting Masekind go. There was definitely something there—they had both felt it.

CHAPTER 16

Knysna SAPS station
Tuesday, 29 November
08h38

Gavin took the eNCA interview in AppleMac's office, because it was bigger than his own. He had asked Van Wyk to grab a few of his criminology and forensics books from his office and place them on the bookshelf behind AppleMac's desk, where there had been only a few Star Wars and Marvel figurines on display. Lucinda Gasant, their admin assistant, lent them a somewhat anemic-looking pot plant from her cubicle. Gavin had worn a tie this morning, and was now also wearing a navy blue jacket, which he had borrowed from Captain Alvin Josephs on the robbery desk, a snappy dresser.

The two cameramen had set up—one with his tripod filming Gavin over the desk, and the other with a handheld camera perched on his shoulder to do a sideways shot with the interviewer and interviewee facing each other in profile. They were both recording after having tried a few angles and adjusting lighting settings on their equipment. A sound guy with a very big nose held a mic, and hovered irritatingly close to the desk, out of shot.

Penny Maseko sat in one of the old chairs in front of AppleMac's desk. She was an attractive woman in her early forties, a popular investigative journalist with the satellite news channel, who had covered some high-profile trials such as Oscar Pistorius, a string of major political exposés, and investigations of Cape gangland killings over the past few years. Gavin didn't know her, but he had seen some of her work on TV in the past, and he respected her as a journo who always appeared to be hard-hitting but fair.

She spoke first. "Colonel Whitall, you are currently engaged in the most high-profile murder in Knysna in recent years, and one of the most interesting in the Western Cape this past year. How are you coping?"

Gavin smiled, but he was conscious to not show too much emotion in the interview. So it was a thin-lipped smile, but one he hoped would look warm.

"I believe we're 'coping' very well. We are a little over a week into the investigation, and we are following credible leads. In my experience, a crime of this nature can frequently be one where there is little if anything to go on from day one. We have been lucky here, I think, to have been assisted by some extremely able officers from our own and other supporting units from the start." He saw that she was ready to jump in with her second question, and he rushed the next part a bit. In his experience, the way to avoid troubling questions was to try and preempt them by providing the answer first. "And I don't mean that we are relying on luck. Not at all."

He allowed the smile to spread a bit wider. "Our people have been doing excellent work, under great pressure, and with limited physical evidence to go on. You also call this case 'interesting.' It is that, certainly, but I hope you and your viewers will appreciate that we don't really go for that sort of thing." He smiled again. "We like things clear-cut, if anything."

Penny nodded and returned the smile, and then she hit back with a harder question. "Colonel, do you currently have any idea who the perpetrator of this violent crime is?"

Gavin inclined his head slightly, cocking it to one side. "As you know, a police investigation of this nature is a sensitive operation. No, we are not at this moment poised to make an arrest, but we currently have a couple of individuals on our radar, and we are investigating them to the best of our ability. Providing any more specific information at this point might jeopardize that investigation, so I know that you will not push me too much in that respect. I know that you understand and appreciate the nature of the work we are doing." He kept smiling.

Penny nodded again. She shifted in her chair after glancing at some notes. "Are you saying that you are investigating two persons of interest?"

Gavin was willing to concede this. He and Josh had discussed things, and he had also spoken to Hlungwane about an hour ago. Even in the face of his commanding officer's total distrust and antagonistic attitude toward the eNCA team, Gavin had persuaded him over the phone that it was in all their best interests to be open and truthful with the media as much as possible, without giving away too much, or opening them up to issues later. The eNCA was planning on interviewing him a couple more times this week, so he knew that anything he said today would be followed up on with further questions later, but they could—and should—try to be as open and transparent as they could be.

"Yes, at present, we have evidence of two separate individuals possibly being involved, who may have had motive and opportunity to commit this crime, but we are also following information that points toward the fact that these two individuals and the victim may all have been mutual acquaintances. And that there might be a link there. More than that I am not at liberty to say, at present." He gave the journalist a charming—and what he hoped would be a trustworthy—smile.

She thanked him. And then she got to the chase. "Is one of those individuals a man by the name of Reghardt Brink?" She butchered the name a bit with her accent. "And is that gentleman not, himself, a victim of murder? Was his body not found in the area around Wellington late last week, while you were investigating the murder of Mark Whitcombe? Are these two murders linked?"

Gavin's smile grew thinner again. He had expected this to come up. The journalists were not idiots, and he knew that the Cape Argus had run a story on Saturday, speculating on a link between the Whitcombe and Brink killings. Nothing official had been released by SAPS in that regard, so the investigative team was in agreement that there had probably been a leak from the Wellington station. It could be elsewhere; Gavin remembered personally requesting that the Whitcombe post-mortem findings be sent to the Paarl pathologist's office before the commencement of the autopsy on Brink's corpse. Before he and Josh had even visited the Brink murder scene, in fact. That may have been a mistake, but he had done so in the interests of expediting the forensic results, a justified decision in light of the delays they had experienced on the Whitcombe forensics results from Mossel Bay. It could be a very probable source of the information leak, but Gavin was still so enamored with the Paarl forensics team's level of service—after the fuck-up that was Mossel Bay—that he didn't really want to consider this too much.

He had mentioned it, however, to the two IPID officers who had stopped by after the Argus article came out; he was duty-bound to do so. IPID would investigate, and if a leak were found to exist and an individual identified, heads would roll. Gavin felt, personally, that the IPID had better things to do with their time, and much bigger fish to fry. But, of course, he understood the protocol. At least the linking in the media of Brink and Whitcombe was not a train smash, especially seeing that Brink was no longer at large. If that had been the case, he would personally have initiated a vicious hunt for the leak, as it might have jeopardized their chase, or put SAPS officers in danger.

"I need to correct you there. Mr. Brink's body was found, that is correct, but the investigation into his death has not been finalized. At this point, Mr. Brink has not been designated a 'victim of murder,' as you put it. We are investigating, and results will be forthcoming shortly."

Penny arched her eyebrows and had a strident tone as she threw out her next question. "But is it not true that Brink was shot in the head and chest? Are you suggesting that this was *not* a murder?"

Gavin's smile was gone now. He stood up, abruptly, the office chair shooting back on its wheels and hitting the wall with a loud clang that made the sound guy wince and pull at his headphones. Gavin waved his hands in front of him. "Cameras *off!*"

The two cameramen stepped slightly away. Gavin decided to be sure, and he also told the sound man to switch off his equipment, which he did with a prissy little pout and an over-exaggerated frown.

Penny was angry and looked as if she would have torn into Gavin if she weren't more professional. But she simply asked him what was wrong.

"I get what you're after, Penny, and I understand that. Really, I do, but please know that SAPS has thus far officially released information on Brink's death limited to the fact that his body was found out in the

Bain's Kloof pass. That's it. *You* know, and *I* know, that what you have just described, in a nutshell, is how the man died." She stared at him, nodding slightly. "Yes, of course we are investigating a murder, but until such time as my superiors decide to release that information, my hands are tied. I will not answer questions on that possible murder here today. Let's see what happens, OK? We will talk again this week, and I may be able to give you a better answer on that, then. But not now, not today. OK?"

She seemed to respond well to this, but Gavin wasn't finished, looking sterner now, more serious. "You are also aware that the information you refer to is not public knowledge and, in fact, it is not information authorized for disclosure by SAPS?" She nodded again, now looking a bit wary.

"I will tell you—and this is off the record for now—that IPID is investigating a leak in the investigation or support services, somewhere." Gavin immediately looked sorry about his choice of words just before. "I am confident that there is no leak within our investigative team. But there are various other places where this information could have come from. I know that the print media broke this over the weekend—so I am not blaming you, Penny, or your employer—but I will not and I cannot respond on the record to the questions you are starting to ask about the Brink killing, and I need you to edit that question you asked me a minute ago out of your footage. Please *delete* it."

Penny agreed, and she actually apologized to Gavin.

They wrapped up the interview with Gavin emphasizing that they were only a little over a week into the investigation of Whitcombe's murder. When she reminded him of the "you'd better solve it in forty-eight hours" chestnut, which even the media appeared to be familiar with, he nodded, but then he told her that in a case of this nature—and if you didn't get that lucky right off the bat, especially with physical evidence—the investigation could take months or years.

However, he quickly told her that this was not the expectation here. He did not mind disclosing this information—and he made an executive decision to do so on the spot—so he told her on camera that they did not have DNA or fingerprint evidence in the Whitcombe murder. Things were not that straightforward. The "Fourth Industrial Revolution" was the new buzz-word everywhere, but they couldn't yet press a few keys and let an expensive computer run down the odds and cycle through data banks to find their perpetrator, leaving the flesh and bone cops with the sole job of making the arrest.

But he made a point of telling her that they did have other leads they were following, and he emphasized that those lines of investigation were promising. He asked for the media and the public to be patient, and to give them the time and opportunity to solve this heinous crime, as soon as possible.

She signed off on the interview and thanked him for his time, wishing them luck in their investigation and promising follow-up interviews later in the week.

KNYSNA SAPS STATION

14H27

Gavin and Josh were both in front of their laptops in the squad room when the call came in, and there was a sudden burst of shouting toward the front of the building. Josh was on the phone to the Cape Town Central SAPS station, checking up on the fingerprint report on the blue Mazda found out in Langa. It was still not ready, and he was holding to speak to a technician. Paarl Forensics had just confirmed a few minutes earlier that the report on Brink's body should reach them no later than 15h00 that day. Some officers ran around the halls outside, and Gavin leaned across to see what was happening.

Word came that a bomb threat had been phoned in, concerning the Knysna Mall, just a few hundred meters or so west on Main Road. There was a state of pandemonium right across the station. While units scrambled to check it out, Gavin and Josh remained at their computers, although Josh excused himself and finished his call to Cape Town.

This was not their baby—they worked homicide—but a few minutes after the call had come in, Christiaanse came jogging in, panting, and looking more serious than Josh had yet seen him on the job. Shortly after the bomb threat call, they had received a report from the security service at the same mall that a security officer had been found dead in the parking lot. This call had still been in the process of being logged, after which it would be dispatched, when the bomb threat was called in to SAPS.

Gavin and Josh grabbed their things and prepared to make their way to the mall. At the charge office desk, Gavin spoke to the constable on duty to get the name of the officer who would be in charge of the mall operation. It was Lieutenant Colonel Phillips, a Coloured officer in his late thirties, and Gavin nodded in approval. He left an order for Christiaanse and Van Wyk to make their way to the mall as soon as they were able. Fourie and Fortuin were in Plett that day, having to testify in court in a domestic violence case that had turned into a murder. Josh was sorry they weren't available.

As they left the building, Gavin suggested that there would probably be a big fuck-up in terms of traffic on Main Road and the surrounding cross-streets, as a number of units would respond, so they shouldn't take a vehicle. The two men jogged down the sidewalk toward the mall.

News on the radio was that a lieutenant colonel and a captain from the satellite office of the SAPS bomb disposal unit out in Mossel Bay were currently on the road to Knysna, and they were expected to arrive within the next twenty to twenty-five minutes. In the meantime, the SAPS Knysna teams under Phillips were already in situ and conducting a sweep of the mall. The SAPS Knysna canine unit had arrived a few minutes ago, and the dogs would go in any minute now to assist in sniffing out any explosive devices.

Gavin had asked Phillips to provide officers to cordon off the immediate area around the security guard's body. It was fortunate for them that the search for the explosive device happened inside the mall. They needed the scene of the crime to be preserved, and a frantic police search could contaminate it in no time at all.

When they arrived, Gavin and Josh spotted three officers in the far western corner, milling around a colorfully painted hippie van, and made their way there. Gavin introduced himself and Josh and he asked the officers—two female and one male officer from traffic enforcement who already looked like they might be a little out of their depth here—to step aside. The men put on latex gloves, while scanning the immediate vicinity of the lot.

The body was that of an African male in his late thirties or early forties. He was dressed in the dark blue-gray uniform of the mall security services, with its red-and-silver logo prominent on the cap that lay next to the body and on the pocket on the left-hand side of the chest. The body lay on its right side, with the face turned down into the asphalt, hiding the features. Blood was pooled on the ground under and around the body, predominantly in the abdominal region.

Gavin asked the three officers to move back a little further, and to ensure that nobody walked up to the scene within a radius of ten meters. Security officers were in the process of cordoning the evacuated shoppers into one corner of the parking lot. They would not be allowed to leave just yet, pending the bomb search, but they were far enough away from the building to be safe in case an explosion occurred inside.

Josh was skeptical. It would have been much safer if the shoppers could have been moved across Main Road to another location, further from the mall. He knew that would be a bit of a logistical nightmare and could provide an opportunity for any guilty parties to make a break for it, but the lawyer in him thought it was risky to keep these civilians so close to a possible explosion site.

But that was not their problem.

There were no footprints to be seen in the pool of blood, and accordingly no bloody footprints around the body, or on the asphalt of the parking lot anywhere they could see.

Josh looked up at Gavin and observed that he couldn't see any evidence of blood further away from the body. Just as Josh had spoken, a police vehicle arrived out on Main Road with sirens blaring. Gavin had to mime that he hadn't heard. Josh repeated his comment, louder, and Gavin grunted, saying that it looked like the man had been killed right at this spot, and hadn't run or stumbled out here after being attacked inside the mall.

At Gavin's request, Josh took photographs from all angles around and above the body. When he was done, he shot a ninety-second video of the scene, of the body in its position, as well as the surrounding area.

He panned over the few vehicles that were parked in the vicinity, making sure to get good stable shots of the registration numbers of all the closest vehicles, especially the Kombi van right beside the body, its colorful flowers at odds with the scene. They would need to check at exactly what time it had been parked in its spot. That could give them a much more accurate assessment of the time of death of the guard—once they got an estimate from the forensics people following the post-mortem—as it seemed pretty obvious that the body could not have been there when the driver had parked the van. They could get that information from the automated parking ticket machine at the entrance. Josh then gave Gavin a thumbs-up.

Gavin took hold of the man's uniform by the left shoulder, where there was no blood, and grunted with the effort as he turned the body onto its back. With the chest and abdominal region of the uniform now exposed, it was clear that the man had been stabbed. There were six or seven tears in the uniform over the abdomen, and one over the right-hand side of the chest area. There was a lot of blood, and it had not yet dried, so when Gavin turned the body, he could feel the stickiness of it dragging on the man's clothing, as if the parking lot was trying to hold on to him, a lover reluctant to part ways.

Josh searched the man's pockets for identification. There was none. He unclipped the man's radio from his belt. There was a number—G-21—on a white label taped to it. He guessed it was the officer's radio call number.

The man was unarmed. Josh remarked on this. In his experience, mall cops usually would carry batons or tasers, some form of weapon, especially in recent years since mall robberies had been on the rise across the country. It was now a category in its own right when the Police Minister released the annual crime statistics. In fact, he believed that in the past ten years or so, it was the third-fastest growing violent crime, after cash-in-transit heists and automatic cash machine bombings.

As they looked over the body, a Coloured man in his sixties, wearing a suit with a name-tag with the security company's logo clipped to one pocket, stood a few meters away, trying to catch the detectives' eye. Gavin turned to him, smiling. He slipped off his gloves and walked up to the man, introducing himself.

Mervyn Sassman, with a craggy face but a wide smile that showed a broad expanse of white teeth, introduced himself as the manager of the on site mall security. Josh guessed that the man had a natural inclination to smile warmly at every new person he met, but once the smile had faded from his face, he looked worried, and quite stressed. That was understandable, between the scene here and the operation inside the building.

After Josh shook his hand, the older man explained the order of events.

A cashier from the Edgars shop in the mall had gone out for a smoke break and stumbled upon the body of the guard. She had run back inside, screaming, and another security officer radioed it into their control room. But about three minutes later, before SAPS could be notified about the body, the control room received notice from the mall manager, a Ms. Danni Clinton, informing them that she had just received a phone call from an unidentified man, who—judging by his voice and accent—might be a black male in his late twenties or early thirties. The caller claimed that there was a bomb hidden in the mall, close to The Bedroom Shop.

The control room immediately phoned this into SAPS, and the security team began evacuating the mall and ordering shops to close their doors once they had checked that there were no customers left inside. Shop management staff were told to report any bags, luggage, or other suspicious unattended objects to the control room or the nearest available security officer, but by no means to touch or search anything of this nature that might be found. SAPS were on their way, and they would take care of it.

While this was all going on, the manager of the security service dialed the number for SAPS a second time, to report the death of one of his guards.

Josh asked Sassman whether a device had been found yet. Sassman said no. The dog unit had done one pass with no success, and they were now starting again from the other side of the building.

Gavin got down to it. "Sir, I know you are pressed for time, so there are just four or five things I need to ask you." Sassman nodded, his eyes wide. Josh thought that, while many especially senior management people in private security were ex-cops, Sassman didn't seem to be. He looked just a little too fazed by the day's events.

Gavin started off with the identity of the body at his feet. "I assume you can identify the victim here as one of your men?"

Sassman looked sad as he nodded. "His name is—was—Elvis Makhubela. He was one of our longest-serving employees. He joined the team just after the mall opened, in fact. He was in line for promotion to a management position in the new year. Dammit, man! He could have been safe up in an office on the Upper Floor, give or take a month."

Gavin commiserated, then he asked whether Makhubela had any history of disciplinary action against him; any disputes or issues with management, or problems in his work. Sassman frowned, probably not understanding the reason for the question. But Josh knew that when it came to private security guards—and, unfortunately, also to members of the police services—one needed to ask whether they might have had any connections to criminal elements. If the man had ever been caught assisting robbers, shoplifters, scammers, pickpockets, or whatever, it could put a very different spin on finding his body out here.

Sassman gave an emphatic, "No." Makhubela had a clean employment record.

Gavin nodded. He then asked where Makhubela had been stationed, and what his route was when he patrolled the mall.

Sassman didn't hesitate. "Elvis was ground floor along with three other guards. They would patrol pretty much at random, but we separate ground, upper, and parking here, so that the guards are assigned to a floor, and they are not supposed to go up or down. They patrol their designated floor, without deviation; unless, of course, we have some kind of event that requires more guards at any given place, but that's happened only a couple of times in the past few years. This is a very safe shopping precinct." That last part seemed to have been thrown in as a pat on the back for Sassman's security company.

"OK, so if Elvis had stayed in his designated patrol area, that means he would have come from there—on the ground floor—and then directly out here to the parking lot?" Gavin pointed over Sassman's shoulder to the closest exit onto the parking lot. Sassman turned to look, then he turned back and nodded. Gavin continued. "If he hadn't deviated and been out here in the first place, of course...maybe for a smoke?"

Sassman shook his head, vehemently. "No, none of our guards are allowed to smoke on the premises, even out here. In fact, we are contractually obliged to fine any of the tenants'—the shops'—employees who smoke within twenty meters of the building. So our guards have to enforce that, and they face disciplinary warnings if they themselves are caught. Building management gets very *kwaai* over that. *Yoh*, they get very serious." He shook his head.

He didn't look like he agreed with the policy, and Josh guessed the man was probably a smoker himself. Josh jumped in.

"Sir, I heard you say that Makhubela was assigned to the ground floor, along with other guards. I assume they all patrolled the whole of that area. But do they, individually, cover the whole expanse of the area routinely, or does each focus more on a quadrant or on a specific area on the floor?'

Sassman nodded. "They do that, yes."

Josh looked confused, so Sassman was quick to explain. "Sorry, I mean the last thing you said. They tend to split up the shops and the restaurants between them."

He looked like he was getting Josh's drift. "I know what you're getting at. Makhubela would mostly cover the clothing shops section—Foschini, Edgars, Jet, Mr. Price and Truworths." He pointed toward the mall building behind him. "The section closest to that exit there."

While Josh asked the last question, Gavin put his radio to his ear and heard Phillips saying that the second sweep of the canine unit had also not turned up anything, but that they were going to do one more sweep on the upper level. Vehicles with sirens on were still arriving, and one was the ambulance for Makhubela's body, which was now cruising slowly into the parking lot. He motioned to the traffic enforcement officer to run down to the entrance and escort the ambulance to where they were. He turned back to Sassman.

"Sir, I have two more questions, then we'll let you go." Sassman looked relieved. "By the way, I just heard that the second dog sweep found nothing, but they are going over the upper level again." Sassman looked grateful for the information, and especially happy at the fact that a device had not been found; at least, not yet.

Gavin continued. "Sir, are your guards armed in any way? We didn't find anything on Makhubela's body, and we need to know whether he might have dropped or lost some form of weapon or whether he may have had it taken from him by his attacker or attackers."

Sassman nodded. "They all carry batons. We decided from day one not to go with tasers—those can be just too dangerous. So each guard has a black rubber baton issued. You'll see there's a loop on his belt there?" He pointed to the body.

Gavin nodded, then looked at Josh. They needed to search for the baton. It might provide them with evidence of where the attack started. If Makhubela had stuck to his assigned patrol area and had not been AWOL, he may have accosted someone inside the center and then chased them—or had been chased—from there out to the parking lot.

Josh understood the look, and moved toward the warrant officers guarding the body. He instructed them to start moving toward the mall building, and to look for a black rubber baton, working inwards from the nearby exit but focusing on the closest shops in the retail clothing section.

Meanwhile, Gavin posed his final question to Sassman.

"Sir, will you please let us know what turns up on your CCTV cameras?" Gavin had taken a casual look while they had been outside. He wasn't sure what the position was inside the building, but he had already spotted three cameras that covered the parking lot, and one that focused on the nearest entrance, from where it seemed Makhubela may have exited the mall before getting knifed.

Sassman said he would, most definitely. They could get that information to the police as soon as the mall had been cleared from the search for an explosive device, and they knew that the building was safe. He took Gavin's card and promised to call him and, if they saw anything, to email him the relevant CCTV footage. Gavin stopped him from putting it into his shirt pocket, and asked to have the card back for a second. He scribbled AppleMac's email address on the back, and asked Sassman to allow their W/O Jantjies access to the control room footage. Whether the security company people found anything on the camera footage or not, he would prefer that AppleMac have a look at it, just to make sure. Sassman promised to do so, and he pocketed the card.

Gavin and Josh both thanked the man and let him go. He jogged back into the building. They turned toward the ambulance, which had just parked a few meters away. The forensics team from Mossel Bay—Gavin didn't look too impressed to see them—had arrived in the wake of the ambulance, in a SAPS Forensic Services van that badly needed a wash. They got out and came up to shake hands. Gavin wished them luck, and then he wandered off to find Phillips, after asking Josh to stick around in case the forensics guys had any questions from their preliminary check of the scene.

Phillips was clearly a bit stressed. He had probably run around like a headless chicken for the past half-hour or so. When Gavin arrived at the main entrance of the mall on Main Road, where Phillips had set up his makeshift control post, Phillips actually looked grateful to have a more senior officer with whom to discuss developments.

Gavin smiled at him, and suggested that he sit down in one of the four collapsible camping chairs that someone had set out a bit haphazardly; they had price tags on and had clearly been "requisitioned" from some nearby shop. Three laptops, being manned by a couple of warrant officers, were positioned on the edge of an indoor flower bed in the lobby of the mall's main entrance. A few officers milled around, and Gavin thought they didn't look very comfortable being there.

"What's the news from the search, Phillips? Have they found anything?"

Not surprisingly, Phillips looked relieved when he said that three passes had been done, two with the dogs, and that there was no sign of any device or even a suspicious bag. All rubbish bins had been cleared (that report had come in just a couple of minutes ago) and the search was now finishing up its final phase—where officers were physically entering every shop which had been closed by their proprietors after the evacuation. They had covered most of the upstairs, and after that they would finish things downstairs.. Phillips hazarded a thin smile; it didn't appear that there would be an explosion in this mall today.

Gavin clapped him on the shoulder and said, "Good job."

An officer from the Mossel Bay bomb disposal unit walked by, appearing very bored. Gavin's smile broadened. That's how he liked his bomb disposal colleagues to look when he encountered them out in the field, which wasn't all that often, fortunately.

Phillips was still scanning the laptop screens, where real-time messages from officers provided a narrative of the search and the broader operation of securing the premises and patrons, who were still being kept in protective custody in the parking lot. Phillips had asked Sassman on arrival where the rally point for fire drills was, and he had decided to use it for their purposes. He now turned to Gavin.

"Sir, did you manage to inspect the body in the parking lot? Any news on that?"

Gavin told him that the crime-scene unit from Mossel Bay currently had the scene. He explained their brief search of the scene and the body, and the identification of the victim by Sassman, as well as further information regarding the missing baton, Makhubela's area of patrol, and the suspected area of encounter with his attacker or attackers. He expressed the opinion that they would shortly receive word of evidence found of an incident within Makhubela's patrol area, where Makhubela was either attacked or had accosted someone. Gavin had already formed a theory, but he would wait to see what turned up before he shared it with Phillips. He didn't have long to wait.

One of the female officers from the parking lot, who had guarded the body when he and Josh arrived, jogged up to Phillips. She hurriedly told him and Gavin that a baton had been found in a corner of the mall, next to the escalator in front of the Sport Scene shop on the ground floor. The escalator was less than forty meters from where they currently stood in the main entrance, and a few meters from the ground floor exit to the parking lot, where Makhubela's body had been found. Gavin called Josh on the radio and asked him to join them at the escalator.

Phillips followed, after having asked a W/O to radio him if there were any developments, and a few seconds later they met Josh. The other female officer from the parking lot stood guard over the black rubber baton, which lay against the edge of the escalator on the marble floor. Gavin nodded to her, and then he turned 360 degrees to scan his surroundings. The second shop he saw was the American Swiss jewelry shop, right opposite the Cape Union Mart. It fit with his theory, and he walked toward its front door. The shop was locked, as expected, and he asked Phillips to phone Sassman to bring the store's manager here as soon as possible.

After a couple of minutes, an attractive Indian lady in her early forties arrived, breathless and wide-eyed. Mandy Patel had been manager of the shop for two years. She greeted the officers and explained that they had followed the security protocol once the alarm of the bomb threat had been communicated to her.

Gavin asked her whether all her employees were accounted for at the rallying point, and she said she wasn't sure. Two of the four employees were not there when she closed the shop, but she knew that one had taken an early lunch, and she suspected that the other, a young Coloured lady by the name of Estelle, had been out for a smoke break and was probably now amongst the mall employees and customers gathered out in the parking lot.

She had not had a chance to check. She mentioned that she had done a lightning check, but seeing that the showroom was one single room of about six by four meters, with no hidden corners, she had been quite quick in getting herself and the other two sales assistants out of the shop before locking up.

Patel unlocked the door. Gavin drew his sidearm and asked the woman to step aside, as he, Josh, and Phillips entered the empty retail space. The lights were still on, and there was a dazzling display of rare gems and expensive jewelry and watches on all sides. When Gavin rounded the corner of the central display case against the back wall of the shop, he cried out and rushed forward, holstering his pistol.

A young Coloured woman lay on her stomach, tucked in close to the foot of the counter. Her short skirt was rucked up, and Josh had the irrelevant—and rather shameful—thought that the woman had stunning legs. Gavin hunkered down on his haunches next to her, and felt for a pulse.

The next moment he turned and shouted to Phillips. "Get an ambulance team here, ASAP! There's one out in the parking lot, by the nearest exit. Tell them we have a young woman, unconscious, but I've got a pulse. *Hurry!*"

Phillips spun on his heels and ran out of the shop, trailed by a couple of officers who had arrived while Gavin spoke to Patel.

A minute or so later, the ambulance team arrived, a male and a female paramedic. By this time, the young woman sat with her back to the display case. She had blood on her temple and on her left cheek. Gavin had stroked her hair and spoken softly to her, and when she showed signs of reviving, he had checked her eyes and reflexes and helped her sit up.

The two medics asked Gavin to step aside and bent down to have a look at her. After a few minutes, they straightened up and the senior one told Gavin that she looked like she had received a nasty blow to the head, but otherwise appeared to be in good shape. They suggested that she should accompany them to the hospital for a check-up, but she said she was fine and could be questioned if required. She smiled, although her frown showed that she probably had quite a bastard of a headache. Now Mandy Patel jumped in, and, taking a seat flat on the floor next to the woman, she took her face in her hands.

"Estelle, sweetie, are you OK?"

Estelle gave a crooked smile, then winced in some pain. She brushed off Patel's gushing entreaty to keep still.

"I'm fine, thanks, just a headache. Really." She stroked Patel's arm. She seemed to gain some comfort from the touch of the older woman.

Gavin hunkered down again, and he asked whether she would mind if they spoke for a few minutes. Estelle looked at him with big eyes, and then she nodded. Gavin helped her up.

Estelle was a stunningly beautiful young woman of about twenty-three, with long curly dark hair and light blue eyes, to go with a caramel complexion. She looked a bit battered and bruised, but was poised, and she managed to give Gavin a weak smile. Until the poise gave way. She grimaced, saying, "Wow, that *fokken naai* packed a punch."

Patel gasped, maybe wanting to admonish her, but Gavin waved a hand in her direction and smiled broadly at the younger woman. Josh smiled as well, trying hard not to laugh out loud.

As Estelle started to tell her story, Gavin asked Philips to put out a BOLO for suspects seen in the vicinity of the jewelry shop. It looked like his theory had been correct, and he wanted to be sure that the word on Makhubela's killer or killers would go out as soon as humanly possible. There had been enough distractions already.

She told them that she had been serving a customer, a white British lady in her sixties, when three black men had entered the shop. They were well dressed, and one carried what looked like a Louis Vuitton men's bag, which Estelle admired from a distance. They smiled at her fellow sales assistant, Gwen, and then they browsed around the men's watches in the display case in the front window of the shop. Just after that, Gwen came over to tell her that she was off to an early lunch, as she had to stop by The Village Pharmacy in the mall to pick up some diabetes medicine for her mom. She had told Mandy, in the manager's office at the back, who was fine with it. Mandy had said that she would come and help out in the store if needed—Estelle just had to call if they suddenly got busy.

Estelle continued to show the Brit two sets of earrings, but the woman left, saying that she wanted to look in a couple of other shops first. She wanted something more African-themed. Estelle had smiled at her and wished her a happy vacation. She then turned away to collect a couple of sales slips she had set aside earlier when the shop had been full, and her attention had to be on some visitors from Gauteng who were loud and crass and demanded to see some expensive necklace.

She hadn't realized that her two other colleagues had quickly stepped into Mandy's office to talk about their commissions scale. Both had mentioned to Estelle that morning that they were going to discuss it with the manager today as soon as things got a bit quiet. They had been bitching for a while now, feeling that they should try and negotiate a raise on the percentage of commission they earned, before the mall got December-busy. The older of the two, Riette, was a bitch, and Estelle couldn't stand her. She was influencing Cindy, their youngest colleague who was fresh out of school. Estelle didn't want to get involved, but she was seriously considering telling Cindy to just ignore her. Riette might be putting Cindy's job in jeopardy.

As Estelle sorted through the sales slips at the counter and was getting ready to staple them together for filing, an arm suddenly came around her waist from behind and squeezed both of her arms tightly to her body, and a hand went over her mouth. She could feel the man pressed up to her from behind, his body hard as a rock. She was terrified, and felt herself screaming, but she couldn't hear a sound. One of the black men, the tallest, came up to her and whispered in her face, demanding the key to the display case. The third man looked desperately to the left and right, checking out the scene.

The key was on a ring on the belt of her skirt, and she motioned her eyes towards it. The man grabbed at it, but it was attached with a chain. He started to grapple with the set of keys, trying to pull her closer to the lock on the display cabinet's glass door.

As this happened, Estelle noticed movement from the corner of her eye, through the front window of the shop. She recognized Elvis, the mall security guard who sometimes let her smoke in the parking lot close to the building in winter when it was raining. The older man seemed to have a crush on her, and she had always liked him. She always called him "Blue suede," which made him laugh.

Her thinking was instantaneous, and talking about it afterwards she didn't know where the thought had come from. While the first man still gripped Estelle's arms in an iron vice from behind, she opened her right hand which contained the stapler she had been using to staple the sales slips. It dropped to her feet with a clatter, and she kicked out at it with her right foot, a Hail-Mary kick. But her shoe connected with it and the stapler went shooting along the floor, a perfect goal, as it sailed through the open front door of the shop and right across Elvis's path as he walked past the shop.

He started and looked up with a frown on his face. He then turned his head and saw Estelle being man-handled.

The tall man reacted violently. He pulled away from Estelle's waist, where he still tried to extricate the set of keys, and he turned toward her with a loud bellow of anger. The next moment he gave her a great big whack across the face with the Vuitton bag in his hand. Estelle said she thought he must have had a fucking bowling ball in there. She felt a huge flash of pain, and things went dark and deathly quiet, except for a ringing in her ear which sounded like alarm bells going off.

Estelle remembered going down, and nothing after.

Knysna SAPS station

19h23

All the excitement of the day was over. The two men sat in Gavin's office, having coffee, Josh ready to take to the road and make his way back to Amy in George. He was going to be in the shit. In all of the hullabaloo, he had never once let her know what was going on. She would give him *kak* tonight, he was sure, and he would probably deserve it.

Gavin had been right in his assessment of the situation. The bomb threat was complete bullshit. Most likely—almost certainly—phoned in by the three men who had attempted to rob the American Swiss shop and had assaulted Estelle January. She had thwarted the attempted robbery, through truly admirable quick thinking, but that had led to the violent death of Elvis, her friend. When Phillips explained to her what had transpired out in the parking lot, the young woman had been reduced to a fit of tears, wracking sobs that were painful to watch. It worried them all, and one of the paramedics had administered a sedative by injection.

Josh knew she blamed herself for Elvis's death. It was all over her; he could smell it on her. They had managed to calm her down, but Josh knew that she would carry that guilt around for a while, and he didn't think she deserved that, but he could do nothing about it, so he put it out of his mind.

They had left things as they were at the scene, although Gavin explained his theory to Phillips and the other officers before they returned to the station. The three men had probably run out of the shop after the tall one had dropped Estelle, with Elvis running after them. He had little doubt that, being outnumbered that way, Elvis had not lasted long in trying to get his baton up to inflict injury on them. The baton was probably torn from his hand and thrown to where it ended up, by the escalator, and the men then made a run for it. Elvis was brave; he must have run after them, and encountered them by the VW Kombi in the parking lot, where one or more of them pulled a knife and ended his life.

It was sad, and as the two detectives discussed it in Gavin's office, the one positive they took from it was that only one life had been lost in the end. They both felt that the young woman had survived because of Elvis.

But now Elvis had left the building.

A high-priority BOLO had gone out. The security cameras in the parking lot did not cover the parking space where Makhubela had been killed. But they had picked up a white Ford Focus with GP plates, from Gauteng, which had driven in and from which three black men had emerged and entered the mall twenty-four minutes before the bomb threat had been phoned in. The three men had gotten back into the car and had calmly driven back out of the parking lot two minutes before the bomb threat call was logged. Estelle had given a pretty accurate description, they hoped— of the three robbers—and now it was up to Phillips and his guys to catch them. Gavin and Josh had their own fish to fry.

CHAPTER 17

The news of the morning, as Josh strolled in, was that the three men from the mall robbery had been stopped and arrested at a garage in Heidelberg heading toward Cape Town. They were currently being transported to George for identification and to be charged with the murder of Makhubela, the attempted robbery at the American Swiss, the assault on Estelle January, and the hoax bomb threat. A number of firearms had been found in the car, and Gavin thanked their collective lucky stars that the men had not been carrying those weapons when they had entered the mall the previous day. Things could have turned out a hell of a lot worse.

On the Whitcombe investigation, the news was a bit less exciting, and much less definitive, although there was at least some forward motion. The Paarl forensics office had sent through the report on the fingerprints found on Brink's body and clothing. It had come in late the previous afternoon, but both Josh and Gavin had been a bit wasted when they had returned to the station after all the excitement at the mall.

They were seated in Gavin's office. Josh saw that the stack of newspapers with reports on the Whitcombe case, sitting on the spare chair by Gavin's desk, was growing all the time. The "tower of power." He thought that the chair would soon overflow and spill newsprint all over the floor, and Gavin would have to find another place to put them. Or they would have to solve the case, soon. He didn't want to be a defeatist, but if he were honest with himself, he'd put his money on the former.

Gavin had a thin manilla file, stamped with "SAPS PAARL: Forensic

Services," open in front of him. Josh paged through the three pages of the printout.

Prints, or FRP'S ("Friction Ridge Patterns," as the report referred to them), in various permutations had been found on Brink's clothing and body. Sets of multiples and single prints, one or two full, near-perfect prints, and quite a few fragments of varying qualities and states of preservation.

A number of latent prints had been found on Brink's skin, notably his left hand (two full and one partial print on the upper half of the back of the hand), and on the left-hand side of his neck (a three-quarter partial). Further latent prints were found on the fabric of his shirt just above the waist on the left-hand side (these hard-to-find prints, the report said, had been found through a process of vacuum metal deposition using gold and zinc), and on the back of his leather belt, three good, full prints. Two full latent prints were found on the ornate belt buckle, and the tops of both shoes also showed some partial latent prints.

The report claimed that all the prints were identifiable as deriving from two separate individuals: the ones found on the back of the left hand, on the shoes, and on the belt buckle, were from subject A. The ones found on the left side of the neck, the shirt on the left-hand side above the waist, and on the back of the belt, were from subject B.

It had not been hard to identify "A" as Brink. After printing him on the autopsy table, the print analyst had simply studied the whorls, ridges, and arches of the latent prints and compared them to Brink's prints, and then had the computer confirm this conclusion. Brink had touched his shoes and belt buckle and had squeezed or scratched his upper left hand with his right hand at some point during the day of his death.

The other prints, and their positioning, were more interesting. The analyst, after having consulted the report of the forensics officer at the scene, Glenda Jacobs, was of the opinion that these prints probably were from a subject who had touched the body and clothing around the time of the killing. As Josh had also intuited, the shooter or another individual had turned the body over after it had fallen face-down in the sand, following the shot to the back of the head. To do so, this individual had touched the fabric of Brink's shirt, before grabbing hold of his leather belt and pulling him up and over onto his back, for the two shots to the chest that followed.

The final, partial print on the side of Brink's neck, was unexplained. Josh speculated—and Gavin agreed that it made sense—that the individual who had turned the body over had probably touched Brink's neck to feel for a pulse.

The most interesting part for Gavin and Josh, of course, was that the computer database had managed to identify "B," whose prints were on record.

The database identified the prints as belonging to a Thapelo Nzimande, a 32-year-old male originally from Soweto, near Johannesburg. Nzimande's prints were on record for two reasons.

The first was that he was printed when he joined the South African National Defence Force in 2006, fresh out of school. He had served in a battalion based in Soweto. The second was after he was arrested on a charge of assault in a Durban waterfront bar in 2014, for which he went to prison for twelve months (released after ten for good behavior). He had been working as a bouncer at a drinking place and had become a little overenthusiastic when three young white men started taunting him. Nzimande ended up in prison for assault with intent to commit grievous bodily harm, and all three of the "whiteys" ended up in hospital. Clearly, the man could handle himself.

When his name was put through the database, it didn't turn up any information on his current whereabouts. He had been honorably discharged from the SANDF in 2012, and after he was released from Westville Prison for serving his time on the assault conviction in late 2015, he disappeared from the radar.

Josh stared at Gavin, who looked back at him, an inquiring eyebrow rising slowly.

Gavin spoke. "At least we know who we're dealing with. And if and when we get the prints from the Mazda, we might be able to identify his companion out in Bain's Kloof. And if we have that, we can start looking for links between the two people, which might lead us somewhere."

"So what next?"

Gavin gritted his teeth. "I'm going to send this through to Erna Pretorius. She has contacts in the military, not only from her position in crime intelligence." Josh looked interested, but Gavin raised a hand. "No, please don't ask. Let's see what she can dig up on this guy's military record, and then take it from there."

Josh nodded and stood. They had another meeting to attend over in George, chasing the Erasmus angle.

George SAPS Station
37 Courtenay Street, George
12H50

The pair drove through to meet with an officer from the SAPS Western Cape Provincial Narcotics unit, at the George SAPS station. Captain Jusandra Chetty—better known to his colleagues as "Juice"—was involved in intelligence for the Narcotics unit, which meant that he mostly ran informants and collated information on drug deals, supply routes, and the like. Juice had been involved in the investigation of the Funky Guys for the past year, and he was the "go-to" guy for information on Erasmus's business dealings and the people with whom he consorted. They were actually quite lucky to catch him in George. He had been in Port Elizabeth for the last week and was on his way to the airport that afternoon, to testify in a trial in Johannesburg of a dealer from Delft who had been arrested up in Kempton Park. The Western Cape Narcotics unit, and Juice specifically, had been intimately involved in setting up the arrest.

After the disastrous interview on Monday at Knysna station, Gavin had picked up the phone and made a few phone calls. He was still less set on Erasmus as the doer in the Whitcombe murder, or at least quite a bit less so than Josh, but the man (and his lawyer) had really pissed Gavin off on Monday, and he decided to officially open up communication channels with his colleagues in Narcotics. They had been confronted with the fact that their suspected connection between Whitcombe and Erasmus was as yet still just a theory, and that they had virtually no evidence. Chauke had been right when he pointed out that the presence of Whitcombe's car at Erasmus's house was circumstantial at best. Of course, they hadn't broached the subject of the Phantom Pass project, which they believed was how Whitcombe and Erasmus hooked up in the first place. But they had even less on that angle, apart from putting the two men in the same room at a number of meetings. Charmaine Dalgleish had not even spoken to Whitcombe at any of those meetings. There was really nothing there until they could find evidence to link the two men directly.

Josh had phoned Dalgleish the previous evening, and she had suggested that they speak to one of her colleagues at the Western Cape's Department of Environmental Affairs and Development Planning, a Werner Grobbelaar. He was her number two on the PPEP and had attended more of the initial and more routine planning meetings in Knysna than she had. Grobbelaar probably met with both Erasmus and Whitcombe; but he was currently on annual leave in Durban with his family, trying to get a jump on the December holidays. He was expected back in the office the first week of December, and Josh made a note to follow up with him, to see whether he might provide a more solid link between Whitcombe, Erasmus, and the PPEP.

Both Gavin and Josh agreed that until such a basis could be established, the only thing to do was to talk to the Narcs and find out what else Erasmus was doing. They were hoping that some connection with Whitcombe might come out of this, but they knew that was quite ambitious. At the very least, both men wanted to get a better handle on Erasmus's activities and the people with whom he did business.

They met in a small conference room at the George Station that showed its age. The place was a mess, with clear signs of water damage on the walls, which were badly in need of a coat of paint. A few desks were scattered around the room, and things generally looked neglected. Apparently, this was where the provincial Narc boys had their makeshift digs when they were working out of George. The place was depressing, and it smelled a bit suspect.

Juice was a pleasant-faced Indian officer in his mid-thirties, with a few visible tattoos and a funky haircut, his hair longer than regulation. Gavin knew that some of the intel officers in the Narc division had come through the ranks as undercover operatives, but maintained their look once they had moved on from undercover operations, simply because their activities and their continued interactions with informants might mean that they would now and then have to meet with people in the business. It made sense to blend in, and not look like the cops they were.

Gavin started off by apologizing for the hour of the meeting; he didn't know whether the man might be someone who was religious about his lunch hour. Juice wasn't, and he shrugged it off. He was also interested in this meeting, having been told that the murder squad was tentatively looking at the head of the Funky Guys for a murder, possibly unrelated to his drug business. Juice was curious to hear whether there was anything the Narc squad could use in their ongoing investigations of the man who had, for the past few years, proved so elusive to them.

Gavin explained their very flimsy evidence and theory about the possible links between Whitcombe and Erasmus. After giving Juice a brief picture of the Whitcombe case, Josh was tasked with explaining Whitcombe's visits to Erasmus's house, as well as the meetings over the Phantom Pass project. Juice was respectful toward Gavin—he didn't want to insult a senior officer—but made it clear that things were really looking very thin. Fortunately for him, both Gavin and Josh agreed.

Gavin then asked him what he could share about the investigations into Erasmus's drug activities, and Juice blossomed. He was clearly no fan of the man, and obviously liked to talk about what they suspected him of and what the Narc unit was doing to try and get him off the streets permanently. But before he got into telling them about the Narc unit's investigation, Juice asked whether they wanted to know their file history on Erasmus, the man.

Both homicide detectives were eager for this information.

According to the best intelligence that the various SAPS units whose paths had crossed with Erasmus had dug up over the years, the man had quite a checkered past before he came to the Southern Cape.

Erasmus was 43 years old. He had been born in Manenberg in 1976, in the tumultuous time of the Soweto uprising in Johannesburg—the heady heydays of the struggle against Apartheid in South Africa. Manenberg was in the heart of the Cape Flats, not far from Cape Town Airport.

Erasmus first came onto the police radar in the early 1990s at sixteen years old, when he was first arrested for drug-running. Being underaged, he served a few short stints in correctional facilities for boys. The last was in the Ottery Youth Care Centre, as it was now known, from where Erasmus was discharged in 1994—the glorious year of the first democratic elections—when he was eighteen. There had been a single mother when he had gone in for that last stint in 1992, but at the time of his release, the Western Cape Department of Welfare showed no living relatives on record.

Erasmus disappeared for a while. But he showed up again a few years later, and on the other side of the fence, as a member of PAGAD.

People Against Gangsterism and Drugs, or PAGAD, terrorized the gangster and drug dealer elements on the Cape Flats for some time in the turbulent 1990s. There were still many people in that neighborhood who wouldn't say a bad word against PAGAD, the organization they had viewed at the time as their saviors from the endemic crime in the city and its surrounds.

In 1996, after PAGAD had built up quite a name, Erasmus was rumored to be one of the less than fifty members of PAGAD's G Force, or "Gun Force," the militant wing with ties to Qibla, the reputed South African Muslim extremist organization started in the late 1970s. Qibla was officially listed as a terrorist organization by the United States Justice Department.

In February 1999, two months after the killing of Jackie Lonte, leader of the Americans gang, Erasmus disappeared from the Cape Town SAPS radar for good.

Much of Erasmus's history was confusing and contradictory, at least to the provincial Narcotics boys. He had apparently, at some point after leaving the Ottery "school," converted to Islam. They couldn't figure out any other way in which he might have become that involved in the PAGAD movement, but when they picked up his trail after his move to Knysna and the events at the end of the Grootman Goliath era, Erasmus had suddenly become a Rastafarian.

Their intelligence showed that around the time he had become initially involved with Grootman, Erasmus had spent about eight months living out in Judah Square, the small Rastafarian community based in a small valley in Khayalethu South, near Knysna. The community had been formed in the year before the democratic elections in 1994. It was an outsider group, which had remained small, but had managed to receive more and more popular and political acceptance. Children from the community were nowadays allowed into mainstream schools in the town wearing their dreadlocks. Narc intelligence couldn't dig up much about Erasmus's time in the commune, or of existing contacts who still interacted with him, but they were pretty sure that quite a few of the members of the Funky Guys—and especially the four or five closest associates of the man, including his bodyguards—had been recruited from this community. Information on Erasmus in Knysna prior to the death of Grootman was scant. But the consensus was that the man was a bit of a chameleon, at least as far as his religious beliefs went. He was clearly happy to associate with whomever suited him. He was a supreme opportunist.

After more than six months of intensive investigation into the Funky Guys, the Narcotics unit had very little to go on. The gang seemed to follow a classic model well known on the Cape Flats, where Cape Town's (and the country's) most widespread drug trafficking occurs. The Erasmus years since Grootman Goliath departed this earth had not seen any large-scale changes to the organization itself. It was still modeled on Goliath's early experience in the Hard Livings gang and then later, in jail, in the 28s.

There was a clear hierarchical structure, based on military ranks, with the lowest level members—the foot-soldiers—being recruited mostly from teens in the townships around the Southern Cape. They followed the creed of "blood in, blood out." The entry ticket was sometimes a hard one. You had to spill blood. If not by killing a member of a rival gang, or by beating up someone (maybe some shop or shebeen owner who refused to pay the gang's exorbitant protection money), then you probably had to rape someone. Rashied Staggie, who established the Hard Livings with his twin brother, was himself convicted to fifteen years in jail in 2003 for ordering the gang-rape of a seventeen-year-old young woman. He had reportedly taken her to an isolated spot in August 2001, and then forced her at gunpoint to have sex with three of his men. The victim was shot in an alleged revenge attack by Hard Livings members ten years after Staggie's conviction.

The blooding of new recruits showed the lieutenants and the higher-ups that the new soldiers could be trusted to obey orders, and to put aside any moral compass. Of course, the fact that those higher-ups would now have easy-to-prove guilt in a violent crime to hold over the heads of the new recruits was priceless for the leaders. That glue was always fear, and guilt. And a healthy dose of desperation.

These young men, and sometimes women, came mostly from desperate, poverty-stricken, and single parent households. Many were already addicted to drugs, and if not by the time they entered "service," they would be soon. The leaders had less trouble keeping their lower rank and file in submission, and keeping discipline, than most military organizations in the world. The areas in which these gangs operated, and the circumstances there, were nearly indistinguishable from war-torn regions elsewhere on the continent.

Juice decided the two homicide cops had enough of an idea of how these gangs functioned for their purposes, so he decided to focus on their investigation of Erasmus and the Funky Guys's activities.

Over the last six months, Juice and his team had investigated countless small-time deals, and small establishments like the shebeens in the townships, stretching from George to Plett and beyond, into the Eastern Cape. They occasionally performed raids based on the information provided by a quite impressive body of informants that the Southern Cape SAPS already had in place before the Western Cape Narc unit had gotten involved, along with a number of new informants drafted in by Juice and his colleagues since. But it was a constant source of frustration for them all. The fact was that all their successes—and there had been a few—were small and occurred mostly by accident or pure luck. Most of those only helped them get to the Funky Guys at the point of sale of the meth, heroin, and other substances these guys were dealing in, but they had never once managed to get further up the food chain on the supply side.

The heroin was coming from overseas. They investigated this, too, with varying success—most productively, the frequent claims of Chinese fishing trawlers bringing the stuff into ports and small coastal towns in the Eastern Cape. The meth, they were convinced, was mostly locally manufactured. Quite a few of the informants closest to the Funky Guys were adamant that Erasmus had set up a meth lab somewhere in the region of Plettenberg Bay. But all avenues for investigation always seemed to stop short of any definitive information on where and how the stuff was produced, and then transported so far afield to the various distribution points across the southern part of the province and beyond. In fact, when Juice and his colleagues started getting more aggressive with the informants, a few of those informants disappeared. Two were found, in separate incidents, allegedly drowned while swimming at beaches in Vic Bay and in Mossel Bay. This was the middle of winter, and hardly beach weather for anyone in their right mind, but no suspects were identified. Three other missing informants were never found at all.

The big break came in late July. On the 23rd, a Sunday evening at around 20h30, there was an explosion at a panel-beater's shop on Paris Street in the industrial area just outside Plett.

When the fire department and the SAPS investigated, it was found that the shop had been a meth lab. Even though the initial explosion and the fire that raged until the early hours of the Monday had destroyed most of the building and workshops, the arson inspectors had more than enough to work with—including about twenty large barrels of chemicals used in the manufacturing of meth, which had been stored in a back corner of the yard and were safe from the fire. They found a lot of batteries (used to extract lithium), sulphuric acid, a number of bottles of flu medicine and packets of diet pills (containing pseudoephedrine), fertilizer (containing anhydrous ammonia), and hydrochloric acid.

The remains of two individuals had been found on the scene, too badly burned to provide any chance of identification, and there was no evidence linking the establishment to the Funky Guys. No informants came forward. There was not even sufficient evidence of what had caused the explosion. They all suspected that it was simply an accident, but in the week to ten days following the explosion, reports started to come in from informants further afield about the Funky Guys's meth deals and previously arranged deliveries to distribution points at shebeens (and even one high school in the Plett area) having been canceled at the last minute. The Narc unit's best people put their heads together, and it did not take them long to conclude that this had been Erasmus's meth lab, the one that had supplied the organization for the past two years at least.

Gavin and Josh were hooked, and Juice was on a roll. He laughed as he recounted how the Narc unit guys took that Friday evening off and gathered at a Plett night club for some welcome release. They knew that at least two positives would come out of this development. The first was that the supply of meth in the area would probably quiet down significantly for the foreseeable future. That would always be a positive, of course.

The second was that Erasmus would need to find a new supplier, or build a new lab; this would hopefully give them an opportunity to move in and to obtain information that could lead to important arrests.

So, they decided to split their investigative muscle between two angles. The first, of course, was to zero in on all informants and to see whether they could trace Erasmus's "scientists"—the "fuck-ups" who had run the previous lab and would no doubt be roped in again to establish a new one. The second was to focus attention on the Funky Guys's heroin supply. With the meth supply chain experiencing hiccups, the expectation was that Erasmus would ramp up the turnover in heroin, while they waited to restock their meth supply. This would undoubtedly lead to opportunities for the Narc unit to get closer to Erasmus and the Funky Guys than they had managed to date. Or so they had thought, Juice added with a grimace.

Gavin gave the Indian officer a quizzical look. "So, nothing came from your investigation into the alternative, the heroin supplies? You couldn't fit him up on anything there?"

Juice shrugged and shook his head. "No. Maybe we were a bit too ambitious. We thought he would move fast—and big—to establish new supply lines, not only for the heroin but also for the meth." He looked defensive. "According to our informants, the Funky Guys had consistently, over the past eighteen to twenty-four months, maintained a balance of about sixty-five to thirty-five percent meth to heroin sales—with some coke and other stuff thrown in, of course, but it was never their main stock-in-trade—and there always seemed to be a steady supply of heroin from Nigerian sources. So, with what seemed like all of his meth cooking operation gone, we thought that Erasmus would ramp up the heroin side big-time to make up for it, you know?" He looked at the two homicide cops as if looking for confirmation that the Narcs' thinking had not been complete bullshit.

Josh nodded sympathetically. "Makes sense."

These guys had a lot more on Erasmus than they had on him for the Whitcombe killing, and he thought that neither he nor Gavin could point any fingers. He understood the Narc guys' frustration, but he was interested primarily in how they could get a hook or two into Erasmus. If not for Whitcombe, then at least on other charges. But things now sounded as if they weren't really going anywhere, for either of the two units.

"So where does that leave you guys? Where are you now?"

He looked as disappointed as he sounded. "There was nothing like the expected escalation of activities from the gang. We didn't see any affirmative moves to cultivate new suppliers, nothing like that, really. Erasmus didn't travel—we expected him to go out looking for new blood, but nothing new came up on the radar. Of course, he wouldn't need to travel if he was making new contacts over the internet, and we didn't have good access to his online activities. To be perfectly honest, we've kind of been spinning our wheels for the past couple of months, waiting for something to happen."

Josh thought of something: the files they had received from the Narc unit after Fourie's quick walk-by search of Erasmus's place in Joodse Kamp, early the previous week.

"What about his financials? What kind of information do you have on the organization and what they've been pulling in during the past few years?"

Juice seemed grateful for the chance to change course on his briefing. He nodded.

"He runs a very tight ship. He's been using a guy out in the Eastern

Cape, a chartered accountant, to take care of the finances and investments. We had an informant who had just made it into the upper echelons of the Funky Guys, around the time the meth lab exploded. He had been there a few months. He gave us some insights into the money, and on how Erasmus was making it and hiding it. Unfortunately, our man disappeared a few days after he reported on this. We have no idea where he is, although we assume that he is in a number of pieces, floating somewhere in the Indian Ocean. Maybe off the coast of Tsitsikamma, apparently one of Erasmus's favorite disposal spots since he dropped a Johannesburg guy's body in the sea there six years ago. Or so we've been told; nothing to investigate, of course."

Juice looked bitter for a moment, and then perked up. The Narc guys knew that you couldn't let all the dead ends and silent witnesses get to you. You just plugged along. The Cape Town units had been doing this for many years—and were usually just waiting 'till the drug guys fucked up. Which they frequently did, spectacularly.

Josh could see all of this on Juice's face, and behind his eyes, but the man was still trying to help them. Maybe he was laboring under the hope that these homicide cops might end up doing their work for them; that they might be able to nail Erasmus on something unrelated to his own unit's thousands of hours of fruitless graft. Josh was feeling more and more certain that, if this was the man's hope, they would dash it.

Juice rallied a bit, probably feeling a little more secure being able to share some information of potential value.

"Erasmus allegedly has a guy doing his financials. An ex-MTLS man, a former partner." Gavin and Josh both raised their eyebrows.

In 2017, the dying year of former president Jacob Zuma's disastrous—and by all reports, obscenely corrupt—tenure at the top, some big corporate names came to the fore in respect of work they had done for the Zuma-linked Gupta family, the Indian family that was still heavily implicated in the corrupt "capture" of the South African state, and especially of its state-owned enterprises.

It was reported that senior executives (including the CEO and chairman, and a number of senior partners) of the South African branch of a world-renowned international auditing firm, MTLS, had resigned. It was the second established corporate name to bite the dust from the Zuma and Gupta fallout. Apparently, the auditing firm had been auditing companies owned by the Gupta family. While an internal investigation failed to find evidence of fraud or actual corruption amongst the MTLS executives, it did find that those involved had failed to conduct themselves according to applicable professional standards.

Juice told them that Erasmus's accountant was one of those partners who had resigned at the time, a white guy in his mid-fifties by the name of Steve Barker. He was now allegedly running a little cottage financial advisory service from his luxury beach house on the Kowie River, near Port Alfred, an upmarket coastal town in the Eastern Cape.

"Three months ago, we got lucky. Barker has a friend, a retired banker I believe, who would join him now and then for deep-sea fishing out of Port Alfred and would also stay for parties at Barker's house. In fact, he's the one who brings the underaged girls from Johannesburg and Durban for the entertainment."

Josh grimaced, and shook his head. He really hated these rich, crooked fucks.

Juice continued. "This time we got lucky. A 21-year-old Coloured informant of the Gauteng Organised Crime Narcotics Unit, a young lady out of Eldorado Park who apparently doesn't look a day older than sixteen, was one of the girls who the banker took out there. She stayed for the party, and she reported on quite a few things, but she also managed to get her hands on a couple of files in the accountant's office while the fat cats were out at sea."

At Gavin's frown, he quickly explained. "Of course, we understand that this material is not admissible in court." He looked a little embarrassed. "But it made for some very interesting reading. Erasmus's name came up a few times—in code, but it wasn't too hard to crack."

Josh thought about the informant. In his eyes, she was a bloody hero, and he tried not to think about what she had to do the rest of that weekend, when not purloining financial files from the accountant's study. If they couldn't use this in court, they could sure as hell try to use it to get as close to a court as humanly possible. They at least owed her that.

Juice didn't have all the details. He hadn't expected to be briefing the homicide cops on the Funky Guys's financials today. He promised that he could get more complete information and that they could have a look for themselves if his commanding officer approved it. But he shared what he could.

The Funky Guys were turning over in the region of 25 to 30 million rand a year from the business, or at least they had in the past two years; all tax-free, of course. From that, it was estimated that Erasmus was skimming an amount of between 5 to 8 million rand. Business was good. Although there was limited information in the files, it did seem that Erasmus had a lot of his income tied up in real estate investment across the country, primarily within the Cape Peninsula and Cape Town CBD.

An informant within the organization, one whose identity Juice wanted to keep hidden even from the homicide cops, was adamant that Erasmus had identified the small village of Pniel, over Helshoogte Pass toward Franschhoek, as his major point of investment. He had reportedly spent upwards of 15 million rand in the past three years buying up land in the hamlet itself and the outlying areas. Erasmus had allegedly stated that he would someday retire on these investments alone; that Stellenbosch was growing fast, and that the natural direction of that growth would be over Helshoogte Pass. The man had dreams of offering student accommodation at grossly inflated prices, once the university town was completely saturated and parents became desperate.

Erasmus didn't seem to be very cash-rich currently, although many of those property and other investments could be liquidated at a later time, possibly with some negligible financial penalties. Some of those investments, however—especially those in Cape Town—appeared to be together with partners, and preliminary investigations of the available paper trails showed that there might be much more substantial penalties if Erasmus decided to dump any of those deals at short notice. There were some names that came up, Russian and eastern European; big names in the Cape Town underworld. Night club owners and bouncers mostly, some more directly into drugs.

Maybe Erasmus should hang onto those for a while, for his own health, if not for the investment value.

The South African Revenue Service was hot for Erasmus, but the Western Cape Narc unit had managed to stall them to date. Any major move on the gangster's income from drug sales and other illicit causes would jeopardize their ongoing investigations, and definitely give notice to both Erasmus and his accountant of the stolen files. So, although everyone was hanging back and no urgent action was taken or even planned in the short term, the Narc unit did try to perform their own "informal" lifestyle audit on Erasmus and his closest associates in the organization. It was from one of these that the information about the 1.5 million rand Audi emerged, which had been bought for cash from the Audi dealership in George in September. There was also a speedboat, which had been purchased in the first week of October—also for cash, in a private sale from a guy in Knysna, for around 350,000 rand.

Gavin yawned, and then immediately looked embarrassed, laughing and throwing his hands up in a sign of apology. It was after 14h15 now, and they had been sitting in this badly ventilated room for more than an hour and a half, probably breathing in all kinds of mold from the walls and ceiling. He glanced at Josh, who also looked as if he'd had enough for the moment. Gavin turned to Juice.

"OK, thanks for all this, it really has been most helpful. But what can you tell us that is current? What's happening with Erasmus's business, the gang, their supplies, and all that? What are they doing at the moment?"

Juice nodded. He looked as if he might want to stifle a yawn himself, but he was still reporting to a senior officer. This was serious shit.

"Sir, it's hard to say, exactly. We have lost some intelligence capacity in the last few months." Before they could ask, he raised a hand. "Sorry, that's just how things work in this business. We are much more dependent on confidential informants than you guys at homicide, and we go through phases. Worst case, some informants die." He pulled a face at this. "Others OD—they are mostly junkies, of course. They just take too much of that shit and they 'go gently into that sweet night.'"

Gavin grimaced a bit at the butchering of the Dylan Thomas line, but he let it go.

Juice continued to look apologetic. "Others get arrested by unrelated units. We obviously can't provide the confidential informants with any kind of blanket cover against arrest or prosecution—that would get out on the streets, and then they would get taken out. It just doesn't work that way. So, we sometimes—often, actually—have to work to get them back out on the streets after the arrests, and then we have to spend some energy and manpower in getting them vetted again by the gangs. There is usually some suspicion; once a CI has been inside for any period of time, the assumption is they might have turned and given evidence against the gangs. It's a judgment call. When things look bleak, and the CI looks compromised, no matter what we try out on the street to 'rehabilitate' them, we have to pull them permanently and set them up elsewhere."

Juice could see that he was starting to bore Colonel Whitall, so he summarized.

"It seems that Erasmus and his guys have not had a very good few months, since the meth lab explosion in July. We weren't wrong that they would try to ramp up efforts to increase heroin imports from the Eastern Cape, via the Chinese, but the word on the street is that this hasn't gone so well for them. We and other units have been pretty successful in the past two years, in slowly cutting down the supply from maritime landings in the Eastern Cape and KZN. The trawlers are less inclined to try to enlist the small towns and the remote spots—you know, a torch or two onshore signaling, and small boats going out to sea to collect. We've really made a dent there, and that's the consensus across the Narc units all over the country. We don't have a lot of success, but that's one thing we're definitely proud of." Gavin smiled encouragingly.

Juice continued. "We've also had success in curbing offloads at the major ports. In the Eastern Cape—that's PE and East London mainly—so there's a definite pinch being felt in that region, in respect of the import volumes of heroin. To make things worse for our 'Rasta friends,' with all this in mind, it seems that the Chinese suppliers have raised their prices. They're not stupid, and they know that Erasmus is between a rock and a hard place. And, all our information says that the guy hasn't been able to find an alternative meth supplier.

"We've looked at that, specifically. We expect him to build a new lab—it's just the most cost-effective, and probably safest, way to go—but we have no real information pointing that way yet. We unfortunately do not know who his scientists are—he could be using new people, of course, but if those guys or gals are still alive, we suspect that he would use them again, as the product he delivered from the Plett lab was generally viewed on the street as being of excellent quality. He would be stupid to let them go, if they were still in the game.

"As for the heroin side, we've been hearing rumors of Erasmus spreading out his tentacles to other regions."

Gavin raised his eyebrows. "Other regions? Where would that be, most likely?"

"Cape Town, sir, Cape Town and the west coast. That's where we're looking, and that's where he'll go, eventually, without a doubt."

Gavin and Josh both thanked the Narc officer profusely for his time. It had been educational, even if they were disappointed to find out that the Narc unit was still quite some way from arresting Erasmus and pursuing any kind of prosecution that might stick.

Gavin did tell Juice—and Josh nodded along in the affirmative—that they would really appreciate it if the officer or his colleagues would inform them in case they received any more definite information about Erasmus's moves, and especially if he extended his operation toward Cape Town, where Gavin still had some contacts. They needed to know what the man was doing.

Juice seemed happy with the idea and promised to do what he could.

As they left, Josh brought up the name of Captain Gershwin Carels, one of Chetty's men, and asked the officer what connection, if any, there was between the cop and the drug dealer. Juice looked concerned, and he frowned as he told them that Carels had been working the Funky Guys intelligence for a long time. He was aware that the captain had met with Erasmus frequently in an undercover role, but beyond that, he was not willing to speculate.

When Josh said that the homicide team had concerns about a possible tip-off of Erasmus before his interview at the Knysna station, Juice seemed to ponder the matter. He assured them that he thought they were barking up the wrong tree, but that he would look into Carels and get back to them.

CHAPTER 18

After the meeting with Juice Chetty, they had driven to Josh and Amy's flat for a debriefing. They arrived around three. Gavin would make his way back to Knysna SAPS later in the afternoon, and he didn't think that Josh needed to drive back out to Knysna just to return to George again.

They were both more than a bit demoralized about the lack of useful information from the Narc officer. Nobody seemed to be anywhere close to arresting Erasmus for anything at all. Josh was a bit nervous about Gavin's commitment to Erasmus as a viable suspect in the Whitcombe murder, but he didn't need to worry. Gavin reassured him that, even if things were still very sketchy, Erasmus was a credible suspect. At the very least, they could eliminate him only once they had convincing evidence that distanced the man from Whitcombe, after the apparent meetings at his house as well as the definite—although hard to prove—link with the environmental project up in Phantom Pass.

They were both sure—as was Juice—that something was brewing, and that Erasmus was about to make some move that might ultimately assist both their investigations. But that could happen tonight, tomorrow, or two weeks from now, and those were all optimistic predictions.

So Gavin insisted they pursue another angle they had not yet investigated: Erna Pretorius's theory. Wild as it had seemed at the time, but with little else to go on, worth a shot.

He asked Josh to look into the whole history of the Whitcombe/Brink association, the 1995 appeal in the Western Cape High Court, and the 1986 murder of Senzo Shabane, for which Brink had been arrested and ultimately convicted and imprisoned.

AppleMac had sourced the relevant documentation. The court files were obtained from the High Court archives in Cape Town, and from Brink's lawyer at the time, who had to instruct Whitcombe because of the archaic Law Society rules back then which prohibited a client from directly engaging an advocate at the Cape Bar without the intermediary of an attorney. The firm was based out in Rondebosch, and the attorney, Lawrence Cohen, was still a senior partner there, approaching retirement. Cohen had apparently made some noises about attorney-client privilege, but after it had been explained to him that both the client and the advocate were dead in suspected murders, he had asked his PA to copy the relevant files still in their possession. He did mention to AppleMac that he was a bit conflicted about this particular case.

Apparently, he had referred Brink's appeal case to Whitcombe, who was known casually to Cohen, and had also come highly recommended by colleagues who specialized in criminal law. However, a few months into their preparation for the appeal hearing, just under a month before the trial date, Brink had fired Cohen. He had not really given reasons; he had mumbled something about his belief that Cohen had apparently "fucked up" his original trial. Cohen was offended but let the matter go. But he was quite pissed at Whitcombe. Even though he had referred Brink to Whitcombe, the two lawyers had struggled to get along from the start. Cohen's recollection was that the advocate could be a real cold bastard, and a slave-driver when it came to trial preparation. He had treated Cohen, at that time an experienced attorney, like a wet-behind-the-ears articled clerk, a mere novice. Cohen had believed all these years that Whitcombe had been pouring poison into Brink's ear and that he had been the one behind his firing in the case.

AppleMac had arranged for a young W/O out in Rondebosch to collect the Cohen file, and it was couriered to Josh's flat in George. An admin assistant at the Cape Town Central SAPS Station had undertaken the massive task of scanning the High Court's hard copy file and then emailing it through. AppleMac had forwarded it to Gavin and Josh earlier that afternoon.

It would no doubt keep Josh busy for a day or two.

Josh dragged himself out of bed, ready for the task. Amy had left for coffee and Pilates with Jenny.

Apart from all the warm feelings toward the Whitalls, at the moment he was less positively inclined toward his new boss. This was really a shitty job he had been saddled with. Paperwork, and the worst kind: the kind with old documents. He kept forcing himself to recall that Gavin had asked, from day one, whether he had a legal background, and had intimated that they could use it. He would just need to knuckle down and do it. He could bitch to himself all he wanted, but these were his orders, and he would give serious attention to it. He remembered Erna Pretorius's quite urgent conviction that this was where the genesis for the whole Whitcombe and Brink angle lay.

So he downloaded the files and started to arrange them into categories, according to source, nature, and relevance for their current investigation. He had decided that he would first read through all the contents of the hard copy file which had come from Cohen to Whitcombe when he was briefed to handle the appeal. He would then tackle the massive data dump that was the file of the court transcripts. Only once he had read everything and had the whole picture of what happened would he then start making a list of points which might be of relevance to their current investigation.

It was more than three and a half hours later that he clicked through the last page of the court file and minimized the document on the screen with a long sigh. His eyes hurt, and he had had an on-again, off-again headache for most of the past hour. He closed his eyes and stretched expansively, before pushing his chair back and getting to his feet. He needed some distance now. Everything was in his head, and it needed to percolate a bit up there. He decided he would take Amy out for lunch, and then when they got back, he would start writing up his thoughts.

He still had a hell of a big task before him—he would need to constantly cross-reference back to the material—but he felt a small tingle of excitement already. There was something there. He couldn't put his finger on it yet, but he knew that he had read something in the past few hours that was important, something that clamored to stand out from the wealth of information he had ingested.

Josh had learned, very early on in his teenage years, that the best thing now was to try and put all of it out of his mind. It was like when you searched for your car keys, or for the TV remote. The harder you searched, the less were your chances of finding it. When you stopped searching, it would invariably turn up. He knew that his brain needed to chill, crawl back into itself, and figure this out in its own time. But he was confident that the answer would come. It almost always did.

They went to a small coffee shop and bistro in York Street. It was a new place that Amy had spotted on her way to the gym the previous week. She had liked the look of it on the outside, and when they walked in, Josh also started beaming. The little shop, called The Naughty Corner, had been decorated in the style of kindergarten kitsch. It had big, very comfortable-looking beanbags in all colors of the rainbow, scattered around the floor, and oversized letters of the alphabet and all kinds of shapes and colors—fruit, balls, fire-engines, dinosaurs, and airplanes—stuck all over the walls, on which patrons were apparently encouraged to scribble, with the crayons to be found everywhere. As Josh walked in and he and Amy smiled at each other, he felt a little of the stress and heaviness from the investigation drop from his shoulders.

They had great coffee, and each ordered an omelet, Josh's ham and mushroom one probably the best he'd had. Everyone was friendly, and when some wit started humming "Old MacDonald Had a Farm," it was infectious; a younger couple started singing the words, and soon everyone—Josh and Amy included—were singing along. They felt very stupid afterwards, of course, but it was fun. They decided that they would definitely go back there again.

When they got back to the flat, Josh kissed her and excused himself to get back to his office. He had a pleasant buzz from the Corona he had drank with lunch. He wasn't in the habit of drinking midday, and he thought it was a subconscious need to prove to himself that he wasn't really all the way back in kindergarten which made him order it. He took off his shoes, and sat in the chair, leaning back and closing his eyes. That thing that was tingling in the forefront of his brain was still just out of reach.

CHAPTER 19

After Brink's conviction in the Western Cape High Court for the killing of a Senzo Shabane, the nephew of a senior ANC leader from Zululand in then northern Natal, he was looking at more than twenty years in jail. At that time, during the democratic transition, there was a lot of talk of peace and reconciliation, and "letting bygones be bygones." But there was also a lot of new information coming out about all the shit the Apartheid government and its shady security forces had been involved in. Top of the page was Colonel Eugene De Kock (or "Prime Evil") and Vlakplaas. But the rot went deeper than that.

The former SAP security units had been operating—highly illegally under international law, of course—in a number of South Africa's neighboring states, for a number of years. Brink's unit had been especially active in the east. In the early to mid-1980s, they had avoided the war zone that was the border between the then northwestern colony of South Africa, South West Africa (now the independent state of Namibia), and Angola. Brink's unit, KC-12, focused their attention on Mozambique and Tanzania up the coast, to the northeast.

But this was work that was, in Brink's case, calculated to take him across the South African border for some time. He had gotten himself into a spot of trouble back home. KC-12 was a counter-insurgency unit of the SAP, an offshoot of De Kock's C-10 unit that was based at Vlakplaas, a farm twenty kilometers from Pretoria. KC-12 was based at a nearby smallholding. Here, in January 1986, officers from the SAP fraud squad in Pretoria had staged a bust and confiscated a large amount of counterfeit currency, rands and US dollars, following a sting operation on a black taxi owner and small-time racketeer in the Alexandra township.

It was discovered that the counterfeiters were their own men. What promised to be a coup for SAP in its continual fight against the black market in the townships around Johannesburg and Pretoria, turned into a public relations (and legal) nightmare for the State. KC-12 had been involved for the past eighteen months in producing the counterfeit money and spreading it around like candy in the townships, whereupon they would buy drugs and illegal firearms, in the process getting leads on the guys who dealt in guns and their clients—often militant anti-Apartheid activists and ANC members.

The whole thing was hushed up, of course, but Brink and four of his men (Josh wasn't surprised to see the name of Jacobus van Zyl, the man whom Brink had stayed with recently in Rheenendal, on that short list) had narrowly escaped arrest. Their operation was, of course, highly illegal, and all that saved them was the fact that the powers that be in the SAP and in the government knew exactly what they were doing and had authorized it. But no one else could ever know about it.

So Brink and his men needed to get out of sight, and KC-12 was sent to Mozambique. They were to undertake surveillance on the revolving door of ANC militants who were making their way in and out of cities such as Lourenco Marques and Beira, on their way across the southern African borders to plot their attacks on military, government, and civilian targets alike in the fight against the white oppressor. After a short stint in Lourenco Marques, Brink had found himself in Beira in May 1986, when Shabane died in a bomb explosion on a Saturday afternoon in a busy marketplace on Mouzinho de Albuquerque Rua.

In Brink's original 1993 trial, the prosecution team was headed by an old hand, Advocate Johan Steenkamp. Steenkamp was a lifer who had started out in the magistrates' courts and regional courts of the Free State and then later had successfully prosecuted a few death penalty cases— mostly political trials—during the 1970s and '80s in Johannesburg. He was in his early sixties in 1993. While he was still working for the State, he was on the other side of the fence, as his target this time around was the

Apartheid security cluster rather than some banned and exiled political liberation party. But he was no less dedicated to the job of putting away his man.

Steenkamp ended up calling surprisingly few witnesses against Brink. There were a couple of retired SAP officers who testified to Brink's involvement in the KC-12 unit. Then there were three civilians who testified to the happenings of Saturday, May 14th 1986.

The first was a Mozambican gentleman of Portuguese extraction by the name of Jorge Ramires, who owned a small pension near the marketplace. Brink and three of his men had rented two rooms there for a week before that fateful Saturday. Ramires testified to Brink leaving his room and walking toward the marketplace sometime in the late afternoon, about an hour before the explosion which shook the area. He had been carrying a bag or a suitcase. Ramires could not exactly recall which it was.

The other two witnesses were a South African couple, a Coloured man and woman in their late forties, who hailed from Bellville South near Cape Town, who had been on holiday in Beira at the time. They testified to seeing Brink on Mouzinho de Albuquerque Rua at around the same time that Ramires had seen him leave the pension. They remembered him, because the husband, Clive Samuels, had nearly gotten into a fight with Brink when Brink whistled at his wife as he walked by. When Samuels accosted him and Brink heard their Cape Town accents, he started throwing racial slurs at them and threatened to beat up Samuels, whose wife managed to pull her husband away into the crowd. They testified that Brink had been carrying a black rucksack over his shoulder. He disappeared down the road, and they decided to hurry the other way.

The two main witnesses for the prosecution did not testify in the courtroom. They testified anonymously. The two black men (who were simply identified to the court reporter and the lawyers as "K" and "S") testified *in camera* in another room of the court building, which was not open to the public. The only persons present were the judge, Steenkamp and his assistant prosecutor, Cohen and his candidate attorney, and the court stenographer. "K" and "S" both wore balaclavas over their heads, which covered their faces and only showed their dark eyes.

These guys buried Brink under a mountain of allegations about the SAP Special Forces activities in Beira.

Brink's defense had a lot of trouble cross-examining them. They just didn't know who they were. There was no way to discredit them, with their identities being withheld. Ultimately, Cohen gave up the fight of objecting to the admissibility of these witnesses' testimony, and let their evidence be recorded as largely uncontested.

It appeared that the legal plan of attack for Brink's defense team—devised originally by Cohen and employed in the original trial, and at least initially endorsed by Whitcombe in 1995—was twofold. It was one of complete denial of guilt, accompanied by some measure of misdirection.

The denial was what appeared to Josh to be a rather poorly constructed alibi defense. Yes, Brink had been in Beira. He had been there with the rest of his unit since a week before Shabane's killing, in fact. They knew the lay of the land and they were busy with an operation targeting the ANC and PAC operatives who were newly-arrived from the training camps in Tanzania and elsewhere and were suspected of planning attacks on South African targets in the city. Their brief was to take out any of these guys who they could pinpoint, and who they could prove guilty to their own satisfaction. These executioners of the Apartheid State acted outside of legal constraints when it came to things like reasonable doubt and the rule of law, and they took action against anyone they were satisfied was either planning paramilitary operations in Beira itself, or who might decide to cross the border into South Africa in the future, to do bad things there. Under cross-examination, Brink admitted to being aware of Shabane, and of actively surveilling him.

The Apartheid government had, by this time, obtained notoriety in international law circles for their interpretation of the principle of "hot pursuit." If a "terrorist attack" (as these attacks were invariably branded by the Apartheid government) occurred within the borders of the country, their forces were often sent into neighboring sovereign states and would retaliate—mostly by annihilating the relevant terrorist units completely and horrifically—without concern for the invasion of foreign sovereign territory in the process. The "hot" part of hot pursuit sounded a bit nonsensical when reports sometimes came out of "terrorist units" having been wiped out three weeks after fleeing across the border. But apart from the international condemnation and the frequent, strident complaints by various southern African governments, it was a highly successful strategy and modus operandi. There was intelligence information at the time showing that quite a few prospective paramilitary operations by enemies of South Africa had been aborted before the fact, as a result of such hot pursuit missions.

There was a lot of fear. The South African security forces and the recce units (the elite South African reconnaissance units at the time) were highly respected for their fighting prowess, courage, equipment, and resourcefulness when on the trail of targets, especially out in the African bush. Many of the young white Afrikaner members of these units had grown up on farms or in the bush. They were, for the most part, natural expert trackers and excellent shots. They needed little outside assistance in mounting operations in such terrain, and were completely at home living off the land and sleeping rough for weeks on end. And, of course, these young men had been indoctrinated by the State (and their own parents and relatives) for most of their lives, to not only feel complete superiority over Africans, but to feel a burning hatred toward communists, which is what their enemies were invariably painted as being.

Brink's unit was, by the man's own admission, in Beira at the time, and he also admitted in the original trial that Shabane was one of the prime subjects of their operation. They knew about the Natal man, and of his training at an ANC camp in Tanzania, and they suspected that he had been sent out to Beira with a bombing or assassination mission. What, for Josh, made Brink's unit of sixteen men especially interesting, is that they were one of only three units of the South African security forces in 1986 who had been accorded "special privileges." "Hot pursuit" was, by its nature and in principle, an ex post facto affair; if a thief stole your sheep and left your farm to transport it across neighboring territory, you were allowed some leeway in pursuing that thief onto your neighbor's farm. That was the gist of the legal doctrine, which the South African government had abused and perverted for years. But Brink's unit, KC-12, had special permission to apply a weird kind of anticipatory form of the doctrine. As soon as they suspected that a terrorist unit was planning to commit crimes on South African territory in the future, they were mandated to preemptively take such units out before any such plans could be brought to fruition. In essence, once you merely suspected a potential thief of planning to steal your sheep, you could take him out, right away—job done.

This was anathema to many principles of international law. So, unsurprisingly, Colonel Louis Germishuys, commander of KC-12, had requested—demanded—and subsequently obtained a special letter of authorization from no less than the then State President's office. Everyone involved in that piece of correspondence was fully aware at the time that, at international level, such letter was not worth the paper it was written on. This was all highly and quite blatantly illegal. But Germishuys had insisted, and the President's office had gone along with the farce, in the hope that any future potential domestic prosecution that might follow from KC-12's activities could be defended on the basis of such authorization.

Josh was fascinated by all of this, but the gist of it was that Brink had brought an alibi defense. After admitting under cross-examination in open court in the original trial that KC-12 had been actively targeting Shabane and had been following him and his associates for a number of days, Brink had testified that on the early Saturday evening in question, he had been off duty, and with someone. He had been in the arms (and between the legs) of a local hooker out in Palmeiras, where he had spent—according to him—the hours between 16h00 and 21h00. He couldn't have killed Shabane, as he had simply not been in the marketplace in Area de Baixa, or anywhere near it.

Notes in the margins of Cohen's file recorded that there was some excitement in the court at the time of this testimony. It was 1993, after all, the year before official democracy and the birth of the fabled "rainbow nation." The irony was not lost on any of the spectators, lawyers, or court personnel, or even the judge, that this racist white Afrikaner soldier had spent—according to his own testimony—five hours in the intimate company of a black African whore, in the bed of her slum apartment on the beachfront in Beira. The Cape Town newspaper, *Die Burger*, had something about this (in a quite stridently shocked tone) as their headline, on the day following Brink's testimony.

Brink failed to prove his alibi. He couldn't remember the prostitute's name, and investigators couldn't find her.

The second prong of Brink's defense in the original trial was one of apparent misdirection.

After having admitted that KC-12 had been in town for some time watching Shabane, and targeting him for future "intervention," and then testifying that he, Brink, was otherwise occupied at the time of Shabane's killing, his legal team presented an argument which implicated others in the killing.

The prosecutor made hay over the fact that it was completely unsurprising that Brink did not implicate any of his own people, either his direct unit or his fellow Apartheid forces. Brink claimed that there were rumors that Shabane had been killed by some of his own people.

In the original trial, this defense flopped spectacularly, much like the one involving the fabled hooker—"Black Delilah," as some journalists were calling her. Brink could not provide any evidence to prove this theory. Under cross-examination, he vacillated between alleging that one or more of Shabane's comrades had planned and executed the killing of the man by bombing, and then later that there had been a technical malfunction with an explosive device that Shabane himself was in the process of planting, in a car in front of the building of a South African agricultural import business.

The court was not impressed. The prosecutors tore great big holes in Brink's testimony. This second line of defense went the way of the first. It crashed, and just as hard. Eventually, on October 13th, 1993—a Friday—the court found Brink guilty of Shabane's killing.

Sentencing followed three weeks later.

And then, in March 1995, Brink appealed to the full bench of the Western Cape High Court. Cohen had instructed Mark Whitcombe, and the two legal minds plotted a multi-pronged attack on the trial court's finding of guilt, as well as sentencing. The conviction was upheld by the full bench and would remain in place until its appeal in April 2017 to the Supreme Court of Appeal.

The grounds for the granting of the appeal were, firstly, that the judges of the SCA held that the original trial judge in 1993, Esterhuizen J, had convicted Brink on scant evidence. The SCA judges felt that the only real evidence that the court had based its finding on had been the testimony by "K" and "S," the ANC operatives who had testified *in camera*. Even though Brink had raised the alibi of the prostitute and had failed to bring any evidence to court to show that he could not have been in the marketplace at the time of the killing, the SCA judges felt—from their reading of Esterhuizen J's judgment and comments that he had made during sentencing—that the judge had accorded undue weight to this failure of Brink's alibi defense. In fact, the majority of the SCA judges were of the opinion that Esterhuizen J had committed an error in law by, in effect, placing the burden of proof on Brink, as the defendant, while the burden to prove Brink's guilt beyond reasonable doubt was fully directed onto the State. This, the SCA judges held, constituted a violation of Brink's constitutional right to a fair trial, as guaranteed in Section 35 of the Bill of Rights, specifically the right to be presumed innocent, to remain silent, and not to testify during the proceedings. The court found that Esterhuizen J had committed a "dialectical irregularity in misconstruing the nature of the case before him, and the applicable law in respect of the State's burden of proof and the accused's constitutional rights."

The SCA judges found, secondly, that Brink's constitutional right to a fair trial had also been violated by the fact that "K" and "S" had been allowed to testify *in camera* against him. The judges held that the State had provided insufficient grounds to justify these two witnesses' identity being protected in the proceedings, and that Esterhuizen J had, in allowing this, come close to displaying bias in favor of the prosecution. The judges frowned upon that.

The SCA judges were also of the opinion that this violated Brink's constitutional rights to "a public trial before an ordinary court," his right "to be present when being tried," and his right "to adduce and challenge evidence." The SCA judges felt that the cross-examination of these two witnesses by Brink's lawyer had been stunted by their identities being withheld, and by the lawyer not being able to investigate and question their backgrounds and all the circumstances surrounding their paramilitary activities in Beira at the time of Shabane's killing. One judge actually expressed the opinion that these two witnesses' testimony should be treated as being akin to hearsay evidence, seeing that Brink appeared to have had little, if any, chance to direct a challenge to the credibility of the witnesses themselves.

Ultimately, the SCA overturned Brink's conviction and his sentence. While Josh looked hard for it, there was little in the SCA judgment which specifically explained the court's opinion regarding the 1995 appeal to the full bench, or which implicated Whitcombe in the SCA's decision to overturn the conviction. The SCA judge who penned the majority judgment in the 2017 appeal, Mposana JA, just made a cryptic remark in this regard toward the end of the judgment:

"It is noted that the appellant was thus denied vitally important constitutional protections offered under our Bill of Rights. Justice delayed is justice denied, and we take note of the fact—although we do not need to express a view on this in light of our above findings—that the appellant was possibly doubly prejudiced in the handling of his 1995 appeal. The fact that his counsel in that matter did not challenge the in camera testimony and proceedings (and may have failed to bring relevant evidence before that court in defense of his client) may point toward the fact that the appellant received ineffective assistance of counsel. We believe that the constitutional grounds are sufficient to vacate the original conviction and its subsequent confirmation on appeal."

Josh found little in this last statement to lead directly to Whitcombe, or to anything he may have done wrong at the time. In the legal and ethical sense, at least. If there was any evidence of this, it would have to be in the Cohen file and the 1995 court transcripts, which he had already scoured.

That something, the thing that he had felt even before he took Amy out to the cool new restaurant, was now playing more and more on his mind. He started to get that creepy feeling that it was like some worm or other loathsome creature writhing inside his head, trying to get out.

Josh got up to make some coffee.

He rolled his head around as he waited for the kettle to boil. His neck was stiff, no doubt from both the hours spent sitting and reading, as well as the tension that occupied his mind. When the kettle switched off, he grabbed it and poured the boiling water into the cup. As he stirred the coffee, he suddenly looked up, a glint in his eye.

There!

The code "BA/SE-17" jumped into his mind; why, particularly, he didn't know. He had encountered it earlier, in reading the files. He corrected himself—in reading Cohen's file, specifically. He had the distinct recollection of seeing it on paper, not on the computer screen. It was mentioned in one of the documents that Cohen had sent to Whitcombe in preparation for the appeal.

Josh had a good memory and he knew it. During his legal studies, he had sometimes thought it might be photographic.

"BA/SE-17" was some kind of code or document numbering system, and he would find it soon.

He decided to finish making his coffee, take a seat at the table, and then search for the reference. He would take his time, act naturally, and not go looking for this. He let his subconscious whisper to him before he started opening files and scanning pages.

A few moments after he had sat down at the table, it came to him. He picked up the Cohen file, and he turned the pages to around the 200-page mark. It took him less than a minute to find it.

On page 212 of the file was a letter from Cohen to Whitcombe, dated June 14th, 1995. The appeal court date was less than two months away at that time. Midway down the page, Cohen was explaining that he was providing access to the original evidentiary material that he had used in the trial in 1993, as well as some information delved up subsequently by the lawyer's investigator, a private investigator from Edgemead by the name of Stan Evans. Josh now remembered that the man's name had come up a few times in the Cohen file, as well as in the 1995 appeal file. And then he saw the "BA/SE-17" reference.

It was on a list of documents that Cohen had either sent to Whitcombe or was promising to send to Whitcombe shortly. The number was the fourth bullet down in a list of nine. The description next to the number was, *"Alternate intel—own goal?"*

Josh now realized why the number and the reference had stuck in his head. It was a weird description of the relevant document. "Own goal?"What the hell was that? Maybe his mind had singled this item out as it was the only one of the nine such codes listed on the page where the description ended with a question mark. The descriptions were just that: very brief explanations to Whitcombe of what the relevant document contained. But this was one where it seemed that Cohen himself didn't know what it contained. It was something that he obviously thought was relevant, and potentially of value to their case, even though he appeared to be unsure as to what exactly it meant.

Before he went digging for it—even though his subconscious was telling him that he hadn't seen the actual document earlier—Josh was playing with the number, the code. He was guessing, with no way of knowing whether he was right, that the "BA/SE" part referred to "Brink Appeal/ Stan Evans," and that the document number referred to its position in the order of documents. Josh made a note to phone Cohen the following morning to ask about this, and to get Evans's contact details. As he lifted his head from the notepad, something struck him.

The court files of the trial and appeal had all been provided electronically, in Acrobat PDF format. Josh said a silent prayer of thanks that he was not working with actual paper copies of the documents as he had been with the contents of the Cohen file, and then he quickly did a word search for the term "BA/SE-17." Just to be on the safe side, he did a couple of searches, both with and without spaces before and after the "/" and the "-" in the search term.

As he had suspected, it didn't turn up anywhere in Cohen's original trial file. It appeared twice in the appeal file. The first reference was the one he had just read, the correspondence from Cohen to Whitcombe, shortly before the appeal trial date, and before Cohen's axing by Brink. The second reference was in the actual court transcripts, and it recorded that a document listed under that code had been removed by Whitcombe from the appeal discovery list.

An appeal of a court judgment was supposed to take place based upon the evidence assessed in the original trial, and new evidence was frowned upon and generally not allowed, unless there were compelling reasons to do so, in the interests of the administration of justice. Some new evidence had been listed by Whitcombe in the discovery list, by means of which the appellant in the case (Brink) would inform the State that new evidence might be tendered at the appeal hearing. "BA/SE-17" had been on that list, initially, but had been removed by Whitcombe prior to discovery, in the run-up to the court hearing. He was allowed to do this if the strategy had changed and they no longer intended to rely on a piece of potential evidence. And it was unlikely that the prosecution would have complained about this. It was less work for them, not having to investigate a new piece of evidentiary material.

Cohen had provided a phone number in a note he had scribbled on the inside cover of the file. He had not seen or spoken to Evans in more than ten years, but he had only good things to say about the man, who had apparently worked as his investigator for more than twenty years prior to his retirement. He asked Josh to pass along good wishes, if he managed to talk to Evans.

Stan was seventy-six now, and in a retirement home in Milnerton. He had been retired for a number of years. The number Cohen had provided, a cellphone number, was not current. But Josh Googled and managed to find the phone number for the retirement home. Within five minutes he had the man on the phone. Google was that good.

After introductions, Josh explained that they were investigating the death—the murder, actually—of a retired advocate. He explained most of the details, and mentioned both Cohen and Brink, and Stan made the connection before he was finished with the rehearsed script.

"I remember the case. A bit of a bastard, if you ask me. Just like that bloody lawyer!"

Josh frowned on his side of the phone. "Cohen?"

Stan was quick to say no. "Larry Cohen is probably the best of all of that rotten bunch of over-educated shits I had to work with, who called themselves 'lawyers,' *men of the law*. Ha! No sir, Larry's a good guy. The rest of them are mostly bastards." There was a pause, then he continued. "But that Whitcombe guy—what a prick!—not to mention his client."

Josh didn't know how to respond. They were investigating the "prick's" murder, after all. But this was good stuff. Evans appeared to remember the Brink case and Whitcombe, even though Josh had not yet mentioned him by name. After hearing about the man's age and present circumstances, he had thought that the call might turn out to be a waste of time.

Josh explained the situation to Evans, starting with a quick recap of Brink's conviction and then the appeal.

Evans said yes, he remembered all of it. Josh was inclined to believe him. The older man sounded sharp.

"What are you after, Captain?" asked Evans. "I can hear there's something specific. I may not be a detective anymore, but that sixth sense thing doesn't go away, or at least I don't think so."

Josh smiled to himself. Then he explained to Evans the reference to a file that he had found in the appeal documentation.

Evans was silent for a minute. So much so that Josh asked, "Are you still there?"

Evans grunted, then said, "Yes."

A few more moments passed. The man was clearly thinking. Whether trying to remember or trying to decide how much of what he did remember he was willing to disclose, Josh couldn't tell.

"I think I remember that. That document. It was a letter." Josh held his breath. "What did you say that description in the file was again? It's a bit strange. Something about an 'own goal'?"

Josh was holding his breath.

He nodded and said, "Yep." He didn't want to talk too much, or risk Evans losing the trail.

"That was a letter I got from an anonymous source, I think. Fuck,

I can't remember what it said, really. But I know it was from someone shady." He paused. "We—Larry and I—couldn't exactly establish its veracity, on the face of it. And then that prick fired Larry. I mean Whitcombe, he fired Larry. He was behind the client's decision, I'm sure of it, and then we were out of the game."

Josh knew that it was too much to expect that this elderly, retired detective should recall the contents of one document in a major case fifteen years ago, but he was still disappointed. He asked Evans whether he could recall anything about the circumstances of them obtaining the letter, and the source.

Evans was quiet again for a minute. Josh wanted to check that the connection had not been broken, but he didn't want to pressure the older man.

"I was investigating the paper trail of reports on the victim's killing, that ANC guy." Josh could picture Evans frowning, trying to recollect the details. "Even though there was a lot of secrecy around those foreign operations, of course, we found some material in the military archives in Bloemfontein. That letter might have…"

He suddenly swore loudly into the phone. Josh jerked the phone away from his ear.

"*Fuck me!* I'm an idiot! I remember now. That must have been the letter I got from the recce."

Evans explained that, in the course of researching the documentation that had been generated in military circles about the Mozambique operations, one of his operatives had run across a retired "recce" from 5 Reconnaissance Regiment, a Special Forces soldier by the name of Van der Westhuizen, who went by the handle "Van." This had been about three months before the 1995 appeal hearing. Evans had interviewed the man at a seedy little pub in Bellville, on Barnard Street, just off Voortrekker Road. Van told him that he had been in a small covert unit that had worked with Eugene de Kock's guys on some of the security police operations in the mid-1980s. This unit, "Red Team," was also monitoring the activities of the ANC and PAC militants who were active in Mozambique.

When Evans asked about Shabane, Van said that they had been surveilling him, and that there were Red Team reports. What had grabbed Evans's attention was the fact that there had been a report on Shabane's death, generated by the Red Team unit commander. Van said that in the early 1990s, as the secret units were being disbanded and evidence of their activities destroyed, he had taken some of the Red Team's paperwork. He didn't say why, and Evans didn't ask. He was guessing that the man might have had plans to supplement a meager pension for his work as an Apartheid storm trooper, and that he might have been planning to blackmail someone.

Van said that the Shabane report was amongst the material he had purloined and stored in his house. Evans's excitement waned when Van told him that the report had somehow gone missing after he had a fire in the garage at his house, and he believed it was destroyed. But then he told Evans that there was a letter, which had formed part of the report, which he must have misfiled because he had later found it in one of the other files which had survived the fire. It was this letter that Brink's defense team had then bought from Van for 12,000 rand, and which then made it onto the appeal discovery list, only to be removed by Whitcombe after Cohen was fired. Evans hadn't known about this last part, of course. After Cohen's firing, he had taken his investigator with him as he exited stage left.

Van had died a couple of years after that. Evans remembered reading something in the paper about the man having been killed in a boating accident in Bloubergstrand. He also remembered thinking at the time that maybe it had not been an accident; maybe the man had decided to peddle the wrong document from his stash of stolen files, to the wrong person.

Evans explained to Josh that, while he couldn't recall all of the contents of the letter, it was potentially explosive for Brink's case. It was a letter sent by one of the top ANC men in Mozambique to another senior guy in the MK intelligence wing. The letter warned of possible fallout from Shabane's killing. While South African security police and special forces units had been in Beira at the time and had been engaged in the surveillance of Shabane and a few other ANC men, and the finger of blame was bound to point at them for the killing, the sender of the letter claimed that Shabane had actually been killed by one of his own comrades. A lightning investigation by the top brass in Mozambique brought up evidence that the killer had been someone who had known Shabane from "B-Camp," where the two apparently had a major altercation for some reason. The man admitted to killing Shabane, but he was being protected by a very senior ANC official. The official's name was not mentioned in the letter, but the killer's was, though Evans couldn't remember it.

Josh was stunned. This was massive, and kind of inexplicable. After thanking Evans for his help, and gently placing his phone down on the desk, he sat down and literally scratched his head.

The rules of evidence are very complex, even more so in criminal trials than in civil cases, and there was a good chance that the letter would have been thrown out by the appeal court for some reason or another. Courts demand that the best evidence be provided. A letter is, in essence, a document that constitutes hearsay evidence, which courts are very loath to entertain if the author is not available to testify and be cross-examined about its contents. Exceptions are made, under certain circumstances, but there was a good chance that this letter, which appeared to throw a huge spanner in the prosecution's case against Brink, would never have featured in determining the outcome of the 1995 appeal. This, however, did not explain why Whitcombe, after having included it in his discovery list in the first place, then subsequently removed it before the appeal hearing. Something was fishy here, and Josh didn't understand it.

If a lawyer doubts the admissibility of a piece of evidence before going to trial, it makes sense to at least attempt to put it before the court, in your client's interest. Whitcombe would surely not have hidden the letter because of doubts as to whether the court would allow it.

This left another possibility, and now Josh got more excited. Whitcombe may have realized that this piece of evidence, which could have played a major role in getting his client's conviction overturned, might be of more potential value for him, Whitcombe, than for Brink. This document claimed that a "Mr. X," and not Brink, had killed Shabane. This letter might be of huge value to "Mr. X," who—if the contents of the letter were true—had at the time of the appeal managed to evade suspicion and capture for the murder for nearly ten years.

Josh had no idea whether "Mr. X" was still alive at that time, or now, for that matter, but the pieces of the puzzle seemed to slot into place.

Josh was convinced that Whitcombe had blackmailed "Mr. X" with the letter. In exchange for something, he had taken it off the discovery file and hidden it, removing it from Brink's case, and the public eye, forever.

It now also made sense why Cohen was fired by Brink, at the instigation of Whitcombe. If Cohen had still been on the legal team at the time of the appeal, he would know that Whitcombe had hidden the letter, and he would question it. What Whitcombe had done was, of course, highly unethical, and Brink would have been able to sue him and possibly get him disbarred for that. So Whitcombe had to get rid of the other lawyer. If Brink knew about the letter—which Josh believed must have been the case, seeing that Whitcombe had initially included it in discovery, before he had decided to keep it a secret—it must have featured in discussions between Whitcombe and his client. Whitcombe could always explain later that it was excluded from the appeal for some strategic reason. In fact, he might even have told Brink that it had been determined that it was inadmissible evidence, and that attempts to introduce it in court could harm their case or open them up to a legal sanction. Some bullshit along those lines.

The second thing that jumped into Josh's head was that this could also partly explain Brink's eventual success in the 2017 appeal to the Supreme Court of Appeal. He had, for some reason, been under the impression that the main ground for the overturning of the man's conviction had been "inefficient counsel" in the 1995 appeal (the reason they had first suspected Brink after Veronica Whitcombe's story of the stalking of Whitcombe and the assault at the restaurant up at Pezula), and they had believed that Brink had been pissed at something Whitcombe had done in the appeal. After reading the SCA judgment, he now knew that the SCA had decided the matter on constitutional grounds, relating mainly to the trial judge's error of law regarding the burden of proof, in respect of Brink's alibi defense, and for allowing the two ANC operatives to hide their identities and provide their testimony anonymously. But he now recalled those cryptic few words from the end of the SCA judgment:

"The fact that his counsel in that matter did not challenge the in camera *testimony and proceedings (and may have failed to bring relevant evidence before that court in defense of his client) may point toward the fact that the appellant received ineffective assistance of counsel."*

This would fit. If the SCA had been told that a relevant document was withheld in the 1995 appeal by Whitcombe, it would explain that statement. Josh assumed that the SCA judges did not make more of this because the document apparently no longer existed.

If Brink had somehow, in recent years, found out that evidence had been withheld by his own advocate, it could have triggered a motive to retaliate, to avenge.

Josh knew he needed to get more information on this before he took it to Gavin or anyone else.

CHAPTER 20

He phoned Cohen's office. It was just before 5:00 p.m. and Josh knew that he was cutting it fine, but he was hoping the man would still be there. He was. After some pleasantries and a brief explanation that he had now managed to work through the files, Josh told him that they had discovered a reference in the 1995 appeal file to a piece of evidence that had initially been included on the discovery list and was subsequently removed. He then explained that he had managed to speak to Stan Evans. He thanked the lawyer again for referring him to the investigator, and said that Evans had identified the document as an ANC intelligence letter regarding the true identity of Shabane's killer.

He got excited when Cohen confirmed that he remembered Evans sourcing it from an ex-security forces operative, and that they had been planning to include it in the appeal, as they both believed it could raise a reasonable doubt over Brink's guilt. Cohen expressed surprise at hearing that Whitcombe had not used it at the hearing. He said that he couldn't think of a single reason, in terms of legal strategy, why the advocate would have quashed this potentially explosive piece of evidence. He remembered that his own candidate attorney at the time had been tasked with researching the rules regarding such a document as hearsay evidence, and how they could get it admitted in the interests of justice. In fact, he continued, the young lady had soon after published an article in a law journal about hearsay evidence, written about the research she had done for the purposes of this one single document in the Brink appeal.

Josh interrupted him, as this was now starting to go nowhere. There were really just two things he needed to know.

"Mr. Cohen, do you remember the name of the man mentioned in the letter? Shabane's alleged killer?"

Josh could feel the tension in his body as he waited for the reply. A lot would hang on it.

Cohen thought for a few seconds. "No, I'm really sorry, Captain. That file was closed when my client dismissed me fifteen years ago. You'll understand that many, many names pass across my desk on a daily basis."

Josh swore under his breath. "OK, of course, I understand. Can I just ask, is there any chance that you still have a copy of the letter on file?"

Cohen again disappointed Josh. "I'm sorry. What I do remember is that I don't have any more files on the work I did for Reghardt Brink, aside from the file from the original trial in 1993, which I sent you a copy of. And I sent you everything in that file."

He explained that shortly after he had been fired in the run-up to the appeal, there had been a break-in at his offices. All the computers had been stolen, and all the files that were in boxes on a desk in the conference room had been destroyed when the burglars had poured household bleach over them (which had come from the ransacked kitchen and staff room on the first floor of the lawyer's offices). These files were awaiting their journey to the lawyer's archive storage unit in Claremont—as, by law, he was obliged to maintain client files for a few years. Seeing that the Brink appeal file had been closed a week or so earlier, it had been in one of those boxes. The damage from the bleach was such that none of the documentation was legible, and it all had to be destroyed. The police never caught the culprits, although if he remembered correctly, the theory had been that it had probably been the work of teenage junkies who needed the computers to sell, in order to buy drugs, and that the thing with the files was just garden-variety vandalism. One officer had told Cohen that he should be glad they hadn't torched the place.

Josh was pissed off, and—he had to admit to himself—quite a way down the road of self-pity, but he thanked Cohen for the man's valuable help.

Once he put the phone down, he shouted, *"Fuck!"* at the top of his lungs—in naked frustration at being so close, but so far still.

Amy came running, thinking that he must have hurt himself. He smiled at the look of concern on her face, and he made a stupid crack about paper cuts not being that painful. She gave him the squinty eyes, so Josh just hugged her and said sorry, he'd had some bad news on the investigation.

But he was still excited, really excited, for the first time in quite a while; they were finally making progress, although he knew they'd have their work cut out to take this lead further.

As Amy kissed him tenderly, he felt a bit guilty, as all he could really think about was discussing the latest developments—what he had found—with Gavin and Erna Pretorius.

68 CAMPBELL DRIVE, KNYSNA
18H45

Josh and Gavin were sitting on the patio by the pool, beers in hand. Josh had phoned to ask whether he could come out to discuss the Brink appeal files. Amy had come along, and upon arrival she and Jenny had taken Jenny's car out to the Thesen Island gallery, where they would work on the plans for the exhibition, now a little over three weeks away. Josh got the impression that both women realized they would be in the way, and that their men needed to talk through something important for the investigation.

There was no braai that evening, but Gavin offered Josh some takeaway peri-peri chicken that he and Jenny had ordered from a Portuguese restaurant in town. Josh had a nibble, to be polite, but was much too riled to eat.

After he had told Gavin all that he had found, including the bad news that he couldn't think of a single way they could determine the identity of the person mentioned in the letter, seeing that Cohen's own copy had been destroyed and the recce, Van, had passed away, Gavin sat deep in thought for a couple of minutes.

He then looked up and smiled broadly. "Good job, son, *great* bloody job." He paused. "Do you believe it? The contents of this supposed letter?"

Josh looked a bit taken aback, so Gavin continued. "I know you—we—

know very little about the original investigation against Brink, but do you think it sounds possible—*plausible*—that Shabane might have been killed by one of his own?"

Josh frowned and thought for a bit on how best to answer. He had been so thrilled about finding evidence referring to a killer other than Brink that he hadn't actually considered whether he believed it.

"I don't know, but I think I do. First, let me mention that I did an internet search and found something that I didn't know, that the old South African Defence Force, possibly with help from some of the old Rhodesian Special Forces soldiers—the Selous Scouts, I think—blew up a big fuel depot in Beira in March 1982. The South African boys were definitely active there, and making a lot of *kak*. But a lot of the court material from Brink's files state that the bomber in this case was Shabane himself. The ANC guys were just as active there. And I think it's possible. This was Brink's original defense, or one leg of it: that Shabane had been killed in the process of placing his own bomb. Is it such a stretch then to think that someone working with Shabane may have been involved?"

He glanced sideways at his superior officer, and grimaced.

"As you say, and you're right, we haven't really seen the evidence in that investigation of Shabane's death. We don't know what really happened there and what they found. What they brought to court, yes. What they didn't?" He trailed off, shrugging his shoulders, and Gavin understood.

In any murder investigation, there was often evidence that the prosecutors might decide not to place before a judge. There were legal, ethical issues with this, of course. Prosecuting lawyers, like their colleagues on the defense side of the table, were officers of the court. They were obligated to disclose any information they had which could lead the court toward making a finding on the facts of the case, even *if* it didn't serve their cause. But both police officers knew that often there was information discovered in an investigation which it was safer to rather lose, misplace, or forget about, if it didn't serve your side all that well. And this must have been exponentially truer for Brink's trial, if one considers the subject matter. There were official State secrets at issue, and draconian legislation at the time (which the courts had since struck down as being unconstitutional in the democratic dispensation), so there could have been many reasons for either side to withhold all kinds of sensitive information from a court of law and from the public eye.

"But I think this ties in with the rest of the evidence, or, at least, the defense strategy in the original trial," Josh said. Brink had been woefully unable to provide any real basis for this theory that Shabane had been killed by his own men (or that there had been some kind of malfunction with the IED), and the court had rejected it outright. But this might simply mean that the accused had been unable to provide the evidence which the letter discovered in 1995 would or could have provided proof of. It made sense. There was at least some basis for the allegations Brink had brought forward in his original trial.

Gavin seemed satisfied on that initial point. He now considered Josh's feeling on what had happened to the letter itself.

"I agree with your theory. About blackmail. I can't see any other plausible reason why Whitcombe would *not* have used that document in Brink's defense."

Josh raised a hand. "Sorry, I forgot just now, I should mention this. I was thinking about the legal reasons why he might decide to deep-six the letter. The fact is that it constitutes hearsay, and might be inadmissible on that basis. Also, I didn't ask Cohen—I will phone him again tomorrow and check—whether the letter was the original or a copy. If it was a copy, a court could exclude it on that basis alone, as not being the 'best evidence,' unless someone could testify as to why the original was not available, and that therefore the copy should be accepted as credible and reliable evidence."

Gavin nodded and said "OK," and Josh continued: "But what I didn't consider earlier, and what I only thought about on the drive over..." he pulled his face in an "aw shucks" gesture, "is that Whitcombe might have decided to exclude it from the discovery list not only because it might be inadmissible, but also because it might have been obtained illegally. As far as I understand, the recce had simply purloined documents from his unit's records when it was disbanded. This material would have been the property of the South African government; in fact, of its most shadowy and dangerous arm. If that was theft, there might have been hell to pay for it. Especially under the then-applicable 'official secrets' legislation—and there was a lot of that, as you'll know."

Gavin nodded—he knew all about that—but he frowned. "But could the legal team, or Brink, for that matter, really get into trouble as a result? They didn't steal it."

Josh shook his head. "I don't know. Sorry, Gavin, I think I told you that I specialized in and taught contract law. Not criminal law or the law of evidence. I'd have to read up on it, or, better yet, we should ask our legal guys, but I don't really think so. They had not been involved in the recce's sourcing of the documents. They had simply purchased it from him. There might be some legal liability for that, especially under the legislation, but I personally would defend any prosecution on those grounds as having simply been a lawyer acting in the best interests of his client, in trying to obtain and preserve evidence which might have proved his innocence."

Gavin agreed. "OK, but are you suggesting that this might still have been a probable reason for Whitcombe to hide the letter? That he was acting in good faith? He didn't necessarily have the intention to use the letter to extort information from the person named as Shabane's killer?"

Josh nodded, but then shook his head. "Yes, and no. In theory, I think the potential legal liability for both the client and his lawyers could have been the motivating factor. But I have this gut feeling…" He smiled at Gavin as he asked him not to tell Major-General Hlungwane.

"I think Whitcombe decided to capitalize on the information. You remember that his background shows that he had a lot of contacts in the struggle movement in the 1970s and '80s? I was thinking that maybe he knew the man identified in the letter, or he knew of him, and might have simply decided that he could extort money from him in order to keep his secret safe. I'm pretty sure that he had no particular interest in Brink's wellbeing, apart from his professional duties. And if he could convince Brink that there was a good reason—or even a bullshit one—to shelve that evidence, I think he might have decided to do so. Especially in the absence of another lawyer looking over his shoulder, having managed to get Brink to fire Cohen."

Gavin accepted this, and agreed, but he looked worried. "You know that your whole theory depends on whether this 'Mr. X,' as you call him, was still around at the time in 1995? If not, the blackmail wouldn't work."

Gavin was thinking that unless the target, or targets, were the sender and recipient of the letter—or, for that matter, the ANC itself—these were their people, and back in '86 the organization was very dependent on foreign and international goodwill in their fight against Apartheid. Especially after it became a violent fight.

Gavin pushed on with his objection. "You know that Mandela himself had been involved in the armed struggle for some time, and that many people in Europe and elsewhere even nowadays have a hard time coming to grips with that. At the time, any inkling of that kind of thing in the outside world could have meant that the ANC would be branded as simply a bunch of terrorists. They would lose that crucial support from the West."

Josh saw this, but he didn't like it. "I really don't think so. Whitcombe would have been crazy to try and blackmail the ruling party of the new government, a year after the democratic elections, right?" Gavin nodded. "And both the sender and the recipient of that letter were just that: the one was the messenger and the other the one to whom it was addressed. Of course we haven't seen the contents, but surely both would have had easy deniability in terms of actual and even vicarious involvement in Shabane's death?"

Gavin agreed, again. "OK, I *do* like your theory, really, and the more we hear about Whitcombe, the more I am convinced that he was no angel, maybe a complete shit. He could have done this, and I think easily. Which brings us back to the fact that the only way that theory would work is if 'Mr. X' were still alive in '95, and in some position where he had a lot to lose. I mean, maybe not only his freedom, in terms of potential prosecution for Shabane." He grimaced and took a long swig of his beer before speaking again. "We need to find out who this man is or was. We need to."

Josh took a sip of his own drink, pondering, and he looked at Gavin. "There's more to it, though, right? My 1995 blackmail theory might explain Brink's need to go after Whitcombe after his release two years ago.

Whitcombe sabotaged his appeal and condemned him to twelve years in prison. With Brink still a suspect, that's good for our investigation, even though we'd have to find the evidence to prove those connections and the motivations."

He hesitated, and then continued. "But if it pans out that 'Mr. X' was alive in '95, and was blackmailed by Whitcombe at the time, it will get very interesting if it turns out that 'Mr. X' is *still* alive and around *now...*"

Gavin squinted at him. "You mean that 'Mr. X' might himself have been involved in Whitcombe's murder?"

Josh said, "Yes," emphatically. "You remember what Erna told us out in Durbanville? Her hunch? That the 'ancient' crime of Shabane's killing could have provided the more recent motive for Whitcombe's killing?" Gavin looked more interested now.

"What if Whitcombe decided to go after 'Mr. X' again? To blackmail him *again*."

Gavin looked sober. "That would give us a second suspect in Whitcombe's killing."

"A third..." Josh looked weary, all of a sudden. "Let's not forget Erasmus."

Gavin finished the remaining half of his beer in a hurry. He scowled, but then patted Josh on the arm.

"Again I say, good work, really. There may be new angles to all this, but they all are valid and require investigation. I want you to keep at this—the 1995 files—and then we can see where it leads us."

They had very little to work on in terms of finding the identity of the mysterious "Mr. X" mentioned in the ANC intelligence letter, with both Whitcombe and Van gone, and Cohen's files destroyed. Gavin had raised the opinion that this might have been intentional, that someone (both Whitcombe and "Mr. X" would be suspects) could have made sure that no record of the contents of the letter would remain. Josh had to agree. Even though the burglars at Cohen's office may have found the bleach in the lawyer's own staff room, it was still strange that they would have used it on the documentation.

Plus, of course, they were very aware of the fact that they didn't have the letter and that they had no clue as to whether it even existed anymore. Gavin thought that they would probably have to build a case against the alleged killer on their own, and that they would probably never get their hands on the letter as evidence to that effect. Thirty-five years on from the events that had transpired in Mozambique, they were both rather skeptical about managing to do so.

Gavin asked the burning question about the only—and sparse—clue they might have, and Josh didn't have an answer.

Josh had also thought of this and had asked Evans what the reference to "B-Camp" meant. This was the single piece of evidence they had from the conversation with Evans that might point to the identity of the killer. They would, of course, arrange a proper face-to-face interview with Evans, to make sure that there was nothing more he might remember, but Josh was not confident. The old man had sounded sharp and he had himself told Josh that this was all he could recall. There was nothing else, apparently, from the contents of the letter that could narrow the scope of the investigation. Evans just didn't know. So Josh planned to ask someone who might. He thought that he should contact the ANC's archives, or the MK Veterans' Association, for an answer.

But then Gavin suggested that he thought they needed help, and that help should be in the form of Erna Pretorius.

She had sent them down this road with her hunch, which now seemed more and more credible by the minute. Gavin was still a huge fan of her investigative prowess, and Josh had little if any reason to disagree.

Gavin said that he would phone her later that evening and ask her whether she could get out of her current duties if she was officially requested through the Serious Crimes division to assist the team here in Knysna on the Whitcombe/Brink case. He would talk to Hlungwane, and he was sure that he could arrange it.

Josh looked skeptical at the mention of Hlungwane. He felt that it might be inappropriate in some way to come from him—this stuff was increasingly going way over his salary level in SAPS—but he thought that the Cluster Commander might not be too keen on following this particular lead. Gavin seemed to read his mind.

"Don't worry, I will be circumspect in dealing with Major-General Hlungwane. He is a dyed-in-the-wool ANC man, and I don't think these theories will make him very favorably disposed toward providing us resources and assistance in running leads." Josh was a bit wide-eyed. The conversation now seemed to be a bit…treasonous.

Gavin smiled at him. "You saw how he reacted about the eNCA interviews. I am not discrediting the man, but I do think that he may lack some objectivity when it comes to political angles. I will think it through and find a way to sell this part of the investigation, and hopefully, Erna's potential involvement. I don't think that I need to provide too much information directly on point, just background. We are simply investigating Brink's past, after all. Period."

He smiled again and then he winked. "Leave it to me. Rank and experience have some benefits."

Josh raised his beer and toasted his commanding officer, smiling himself, if a little less broadly than his C/O.

CHAPTER 21

Josh was working in his own office for a change, cleaning up his files on the laptop for the Whitcombe case, trying to organize everything for quick access. He had transferred the file with his own notes on the Brink trials, which he had typed up the previous day, to his office laptop. He was planning to phone Erna Pretorius before lunch to see whether she might be able to assist him in tracking down the reference to "B-Camp," what he and Gavin believed to be the only viable clue available to put them on the track of the killer mentioned in the mysterious letter.

He had just gotten up to grab a cup of coffee and stretch his legs when his desk phone rang. When he picked it up, he was pleasantly surprised.

"Mr. Gibson, I presume?" It was Erna, up to her old shit. "I've been dreaming of you, you know. You must be a *mad* man in bed, doing everything to the *max*!" He heard her chuckle, and smiled, closing his eyes in exasperation. He was embarrassed that he got the silly *Mad Max* reference.

"Sorry, madam, you must have the wrong number." She laughed on the other end, as Josh told her, again and with shades of their first meeting, to "fuck off."

She sobered up quickly after he greeted her properly, and then she explained the reason for the call.

"Your boss phoned me last night. Told me that you boys are missing little old me over there in paradise. And that you want Aunty Erna to come spend a few days. Is that right?"

Josh said yes, surprised that she was responding so soon. He hoped she wasn't going to turn down their request.

"I am delighted to come visit! I've already arranged with the old ball-and-chain. Francoise says she will miss me like crazy. Of course she will! And no one can blame her. But I deserve a holiday."

Josh smiled. That wasn't exactly what this was about, but he knew she knew that. He remembered that Francoise was Erna's French partner, a winemaker on a farm a little way outside Durbanville.

"That's great to hear," he said, meaning every word.

She started to explain that after phoning her the previous evening, Gavin had emailed a request to his own commanding officer and to hers, explaining that Serious Crimes needed her expertise out in George. The request said that she had already been of value with the formulation of strategy in both the Whitcombe and the Brink investigations, and they were seeing that strategy pay off. Earlier that morning, Hlungwane had, resentfully, agreed to the temporary move.

Shortly afterwards, she saw the email from Brigadier Annette Stevens, who was not only Erna's commanding officer in Durbanville but also, to-gether with her husband, a frequent visitor to Erna and Francoise Pettifer's charming cottage on Contermanskloof Road. Annette was very happy with the proposed arrangement but said that the staff at Durbanville Station and the Crime Intelligence team would miss her while she was gone.

So, as Erna now told Josh, she would be flying into George Airport late Sunday morning, and would stay the following week with Gavin and Jenny out in Knysna. All the arrangements had been made, and Gavin would fetch her from the airport on Sunday around noon.

Josh was happy to hear this. He couldn't wait to sit down with Erna, now that they had so much more information related to her theory. He would love to hear whether she agreed with the deductions he had made—and Gavin had endorsed—based on the Brink court files. But for now, he only needed help with one thing.

He explained to Erna that they had found some information in the documentation around the Senzo Shabane murder trial and Brink's ap-peal. She was delighted to hear this, and he could picture her with a smug little smile, as she had been the one to send them in that direction.

When she asked him about it, he hated having to do it, but he asked whether she would mind waiting for him and Gavin to brief her personally once she was in Knysna. Things were still a bit sensitive, he said, and then he remembered who he was speaking to and decided to tell her that the angle they were looking at might not amuse some higher-ups in the force. He didn't mention Hlungwane, but Gavin had mentioned at some point that Erna knew the man, so he suspected he didn't need to.

Erna grunted, then said it was fine. She would get the story soon enough. She asked how she could help in the meantime.

Josh explained that they were looking for the meaning of a reference—it could be a code—to "B-Camp," in connection with the ANC's activities outside South Africa in the 1980s.

She jumped right in. "Reggie! You need Reggie."

Josh was silent. He wasn't sure whether he'd heard her right.

"Dear Mr. Gibson, don't sound so surprised." He sniggered, as he hadn't said anything. She came back with, "Aunty Erna to the rescue again!"

He laughed as she explained that Reggie was Reggie Nxumalo, an old "friend *slash* contact" she had known for more than twenty years, following a case she had been involved in when she was still working as a private investigator in Cape Town (or, as she put it, "back in the days when I could still use these long and sexy legs that always drew stares wherever I went").

Nxumalo was a member of the MKVA, the Veterans' Association of the ANC's Umkhonto we Sizwe military wing, which had been co-founded by Nelson Mandela after the Sharpeville massacre, when the exiled political organization's leaders decided they now needed an armed extension called the "Spear of the Nation." He currently worked at the Liliesleaf Museum, a Heritage Site located out in Rivonia in northern Johannesburg. Erna said that Reggie was the man to talk to about everything relating to the ANC's military and paramilitary activities outside of South Africa's borders in the 1980s. She promised to email Josh the man's number within the next ten minutes.

After receiving Erna's email, Josh had waited impatiently, only phoning Nxumalo at the museum just after 14h00, having guessed that the man might be on lunch 'till then. The voice that came over the phone was rich in timbre and reminded Josh of the actor John Kani. Josh formed a picture of the man in his mind which looked very much like the actor. He knew it was false, but he couldn't shake it as he spoke to Reggie.

The man sounded sharp for someone in his mid-sixties. Josh silently berated himself again for his ageism when speaking to an older witness, as he had felt when speaking to Stan Evans the previous day.

"How can I help you, Captain?" he inquired after Josh had introduced himself and told the man—who insisted on being called Reggie—that Erna Pretorius had referred him.

Josh laughed heartily when Reggie commiserated with him for having crossed her path in some way or other, with him sounding so young and innocent and all.

"Reggie, we're looking into an old case. The murder of an ANC man in Mozambique in 1986." He could hear the interest in the man's voice when he asked for a name.

On hearing it was Shabane, he whistled. "That was a big one, I remember it. They tried a white policeman for it, didn't they? One of those Vlakplaas devils?" He sounded to Josh like he was spitting the words on the other end of the line.

Josh grunted in the affirmative, and gave him the bare bones of Brink's conviction, and then told him that Brink had been released on appeal in 2017.

"What is your interest in the case?"

Josh explained that Brink was a suspect in the murder of his former legal counsel who represented him back in 1995. So they were really just looking at the Shabane matter tangentially—it was not a main focus of the investigation, and very much on the periphery of the lines they were currently pursuing; but it was something they needed to check, just to cross those t's and dot those i's.

Josh didn't like lying to the man, but he was well aware of the fact that Reggie was MKVA and, recalling Hlungwane's attitude, he thought that the ANC people might be sensitive about disclosing information about the organization. Even though it was the country's governing party, and one would expect a significant measure of transparency, Josh could understand that many members and senior officials might be a little punch drunk after the media blitz of negative reporting in the past few years, especially during and following Zuma's presidency. He also didn't think it was necessary at this point to mention that Brink himself had been murdered. The man remained a prime suspect in Whitcombe's killing, after all.

Reggie said that he thought he understood and asked again how he could help.

Josh explained that they had come across a puzzling—if maybe not an important—reference to something called "B-Camp" in correspondence, dating back to Brink's trial in the '90s. He wanted to know what it meant, and whether Reggie could narrow this down at all.

Reggie was quick to react. "Oh yes, oh yes. Tell me, was this correspondence in any way connected with the ANC operations in Tanzania?"

Josh thought for a second, then said yes, it was. Evans had said that Shabane and his claimed killer had known each other from the camp, and Josh remembered reading a brief mention in the Cohen court file that Shabane had received his training in Tanzania prior to being deployed to Mozambique.

"OK, then that was a reference to Bagamoyo, definitely. You know it?"

Josh had to plead ignorance but was interested to hear more. He recalled some mention of the name in something he had read, or maybe seen on TV, long ago. Nothing to do with the case, but he had definitely heard the name.

Reggie explained that there were a number of ANC training camps that had been set up in Tanzania from the early 1960s. Here, exiled members of the organization were trained, both for paramilitary roles as well as more diplomatic work in southern Africa and elsewhere. This was one of the countries where the ANC and some of their fellow liberation organizations received direct assistance from the Soviets and the Chinese, with many instructors in the camps having flown in from the East to train their revolutionary brothers and sisters in southern Africa. Reggie explained that two of the main camps in Tanzania were Ithumbi, in the west of the country, and Bagamoyo, on the east coast.

Reggie couldn't provide much more information without being asked more specific questions, which Josh couldn't ask at this time. He did inquire as to whether the MKVA still retained membership information on the people who had been trained at these camps, and Reggie said that he would have to search the archives, as he hadn't been asked that in more than ten years. He joked that the ANC had enough problems in the new millennium without people dredging up the ghosts of the past. Thinking of the Zuma years, Josh thought he was probably only half-joking.

Josh asked whether he would check any records that they might still have for the Bagamoyo camp between 1984 and 1986. He remembered reading in the Brink trial file that Shabane had still been in northern Natal in late 1983, and he had, of course, by mid to late 1986 already gone to Beira, where he would eventually die. He asked Reggie to focus on the names of camp personnel, both instructors and officers, as well as trainees, if that kind of information was available. He needed confirmation that Shabane had been at the camp but would prefer a full list of personnel at the time if possible.

Reggie agreed to search the archives and gave Josh his cell phone number. He asked him to give him a couple of days, and phone back on Monday. Unfortunately, the MKVA had not gotten around to digitizing much of their pre-1990 material, so he would have to do a physical search through dusty files. He would do it over the weekend.

Josh objected, not wanting to ask that much of the man whom he didn't know, but Reggie insisted, saying that he was now interested himself. Josh thanked him sincerely before Reggie asked him to pass on his love to Erna, which Josh said he would be too scared to do, as she might get the wrong idea and jump him. He rang off with a smile, to the sound of the man's booming laughter.

Josh was pleasantly surprised that Reggie did not seem suspicious or secretive in any way. He seemed perfectly willing to share any information about the Bagamoyo camp that he might find. He guessed the proof would be in the pudding, and it would depend on what Reggie managed to find and was willing to pass on.

He resolved to spend the evening on Google, finding out all he could about Bagamoyo—both the town and the ANC camp there decades ago. Here was an angle that might, finally, get them closer to Whitcombe's killer, and to connecting the dots between Brink and the advocate. It might also tell them why Brink had ended up with a massive hole in his face and beetles crawling over his lifeless body, in a quiet spot in the mountains above Bain's Kloof.

THERE ARE
MONSTERS
OUT THERE

CHAPTER 22

He was making his way to Thriller Tavern on Pine Road out in New Horizons. They were east-bound on the N2, and he was keeping to the speed limit, fastidiously. It was a Friday evening, after all, and the traffic cops were always out in force looking to bust drunk drivers and speedsters and make their arrest quotas. He was driving the Ford Ranger, with Bangjan Davids in the passenger seat and Skollie September in the seat behind them, in the second row of the double cab. And he was pissed off.

Erasmus had spoken to the owner of the shebeen, a Nigerian by the name of Sam Adeyemi, who went by the handle "Bull," earlier in the afternoon. He was a mountain of a man, and by all accounts an ugly mother fucker, more flab than muscle, but intimidating when you were in his presence. The two of them had agreed a couple of weeks ago that Erasmus would buy about seventy percent of a shipment of heroin that Bull had received from up north, for what Erasmus thought was a pretty fair price, in light of his circumstances. He would be paying about twenty percent over the normal wholesale price, but that was understandable, even if it pissed him off a little. The Chinese had decided to fuck him a few months ago. It made him mad, but he also understood it. This was just business. It was what he would have done if he had found out a buyer was having supply chain trouble, which he'd had a shitload of since July when his fucking meth lab had gone up in flames. He had been struggling for some time to keep things going on the horse side, until he could start producing tik again, his staple product. And now this...

Bull had phoned him earlier in the afternoon to say that the scheduled pick-up this evening might have to wait 'till next week; and that the price had gone up. Erasmus kakked him out. He couldn't wait, although he wouldn't say this to the man. He needed to get stuff to his sellers out in Knysna and George. The junkies were lining up and there were rumors that they were starting to buy from some of the African suppliers (the few who, unlike Bull, were willing to go to the effort of going beyond import and wholesale).

Erasmus prided himself on the fact that his prices were the best. Many years ago, on the Cape Flats, he had learned that there were various ways to hook the crowds of the somewhat addicted and the seriously fucked-up. Some dealers tried to pride themselves on the quality of their shit, seeming to think that the poor fuckers would be return customers as long as you provided the best product on the street, with no product laced with too much baking powder or worse. But Erasmus hated these pathetic end-users, even if they put bread on his table, and he didn't give a shit about their experience of the product, or their health and safety for that matter. From back in the Bonteheuwel days, he had decided that the only thing that mattered was price. The idiots would buy if they could afford it; and if they could afford to buy more often, they would do that too. If the shit killed them, fuck it. It would kill them all eventually, anyway; and there were always new customers. So price was the major factor in his business equation.

Which was why Bull had pissed him off. The man was fucking with him. He had said that there had been some problems getting the stuff to Plett— that they'd unexpectedly had to bribe some extra railway officials on the way down from Johannesburg, which had loaded the front end a lot. So, he was no longer willing to sell at the price he and Erasmus had agreed upon. The overheads were higher. But Erasmus didn't give a shit. That should not be his problem. They were both businessmen. If you ran into shit, you had to take the hit and try to make up any loss on the next deal, or with the next buyer. They had a fucking contract, even if it was a verbal one.

Bangjan looked a bit wary. He knew his boss's moods, and this looked like a bad one. "What are you gonna do to the darkie?"

Erasmus looked at him sideways, then back at the road. "Ek het djou gesê. Ek gaan nie sy kak vattie." He snorted. "I'll sort this poes out. You don't fuck with Erasmus."

Skollie jumped in from the back. "Boss, you know he's got some new guys in? Remember, we heard from the Damons boys out in Kwano, they dealt with him last month. They say he's brought in some muscle from Lagos."

Erasmus laughed scornfully. "Fokoff, Skollie! I told you then, I don't care how many guys he has around him. We'll take them all out if we have to. There's a principle here man, fok."

"But he wants more coil, boss. You gonna pay it?"

Erasmus looked at Bangjan for a few seconds, and then at Skollie in the mirror. He gave that slick smile they were so used to. "Ease up, my bredren. Masekind will provide. I will sort out this kak, no worries. You just keep your hands on your gats and your eyes on those fucking darkie bouncers. Tonight, we're gonna have us a lekker time. And this cunt won't fuck with us again."

Bangjan took the Glock from his pocket and ejected the magazine, then punched it back into the slot and cocked the weapon. Skollie gave a loud whoop from the back and lit a joint, which he passed over to Erasmus after taking a couple of drags, making sure that he didn't get any spit on the joint. Masekind didn't like that and was likely to throw it back in your face, literally.

They arrived at the shebeen just as a SAPS patrol van pulled out of the small parking lot. The cops slowed down and stared hard across at Erasmus at the wheel of the Ranger. He smirked and showed them a peace sign. He was pretty sure the cops knew who he was. He was fucking royalty around here. And if they didn't, they might know after tonight.

The cops just stared, looking like they wanted to get up in his face, but they continued driving, and Erasmus burst out laughing as he took a drag from the joint and blew the smoke in their direction, and then spat out the words "Fuck Babylon" at them. As the van turned left onto Ashwood Road, Erasmus reversed the Ranger into a parking spot next to a rusty VW Beetle of unknown vintage, facing the big vehicle out toward the street.

As the three men walked in, they could hear that the music was already pumping. Just before seven on a Friday evening, the place was packed with people who had come off a hard week of work, with a few bucks in their pockets. They were there to get drunk, and fucked, and fucked-up.

Gavin and Jenny were hosting a dinner at Jenny's gallery for a visiting group of Norwegians. It was a big deal. And a huge coup for Jenny, as there were quite a few upmarket restaurants in the island's Harbour Town development that they could have picked, and it really was great, if a tad surprising, to have the high-profile event held at *Jen-Jen's*.

The original Thesen family who had settled in the area in the late 1800s hailed from Stavanger. They had settled in Knysna quite coincidentally. Arnt Thesen and his brother, Mathias, a sea captain, sailed in 1869 on the *Albatross* to move their large family to New Zealand in the face of an economic depression in Norway. After stopping for supplies in Cape Town, they encountered heavy weather and had to turn back to the continent's southernmost city's port to have damage to the ship repaired. While there, they were approached by traders who wanted them to use the ship to deliver supplies along the Southern Cape coast, and following positive reports about Knysna's potential as a harbor, the Thesens decided to ditch their New Zealand plans and settle in Knysna instead. The family established a successful trading company, which included woodcutting and timber trading. In 1904, Arnt's son Charles Willem bought what had become known as Paarden Island, or Horse Island, in the Knysna River estuary, named after the rare and endangered Knysna sea horse endemic to the estuary. He later established a timber processing plant on the island, which became known as Thesen Island.

This historical connection was now being exploited by the Western Cape tourism department, which had first approached Stavanger's government in 2017 to explore investment in the Knysna area for the upliftment of poorer communities. Stavanger, which is now Norway's oil capital after the largest oil field in the North Sea was discovered there in the late 1960s, had pledged financial support from Norway's global government pension fund, which is the world's largest sovereign wealth fund holding, with assets exceeding 10 trillion kroner—more than a trillion US dollars.

The Stavanger government delegation, accompanied by a few professors from the University of Stavanger, were on a ten-day visit to the Southern Cape, including a few days on Thesen Island to speak with local businesses and Knysna's municipal authorities.

The South African ambassador to Norway and a senior official from the South African Department of International Relations and Cooperation, DIRCO, were also present. Tonight they were treated to a small dinner at the gallery, where the head of the Stavanger delegation, Lars Moen, would unveil a scholarship program that would send ten local, underprivileged young people to the University of Stavanger for undergraduate studies. This was just one small part of the greater cooperation project. Jenny—or rather, her caterer—was serving pickled herring and *Fårikål*, made with mutton. Everyone seemed to be having a good time, and both Gavin and Jenny were delighted.

Moen had chatted to the couple just after the delegation's arrival, and he was a charming person. He joked about the fact that the Norwegian government, and a significant proportion of its people, were embarrassed by the young Swedish climate activist, Greta Thunberg, and how she was shaking up the world. They were very aware of the fact that oil—"old energy"—was fucking up the planet. They were sitting on a shitload of money (pronounced a "*sheetload*") deriving from its extraction, and felt a moral obligation to spend that money on things for the future. Which is why the Stavanger contingent had jumped at the chance of investing in the future of those less privileged, especially on the African continent, where generations had been born into exploitation and neglect, and where those oil dollars could make the most significant difference.

Moen mentioned to Jenny that his city was nowadays one of the art capitals of Europe, and that the city paid famous artists to come and decorate their buildings with graffiti and "street art." He had personally chosen the gallery for the evening's event; he wanted to get away from "the self-destructive environment of the posh restaurant" and rather spend some time in the "self-affirming world of art." His accent was thick, but his speech pleasant, and his general demeanor so endearing that both Gavin and Jenny loved the man, and what he appeared to stand for.

A few minutes later, as he was having a highly amusing discussion on the differences between football and rugby unions with one of the professors, Gavin felt his cell phone vibrate. With regret, Gavin excused himself and stepped outside to take the call. It was AppleMac.

"Colonel, we got a call from Juice Chetty a couple of minutes ago. They think Erasmus is doing a big drug deal out in Plett tonight. A couple of patrol cops spotted him at a shebeen owned by a Nigerian dealer in New Horizons, and Juice says this fits with their intelligence. Apparently. Erasmus has been in contact with the Nigerian on a number of occasions in the past few weeks, and there may be a shipment of heroin coming in."

Gavin was interested. He thought for a second and then spoke into the phone in a low voice as he watched the festivities inside the gallery.

"Apple, we need to get involved with this. But I can't make it, man. Sorry. I've booked myself off for the evening, I'm at an event here on Thesen all night. I really can't skip it; it might be good for Knysna. Phone Josh and ask whether he can go through with a couple of guys." He thought again. "Are Fourie and Fortuin on duty?"

AppleMac said they were not; they were away on a case.

Gavin was disappointed. "OK, ask Josh to go through to Plett. And get Christiaanse and Van Wyk to go along. Do you know whether the Narc boys are sending people? Surely they must."

"Yes, sir, Juice said they have a unit going, and he's going to join them."

"OK, see if Chetty's going from George, then tell Josh to try and ride with him. Let the others make their own way and they can organize themselves when they get to Plett."

Gavin asked him for an update as soon as he had news. He would leave his phone on. Gavin sent a quick text to Josh giving him a heads-up that AppleMac would phone him, and then he turned around and walked back into the gallery, greeted by the sounds of Edvard Grieg and raucous laughter from some red-faced Norwegians at a table near the door.

THRILLER TAVERN, PINE ROAD

19H35

The place was rocking. Loud kwaito *and hip-hop music was blaring from* speakers everywhere, a couple of different songs at the same time. Some people were writhing, others grinding together on the makeshift dancefloor in front of the extremely busy bar. The bar counter was constructed of old house doors, painted bright red and dark green, and set on trestles that didn't look all too steady. Especially as a few clearly drunk people were hanging onto it and swaying to the beat of the overpowering music.

A couple of very obvious prozzies—one in only underwear that left less than little to the imagination—were making eyes at Erasmus and his boys as they walked through the front room, over the dance floor littered with crushed beer cans and cigarette butts. Skollie looked too interested, and Erasmus had to mouth "fokoff" to him as he swept toward the door in the back wall. A very large black man was standing in front of it, picking something out of his teeth with a small penknife. As Erasmus got closer, he saw that the knife was not that small, the man's hand was just huge. The giant, who towered over them, eyed the three Coloured guys through little slits, his brows furrowed to the point of confusion.

Erasmus came up very close to him, and the man pulled himself up to his full height.

"Chill, my man!" Erasmus smiled, and produced a 200 rand note from his pocket, which he waved in the bouncer's face. "We've come to see the manager. Adeyemi. He's expecting us."

The black giant looked at Bangjan and Skollie, then back at Erasmus. He took the knife from his mouth and made it dance between the fat fingers of his hand, staring at Erasmus.

"We're here on business. We come to have an indaba with your boss, man."

In a voice which sounded like he was gargling gravel, and in very broken English, he asked them to take a seat by the bar, while he checked with the boss. Erasmus slipped the note into the man's huge fist, from where it disappeared into a pocket in a well-practiced flash, and then he motioned to his companions to step back toward the dance floor.

Bangjan shouldered his way through a few rough-looking characters in the direction of the bar, where he ordered three Black Label beers from a topless young black woman with a purple weave and a nose-ring. Skollie had grabbed a seat at the bar, and was staring at her tits, smirking and trying to catch her eye. Erasmus grimaced from the volume of the music and the sheer stench of the place. It smelled of booze, urine, smoke, and unwashed bodies. And there was quite a big chunk of naked desperation. These were people who worked long hours, for short money, and probably couldn't see a future beyond this Friday night or the weekend, except for having to go back to the long hours again on Monday to start that whole fucking demoralizing cycle again. And that was just the ones who were gainfully employed.

Erasmus wanted to get out of here and get his business done. He was feeling the start of a headache behind his right eye.

When Bangjan passed him a beer, he downed it in one swig, keeping an eye on the ebony giant by the door. The man was now whispering into a cell phone, no doubt talking to Adeyemi.

Erasmus turned and looked around the small crowd gathered in the room, until his eyes lit on the friendly face he had been expecting. He raised an eyebrow as he saw the man return his look, and the man nodded slowly, twice, then turned away and disappeared behind some other patrons who were starting to really get into the music.

Erasmus smiled to himself and turned back to the giant by the door. When he brought the phone down from his face, his eyes sought Erasmus's, and he nodded slightly, while turning to unlock the door. Erasmus put a hand on Skollie's arm and pulled him up off the barstool, catching Bangjan's eye. Erasmus's companions left their largely untouched beers on the counter, and they were instantly snatched up. Skollie wanted to say something to the guy with the Adidas cap who grabbed his beer, but Erasmus pulled him away.

The giant ducked a little as he stepped through the door behind them, into a dark corridor with glow-in-the-dark stars pasted all over the ceiling. He stopped them with what sounded like the bark of a deranged and pissed-off dog as soon as everyone was through, pulling the door closed behind him. He was so black that Erasmus had trouble seeing his face, until he opened his mouth and his white teeth glistened brilliantly in the low-volume fluorescence. Erasmus was wearing a shiny, bright yellow Bafana Bafana windbreaker—he had thought that showing some allegiance to the piss-poor national football team might go down well with the darkies in the *shebeen*—*and was the only one of the four men who was relatively visible in the passage.*

Erasmus gave a thin smile. "What you want my man, huh? I paid you already. You need some more of the green stuff? We come in peace, my brother."

The man pulled the fingers on his right hand into the shape of a pistol. "You got the guns. Huh? You tell me now and give them. Now. Before you see the boss, okay?"

Erasmus nodded, and motioned to Bangjan and Skollie, who stared at the bouncer with naked animosity, which was wasted in the near dark. And probably would have been wasted on the man, anyway, had they been in broad daylight. But they put their hands in their pockets and each pulled out a Glock, which they handed over grip first. The giant took them, his huge hands closing over the weapons and making them look like toys. He turned to Erasmus, with a grunt.

"I'm not carrying, my man. These are my boys; they do the protecting part. I pay the bills." He rubbed his fingers together as if he was fingering notes, and glanced at the man's pocket where the 200 rand had disappeared.

The man stared back at him for half a minute at least, until it got uncomfortable. Then he nodded, pocketed the two Glocks, and showed Erasmus the way toward Adeyemi's office. As they walked, with the bouncer following in their wake, Erasmus mentioned in passing that they would want the weapons back following their meeting, or his boys would not be happy. There was no response. As they came to a left turn in the passage, the gravel voice spoke up from behind them.

"Me must look dancing floor, all night. You go, there." He pointed to a closed black door at the end of the passage. "You knock. Boss expect you." He turned and disappeared around the corner. Erasmus gave him a few seconds to get back to the door. When he saw light entering the passage and heard the music from out front pick up as the man stepped through the door, he lifted the back of his windbreaker and pulled two pistols out of his pants, handing them to his colleagues. They cocked them and made them disappear in an instant.

Erasmus looked at Bangjan. "OK, you know how this is gonna work, bredren. You look at me, okay? If things get out of hand, I'm taking the fucker down. Be ready. I want those gats out in less than a fokken *second*." Skollie was nodding feverishly. "And keep your eyes open for those Nigerian boys, okay?"

Erasmus turned around and made his way to the black door. He looked back briefly at his men, and giggled. Bangjan's eyes widened. That giggle never boded well.

Then Erasmus knocked loudly, three times, and a muffled voice told him to, "Come!"

CHAPTER 23

On the N2 past the Harkerville turn-off
(en route to Plettenberg Bay)
Friday, 2 December
20H12

Juice was excited, Josh could see it; the man was positively fizzing. They were racing along in a Golf GTI patrol car, sirens going, the traffic opening up smoothly as they crisscrossed the lanes on the N2 toward the western outskirts of Plett. Josh was in the back seat with two of Juice's men. Juice was in the passenger seat, turning around every few seconds to make some observation about what was likely to go down that evening.

AppleMac had phoned Josh about a minute after he had received Gavin's text, and he had told the IT tech that he could meet Juice at the George SAPS Station within ten minutes. When he got to the station, Juice and his men were in the car, the engine running, so he quickly parked the BMW and jumped into the VW.

Josh regretted that Gavin couldn't make it. If the Narc guys could nail Erasmus tonight on a major deal, they would. Josh was looking forward to Erasmus being in custody the next time they interviewed him about Whitcombe. It might make the man less arrogant, even if he brought Chauke along for the ride. But, still, Josh would have preferred to have Gavin along.

They were nearing Plett now. As they turned left at the traffic circle near the Shell garage, Josh saw they were entering the industrial area, where the explosion in July had destroyed Erasmus's meth lab. This was Masekind's backyard, he told himself, and they shouldn't forget it.

Juice asked the driver to switch off the sirens, as they were approaching New Horizons. When they went off, the driver started slowing down, and they traveled on in a somewhat eerie silence. It made Josh nervous after all the noise and the rush of high speed on the N2. They were getting close now.

The three men stepped into a surprisingly large office. It was well lit, and the sudden sensory onslaught after the few minutes in the dark passage made the Rastas narrow their eyes and blink. Erasmus felt the headache coming back.

There were shelves on two sides, one containing what seemed like a collection of tribal military artifacts. There were daggers and pangas, a shield and a couple of spears, and even a homemade revolving shotgun. Erasmus had heard of these but had never actually seen one. The other shelf was filled with an impressive collection of porn magazines, looking as if they went back many years and covered surprisingly diverse tastes.

A large desk dominated the back wall, and was cluttered with papers and takeaway food wrappers. One side of the desk contained a large wood-carved figurine—a traditional Nigerian artwork, Erasmus guessed—of a funny-looking man with a necklace of what looked like sea snail shells around its neck. On the other end was an ornate—but Erasmus guessed fake—red-gold desk lamp. To the left of the room there was a rather grotty-looking couch, with some scatter cushions in colorful ethnic prints.

In a swivel chair behind the desk sat another huge man, even darker than the big bouncer; he seemed to spill out of the chair like soft-serve ice cream melting down the sides of a cone. He was wearing a tank top with sweat stains under his arms and around his neck, under a heavy gold chain. His head was bald and shining like a bowling ball. He squinted at them and rose halfway out of the chair—it looked like quite an effort—and then he focused on the tallest of his visitors.

"Erazzmus?" The voice was surprisingly high, even effeminate, and didn't seem like it could possibly come from the barrel chest from which it emanated. The way he pronounced the name sounded almost American, and he had a weirdly disarming lisp.

Erasmus nodded, and moved forward, stretching out his hand to the man over the desk. "Jah live *my brother.* Mavo!" he greeted him, as Adeyemi's hand grabbed his in that particularly African double-shake.

The man's palm was sweaty and gross, Erasmus thought, and when he dropped his hand, he wanted to wipe it on his jeans, but didn't want to start this off by showing the man disrespect. That would come later.

As Bull settled back down into the creaking chair, Erasmus turned to find his own seat across the desk, motioning his guys to move back toward the door so that he could have a discussion with the man. He had to move his chair to the right a bit to be able to see Bull past the wooden figurine.

As Bangjan and Skollie stepped back, a door behind Bull's desk opened, and two men walked through it. It had looked like the door to a cupboard, so Erasmus guessed it might be a passage leading out to the back of the shebeen. He filed the information away for future reference.

Erasmus heard the rustle of Bangjan's jacket and guessed that he was reaching for his Glock, but Erasmus gave a low whistle through his teeth, and with his left hand behind his seatback signaled for the two Rastas to chill for a minute. The door closed as the two black men, dressed in what looked like cheap suits, walked slowly up to Bull to take station next to the man's chair. He had a broad smile all over his face and spoke in his broken English.

"You don't mind my men, huh? They are part of my business. I make them shareholderzz!" He laughed, in that incongruously high tone. "They just want talk, want part of action, okay?"

Erasmus nodded, but wasn't impressed. He knew these two guys were half of the rumored four-man team of heavies that had joined the Nigerian recently. They were imported muscle, nothing more.

He was gonna give this guy shit tonight. He had come for his stuff. And he had a contract. So fuck the muscle, and fuck Adeyemi.

NEW HORIZONS
20H27

The SAPS units converged on the parking lot of the USave shop on Mimosa Street, about a hundred meters from the shebeen, with all sirens off. They parked and killed their lights. A couple of officers in an unmarked car had cruised by the place a few times in the past fifteen minutes and reported that it didn't look like there was anyone posted outside. So they felt safe parking this close, just around the corner and out of a direct line of sight of anyone at the tavern. There were quite a few revelers having drinks outside on the pavement.

Josh got out of the GTI and walked with Juice to the officers already there, who were looking nervous, excited, or both. There must have been a dozen officers on the scene, and a discussion was taking place about how best to approach the shebeen, and what they would do when they got there. Christiaanse and Van Wyk started talking loudly, and Josh frowned. They were hardly into operational logistics, and the two men were clearly hyped-up on adrenaline. He guessed they were looking forward to this and wanted some action to go down.

Juice took command, naturally, as this was a suspected drug pick-up. Josh was fine with that. His own interest, and that of the Knysna boys, was in Erasmus for the Whitcombe murder. If they caught the Rasta red-handed tonight it would help their investigation. They would have him, and they could sit on him while gathering evidence. He was also very alive to the fact that the Narc guys knew their targets, and how they operated. He was more than happy to relinquish command. He would stay on the sidelines, and he meant for the Knysna boys to do the same. So, he told Christiaanse, in a firm voice, to stand back and let the Narc boys formulate the plan. Christiaanse gave him a dangerous look, one that Josh did not appreciate, but he let it go. The man did as he was told and shut up, with a hand on Van Wyk's arm, motioning him to do the same.

Juice didn't know whether all the units that had arrived in the past few minutes were up to speed with what was happening. He had been on the radio just before they parked, and he began by saying that they knew Erasmus and two men had entered the tavern and left their green Ford Ranger *bakkie* parked outside. This had been nearly three quarters of an hour ago, so it was unclear what was going on inside.

They didn't know whether this was a social call, or whether the three Rastas were simply in there getting drunk, but the information they had received from informants in the past week all pointed toward a deal going down with the owner of the shebeen. They would proceed on that basis. Juice was very aware of the fact that both Erasmus and his guys, as well as the Nigerian and his men—the informants had indicated that Adeyemi received some back-up recently from across the border—would be armed. He did not want to see the SAPS officers rush into a bloodbath. Or worse, to precipitate one by moving in and causing a reaction that might be avoided with cool heads.

The discussion started with Juice and his deputy setting out objectives. Josh listened, and glanced toward Pine Road, where the sound of music, laughter, and the occasional threatening shout of anger from some drunk or stoned patron could be heard. Josh felt a stab of nerves as five officers from the most recent vehicle to arrive came walking up, cradling their R5 selective fire automatic assault rifles and looking ready to rock and roll.

THRILLER TAVERN

20H35

"I don't give a fuck what you want! We have a deal. A fokken *contract!"*

Erasmus was still in his seat, but both his elbows were on the desk and he was leaning forward threateningly, right in Adeyemi's face. The volume of his voice had come dangerously close to a scream. He spat violently to the side, mouthing the words "ma se poes," just loud enough for everyone to hear, although the Nigerians didn't seem to get the meaning.

From the edges of his vision, Erasmus could see Adeyemi's men move their hands down to their waists. He expected they were close to taking out their weapons, but they were also constantly eyeing Bangjan and Skollie by the door, unsure whether making the wrong move might set things in motion. So far, they seemed to have decided to leave things up to the fat man on the other side of the desk.

Bull had both his hands up, the insides of his palms a pretty, princessy pink color. Erasmus smirked at the sight, and the thought.

"Erazzmus, please! We are business people here. We like each other, right?" He glanced sideways at his men, and then turned an imploring look to Erasmus. "At least we understand each other, huh? We do business, we both happy. We all get money! Much money!"

He gave a broad smile, all brilliantly white teeth, but Erasmus noticed that the smile didn't seem to travel north very well, and didn't touch the man's eyes at all. So he returned it, tit for tat.

When he spoke, his voice was harsh. "Bull, you are fucking me around here, my man. You know what I've come for. And you know you get the money immediately on delivery. But now it looks like you won't deliver. And that makes me mad. It makes me pissed off, my black brother."

There was a hissing sound to his voice, and he stared hard at the Nigerian, until Bull broke eye contact as he reached for a pack of Marlboros on the desk and proceeded to light one. He seemed careful to blow the smoke out sideways, and not into his angry visitor's face.

Erasmus decided that this was taking too long. He needed his stuff, and he was starting to think that the Nigerian was just stringing him along. That there was no stuff in the first place. So he slammed his fist hard on the table.

"I've had enough of this now, my man! Are we going to do a deal to-night?" He looked pointedly at the two guys in black suits to the side of the desk. "Or is this going to go badly for you?"

Adeyemi seemed to sense that Erasmus was not going to be patient much longer. He took a deep drag from the cigarette and tipped ash into an ash-tray, and then looked at the Rasta with hooded eyes.

"Erazzmus, I cannot do this. We need more money. Your big hurry makes more expensive." He looked at his men, and there was a twitch to his right eye.

Erasmus saw the man on the left lower a hand to his outside jacket pock-et, which looked like it contained something heavy. Erasmus felt Bangjan and Skollie move. The moment was here.

He stuck out his left hand toward the wooden figurine on Adeyemi's desk, grabbed it, and flung it violently into Bull's face. It was surprisingly heavy, but it flew as straight as an arrow, and hit the Nigerian squarely in the jaw.

Adeyemi seemed to go down in a heap in the chair, as he shielded his face with both hands—too late—and jerked back. The chair turned over backward and dumped noisily onto the floor. The big man hit his head on the wall behind him, and Erasmus grimaced at the sound of the collision. He swore he heard the man's neck shatter.

As Erasmus scrambled forward onto the desk to launch himself toward

Bull, he heard the noise of three shots from behind him and saw the Nigerians blown backward and down. One had his weapon out, and the other one went down without even managing to present arms.

Erasmus landed heavily on Bull's stomach. There was a muffled grunt, but the big man was still disoriented from hitting his head on the wall. Erasmus didn't care; as he lay on top of the Nigerian, he started hitting him in the face and stomach with alternating blows. It was hurting his hands, but he barely felt it.

Bangjan was shouting from behind him. "Fok boss, they down! Hulle is opgefok! Wat maak ons?*"*

Skollie was saying something, but Erasmus couldn't make it out. He stopped hitting the immobile mountain beneath him, and slowly got up. He had hurt his left knee when he had jumped over the desk, but he could stand on it. He could move. He knew that they would have to hurry up and get out of there, and they might have to move fast. The sound from the bar up front was muted back here, but the constant noise from the hypnotic bass drumbeats coming through the walls had probably covered up the shots.

He wasn't done with Bull, and he needed the shit he had come for. But he also knew that there was probably more muscle around, even though his friend on the dance floor had indicated only two.

He turned to Skollie. "Lock the door."

USAVE PARKING LOT, MIMOSA STREET
NEW HORIZONS
20H38

They were ready to roll.

Chetty and his unit would enter from the street through the front entrance of the tavern, with the R5-toting officers right behind them. They were fully aware that the shebeen was packed, and that they would be facing a bunch of drunk, drugged, and probably riled-up patrons. There would be opposition, but these guys were innocents, or at least nominally so. Josh had wanted to say it, but Juice fortunately preempted him by turning to the armed officers and warning them that they should go in with safeties on until he gave the order for them to go live, once they had a better idea of where the players were. Juice had the added pressure of having to show probable cause; they all suspected that this was a major drug deal, but they had no idea where the product was and whether, if at all, a delivery was taking place tonight.

Another two units would cover the sides of the building and the back entrance, in case the Rastas made a run for it. One of those units comprised Christiaanse, Van Wyk, and Josh. They would hang around outside and listen to what occurred inside the shebeen. Their intelligence was that Adeyemi had an office to the rear of the building, and they guessed that this was probably where Erasmus and his boys currently found themselves.

No one was a hundred percent sure about the Nigerians. They knew that Adeyemi had five guys working protection in the establishment and in Adeyemi's operation. One was the local bouncer, a giant of a man, and four guys, obvious muscle, who had recently appeared on the scene. But Juice's undercover captain said they were pretty sure that two of the newcomers were currently in the Eastern Cape for a buy from a Chinese supplier operating near Jeffreys Bay. But the intelligence was not bulletproof, so Juice suggested that they should expect more Nigerians on the scene.

THRILLER TAVERN

20H39

Adeyemi had regained consciousness. Erasmus was right up in the man's grill, raining spittle in his face.

"You fokken *piece of shit! Ha! You don't even know it, kaffir. I would have paid you. But you try to kill me? A'a, no fokken ways, brother. My boys will take all your stuff. I know you brought some in last week. And we gonna take all your cash, your makati, eh? Everything you have here." Erasmus looked around, then back to Adeyemi. "You don't pay me now, right now, you will visit your forefathers. Tonight."*

Bangjan had his eye to the keyhole, looking for any movement in the dark passage they'd arrived through. There was none yet. Skollie had joined his boss on the other side of the desk, after having searched the two dead bodyguards and pocketing their pistols (and the one man's fancy-looking but likely fake gold watch). He was grinning, sensing blood in the water.

Cash was now item one on the agenda, Erasmus told Adeyemi. Once they had disposed of that, they would get to item two. The "horse." And then they would get to item three: deciding whether the Nigerian poes would live past tonight.

Adeyemi's eyes were open and trying to focus on the angry Rasta's face. He was murmuring something Erasmus couldn't make out, but he was pretty sure it was bullshit. He was fully awake and trying to kill time until reinforcements arrived. But Adeyemi didn't know that Erasmus's friend out on the dance floor had confirmed that there were only two bodyguards in the place tonight. There was nobody coming, and "Bull" would be turned into steak tartare tonight if he didn't play along, right now.

Erasmus asked Skollie to make sure that the Nigerian would never walk right again.

He was pleasantly surprised at the speed of Skollie's response. Before he had even received the whole instruction, Skollie had pressed his Glock into the side of Adeyemi's left leg and fired a shot right into the knee cap. The Nigerian bucked, threatening to pitch Erasmus off. The Rasta grabbed one of the ethnic pillows from the couch and smashed it down on Adeyemi's face to hide his scream of pain. Erasmus gave a crazy-looking grin as he had a crazy-sounding thought. The deep red crimson of the pillow totally matched the color of that scream. It must have been destiny.

USAVE PARKING LOT, MIMOSA STREET
NEW HORIZONS
20H42

They were moving in, finally. Everyone seemed on edge, and the waiting around hadn't helped.

Juice had started down the road toward the front of the tavern with his team, followed by the response unit armed with the assault rifles in close support. Josh, Christiaanse, and Van Wyk were running across the field at the back of the USave supermarket building, planning to cross Pine Road and circle behind the shebeen.

As they ran, Josh glanced to his left and saw Juice and his boys walk rapidly across the road and onto the pavement in front of the tavern.

Just before he lost line of sight, Josh saw that the first revelers out on the sidewalk notice the police presence. Some turned away, hiding their faces, while one young guy in a red t-shirt threw down his beer can and started running north up the road. Juice and his unit ignored him, although Josh saw one of the rapid response cops just behind them swing his R5 to follow the man, then turn back, following Juice's lead into the tavern.

THRILLER TAVERN, PINE ROAD
20H42

Erasmus ended Adeyemi's screams by smashing his fist hard three times into the cushion covering the man's face. The bullet to the kneecap had been a good idea. A real conversation-starter.

Adeyemi directed them to a hidden cupboard door below the shelf filled with porn. Bangjan opened it and removed what looked to be roughly 30,000 to 40,000 rands in cash. Bangjan distributed the notes between his pockets and then returned to the door to keep watch.

Erasmus was now working on item two on his new agenda, but Adeyemi seemed to have grown a set of balls since he saw his cash being pocketed by a Rasta enforcer. He refused to say a word about where the heroin was, even after Erasmus had slapped him repeatedly in the face, and grabbed the man by the ears and slammed his head back against the wall. By now, the Nigerian was disorientated all over again, and spit was drooling down his chin, as he stared back at Erasmus with empty eyes, his big, fat lips pursed tightly. He lashed out weakly with his left hand and struck Erasmus a glancing blow to the side of his face.

That was it. The Rasta had really now had enough. There may not have been other bodyguards on the premises, but he was not so stupid as to imagine that no one would suspect something was wrong back here, and come to check things.

So Erasmus looked at Skollie and asked him to fetch one of the pangas off the shelf with the tribal artifacts, and then to come and relieve Adeyemi of the hand that had just had the fucking nerve to slap him.

Again, Skollie acted like a dog reacting instinctively to a tossed stick. He was up before Erasmus had finished his order, and before it even reflected in the Nigerian's eyes, which now opened wide, showing yellow around his black pupils. Erasmus was ready, and he smashed the cushion back into the man's face to drown the new screams of anguish.

Skollie returned with a panga that looked old, and not very well cared for. It had a rusty blade, and the strips of leather that had been tied around the haft had come loose and were swinging around like the big Rasta's dreadlocks as he pointed his chin at Adeyemi's left hand.

Skollie did not hesitate. He grabbed Adeyemi's arm just below the elbow and brought the panga down, slicing the hand cleanly off at the wrist. As the hand skittered away across the floor under the desk, Erasmus could swear he saw it twitching. Skollie threw the blood-smeared panga into a corner, where it rattled to a stop against the wall.

Blood was pumping from Adeyemi's left wrist, dousing Skollie's shirt and the front of his pants. Erasmus was putting more weight on the cushion over the Nigerian's face, as the man tried to wriggle out from under him, screaming his lungs out. Erasmus looked over at Skollie and shouted at him to get the man's arm up in the air to stem the heavy flow of warm, bright-red blood. Skollie did as he was told and was soon sitting with the man's arm in both of his, holding it heavenwards.

Erasmus moved to one side while keeping his grip on the cushion. Then he brought his mouth close to the man's ear and whispered again.

"Where's the heroin? Answer me you fucking kaffir prick, or I will cut off your balls next."

Erasmus knew that he had finally gotten through to the man. He could feel the resistance going out of his body. Bull was nodding his head under the cushion. Erasmus took it away and looked into the face of the man whose eyes now reflected nothing but pain, terror, and resignation. There were tears streaming down his cheeks.

Adeyemi spoke in a halting voice, as he fought for breath. He told Erasmus that the shipment was still in a warehouse in Johannesburg. He had never moved it to Plett, as he'd thought he would have more time to negotiate with Erasmus over a higher price.

The Rasta felt his anger surge. This was what he had feared. The man had fucked him again. He was considering what to do next when Bangjan *called urgently from the door.*

"Boss, fok, someone's coming!" He had spotted a figure moving along the passage, stopping then walking again, like an intruder trying to approach with stealth.

Erasmus put out his hand to Skollie, who placed his Glock in the tall Rasta's hand. Erasmus slipped across to Bangjan and shouldered him aside, dropping his face to the keyhole. The figure was about three meters away from the door.

Erasmus thought quickly. He saw that there were two light switches on the wall. The one was for the office lights. The second, he guessed, was the light for the passage. He unlatched the office door, and then flicked on the passage light. He then violently pulled open the door and raised the Glock.

The man had turned in surprise as the light blazed into life, offering his back to the office door. Erasmus shot him three times in the torso and neck. The figure went down in a heap. It was his friend he'd seen on the dance floor.

He pulled the door closed again and latched it.

Then he walked calmly over to Adeyemi and bent down to look the man in the eyes. He was smiling an ugly smile. The Nigerian looked resigned, which disappointed Erasmus. But he still took pleasure in putting a bullet in the man's forehead.

THRILLER TAVERN, PINE ROAD (AROUND THE BACK)
20H43

Josh, Christiaanse, and Van Wyk were in position. They had managed to sneak over a fence in the cluttered alley between the tavern and the adjacent building. The backyard of the tavern was littered with rubbish and junk, including the wreck of a rusty Ford *bakkie* and some old, bald tires stacked up in a corner. It was bordered on two sides by a chain fence, and on the east side by a low brick wall, unpainted and showing its age, even in the dim light. The back door of the tavern opened to rows of rusty shelves, about three meters in height, which were covered in crates of empty beer bottles, beside a big plastic bin of empty spirits and wine bottles. The air was heavy with the smell of stale beer and rotten food.

Josh had ordered his subordinates to take cover behind the rusted wreck of the *bakkie*, which provided the only real cover. There was a half-moon in the sky and no cloud cover, so even though there was no lighting in the yard, they could see everything quite clearly. He was confident that if anyone exited through the back door, they would be able to identify the person and engage if necessary. They all had their sidearms out, and Josh was on the radio with the units inside.

Juice had just informed him that they had entered the tavern and were calming people down. The unspoken consensus amongst the revelers was that this was a raid on the shebeen. Some guys, drunk already, were getting a bit agitated, and two of the response unit's boys were lining them up at gunpoint at one end of the dance floor. The order had gone to the bar staff to kill the music. The other response unit officers were at the entrance to avoid people sneaking out. Apparently, there was a giant of a guy working as a bouncer, who looked nervous, and Juice was about to question him about Adeyemi's and Erasmus's whereabouts. Juice told Josh to hang on.

As Josh signed off, the back door flew open with a bang against the wall, having clearly been slammed open from the inside. Christiaanse jumped up next to Josh, who stuck out an arm and forcefully pushed him back down into cover behind the rusted Ford.

THRILLER TAVERN, PINE ROAD (ADEYEMI'S OFFICE)
20H43

Erasmus motioned to Bangjan and Skollie to join him at the back door to the office. This was their only exit. They had heard the music go dead up front, and that, together with the guy who had come up the passage from the bar side, made Erasmus think that the boere *had arrived.*

They needed to get the fuck out of there. He was not going to get caught up in a drug bust in fokken *New Horizons. It was a shithole, and the only reason he ever came here was for a young whore he knew, who stayed close to the Community Hall, three blocks up Pine Road.*

Thinking of her made him decide that they should go that way. The Ranger was out of the question now. If they didn't find another, faster way out of the suburb, they might be able to crash there, although she had a mo-erse small outside room that she rented, on a property belonging to an old Muslim guy and his wife. But it was something. He knew they could regroup and get the fuck away from the boere if only they had a few hours to lay up and plan the way out.

Skollie was drenched in Adeyemi's blood, and Erasmus grimaced as he stood aside, not wanting to touch the man, sure he might get AIDS. He barked at Bangjan to check the back door, and the shorter man bent to the keyhole to have a look. It was dark outside, but there was a little light coming from a few meters away.

"I think it's clear, boss. I think there's a short passage that leads outside."

Erasmus nodded, then took a look back at the office. It was like a slaugh-terhouse, with the two Nigerians in suits laying in a heap in the corner just behind them, and the fat fuck in a massive pool of blood against the wall. Erasmus tried to remember what they had touched, what evidence they may be leaving behind, and then said "fuck it" to himself as he thought of Chauke. He could protect him if they ever went to trial for this. It was more important to get the fuck out than to try and clean up. He tapped Skollie on the shoulder, telling him to open the door.

It opened smoothly. The three men moved slowly and cautiously into a short, unlit passage. There was the open door of a small bathroom to the left which smelled terrible. There were some posters on the wall to the right. Beer advertisements. Moonlight shone through a small, dirty window beside the green door at the end of the passage.

Skollie turned the handle and pushed, but the door was sticking. He tried again, with little result. So Erasmus told him to "fokoff," and as he stepped aside, Erasmus came from behind and threw his shoulder into the door. It sprang open violently, and the door slammed against the outside wall, break-ing the silence of what was a peaceful evening out here at the back of the tav-ern, away from the noise in the front room, which seemed continents away. Skollie was still to one side, and Erasmus had startled himself a bit barging into the door, so Bangjan was the first one through into the moonlight.

Josh saw a chubby Coloured man come out into the yard. One of the Rastas, he guessed. He looked to be carrying a pistol in his right hand, and there was movement behind him.

Josh raised his head over the rusted cab and shouted. "SAPS! Police. Hold up and raise your hands! *Staan stil!*"

The man's head turned toward his voice and the hand with the dark pistol was raised and turning in his direction. Josh was about to shout again when he heard movement next to him. Christiaanse jumped up and raised his own weapon, firing wildly toward the man. His shots, half a clip, all went left, and Josh could hear beer bottles shattering.

He cursed under his breath, then hissed "get down!" as he reached across again to pull Christiaanse into cover. He had just grabbed hold of the officer's sleeve when bullets slammed into the Ford—metal pinging against metal—and then into Christiaanse, a split second before Josh heard the sound of the shots. Christiaanse went down in a heap. Van Wyk was now up and aiming his weapon to return fire, but Josh kicked out sideways at him and managed to catch him a painful blow in the thigh with his right boot. The younger officer fell to the ground, swearing in a high-pitched voice, which a part of Josh's mind somehow—quite irrationally—found funny.

Josh looked through the opening of the nonexistent side window of the *bakkie* and could see that the shooter was now a few meters away from the door, two more men behind him. Even though there was no backlight and the figures were still mostly in darkness, he recognized the profile of Erasmus—tall, with long dreadlocks swinging. He immediately radioed Juice, in a low voice buzzing with tension, to tell him the Rastas were at the back, running into the yard, and that they had an officer down. Josh had not had a chance to look over at Christiaanse. The three men were now sprinting toward the brick wall.

Without waiting for a response from Juice, Josh moved to the right and sighted his pistol on the running figures as best he could in the near dark. The smaller guy had stumbled—Josh thought he must have tripped over something hidden in the long, unkempt grass—but he was up again in an instant. He called out to them again, identifying himself as SAPS and ordering them to stop, but they were at the wall, and the overweight guy jumped and, surprisingly, scaled the wall in one smooth movement. Josh opened fire just as the tall figure also cleared the low boundary with ease. Josh didn't know whether he had hit anyone, but he heard the reports of his bullets thudding into the wall, just as the short guy disappeared over it.

Josh was still in the moment, heart hammering. He wanted to follow them but knew he had a man down and protocol demanded he stay where he was. He would also be running in near dark, not being able to see whether they might be crouched on the other side of the low wall, ready to open fire at his approach. He had been slightly deafened by the reports of his own shots and couldn't hear any movement across the wall.

After asking Van Wyk whether he was okay, and getting a sullen mumble, he pressed the button to eject the magazine from his firearm and moved the weapon's selector switch into safety mode. Then he glanced back at the wall where the Rastas had disappeared. They were gone now, in the wind. He knew that they would have to pursue them, and that it would be dangerous, and would doubtless endanger many others along the way. But, to his embarrassment, he felt only relief.

They were gone, and he was safe.

Thriller Tavern, Pine Road (around the back)
20H45

Juice and his Narc unit arrived seconds later, although it seemed longer to Josh. They identified themselves loudly, and repeatedly, as they exited the back door and met Josh halfway toward the old Ford. Josh immediately pointed to Christiaanse, who was lying at the side of the wreck, and one of Juice's men scrambled to his side and knelt down to have a look. Juice had called for an ambulance when he received Josh's call, but it would be a while before it arrived.

The officer kneeling next to Christiaanse looked up and made it clear that there was no real urgency. Two bullets had entered the officer's chest, he was not breathing, and he had no pulse. It was too late.

Josh turned away, sick to his stomach, although he managed to avoid embarrassing himself by vomiting in front of the Narc guys. He knew he had done nothing wrong. And even though it hurt him to think it, he knew that the flashy cop had been the engineer of his own fate. He had not stuck to protocol and had broken cover and fired at their targets without checking with his commanding officer or checking his surroundings.

Josh couldn't blame Christiaanse, and he wouldn't, but he resolved in that instant not to ever blame himself. He had done nothing wrong, except maybe being such a shitty shot when he had fired at the guys by the wall. But he knew that even if he had hit one, or even all three of them, it would have been too late for Christiaanse. So, he would let that shitstorm of self-criticism and sleepless nights take a walk, a long one, one which bypassed him by as wide a margin as he could manage to clear in his head.

KINGDOM HALL OF JEHOVAH'S WITNESSES
SARINGA ROAD
NEW HORIZONS
20H45

Two of the three Coloured males, all in their early twenties, were busy drinking lukewarm beer from cans and sharing a spliff as they watched Jarryd Kleynhans tighten the last two nuts on the front left wheel of his neon purple Honda Civic Type-R. He'd radically pimped this 2003 model in the past three years, though it still showed some rust damage on the back and hatch. They had replaced the wheel, which had gone flat since Jarryd left his job at Build-It in Plett just before 5:00 p.m. and picked up his posse at the Spotlight Night Club, where the two were having a beer and talking *kak* to the bouncers coming onto shift.

They spent most Friday and Saturday nights cruising the neighborhood, and sometimes out to Plett and the beach, in the car, which all three—but especially Jarryd—were convinced was a real pussy magnet. They got lucky most weekends, even if most of the skanks they picked up were repeat offenders. Zane had said just last night—and it had cracked all three of them up—that he would stop using condoms as he was pretty sure that he was the only guy fucking Melissa, Tracy, and Janine with any kind of regularity. Marlon was disappointed that they didn't meet more new chicks, although he supposed for that you probably had to change your grazing patterns once in a while, which they hadn't done in quite a while. Hey, if it works, it works, and even though all three kept complaining, they were getting laid every weekend. Back in school, they would have jumped at that.

They were parked on the lawn in front of the church, where they often hung out while deciding where to go, what shit to take, and which chicks to pick up. The trees surrounding the property shielded them when the odd *boere bakkie* drove by on patrol, even though they knew their movements were pretty well known to the cops. Jarryd had been out of the *tjoekie* for four months now after he was busted for dealing *tik* down at the high school. He had served ten months, but the cops were still keeping an interested eye on him whenever he came into focus. Jarryd kept saying how unfair that was, and they agreed when he called it "racial profiling" and "police harassment."

They blamed it on the ANC and felt that they needed a Coloured political party to run the 'hood, although none of them could identify any viable candidate for the job.

Even though all three were filled with righteous indignation about the *boere*, the music coming from the Honda's expensive sound system was muted. They didn't want to attract too much attention.

But they did.

Kingdom Hall of Jehovah's Witnesses
Saringa Road
New Horizons
20H46

Erasmus heard the soft beat of the music as the three Rastas jogged north from the tavern, threading through backyards on Pine Road. They had jumped a few fences, and encountered only one dog, a Jack Russell. Skollie kicked it in the head and he guessed it was bye-bye doggie. It didn't bark again.

When they scrambled over the last fence and were coming onto Saringa Road, Erasmus heard the muted "doof doof" of the beat, and then the subdued melody of the music coming from the yard of what looked like a church. He had been planning to turn left toward the Community Hall, and the house where Liezl stayed, but decided to check it out.

There was some street-racer kind of purple car, something Japanese, and three young brass who looked like they were on their way to a party, drinking beer and having a good time. The one was seemingly arguing with the other two, and Erasmus heard "new pussy!" shouted. He recognized the oldest of the three. He was a small-time dealer who had worked for the Funky Guys for a short while, and had been busted about a year before, selling drugs at a school in Plett. He couldn't remember the guy's name, something with a "G" or a "J," he thought, but he remembered that the cops had taken too much shit off the little doos when they busted him, and that had cost him money. Erasmus gave a sign to Skollie and Bangjan to keep down, and they stopped at the boundary of the church premises, seeking shelter behind a tall pine tree. Erasmus thought for a few seconds.

They needed the car, but this dude might recognize him. Erasmus wasn't too worried about it. Once a car theft was reported so close to the tavern and so soon after all the shit went down, even the fokken stupid boere would make the connection. But he would still prefer not to be identified right off the bat. So he took his long dreadlocks in hand and tucked them inside the back of the Bafana Bafana jacket he was wearing, so that a casual observer wouldn't be able to spot the length of his hair. Then he smiled at Bangjan, and at Skollie, and told them that they were gonna get a car, right now, and get the fuck away. He grabbed Skollie and whispered to him to shut up before he could object, then tore a strip of cloth off the lower part of the back of Skollie's shirt. Erasmus then tied it across his face like a mask and winked at his boys. Let's do this.

They strolled up to the men at the car. Erasmus didn't want them to be seen running, and seem desperate, like they were being chased. As they approached, Marlon was the first to spot them, and he whistled at Jarryd to check it out, they had visitors. He wasn't nervous, not yet. He should have been.

The results of the evening's events were disappointing, and the fallout promised to make life difficult for the SAPS units involved in the coming weeks.

The first disappointment was that Jerome Erasmus and his boys had gotten away. There were no arrests at the shebeen, but there were a few dead bodies. Photo identification by the waitress at the bar and the big bouncer were definitive. It was definitely Erasmus and his men who had entered the owner's office earlier that evening.

Even though they could cover identification, SAPS didn't have any physical evidence of the suspected drug deal, as nothing had been found on the premises or in the vicinity. This was of special concern to Juice and his men, as their involvement in the night's activities had been based on the intelligence they had received, all threads of which promised a large movement of heroin. But there were no drugs found, and after a search of Adeyemi's office, no money.

And then there was the significant fallout, on the SAPS's side, of dead bodies. Two of them were SAPS officers.

Apart from the Nigerian and his apparent bodyguards, Christiaanse had died on the scene. There would be hell to pay for that, Josh knew, as IPID would invariably launch an investigation into their tactical response. Josh was thinking too many things at once, all of them troubling.

Had they been in the right location? Was the old, rusty Ford the safest spot to find shelter and a firing position in order to attack or defend against the gangsters exiting the tavern? Could he have done more to keep Christiaanse safe from harm? Did his fucking pathetic attempt at shooting—and completely missing—the three Rastas mean that he had single-handedly screwed up the night's operation? He didn't want to think about that too much.

He had managed to send a WhatsApp message to Amy to let her know he was okay. He suspected the media would run something about the operation first thing in the morning, and he didn't want her to hear about it from someone else. He knew he wouldn't be returning home that night. He'd probably stay holed up at either the Plett or the Knysna SAPS station to ride this out.

She didn't know where he was. He hadn't had a chance to tell her when he'd left their flat in a hurry. He'd just said that he was needed in Plett. He was glad he hadn't worried her, but Christiaanse's death was a wake-up call. Things could have been a lot worse. Amy could have been receiving some really bad news right now.

The second SAPS officer who was found in the passage between the dance floor and the office had been identified as Captain Gershwin Carels, a Narc officer based out in George. He was identified by one of his colleagues, who had been riding with Juice for the operation. Juice confirmed the identification.

Josh recognized the name. This was the man whom Gavin had asked to inform Erasmus about the interview the previous weekend. And the man Josh had suspected of working with Erasmus and warning him up front of the cops' suspicion of him in the Whitcombe murder.

So far, nobody had been able to explain Carels's presence at the she-been. He had not been officially on duty. He may have been there coincidentally, having a few drinks or looking for a good time, although he lived out in George. Thriller Tavern was definitely not his local hang-out.

Or he may have been there on the instructions of Erasmus. Although this last option didn't explain his killing, something looked wrong. They would have to investigate. And IPID was, by all accounts, already on it.

CHAPTER 24

It was little more than a fucking shanty, an old cabin in the forest that was falling down around itself. It was hardly the place he would have picked to spend a few quiet days out of the spotlight. He liked to do things in a more five-star kind of way—and he was already regretting the decision to come here. But at least it was off the beaten track. It was a shithole, but it would serve its purpose.

Shaileen had told him a couple of months ago about this place, where she had grown up. It had been her grandfather's house, but her elderly parents were still living there.

This kind of poverty reminded him of his upbringing in Bonteheuwel and Mitchell's Plain, and those were memories he had made a great effort to bury. It wasn't like Shai was poor. She had some money (a lot of which he had given her) and was living the "high life" in Plett, doing some escort duties in the holiday months, taking a few euros from some faggoty tourists for the odd blowjob and bragging rights of having had some fun with a relatively classy local. He knew the Germans, especially, loved to slum it out here, but recent years and all of those crime reports had made most of them a bit wary.

But seeing this piece of shit place now, he thought that he would, from now on, probably smell it on her every time he saw her; poverty and desperation, his own past.

He had put the old folks in an Uber, with a couple thousand rands in cash in the old man's pocket, sending them off to a guest house near the Beacon Isle Hotel for the week. And he had brought Bangjan and Skollie along; not because he liked to spend time with them, not at all, but because he couldn't trust them being back out on the street. It would not take much for the cops to roll one or both of them on the shebeen thing, and to come calling out here not too many hours later.

The girl was a risk. He didn't like having her out here and knowing where they were. He sipped his glass of brandy as he walked from the small kitchen through the tacky beaded curtain—having to shake his head to disentangle beads from his dreadlocks—into the only bedroom.

She was on her back on the bed, naked, her head propped up on two pillows. She was wearing a reddish-brown wig, which was sitting askew. Skollie was standing next to the bed, wearing only his favorite Bob Marley t-shirt, his little dick in her mouth, and she was making enthusiastic noises as she sucked him. Bangjan was naked, planted on his knees on the bed between her thighs, deep inside her and pumping away while he was kneading one of her huge tits in his hand. His rolls of fat were jiggling with every movement.

Erasmus took another sip of his drink while he watched them. Skollie looked over his shoulder and asked his boss if he wanted to join in. Erasmus grunted an emphatic, "No," even though he could feel himself getting hard, and he turned slightly away, so they wouldn't see his erection through the thin material of his pants.

"You know you guys are gonna fuck this up, right? This bitch is gonna bring the boere out here as soon as she leaves. I can smell it on her."

Bangjan shook his head. "No boss, she gonna be a good girl. Right?" He looked in Stacy's direction and gave her nipple a hard squeeze.

She opened her mouth and Skollie's member dropped out, and she squealed in pain. "Nee man fok, oubie! Moenie my seermaakie!"

Bangjan countered with, "Maybe we won't let her leave," while Skollie was stroking himself and looking pissed. She smiled and licked her lips, trying to look sexy, with her left hand going up to pull the wig straight. Maybe she was anticipating more money for a longer visit.

Erasmus was amused. She was not much older than sixteen, he guessed. She had assured Bangjan that she was twenty, a hairdressing student at a nearby technical college, who just needed some extra pocket money and was looking for a nice gentleman to "bless" her. But none of them were under any *illusions. He had paid her five hundred rand when Skollie had picked her up on the N2 near Kwanokuthula, after they arranged it over the phone. It was a burner, which Erasmus always carried around in case he needed to make a call or two and not have the Narc squad listen in or follow him around. Her number had come from an ad in the* Plett Herald's *adult entertainment section, where she was listed as "Busty Stacy." Erasmus thought that at least it hadn't been false advertising, as was so often the case with these bitches.*

Skollie and Bangjan had taken the drive out to pick up some booze and the pussy. They didn't have any stuff on them, except for a bit of tik *that Skollie had been carrying when they went to Thriller Tavern. They were trying to keep that for later, until someone could get away to pick up some stuff in Plett.*

Skollie's dick was back in her mouth, and he was squeezing both her cheeks in his hand, maybe trying to ensure she wouldn't drop him again. She was trying to sound enthusiastic, but Erasmus could tell the moaning was an act. He didn't care. She was a bargain at the price, to keep his boys happy and occupied, and not bitching as the realization slowly kicked in that they were being hunted and that they would have to give up their lives as they knew them for a while.

He shifted his equipment around in his pants and strolled out of the room to pour another drink and light a cigarette, accompanied by the increasingly loud noises from the bedroom. He was thinking that she was earning her money now, and that was good, but that he would get a little extra out of her later. He had a lot more cash on him, most of it from Adeyemi's little slush fund, and he would give her some danger pay. She would need it.

He gave that little schoolgirl giggle as he thought how much the fat Nigerian doos *would have hated knowing he was paying for Erasmus's entertainment.*

Knysna SAPS Station
Saturday, 3 December
20H13

They were seated in Gavin's office. There was a grim silence, and a tangible air of desperation, as Gavin, Josh, and Juice tried to figure out just what the hell had gone wrong the previous night. They had received very few answers all day, and those they did get, they didn't like.

That morning, they had decided to base the command center at Knysna Station to deal with the inevitable fallout. The two younger men had slept on bunk beds at the station, after checking the reports coming in from all units until about 04h00. It was closer to Plett anyway, just in case they needed to pop out there again. Gavin had joined them just after 08h00 that morning, having had a late night with Jenny at the gallery party but also having been up since 05h00 to start dealing with the shit that had gone down.

They received news of the stolen Honda late the previous night, and a BOLO had gone out just after 00h30. No results so far. The three Coloured guys couldn't provide anything of real value, beyond the description of the tall Rasta with the long dreadlocks and the two other men, one fat, and one small and shifty looking. It was definitely Erasmus, and Juice had sent away for a file from the provincial Narc unit that might identify these two of Masekind's closest acolytes.

The three Rastas had gone ballistic on the group of young Coloured men. According to their statement, Erasmus hailed them, then started talking about the weather, of all things. Marlon Jacobs made a sarcastic remark, after which the short guy, who had circled around the car, had grabbed the tire iron Jarryd Kleynhans had used just minutes before to change the car's wheel and hit Zane Davids in the side of the head with it. The young man immediately went down. Erasmus then pulled a pistol and put it to Kleynhans's head. In the process, some of his dreads came loose, and Kleynhans thought he recognized someone from his past. But he was not willing to be more specific.

The Rastas were not fucking around, and they wanted the Honda. Kleynhans managed to dig the keys out of his pocket and handed them over. The Rastas left in a hurry.

Davids was okay. His left cheekbone was broken, and he had a concussion, but the doctor was sure there wouldn't be permanent damage. The other two were just traumatized.

They didn't manage to get any report on the Honda within the first

twelve hours, and chances were that the car was already hidden somewhere, but they would keep looking. Josh was committed to finding the
Rastas. He had finally seen them in action. He wanted now more than
ever to be the one to put Erasmus away.

HARKERVILLE
SUNDAY, 4 DECEMBER
15H42

*He had sent Bangjan and Skollie to the local shop. He hoped the place would
be open on a Sunday afternoon. Harkerville was a small, out-of-the-way
community, made up of a few Coloured families who had lived in the area
for many years—like Shaileen's grandfather and parents—and some more
recent inhabitants. Rich people who had bought large properties out here,
and built huge "environmentally friendly" homes, some of which looked like
prehistoric alien spaceships. There was no real community, and no real village, but there was a small general shop a couple of kilometers from the
Davids's cabin. Erasmus's boys were under orders to get them something
to make for dinner, and something to drink. The non-negotiable part was
plenty of cigarettes, a carton if they could get it, and they were to talk and act
like they were just a couple of guys driving through, not staying in the area.*

*When they were gone, Erasmus poured himself another drink. He was
thinking to himself that he was drinking far too much out here as he walked
into the bedroom. She was lying on the bed, half asleep, playing lazily on
her cell phone with hooded eyes. He walked to the bed and took it from her.
She started to complain, and he slapped her hard in the face with the hand
holding the phone. Then he threw it on the scarred bedside table. Her eyes
opened wide, and then she looked as if she might respond. But she saw his
crooked smile and shut up, and averted her eyes, coyly, asking him whether
he wanted to naai.*

*He took a long sip of the drink and pulled the thin fleece blanket that
covered most of her off the bed. He glanced down at her body, and against
his better judgment once again found himself getting an erection. Her legs
and arms were bruised; Bangjan and Skollie sometimes got a bit rough. But
those large breasts did something to him. They seemed so out of place on her*

young and slim body. He rubbed a hand over his cock through the denim of his pants, then downed the rest of his drink. Her eyes dropped to his crotch and he saw her notice his size. He gave her a knowing smile and threw the empty glass violently against the wall behind the bed.

She gasped and swore, jumping up to escape the shards of glass showering the bed.

He laughed wildly, shaking with pleasure, as he grabbed her arm and pulled her so she was standing beside the bed. She trembled, those large breasts jiggling. He grabbed one and squeezed, hard, then slapped it. She gasped again, this time with some pain, and started to sob. She was afraid. And he loved it. This was gonna be fun.

He ordered her to put on his Bafana Bafana windbreaker. She was naked underneath. He pushed her into the kitchen and told her to sit on the floor, while he poured himself a drink.

He then made a show of letting her see as he took a condom in its shiny silver packet off the counter and put it in his jeans pocket with a wicked grin. After taking a sip of the drink, he bent down toward her and rubbed his swollen crotch against her cheek. She automatically, if a little feebly, reached up a hand to take out his cock.

But he straightened up again, suddenly, so that she dropped her hand, and then he lit a cigarette and ordered her to get up. He pushed her out of the front door, and then toward the side of the cabin, where the forest lurked only meters away. It was quiet out here; he couldn't hear a single bird or car. The wind was coming up, and there was a steadily rising shooshing sound as the boughs of the pine trees swayed. They walked. He steered her with a firm hand on her right shoulder, his mug of brandy in his left hand, and the cigarette parked between his lips.

About twenty meters into the treeline, he squeezed her shoulder and brought her to a halt, turning her around. The tears were now flowing freely down her cheeks, and she was murmuring something he couldn't make out. He slapped her across the cheek again, telling her to speak up. She sobbed loudly.

"Meneer, 'seblief, moenie my seermaak nie. I'll do anything!" She struggled for breath. "Please don't hurt me, sir. I have two little ones, waiting *for me at home, please* meneer."

He burst out laughing. The smoke from the cigarette caught in the back of his throat and he started coughing, spitting out the cigarette, which fell amongst the pine needles at his feet.

He doubled over, coughing harder, and she suddenly broke left and started running. He straightened up and watched her go, an ugly smile replacing his grimace, as he bent to carefully place the mug of brandy on the ground. Then, just as carefully, he put his foot on the lit cigarette and mashed it into the soil—don't want to start a forest fire, do we?

And then he broke into a run after her, his long dreadlocks trailing behind him as he moved with a terrible purpose and surprising speed. He just loved the chase.

CHAPTER 25

Josh had been up since just after 06h00. He was struggling to sleep. Indications were that there would be shit hitting the fan from Christiaanse's death, and he was expecting a call from Gavin any minute to tell him that IPID wanted to interview him. He was nervous and agitated at the prospect of an investigation into his conduct, at this point of their investigation into Whitcombe's murder. Both he and Gavin were still painfully aware of the fact that they had failed to establish any definitive link between the Rasta drug dealer and the killing of Mark Whitcombe. And yet they had been riding along with Juice and his guys.

But SAPS's biggest concern right now seemed to be Captain Gershwin Carels's presence on the scene. Juice had recalled Gavin's questions about the officer at their first meeting and had been obliged to share this information with the IPID team, headed by a Major Sello Motsepa. It seemed that Motsepa's guys were now actively suspicious of Carels as a possible Erasmus and Funky Guys collaborator, someone who might have been deep in the Rastas' pockets. Josh imagined the ugly media reports should that turn out to be true.

Josh was turning on the TV, not wanting to wake Amy, when his cell phone beeped with a text message. He had saved Reggie Nxumalo's number under "Reggie ANC." It was a message asking Josh to phone him whenever he had a chance. Josh punched in the number immediately and heard it ring on the other side.

Reggie sounded a lot more subdued than he had been when they had talked a couple of days before, as if the man had a cold.

"Captain Holland, thank you for phoning. I hope all's well your side?"

Josh wasn't about to share his personal and professional turmoil at the moment, so he tried to sound upbeat as he greeted Reggie and asked him to please call him Josh.

The news was not great. Reggie reported that he had gone through all the relevant files he could find, mostly hard copies filed in the Liliesleaf archives. As requested, he had checked the records on the Bagamoyo training camp for the years 1983 to 1986. There was a lot less information than he had suspected.

He had a theory that some of the material may have disappeared over the years—and he sounded frank when he told Josh that his personal opinion was that some of his colleagues in Umkhonto we Sizwe may have destroyed records in the early to mid-1990s. Apparently, at the time of the Truth and Reconciliation Commission hearings, there had been some talk of push back from the old Apartheid security forces and their officers who were being investigated. A fear that the legal teams might start to subpoena information from the liberation movement, and information about the training of what they were calling "terrorists," might open things up to mudslinging from the other side. So a lot of information was buried.

It sounded plausible to Josh, but he was still disappointed. All Reggie could give him was confirmation that Shabane had been in the Bagamoyo camp, roughly between September 1984 to July or August 1985. There was no other information regarding staff and other recruits during Shabane's stay, or, at least, Reggie said he was uncomfortable providing the little information he had found for certain months within that time frame, as he personally thought it was unreliable. And he also said that, seeing that a lot of the files had been seemingly "cleansed" in recent years, it would be irresponsible to provide only part of the picture, when more relevant information may have been removed, and that this might prejudice any persons whose names were still contained in the files and traceable today.

Josh thanked Reggie profusely, as he had done on Friday when they had first spoken, but something was bothering him as he put the phone down.

What Reggie had said made sense to Josh, but he had a nagging doubt in his mind as he just sat on the couch in front of the blank TV screen saying "no signal." The man had sounded different, tentative, cagey. Josh had a feeling that Reggie had lied to him, or at least had not told him the whole truth.

He was thankful that Reggie had at least confirmed Shabane's presence in the camp. But something didn't seem right. Josh guessed that Reggie may have found something a little too close to home. Whether it involved Reggie, the MKVA, or the ANC, Josh didn't know. But something was definitely off. He was charged up, more than ever, to find out the truth.

Gavin had told him on Friday that he had contacted Hlungwane and obtained approval to send someone out to Tanzania to follow up on the alternative murderer theory regarding Shabane. He also spoke with Hlungwane about their theory on Brink's appeal case, which Gavin explained might point to a motive for Brink having dispatched the advocate.

Gavin had asked Josh to be ready to move at short notice as soon as he had the travel sorted out with the finance department. But with everything that had happened since Friday night, Josh didn't know if he was still on for the trip. He would see Gavin in a couple of hours when they met Erna Pretorius at George Airport. He was hoping he would find out then.

He thought to himself that he wouldn't mind getting the hell away for a couple of days, if only to avoid the IPID investigation.

THE FAT FISH RESTAURANT
YORK STREET, GEORGE
12H32

Gavin ordered for them all, which earned him a mock tirade of feminist indignation.

They were sitting outside on the veranda, and the weather was nice. Erna was in high spirits, cozied up to the table in her kick-ass, rock 'n roll-adorned wheelchair—with stickers guaranteed to offend almost all members and factions of the general population—having a Black Label beer, while Gavin and Josh decided to stick to coffee. It turned out that both men had slept badly for two nights in a row, and by midday Sunday they both needed a caffeine lift.

Erna had come in on a SAPS flight that landed a little after 11h30. She was going to stay with Gavin and Jenny in Knysna for the week, maybe longer if her assistance was further required, but they decided to have lunch and discuss the case with Josh here in George. Especially as Gavin had the good news, for Josh, that the younger man was to be on a plane to Dar es Salaam in Tanzania the following morning, to check out the Bagamoyo angle on Shabane and Brink.

Josh still enjoyed being around the older female officer, and she was her inimitable self, as always. She joked with him in the car all the way from the airport and had finally needled him enough to tell her about Amy, at which she had predictably acted like she was throwing her toys out of the cot over the "competition." She had insisted on seeing pics and had then asked them to stop so that she could phone Francoise back in Durbanville and "call the whole thing off," as she needed to be with this young, blonde bombshell in George. Josh needed that, just to give him the opening for the obligatory "fuck off" greeting they seemed to have cultivated, and afterwards they were all comfortable in their somewhat more than collegial bonhomie. But there was serious business afoot now.

Gavin opened the floor. He told Erna the details of Friday night's fuck-up at Thriller Tavern, and how Erasmus and his men had escaped, with a significant loss of life both on the side of the Nigerian drug dealers and SAPS. This was a huge embarrassment for the police, and they were expecting big shit down the road. He said he would elaborate on that later.

Juice had since communicated the news that they had managed to identify the two Rasta henchmen as 32-year-old Elroy "Bangjan" Davids and—as Juice put it, "wait for it"—25-year-old Darwin "Skollie" September. Juice joked that September's childhood must have been especially disappointing, "going from 'Darwin' to 'Skollie' in so few years and all."

The two men hailed from the Judah Square Rastafari settlement, where they suspected Erasmus had met and recruited them. Their records were grim: there were stints for armed robbery, drug dealing, and attempted murder for both men, and a couple of rape charges for September, who seemed to have managed to dodge them in both cases, because witnesses failed to testify. The word on the street was that they had both buried a few bodies in their past, though still less than Erasmus. These guys were currently in the number one spot on the Southern Cape SAPS hit parade, and the search was intensive and widespread.

They had, of course, found the Ford Ranger registered in Erasmus's name in the parking lot of the tavern, and they knew that the Rastas had escaped on foot and then stolen the Honda at the church, but in which direction they had gone was unknown. The first roadblocks had only gone up about an hour after the BOLO had been issued, so they had quite a radius around Plett to cover.

A warrant for Erasmus's house in Joodse Kamp had been issued in the early hours of Saturday morning and the property was only searched around 06h00. The search unit had little to report. Three young guys, obviously junior soldiers who guarded the place, had been arrested and were currently being questioned, and some Mandrax pills and a large quantity of marijuana were seized. Erasmus wasn't really known for dealing in dagga, so the feeling amongst the SAPS people was that this was probably more of a kindergarten situation, with Erasmus allowing the young guys to get into trading lightweight shit as a means to develop skills he could exploit in future.

The only meth they found looked like it was the young guys' private stash, so this aligned with Juice's intelligence about Erasmus's inability to manufacture the drug after his lab explosion; unless it was just being stored somewhere else. Juice and the Narc boys were still convinced that Erasmus was on the prowl for a deal to buy *tik* from elsewhere and get his street-level supply capacity rolling again. The general consensus was that Erasmus was hemorrhaging money.

The officers out in Joodse Kamp also reported that the fancy Audi was nowhere to be found. They had been in touch with the Audi dealership in George but had been told that they couldn't track the car on GPS through its electronics. Juice wasn't sure whether they couldn't or just wouldn't; the dealership manager claimed that doing so would violate the client's privacy. They also traced the insurance company and had managed to speak to someone there after hours. But they were told the Rasta had opted for a more expensive insurance premium by declining to install a GPS tracker in the sports sedan. That was probably how all drug dealers roll, Josh thought.

The RS5 Sportback was a priority in the search, as it was a relatively rare vehicle and should be easy to find. Or so they all hoped.

A unit was also tasked with tracking and shadowing Erasmus's young girlfriend in Plett, as they expected he might show up there any time or that she might be hiding him already.

They would just have to wait for developments. In the meantime, they needed to keep up the momentum in the Whitcombe investigation, so Gavin wanted to talk about other angles.

Erna was glad and, Josh felt, justifiably proud, that her earlier suggestions to look into the history of Brink and Shabane seemed relevant. Gavin had told her about Josh's research and how he had unearthed a potential alternative killer in the Shabane case. Josh felt like a schoolboy being praised by two senior and much-respected teachers. It felt good.

Gavin turned to Josh. "Are you okay to leave tomorrow morning?"

"I can't wait. I really think this is where we should be looking now."

He saw Gavin's raised eyebrow and the slight lift of one end of his mouth, and knew that he, Josh, had been gung-ho for Erasmus as the Whitcombe killer all along.

"Don't get me wrong," Josh continued. "You know how I feel about the Rastas for this, but I think once we get a name—if we get a name— to put into the equation on Shabane's killing, it might get us closer to finding out how Brink was really involved with Whitcombe." He sipped from his coffee mug. "Meaning, specifically, why Brink may have been taken out, in what we both think was an execution. Right?" Gavin nodded, and Josh saw Erna also agreeing, as she mumbled, "Me three."

She was next to speak. "I support this one hundred percent. It was just a hunch, but I still feel—and even more now—that there seems to be some substance to it."

She took a big sip from her beer, as her face changed into a scowl and she frowned intently at a classy society lady in her mid-fifties at a neighboring table, feeding scraps from her plate to her expensively coiffed poodle. Josh heard her say, "Fucking savage," under her breath before she continued.

"The only way we can nail this alternative Shabane theory down now is for young Mr. Gibson here to go find us a name and a motive. Without that, we are going to run into a brick wall with the Brink angle, I think." She looked at Gavin for confirmation, which he gave with a nod. She continued. "You know that old saying that you can't unring a bell?" Josh nodded.

"You've opened this can of worms, my young lover. As long as this alternative possibility hangs in the air, like some particularly unpleasant fart, I don't think it would matter much what else you might discover on the Brink/Whitcombe relationship, and whether Brink was the guy who did him. Even though the Apartheid *doos* is out of the picture now, and we won't see some messy, high-profile trial, should it turn out that Brink was our guy, if—*when*—this Bagamoyo angle eventually gets out there, it will forever cloud the outcome of your investigation. Mark my words, I am a genius."

Gavin didn't look happy, but he agreed. He turned to Josh.

"Josh, I need to be up front with you. It's not just the Shabane thing that has me happy to see you leaving for a few days. I know you're worried about Friday night, and the IPID."

Josh nodded slowly, looking grim. He hadn't known he was such an open book.

"Son, I've gone through about a dozen IPID—or their former equivalent—investigations, in the last twenty years or so. Everyone is always second guessing what we do. Don't get me wrong, they have their job to do, and I agree with their mandate, I really do, but there is nothing more demoralizing to a good cop than being caught up in such an investigation. It is the dictionary definition of a shitstorm. I think you're feeling it already, doubting yourself, and what you did. Right?"

Josh swallowed hard as he nodded, then produced a somewhat scratchy, "Yes," from his throat.

Erna was nodding along merrily, while actively trying to puff smoke from her cigarette in the direction of the poodle-feeder.

"Sorry to break this to you," Gavin continued, "but Penny Maseko from eNCA phoned me this morning on my way to George, asking about possible IPID involvement in 'violent police action' in Plett on Friday. She had accurate numbers on the body count, although I don't know whether she has Carels's identity and backstory yet. That's the thing that might fuck us up.

"The vultures are circling, my boy. And you—we—do not need the distraction right now. So go up there, clear your head, and think of the mission. We can't do anything about the past, except uncover crimes committed there, so that they can lead us to an arrest—and a conviction—in the future. What was that old movie? Timecop? That's what you are here, son." Gavin smiled at him.

Erna stubbed out her cigarette and told Gavin, in an exaggerated English public school accent, "Well said, old chap." She touched Josh on the arm and told him to buck up, be a *lekker ou,* and go do his job.

Josh tried a confident grin and thanked them both. After Friday night, he wasn't quite so sure that he knew exactly how to "do his job," in all respects; but he sure as shit was going to try.

On the way to drop him at the flat—Josh worrying all the time about how Erna meeting Amy would turn out—Gavin told Josh to phone Lucinda Gasant on her cell. She had arranged Josh's booking on an early morning flight from Cape Town International on Tuesday and had also arranged for a SAPS transport officer to drive him through to Cape Town on Monday afternoon. He would stay Monday night at a hotel near the airport, in Bellville. Everything was arranged, but he had to get the details from her.

As Gavin and Erna drove off, they couldn't have known that Josh would not be leaving the next day.

MAN ON
THE RUN

CHAPTER 26

When the phone rang, Amy was awake. Gavin gave her a quick greeting, apologized for the hour of the call, and then asked her to hand the phone to Josh.

Amy elbowed him, and he woke with a start. He wanted to elbow her back, but she gestured at the phone.

Josh took the handset, frowning, and then said a croaky, "Hello?"

Gavin told Josh there was news, and it was big. "Erasmus seems to have turned up." Josh raised his eyebrows, his brain kicking back into gear as Gavin continued to say that the Tanzania trip would have to wait.

Josh could hear a smirk in Gavin's voice. "Remember how cute he was with us the other day in the interview? When he was so happy to tell us about his 22-year-old *stukkie* out in Plett?"

Josh nodded, yep—then he realized he was on the phone, and said, "Yes."

"Well, it seems that her parents stay out in Harkerville, in the forest. It looks like Erasmus stayed there since the shebeen thing on Friday, and then left there early this morning. The Narc guys only got a stakeout going yesterday when they managed to trace her to her parents, and they only spotted Erasmus when he left. And then lost him." Gavin swore softly. "Fortunately, he's been picked up again."

Josh sighed. He had been about to explode at the news that the gangster had disappeared again. Gavin continued.

"By the way, a patrol unit from Plett picked up a young Coloured prostitute around two this morning. Seventeen years old, named Stacy Van

Wyk, by the side of the N2; in a state; bleeding and unable to walk. She says she spent the weekend with three Rastas in a cabin out in the forest, and that she was raped multiple times, and beaten. Someone burned the soles of her feet with a cigarette a few times. She said one of them is the Devil. She had 1,500 rand on her. Wouldn't let our boys touch it."

Josh was disgusted, wide awake now. The more he heard about this guy, the more he wanted to fuck Erasmus up, personally. He was an animal.

"We're not sure which road he took, but he skipped most of the N2. It looks like he went through Uniondale and then De Rust, through the Meiringspoort Pass. He was clocked on a speed camera going through Klaarstroom toward Prince Albert doing more than 180 km/h. We asked the provincial traffic guys to step down. They would have broadcast it all along the route to the N1 and down to Cape Town. He must have hit the N1 after Prince Albert, southwest of Leeu-Gamka, and he was clocked on a speed camera again between Matjiesfontein and Touws River doing more than 200 km/h. It looks like he's driving that gray Audi Fourie spotted at his house. He's on his way to Cape Town. No doubt."

Josh was excited. They were finally onto the *doos*. Erasmus was clearly thinking himself safe on his way west. The Southern Cape was a bit too hot for him and his boys at present.

Josh thought, somewhat irrelevantly, that it was a good thing it wasn't two weeks from now, when the provincial traffic authorities would step up their December holiday road traffic safety campaigns and Erasmus may have been stopped and arrested outside Klaarstroom, on the first speeding charge. Josh's mind jumped to Desmond Chauke, and he thought that he much preferred Erasmus on the run rather than in touch with his asshole of a lawyer on a speeding charge.

Gavin continued. "We contacted the Narc division; they have a huge hard-on for him. They've checked and said there's some news from Cape Town, I'm waiting for their call now. Apparently he's expected there on some Narc lead they're working, and Chetty will call me once they know what's going on. I told them we want to go along for the ride. That okay with you?"

Josh smiled a broad grin. "Fuck yes!"

Now to explain it to Amy, who was lying on her side, pulling the sheet over her bare breasts and looking at him with what looked like the start of an argument in the lines around her mouth. He offered her the phone with the cutest smile he could muster this early in the morning. Even with dimples on full display, he knew he was pushing his luck.

Cape Town Central SAPS station
Buitenkant Street
Cape Town
12H32

They had driven to George Airport just after 08h00 that morning. Gavin had left his car at Josh and Amy's flat, and Josh had driven them the rest of the way in the BMW. There they boarded a SAPS Pilatus P-6 Porter plane, a high-wing turboprop. The flight took them two and a half hours, and they landed at Ysterplaat Air Force base near Milnerton, just outside Cape Town, a little after 11h00. From there they were driven in a patrol car by a W/O Terblanche to SAPS Cape Town Central on Buitenkant Street, where a Sergeant Sidumo took them to the office of Brigadier Maduna. They were welcomed warmly, and then introduced to Major-General Ernie Sithole from the Hawks' Narcotics Enforcement Bureau, SANEB.

Sithole was a man who looked perpetually like he was about to tell you the funniest joke you'll ever hear at a cocktail party. Gavin had heard of him, though, and he explained to Josh that the man was a twenty-five-year veteran who was hands-on and had a solid reputation. He was also one of the few officers who had found his way into the narcotics scene in Cape Town from elsewhere—in his case, from KwaMashu near Durban—and commanded respect from the SAPS special Anti-Gang Unit, the AGU, who were the main drug enforcement guys on the Cape Flats. The AGU was established by order of the President and the National Police Commissioner, and had been in operation since around October 2018, initially deployed in the Nyanga cluster, including Bonteheuwel and Bishop Lavis. Since then, the unit had expanded its operations around other areas of the Cape Flats and Cape Peninsula area, and it had worked closely with the defense force when the latter had been deployed, controversially, to patrol sections of the Cape Flats in 2019, following increased gang violence in the areas.

Everyone appeared to be rushed, but Sithole insisted that Gavin and Josh settle down for a few minutes. He told them that a Captain Chetty at the Western Cape Provincial Narcotics Unit had suggested they be allowed on board for all of the action; that they were already privy to most of the information on Erasmus and might in fact be able to add some value. Gavin and Josh both expressed their appreciation. Sithole waved it away, and then, after graciously asking the brigadier's permission, he asked Sergeant Sidumo to fetch everyone some coffee while full introductions were made. After the coffee came, they settled down, and Sithole briefed them personally.

SANEB and the AGU had been tracking heroin imports into Cape Town from the East via Chinese trawlers and other vessels for the past year. There had been a few small sting operations, with varying success, and while they had managed to curb the traffic in that period by at least thirty percent, there were new players arriving on the scene every month and it was hard to keep an eye on everyone.

One such new player was Cheng Ziu, the owner of a small fleet of fishing vessels who had shifted his fishing operation—if there was actually such a thing—from further north up the east coast in Mozambique and KwaZulu-Natal over to Cape Town a few months before. Reports about illicit drug shipments from his vessels were not long in coming, and the joint operation had been tracking the fleet and Cheng Ziu and his lieutenant, Ernie Huang, for the past two months. The previous morning, they had received information from an informant—and then shortly afterwards, confirmation from a wire-tap on Huang's rented townhouse in Bloubergstrand—of a meeting to take place around midday today with "the man from the Southern Cape."

Surveillance for the past three weeks had turned up the news that Cheng's organization was linking up with a crew operating in the George to PE area who were interested in establishing an import route for heroin and meth into Southern and Eastern Cape, via Cape Town. According to the intercepted communications, PE and the Southern Cape drop-off points for shipments from the sea had become too hot in recent months, and the Southern Cape crew—going by the name of "Twelve Tribes"—was looking into collecting shipments around the peninsula and then transporting it east by road to Plett and PE.

The exciting part was that the "big man" from the Twelve Tribes group—referred to in the chatter as "No. 1"—was to come through to meet with Cheng personally, and then to accompany the first shipment, believed to have already landed and awaiting pick-up in a warehouse near Woodstock—back to his home turf. The AGU cops suspected that these guys were using mainstream courier companies, with the necessary people bribed to do the actual transporting. It was unclear whether money was to change hands, as Cheng was known as one of the pioneers amongst the smugglers in the southern African region who had initiated online payment through bitcoin and other means.

The Hawks and AGU were convinced that the Twelve Tribes's "No. 1" was Jerome Erasmus. When confidential communications of the proposed sting operation reached the SAPS Narcotics unit in George, asking for further information on the Funky Guys's activities, Gavin had been contacted because of SAPS Knysna's investigation into Whitcombe's murder, and its ongoing links with Erasmus.

By the time they had all finished their coffee, Sithole had briefed them on the plan. Erasmus and two companions had arrived in town that morning and had taken rooms at the Westin Cape Town Hotel on the Foreshore. There were three unmarked units sitting on them, from the AGU, and they were being watched with the expectation that they might leave the hotel any time now, for the meeting somewhere to the east of the city between Sea Point and Camps Bay. It was known that Cheng had been booked into a guest house in Fresnaye for the past week, and two more units were surveilling him and his small entourage.

It was one of these units who phoned Sithole directly to his cell as they were getting ready to move out. They were planning to park their vehicles at the Shell garage on Beach Road near Mouille Point, from where they would be able to respond quickest to any address on the seaboard.

But now they heard that Cheng, his mistress—the 34-year-old owner of an upmarket escort agency on Kloof Street in town, a stunning, tall Ukrainian blonde—and three men had just left the guest house, driving in the direction of nearby Sea Point. Sithole said he wanted an update as soon as the vehicle stopped anywhere. He smiled at Gavin and Josh, and they all said goodbye to the brigadier as they trooped down to the waiting cars outside the station. Gavin and Josh were shown into an unmarked white van, with two men up front. The van was full of surveillance equipment, video and audio, and Josh knew that one of the officers up front would join them in the back to man the equipment once they arrived.

While on Helen Suzman Boulevard, after passing the V&A Waterfront on their right, their driver received word from Major-General Sithole's vehicle and conveyed it to the two Southern Cape cops in the back. The large Mercedes-Benz SUV carrying Cheng and his group had stopped outside Mojo Market on Regent Road in Sea Point, a modern indoor market with international food stalls, bars, and live music, and some clothing boutiques. The group had entered the building. Gavin was wryly telling Josh that he hoped it was not a shopping spree for the mistress, when Sithole phoned again, saying that the other units in Foreshore were following Erasmus's Audi. He and his men had left the Westin a few minutes ago and were driving in the direction of Sea Point. Josh smiled. It looked like the meeting was about to get underway.

CHAPTER 27

The white van was parked on Clarens Road about seventy meters from the market. Josh and Gavin were listening to the activity on the radio as Sithole's men reported in from their various stations. Cheng had left the mistress just after entering the market, and he and two of his men had gone into a restaurant, Merle's Schnitzel. Two officers were following the mistress and the other man as they moved from boutique to boutique, spending a lot of cash on clothes and "bullshit accessories."

Erasmus had joined Cheng at a table in Merle's about twenty minutes later. Erasmus's Rasta friends had sat down with Cheng's men at a table closer to the door. The cops knew that Cheng spoke English. All four of the bodyguards were only a few meters away, and out of earshot, and Cheng and Erasmus had cozied up to each other, sitting so close that a casual observer may have thought them lovers. No doubt they wanted to speak in low voices.

Sithole's men were at a disadvantage. The restaurant was not exceedingly busy, and they couldn't get too close for fear of being observed. The bodyguards were not talking to each other and all seemed to be keeping an eye on activity within the room. The closest the two undercover officers, a man and a woman, could get was a seat at the bar, about fifteen meters from Cheng and Erasmus. They couldn't hear anything. A team outside the restaurant was scrambling to set up a parabolic microphone, as unobtrusively as possible.

Five minutes into the meeting, Sithole reported to Josh and Gavin that the mic wasn't working. There was too much movement of people across the line of sight, and Cheng and Erasmus appeared to be whispering in each other's ears for the most part, while covering their mouths. Some deal was clearly going down, but there was no way for them to know what it was about. They were all starting to worry that this could all be a big and expensive waste of time, and that the targets would shortly split up and go their separate ways, with the cops being none the wiser about what had transpired and what had been planned.

But then Cheng abruptly stood up and walked to the counter at the entrance of the restaurant. He grabbed a brochure from a stand and walked back to the table. He sat back down and paged through the document, pausing and then folding it open at a page. He took a pen from his pocket and drew or wrote on the page, then handed it to Erasmus. Erasmus stood and shook the Chinese man's hand, as the latter got up and walked out of the restaurant, his men following him without a word to the two Rastas they had been sitting with. The Rastas immediately moved to Erasmus's table and sat down. Erasmus was scrutinizing the brochure and then showed it to one of his men, the one with the jeans and a green shirt, whom the cops identified as "Skollie" September. He then put the brochure in a pocket of his jacket and took out some cash, large bills, placing a couple on the table. All three men got up and strolled casually out of the restaurant.

Gavin and Josh got ready for a ride. They heard on the radio that Cheng and his men had joined the mistress, and it seemed that they would remain in the market, shopping. Erasmus and his boys were making their way to the Audi, which was parked on Regent Road.

As the van started up and they prepared to follow, Sithole came over the radio. The female officer who had been stationed at the bar had, just after the Rastas left the restaurant, run to the counter and grabbed a brochure similar to the one Cheng had handed Erasmus. Paging through it, she could identify the page Cheng had written on.

It was a map of the Cape Town CBD, stretched across the brochure's centerfold. She had noticed the page Cheng and Erasmus had been studying was light blue-colored at the top, depicting the Cape Town Harbor. It was the right-hand page of the map, depicting the Foreshore, Woodstock,

Salt River, and Paarden Island.

They were hoping Erasmus was moving in that direction now, which they assumed was the pick-up point for the drug shipment. As Sithole had informed Gavin and Josh in Brigadier Maduna's office, their intelligence was that the shipment of heroin was waiting in an unknown warehouse in Woodstock. But they couldn't be sure yet.

If Erasmus went back to his hotel now, today's operation was a complete waste of time. They could arrest Erasmus as the "No. 1" man from Twelve Tribes, but as Chauke had made it so clear in the earlier interview, there was very little that SAPS or prosecutors could pin on him. Even for the shebeen shooting where Erasmus had been identified by the bar staff, the forensic investigation was still under way.

The van pulled out and made its way down the M6 along the Sea Point Promenade, back toward the city. Three other unmarked units were following the Audi, and they would await word before they picked up the tail.

Ten minutes later, the call came through. The Audi had taken the N1, bypassing the Westin, and had taken the M176 off-ramp toward Woodstock. Gavin grinned broadly at Josh and gave him a playful punch on the arm. They were in business.

Salt River
Cape Town
16H42

The two detectives were still in the back of the van, starting to feel the heat. They were parked at the corner of Westminster and Foundry roads, near Salt River Railway Station, about two blocks from where Erasmus's Audi was parked.

Erasmus had driven from Sea Point and turned off Albert Road into Salt River, a little after 14h00. He had driven down the street and then did a U-turn and drove back, parking in front of an old, decrepit house just across from an even worse-looking building with the big sign reading "Christian church—All welcome." Old, faded paint was peeling off both buildings, like most of the other buildings on the street.

The Rastas had entered the house about two and a half hours ago, leaving the shiny gray Audi with its carbon-fiber wing mirrors folded back. It looked out of place. A couple of young kids, around eleven or twelve years old, were hanging around the car, but they weren't eyeing it and they didn't seem to be interested in making *kak*. Erasmus had probably given them a few bucks to watch the car while they were inside.

There were plainclothes units moving up and down the street at random, both male and female officers, and a couple of unmarked cars doing a drive-by every few minutes, trying to switch vehicles to avoid suspicion from anyone who might be watching the road. There were four CCTV cameras pointed in different directions, looking out on the street from the house. No one had entered or exited the house since Erasmus's arrival, and there did not seem to be a back door, but a couple of officers were sneaking around in the block behind the house in case anyone left that way.

Both Josh and Gavin, and most of the cops on the operation, were aware of the irony surrounding this specific address. The former leader of the notorious Hard Livings gang—one of Cape Town's worst for many years, which had ruled Mitchell's Plain for most of that time—Rashied Staggie, was recently assassinated in this very road. He had died in a rain of bullets while sitting in a car in front of his house. The house was only a few doors down from where Erasmus was now holed up.

News reports at the time commented on the fact that Rashied's brother, Rashaad, had been murdered in this very street twenty-three years earlier, set alight by an angry mob—incited by members of PAGAD—and then shot.

Rashaad Staggie had died, terribly and very publicly, in August 1996. Josh pointed it out to Gavin that Rashaad had been a client of Mark Whitcombe's in the year or two before his death—at the same time that Whitcombe had been defending Reghardt Brink in his murder appeal in the Cape Town High Court. It was ironic, but likely unrelated. SANEB had, in the last hour, run the records of the house where Erasmus was currently ensconced, and there was nothing to link the owner to the Staggies.

The house was being rented, and had been for nearly two years, by a foreigner who owned a furniture shop on Albert Road, near the Old

Biscuit Mill, a local food market attraction. The Congolese national, Ignatius Irumba, made custom furniture from repurposed wood, and was starting to hit the big-time, after some bespoke items were featured in a UK home décor magazine. Tourists, local and foreign—the latter with their much sought-after euros and pounds—were starting to flock to the place, and Irumba would likely relocate soon. But SANEB and the AGU were now convinced that Irumba and his overpriced African-inspired objet d'art might be a front for something else. Officers were already looking for links with the Chinese drug cartels, specifically Cheng's group. Erasmus's visit lent credence to the theory that Irumba was a bad boy.

Half an hour later, they were making a conscious effort not to discuss the case. The Tanzanian connection of Shabane's killing was top of mind. Josh was burning to discuss it, but Gavin had said that he wanted them to wait and see whether Erasmus would be apprehended here in Cape Town. If he was, they would have to turn their attention back to him for the time being, to try and get serious answers to his connection with Whitcombe. They'd let the other possible suspect simmer on the back burner for now.

They were discussing the history of the neighborhood when a fist rapped on the outside of the van's door, startling them. They blinked in the sudden glare as the door opened to the scowling face of Colonel "Toppies" Tobukwane, the unit commander of the AGU for the Cape Town CBD and southern suburbs.

Colonel Toppies, as he liked to be called, was a funny character. Gavin had met him a few times in the past, when he was based in Cape Town, and Toppies was working his way up the ranks after starting out in the northern suburbs at Bellville SAPS. Gavin had huge respect for the man, who hailed from the informal settlement of Khayelitsha, and had moved through the ranks of SAPS for twenty-five years with a reputation of incorruptibility.

Toppies's scowl turned into a very broad, and very genuine, grin when he recognized Gavin. Josh relaxed as the two men embraced, Toppies giving Gavin a crushing bear-hug.

After introducing Josh, Gavin explained their angle on the investigation, and why they had followed Erasmus all the way to Cape Town.

Toppies nodded now and then, and when Gavin was finished, he pulled a black cheroot out of his shirt pocket and lit it from a box of Lion matches—something Josh hadn't seen in a while. Toppies seemed to think deeply for a few minutes, looking vacantly toward the train station, where an old white Toyota Tazz was practicing parking in the mostly empty parking lot; a learner driver, with a very patient parent. Then he turned back to Gavin.

"He sounds like a bad man. And we think he's meeting with some of our own bad men here." He paused to gather his thoughts, having been called off an investigation in Claremont involving the large-scale trafficking of drugs onto a primary school's premises to be here for the Cheng/Erasmus operation. "I was told that the Sea Point meeting was with a locally-based guy who works with the mainland Chinese to organize drug shipments into Cape Town. That seems to fit with what you and my own people have told me about this man Erasmus's background."

Gavin nodded, and looked at Josh. Josh knew that Gavin was still not one hundred percent behind the theory that Erasmus might be good for Whitcombe's murder, and he felt the unspoken invitation to put his own feelings across to Toppies. Josh explained that Erasmus was linked to the murdered man through the latter's visits to the Joodse Kamp house, as well as the environmental project out at Phantom Pass, in which both men apparently took quite an interest. As he explained it to the senior officer, he heard how thin it sounded; and he remembered, with embarrassment, their questioning of Erasmus at the Knysna station, and how the gangster's expensive lawyer had torn rather large holes in their theories.

Toppies was sympathetic, although Josh got the idea that it was probably more a case of the officer understanding the plight of a young detective and the need to pursue a hunch—even if it turned out to be wrong.

Toppies replied after he had flicked the half-smoked cheroot into the gutter, saying, "There might be something there. Your man is certainly capable of the crime, but I think you might need to tighten the noose around him a bit more as to motive."

Josh had to agree.

Toppies continued. "Well, it doesn't matter, eh? How did they catch Al Capone? For tax evasion, right?" His smile showed very white teeth.

"It doesn't matter how bad the apple is and what he may have done in the past. If we can't nail him on that, we can nail him on what he's doing right now, under our noses. And I say we go for that. Right? Make sense?"

What Toppies said made a lot of practical sense. If Erasmus was busted here in Cape Town on a big drug deal, they would have their man; they didn't need to be able to take credit for the arrest. They could continue investigating the Whitcombe killing and could always charge him in future if and when they had a strong enough case. Plus, having the man in custody and charged with other crimes could give them access to additional evidence that they would not otherwise have, such as DNA.

ALBERT ROAD, SALT RIVER
CAPE TOWN
MONDAY, 5 DECEMBER
18H25

After the second hour, the van moved a few blocks southeast. They found a parking spot in front of Palace Fisheries on Albert Road, just around the corner from London Road and the Irumba house.

Josh was trying to get used to the boredom and sheer frustration of the stakeout. This was not something that could be taught in a classroom or learned from a manual. It was a lot of waiting around for something to happen, knowing that you had to keep yourself alert because you had to be ready to move at a moment's notice. It was bloody irritating, just sitting there in the back of a vehicle, counting the minutes and the hours. Gavin had a lot more experience with it, and he was trying to use the time productively, talking through loose ends in the investigation.

Gavin had received an email that morning from the SAPS Forensic Sciences Laboratory out in Plattekloof about the fingerprint report on the Mazda, used in the Brink kidnapping in Bain's Kloof. They had still not received the results, even though Josh had phoned every few days for the past couple of weeks. It shouldn't have taken that long, and Gavin was reaching levels of frustration last reserved for the forensics guys in Mossel Bay.

The email said that there had been a bit of a fuck-up. The prints had inadvertently been mixed up with prints from a jetski theft in Langebaan on the west coast. Power outages, IT issues at the Plattekloof lab, and a court officers' strike out at the Langebaan Magistrate's Court added to the mess. It was a tragedy of bureaucratic ineptitude, poor labor relations, and just plain dumb luck, in a few pathetic acts.

In the end, Gavin had to pick up the phone and contact the investigating officer at SAPS Cape Town Central. Thankfully, the blue Mazda was still under lock and key out at the Stikland impound lot in Bellville, and Gavin requested that the fingerprint analysis be done again, and the report expedited for dispatch to the SAPS Knysna station. He also phoned AppleMac and asked him to resend the fingerprint report from Brink's body, with Nzimande's prints, to the investigating officer in Cape Town. They expected to wait another few days for the results. Gavin was not impressed, but decided to let it go in the interest of his blood pressure.

He turned the conversation back to Erasmus. The fact that one of the biggest Chinese players was willing to make a deal with Erasmus suggested that his local reputation in the Southern Cape was just the tip of the iceberg. Yet, on the Whitcombe killing, they still had only the evidence of the victim's visits to Erasmus's house—which (as Chauke had impressed on them at the interview) was purely circumstantial, with nothing in the way of proof of anything untoward. The Phantom Pass project was an interest which they both had seemed to share, even if why it interested these two disparate men remained elusive. Josh had been mulling things over, and thought that he had something else worth considering.

"You remember the payment of the money from Whitcombe's bank account? The money that had been taken—or stolen—from Veronica Whitcombe's UK investment?" Gavin nodded, looking interested. "You remember the name of the recipient? 12 Tri Pharma…"

Gavin lifted an eyebrow. "Twelve Tribes?"

"Yep, that's what I'm thinking."

Gavin thought for a moment. "If there is a link, does that mean that Erasmus was the recipient of the money? Why would Whitcombe be paying that kind of money to Erasmus?"

Josh shook his head. "I don't know. Although, if you consider that the money came from one of Veronica Whitcombe's investments….what if that was also an investment?"

Gavin looked skeptical.

"You mean Whitcombe stole money from his wife and invested it in Erasmus's drug business?"

Josh nodded, shrugging. "I'm curious to look into that company, 12 Tri Pharma. We're still waiting to hear results from the FICA check with the bank."

Both men knew that the results might take time. The banking group was currently in the news on a daily basis, embroiled in strike action by its employees after recent large-scale retrenchments.

Gavin seemed to like Josh's theory.

Erasmus and his boys had now been in the house for more than three and a half hours. The curtains in the windows remained closed, according to the officers manning the TV equipment.

Gavin had just taken out his cigarettes to step outside for a quick smoke when their radios crackled. They got the gist of the frenzied conversation over the airwaves, and then Sergeant Roelofse, who was manning the headphones and TV monitors in the van, informed them that three shots had been heard coming from the house, and the parabolic mics were picking up loud voices and what sounded like heavy items being moved around.

Something big was happening. They could hear the urgency in the voices of the responding officers, a tactical response unit from SANEB, who were moving in to breach the premises, do a sweep of the interior, and apprehend its occupants. The AGU guys would remain outside in the street and monitor the vicinity, and it would be their responsibility to apprehend any occupants who exited the house.

Gavin opened the back doors of the van and they jumped out, running west down Albert Road until they reached London Road. They sprinted toward the house, drawing their sidearms as they ran.

Sirens were going now and there was a busy scene up the road, near the Audi. The kids who had been watching the car had disappeared like smoke in a strong breeze.

Gavin and Josh were huddled closely together behind a red VW Polo parked about forty meters south of the house, listening to the pops of gunshots and keeping their heads low. Gavin was wheezing a bit from the sprint. Three members of the AGU were behind a silver *bakkie* about fifty meters up the road, exchanging fire with Erasmus's bodyguards.

Erasmus and his two Rasta bodyguards had walked briskly out of the front door into the street, where they had immediately spotted the SANEB tactical team approaching the house.

The SANEB guys turned on their heels and tried to get behind cover. The Rasta with the green shirt—Skollie—had a Heckler & Koch MP5 sub-machine gun on a sling over his shoulder, which he had pulled from under a leather jacket over his left arm. He turned, spraying a long burst of fire at the retreating tactical team, but they made it to cover behind a couple of cars down the road. He then fired a few shorter bursts at the *bakkie* and the AGU cops, while his partner with the red and green *tam*—they identified him as Bangjan—was running and trying to usher Erasmus into the driver's seat of the Audi.

Gavin and Josh rounded the Polo, trying to get closer to the Rastas. Erasmus saw them, and recognition was instant. He gave a great bellow of anger. Josh's mind flashed to the report of the young woman, no more than a girl, who they had found by the side of the N2, eaten up and spat out by this animal. Josh wanted to put him down.

He lifted his pistol, gritting his teeth. He was going to do this and fuck the consequences.

But Gavin pulled him by the arm, back into cover. They had miscalculated their approach. They were at the opposite end of the narrow street from the AGU cops, and they were all at risk of crossfire.

Erasmus turned away and got into the driver's seat of the Audi. Bangjan opened the back door on the driver's side—the car was parked too close to the wall to get in on the passenger side—as a burly, blonde AGU cop stepped out from behind the bakkie and fired three shots. Two hit Bangjan in the upper body. He spun around, one leg still in the car, and then dropped unceremoniously to the sidewalk, the pistol dropping from his hand and sliding across the pavement into the road. He was clearly dead.

As the powerful engine fired up, Skollie gave one last burst of fire from the MP5 in the direction of the AGU cops, sending them diving for cover. He kicked his dead partner's leg away from the door and dove head-first into the back seat, and the Audi raced off in the direction of Albert Road, past Gavin and Josh. They stepped out from behind the Polo, guns at the ready. The Audi's back door was pulled shut, and it turned sharply around the corner, tires screeching.

Gavin and Josh flagged down the approaching patrol car, a small BMW, driven by an AGU captain with a sergeant in the passenger seat. They jumped in the back, and the car picked up the chase, siren blaring in Josh's ears.

They followed the Audi's course, turning the corner and accelerating toward Salt River Circle. They could see the Audi weaving around slower traffic. Erasmus must have felt some indecision as to which way to go, as he braked suddenly and started to go around the circle to the right, but then turned back onto his original direction. A right would take him down Voortrekker Road to Maitland and eventually Goodwood. It was a single road which promised traffic snarls.

The Audi turned left at the circle and raced up Salt River Road. The patrol car was much slower, but Erasmus was hitting traffic and had to weave around it to avoid getting caught in the gridlock.

Just after passing James Street, the Audi's brake lights flared and the car rocketed around the corner to the right, onto Main Road, then took an immediate left onto Roodebloem. An oncoming delivery motorcycle tried to get out of the way, but was hit a glancing blow as Erasmus skillfully drifted the corner. The biker went flying through the front window of a KFC.

The patrol car, seconds behind, nearly hit a couple of terrified patrons who ran out of the restaurant into the road. Their driver was frantically wrestling with the wheel. When they were past, Josh looked back and saw a black woman with a long weave run straight in front of an oncoming Golden Arrow bus. He grimaced as he saw the woman disappear under the big wheels like some child's teddy bear caught in a washing machine. He shuddered and turned back to the Audi, which was racing toward the N2 highway.

As they sped up Roodebloem, a heavily tattooed arm came out of the back window of the Audi. Josh saw the muzzle flashes of the submachine gun as Skollie started firing at the BMW. They all ducked instinctively, including the driver, but the shots were wild and came nowhere near the vehicle.

The red-faced captain, by the name of Louw, floored the accelerator while swearing loudly in Afrikaans. The BMW picked up speed but only marginally closed the gap.

About twenty seconds after passing Jamaica Me Crazy—a funky Caribbean restaurant where Josh had brought Amy about six months ago, when he was in Cape Town for a training workshop—the Audi took the onramp onto the N2 outbound at high speed, barely avoiding hitting the barrier on the driver's side. The BMW followed. This late in the evening, the traffic was light.

The cops had the advantage of the siren and flashing lights. What few cars there were pulled out of their way. Erasmus had less cooperation and had to weave around other vehicles. *"Just another wanker in a fast car,"* seemed to be the message conveyed by the car horns blaring at the speeding Audi as it went by.

Skollie continued firing back toward the BMW but must have realized that the movies made this look a lot easier than it was. He pulled the MP5 back inside the window and seemed to be gesturing wildly to Erasmus with his free hand.

The Audi was doing more than 240 km/h on the empty stretches as it sped down the N2 past Groote Schuur Hospital. The BMW was having trouble keeping up. The AGU sergeant, February, was on the radio, broadcasting their whereabouts and the direction of the chase to all units, his voice high and fast.

Their hope now was that a unit up ahead would join the chase. They knew there would not be enough time for a roadblock. Gavin swore, saying that Sithole should have had an aerial unit in the area, but hindsight was a wonderful thing.

There were a number of off-ramps coming up, any one of which Erasmus might take, although Gavin expressed his doubts. He thought the Audi would stay on the N2, where he had a chance to pull away from them and only take a turn-off once he was out of sight. He could also get onto the M3 up ahead, which ran to the southern suburbs. The Cape Flats lay that way. The Rasta would know that territory all too well.

All four of the officers in the car understood that slow traffic might increase their chances of catching Erasmus, but they also knew that such delays would make the gangster even more desperate and could endanger the lives of countless civvies. The last thing they needed was a no-holds-barred shootout with an automatic weapon on a crowded street.

CHAPTER 28

Sergeant Lionel Davids was driving his metro police cruiser on the M3 inbound toward Cape Town CBD. He was in the left lane, cruising at ninety, keeping an eye on the light traffic. Davids knew that patrolling the highways around the city would be more challenging later that evening, but he was knocking off shift in a little over an hour.

He had quite a broad mandate to check for taxi overloading, reckless driving, and the increasing problem of pedestrians who crossed the busy highway, running in front of cars traveling at high speed. And now and then, of course, he would have to stop to get goats or cattle off the sides of the highway, and to reprimand the herders who never earned enough to pay any fine the City of Cape Town could mete out.

Before he reached the University of Cape Town's upper campus, he heard the report on the SAPS channel about a car chase coming south from Salt River.

He sped up when he heard that the dark gray Audi had turned onto the N2 outbound off Roodebloem. The dispatcher's voice informed units in the vicinity that shots had been fired from the Audi at a SAPS vehicle, and they suspected there was a fully automatic firearm being used. He knew that the car was coming his way, and if he wanted to do anything about it, he would have to punch it down the road.

Sirens blaring, he raced toward Hospital Bend, which was notorious both for its bottleneck which stifled traffic flow in peak times, as well as some spectacular high-speed vehicle accidents over the years. The Bend had been upgraded a few years ago to address these problems, but the stretch of road was still a major fuck-up. They got pretty regular calls to come out here to deal with some kind of problem, and in his first year on the job he had to help scrape a body or two off the roadway.

He was doing 160 km/h when he rounded Hospital Bend, having not yet seen the Audi or any police vehicles. He made a split-second decision and screeched to a violent stop in the yellow line at the off-ramp for Philip Kgosana Drive, about halfway into the Bend. He jumped out of the car, pulling his service pistol in one smooth move. The Audi should be approaching from up ahead any second now.

He didn't have long to wait. About ten seconds after he exited the vehicle, the Audi came into sight. It was going at a tremendous speed, weaving in and out of the traffic, horns blaring at it from all around.

Davids steadied himself, the pistol pointing north at the oncoming car. He had never before pulled his service pistol on duty. Something in the back of his mind nagged at him that this might not be the appropriate response protocol; that he was about to fire into oncoming traffic on a major highway.

But hearing the dispatcher relate breathlessly that someone in this car was shooting a bloody machine gun at police units overrode that little voice. He gritted his teeth and bit his tongue hard, causing blood to flood his mouth.

The car was approaching head on, having taken an open gap in the middle lane. When the Audi was no more than one hundred meters away, he opened fire. He didn't know how many times he pulled the trigger, but one hit the windscreen, and another the front left tire. It blew instantly, and the Audi veered drastically to the side.

Erasmus was fighting the wheel and stamping hard on the brakes, trying to slow down. He managed to get the car straight, but as it went past Davids, he could see it shuddering, smoke coming from underneath the front. A puff of smoke erupted as the right front tire burst. The Audi's low-profile tires were not made for this kind of abuse.

The car was nearing the end of the short, straight bit before the road turned to the right, moving too fast and out of control. It slammed into the barrier with a loud screech. Whether Erasmus had flipped the steering wheel, or if it was just a result of the violent meeting with the barrier, Davids couldn't know, but the car suddenly cannonballed to the left, colliding with the left-hand barrier and flipping over it.

The Audi barrel-rolled in the air, plunging onto the N2 carriageway below, where it hit a Maersk shipping container on the back of an eighteen-wheeler. The truck's driver slammed on the brakes and the truck slewed to its right, toward the concrete barrier bordering the fast lane.

The Audi hit the road hard and rolled once, twice, five times, before ending on its roof. It hit the concrete barrier and bounced back into the middle lane of the N2. It came to a rest in the middle of the highway, spinning around on its badly scarred roof. Moments later, a minibus taxi doing at least one hundred km/h smashed squarely into its side, and it erupted in a ball of flame. The taxi overturned and then took a yellow Nissan *bakkie* with it into the left-hand barrier.

Davids was staring, frozen like a statue with the gun still raised. Smoke was coming out of the barrel, the slide having kicked back. He would later explain to his girlfriend that he hadn't even realized he fired the whole clip.

He blinked once, twice, petrified at the carnage beneath him, convinced that he was going to lose his job and go to jail. He only looked up at the sound of the sirens when the SAPS BMW raced past him. He saw its brake lights go on, as the driver spotted smoke and fire.

The chase was over.

CHAPTER 29

Gavin and Josh stayed on the scene for more than an hour. It was a mess. Emergency vehicles were battling to get to the crash. Traffic was at a virtual standstill over a three-kilometer stretch, both inbound and outbound. Sithole had to fly in on a police chopper.

Erasmus and Skollie were little more than ash and a bad memory. The Audi was still burning, and two fire vehicles were spraying the car with foam. There was some excitement when a couple of firefighters had to scramble for cover when the last few shells in the MP-5 on the back seat discharged from the heat.

The truck had managed to come to a stop without hitting any other vehicles. Three badly injured occupants of the minibus taxi, as well as the injured driver of the Nissan *bakkie*, were airlifted away. The driver and two others in the taxi had died on impact. There was pandemonium all around as media started to arrive. This would be a late night for all involved.

Josh knew that this was just the demise of one more drug dealer, and the Cape Town papers were full of those kinds of reports every single day. But even so, it did seem as if the world—at least the world of the four million plus people of this city—had shifted just a little bit on its axis this evening, here at Hospital Bend. He was just happy to have come out of it all in one piece.

After things had settled down and enough units had arrived at the scene to take over the mop-up, Gavin looked at Josh with a sense of desperation. Their investigation into Erasmus for the murder of Mark

Whitcombe was far from over, even if the man himself was now gone.

Josh knew they would have to continue to search for answers to what linked Erasmus and Whitcombe, but he also knew that the remaining angle of their investigation, the Tanzania angle, now suddenly featured much more strongly.

Somewhere out there was evidence of what may have started this whole rollercoaster ride—Brink's crime in Mozambique, if it actually was Brink's crime after all.

Someone out there knew the truth, and it was his job to go and find those answers.

With Erasmus gone, Josh felt like he was reeling.

As there was not much else they could do at the scene, Sithole gave Gavin and Josh a lift in the chopper to Cape Town Central SAPS. After the high-speed chase, both detectives were more than happy to be traveling high above the motorways.

It was a stunning Cape Town summer evening, incongruous with the scene below. The sun was setting spectacularly over the harbor and glinting off a couple of shiny cruise liners. Josh was thinking that this busy little place of noise and lights at the bottom of the big, Dark Continent—this city he had once called home—looked much more magical from up here than it ever did at street level.

Maybe it was because there were people down there.

All kinds of people.

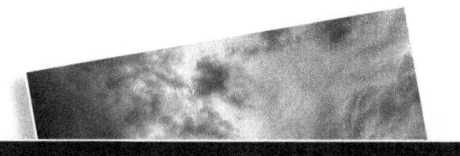

Chasing Ghost concludes the Catalyst International Crime Duology started in *Phantom Pass* as a killing spawns a hunt through a tangled web of drug gangs, political intrigue, and old Apartheid mysteries that crisscrosses southern Africa.

As clues smolder on the freeway of Cape Town, Captain Josh Holland and Colonel Gavin Whitall of the SAPS Serious Crimes Unit in George, South Africa are sucked into a dangerous world of corruption overseen by politically appointed leadership as they search for the killer who left a prominent lawyer mutilated and floating in a small rowboat on the tranquil waters of the Knysna estuary on South Africa's southern tip. As Josh and Gavin dig into the victim's past, the body count rises while tantalizing clues from the war in Apartheid South Africa point to old hatreds and past murders as potential instigators of the whirlwind of violence the detectives find themselves in. The sprint is on to prevent more killings even while careers and lives are threatened by powerful people and bureaucratic deceit in this twisting and relentless conclusion to *Phantom Pass*.

The Knysna Murder Duology explores the intricate thought process of solving a murder while navigating the modern reality of politicized policing.

ACKNOWLEDGMENTS

I need to thank Rowena, for all her brilliant ideas—most of which found their way into the book—and for helping to add that genuine "Capie" touch to most of the Cape Town scenes. You can take the girl out of Grassy, but you can't take Grassy out of the girl. Above all, thank you for putting up with me and the long early hours of the morning, when I was in another world, far away. You were always there when I returned. I owe you a proper December holiday, and so much more. Someday soon, I promise. Without you I couldn't have done this.

For Carl, thank you for keeping me on my toes—you kept telling me this would not be a "gripping thriller." I still think you're an idiot, even though you may be right. But I still hope you'll read it someday, just for the heck of it.

To my "beta readers":

Vandy, without you, this would have read like a Bambi book, so I hope it's "gritty" enough for you now. Thanks for being my first reader, and for encouraging me to finish it.

Willene, thank you so much for caring enough to not only read it but to give me real and thoughtful criticism—I sadly did not manage to do much, if any, of what you suggested. But please know that you gave me confidence to finish and publish it. And that was a big deal for me.

Yolandi, thanks so much for the continued support; when you didn't even know me, you were willing to read this story, and to tell me so enthusiastically that you loved it. I really appreciate your time, and your encouragement. I owe you a copy or two for the library.

This book was originally produced for self-publishing, which didn't happen (as I lost my nerve). Thank you to Brenda (and Hugo) for the editing, to Jane for the typesetting, to Tallulah for the help with the cover, and to Grant for the great service with the printing of that edition. A special word of thanks to Phillipa Mitchell for so generously giving me, a stranger, so much of your time and sage advice about pursuing this treacherous route of getting my baby out into the wide, wild world.

Thank you to SarahBelle Selig, for her wonderful editing and sensitivity towards the story and what I intended. And to Jessica Powers and Catalyst Press for your willingness to publish this, and to get the story out beyond South Africa.

To the government, who giveth (rarely) and taketh (frequently) so easily: thank you for putting me on lockdown and giving me the time to finish the book. For taking my whiskey and cigarettes, I have some choice words I won't include here.

And then an obligatory word of thanks to the many authors whose work I love and who first got me interested in the crime thriller, a wonderful genre to write in. I mean you, Deon Meyer (particularly for showing me that a local boy can also do this), Stieg Larsson, Michael Connelly, Jo Nesbo, Robert Harris, Mark Billingham, and the rest of you.

No. 1 in my book—excuse the pun—will always be the undisputed master, Stephen King. For aspiring authors, you must read his *On Writing*.

THE AUTHOR

Andre M. Louw is a law professor and a non-practicing attorney. He has published books and academic articles on sports law and employment law. This is his first novel.

He lives in a little house by a stream, in a small town at the foot of a mountain in the scenic rural Overberg, two hours' drive from Cape Town, the most beautiful city in the world.

He has no cats or dogs, but he still has most of his own hair.

For more information, including images of locations from *Phantom Pass*, visit www.andremlouw.co.za.

GLOSSARY OF TERMS

43	*doos* asshole
49	*laanie* (Cape Town slang) upmarket, fancy, expensive
50	*skollie* (Cape Town slang) criminal
50	*laaities* boys (young boys)
80	*onnie* mens underpants (briefs)
89	*fokoff* fuck off
92	*tannie* Aunty
93	*roosterkoek* A South African bread which is cooked over the braai (barbeque)
94	*Ag nee man Apple. Fok man!* Oh no man Apple. Fuck man!
94	*kwaai* (Cape Town slang) nice
132	*grootman* big man (nickname)
135	*Wat soek djulle met my?…* *Het djulle fokol anners om te doen nie?* What do you want with me?… Do you have fuck-all else to do?'
142	*kwaai stukkie* (vulgar) a nice piece of ass
143	*Daai goed is kak.* That stuff is shit.
148	*he was gatvol* he had had enough
149	*Fok dit. Genoeg gehad van djulle kak.* Fuck that. I've had enough of your shit.

166	*fokken naai* fucking asshole
234	*Ek het djou gesê. Ek gaan nie sy kak vattie.* I told you. I'm not gonna take his shit.
234	*poes* (vulgar) vagina
235	*coil* money (Rasta slang)
235	*lekker* nice
239	*prozzies* prostitutes
239	*indaba* meeting
245	*pangas*—(*panga*; plural) Large, broad-bladed knife used as a weapon or as an implement for cutting heavy jungle growth
245	*mavo* (Nigerian (Urhobo) hello (greeting)
247	*ma se poes* (vulgar) mother's vagina
249	*Hulle is opgefok! Wat maak ons?* They are fucked up! What do we do?
251	*horse* heroin
255	*boere* cops
256	*moerse* very
257	*Staan stil!* Stay put!
260	*tjoekie* jail
265	*Nee man fok, oubie! Moenie my seermaakie!* No fuck, sir! Don't hurt me!

268 | *naai* (vulgar)
    | have sex

269 | *Meneer, seblief, moenie my seermaak nie.*
    | Please sir, don't hurt me.

278 | *lekker ou*
    | Nice guy